AUTOMATIC LIVING

Automatic Living

Paul Outhwaite

D M PRODUCTIONS

Copyright © Paul Outhwaite 2000
First published in 2000 by D M Productions
PO Box 83
Coulby Newham
Middlesbrough
TS8 0FX

Distributed by Comberow Publications
3 North Street Winchcombe
Glos GL54 5LH

British Library Cataloguing in Publication Data
A catalogue record for this book is available from the British Library

ISBN 0-9537461-0-0

Typeset by Amolibros, Watchet, Somerset
This book production has been managed by Amolibros
Printed and bound by T J International Ltd, Padstow, Cornwall

"The next revolution will be a revolution of ideas".

Bill Hicks

PROLOGUE

He had reached the same point. This wasn't through routine though: a routine would suggest a plan, something followed meticulously. He had no such control. Each re-acquaintance with the point was a reflection of a projection in a downward spiral.

As by period five every Friday, he felt empty, like there was nowhere beyond but convalescence. His tie had loosened from the cheap, stringent, work-only white shirt, dragged to a knot by each desperate tug for order; looking the shambolic idiot he was forced to play.

"Be quiet!" had by now lost its anger, more a plea than a command.

Few of his pupils noticed, talking and laughing amongst themselves, a freedom won through careless, ignorant belligerence. For that he hated their parents, frowning beads of sweat, clutching to anger in the face of despondency.

He pushed back his hair, felt the wetness on his fingers, imagined he could turn it to salt, holding the world on the tips of his fingers.

Slumping into his chair, he turned to the window for solace. Ratiocination in his memories perceived that some beauty should be there, but he couldn't get the feeling back, and he didn't know why, save that his childhood had become so trammelled by experience. Only a numb emptiness existed.

Even the shy innocents were taking advantage of the breakdown, excitedly giggling in their chaotic freedom.

Wiping clammy hands on his trousers, he felt himself becoming detached, out of this world. He pulled open a desk drawer. Beyond the paperclips, stumps of pencils and half-eaten rubbers, a gun. To find order, he took it out.

"Now fuckin' be quiet!" seemed to rip the vocal chords from his throat as it drew attention.

The gun pointed at no individual, yet exercised unquestioning authority over the class. His disequilibrium in the twitching barrel held more menace for the pupils than if he'd been calm and calculated. Their silence communicated their intimidation, against a threat they could not resist.

He took air from the quiescence, momentarily healed.

"Now," dropped, weak. He paused, dripped out, "Open your books," digitally.

Papers flapped, bursting to stay alive, to mask the whimpering.

"OK. We, are, going to do—a bit of—creative writing," he said, every word falling slowly into their consciousness, uttered glaringly through disappointment.

"The title—is—My Last View of Life."

Their muteness hung heavy, unsure, needing guidance.

"What—would you write—if, you knew, you were going to die?"

Nervous eyes flinched glances, their faces holding a position as they desperately sought assurance from their peers.

"Write it!" echoed around the cylinder of the prompting gun, furious chatterings scurrying onto bare pages.

Some eyes filled with tears, whilst some – hardened by modern life – received the directions without expression, hid fears behind thoughts of revenge.

The gun grew warmer in his hand, so warm that both hands were needed to steady it from explosion. He breathed audibly, to himself and within himself, seeking calm.

A voice in his head told him everything. It told him how to suppress the chaotic messages running to his brain, told him how to organise the anarchy so it had some purpose. He paused between messages, heard the parental tones, and then proceeded.

"I want you to write down everything you see. Write about what you think, how you feel. Describe it. Use your imagination. Write it, now."

Some disharmony filtered from the audience, and he almost crumbled, almost wanted to stop and comfort the suffocating whine. He had gone too far though. To show emotion now would be weak.

Fretfully, hands jigged the pens, pencils, stubby felt tips, intellect sending missives to hands, composing manic readings.

"*My teacher has a gun*" in mutant letters; lines crossing lines, crossing lines, dashing for a connection to end the letter, to move on to the next, bludgeoning obstacles of reason, keeping going to maintain an existence. "*He's not himself. Everyone's scared. We have to write. Scary bad, bad scary. Bad not good. Write on. Frightening. Nerve-wracking. Just keep writing. Write anything. Just look like you are writing. Just write down everything. Even repeat things. Repeat, repeat, repeat. Tell everybody to repeat the same. By ESP. Get into their heads. Tell them to imagine. Keep repeating. Fuck. Fuck,*

fuck, fuck. These words won't be marked. Keep repeating fuck, fuck, fuck. You'll only be seen if you stand out…"

Rigidly his figure stood, eyes frozen in horror, a realisation evaporating the air in a stare above their heads. The mechanical movement of his right hand placed the barrel of the gun into his chin, digging in there to stay calm. A red mark glowed beneath his stubble, the static position assumed. A restlessness shuddered, burning from the mouth of the barrel, waves sending shakes through his fragile body.

Branded by the metal zero squirming over his sweat, easing off his chin, he steadied, pulled it back, grew tenser, lost all shape and blinked. A thought crossed his mind.

"Keep writing. Try. To—see—some—beauty."

His words were being shaken out, scattering to a conclusion like dice. The warm red halo itching around his chin couldn't be controlled.

This paradox, this efferent conclusion, would rip, cut, paste his name, to and from the history books. He could return to his birth name, give them answers, conclusions to their analysis. There was reason, and on that he focused. Born under a bad sign.

"Write down everything you see. Every fuckin' thing! Even after I've blown my fearless brains out!"

One click in time before screams: Mad, distorted screams; confused primal screams. They echoed in an empty chamber, smouldering.

Some ran from the pretty pattern; an imagination splattered on blackboard, dripping from a dissection of Antony and Cleopatra's love. Correct spellings bled indistinguishable; calmly, painfully descending onto punctuation. Brilliant red flicked around the room that wasn't his own, where rulers measured reluctantly the expansion of creation over formula.

His lobotomy was complete. The calm, faceless representation had lost emotion, blood dripping like regression.

One boy remained, his classmates screaming in distant corridors. He listened to the crying grow vague, a sense of nirvana reverberating in the bleats until they were like bleeps. Then he could imagine.

DEMOCRATIC COMA

I see life through dead eyes. I live through paralysed limbs. I talk to myself, my other selves. I talk to my other selves' friends, in my kingdom, my world, from which they can never escape. These are my voiceless people, screaming in silence.

I re-run memories every day, to remember who I am, or was. There are my idols, living in the same space as the man with the shaved head, on that Sunday bus, who stared at me, stared at me as we got off at the same stop, stared at me like he wanted to kill me. Or the woman at the train station who was waiting for me to use the ticket machine, who made some footloose comment about it, who smiled and laughed and seemed human.

Every second a "Bleep!" to the past. My heart fakes its emotions; such is Fate. My mind is distant, save for the times when I can haul it in, use it, ride it, and try to escape. My love is impermeable.

I am turned on my side, flashes returning me to the living dead of here: reality. A character screams: "I am still alive!" but only I hear, and I am mute. Pity, sympathies' flowers and gravestones await.

I have run through fields, I remember. I have felt the bark on my bone. I have chased clouds around my head, I remember. "Bleep!" every second of every day.

Passing me by, the bleeps of life.

Faces, processions, the shouting silence to keep me alive in bleeps. "Bleep!" I can see in their tears the act of my funeral. It's rainswept. "Bleep!" It's heroic. "Bleep!" It's the end of an era, the end of me. "Bleep!" I can feel their warm hands releasing me to the air. I am a kite; exuberant, free, out of control. "Bleep!" as I drift away into the bleak eye of the moon.

I will be the star on which you lament, or hope, depending on which you feel lucky with. I just need to get into your head so I can get out of mine. I will be "Bleep!" to your past, present and future, life to your ephemeral hope. Take my heart and soul and treasure them, if the TV doesn't bleep you to bed.

I can hear bleeps, continual, persistent, puncturing the broken circle of thought; the uniform cortège to "Bleep!" A round roll is halted by "Bleep!" with monotonous regularity, getting up to try again.

Shut Up, Be Happy

Freewheelin', the unbroken road stretched ahead.

Like I was better than them, like I'd risen above it. Freewheelin' in my imagined freedom.

Trees crowded, kept secrets, held nature's transience amid their skulking claw-branches. In and out of the ammonia hand-mask, I tried to savour it, the wheels of my bicycle infiltrating, feeding in and out of consciousness. The wide, refreshing creaks came carefully regulated, yet I only appreciated them intermittently as a calming influence.

As always on working Fridays I blew the cobwebs away, cycling apart from the fixed, seeping, insidious routine. Taking the country road home took longer but was wholly more satisfying than choking and dodging the traffic.

I moved leisurely, my sinecure taking in the melting sun before it disappeared, turning over the season. Another week slipped away, strains and stresses eked out; my body cut in two. I twisted indolently, under shimmering trees carelessly dashing the remains of sunlight onto hooded roads.

Levelling off, I slowed to an unused bus stop, dismounting to amble towards an unused bench. Seating myself, I glanced at messages carved deep into its surface, taking them in as my hands acted separately to locate a cigarette. Here's where Kath and Rob snogged and left their love, added to each other's experience, bound inextricably – yet not always prominently – in their futures.

There was just time in the drag of the life to contemplate the sky's lavishness, breathing red bulges into oncoming dusk.

I dropped back my head, scanning the heavens where jet planes had left their fuel and faeces. Inhale, exhale, gushing smoke to hang around a while in the still air, striving to relax.

Above the solace a few birds chirped from branch to branch, mimicking the bleeps of mobile phones. And somewhere in imaginary England the sound of stumps clattered by cricket balls before a smattering of numb applause and the chink of teas carried on a tray.

A car engine interfered with my reverie, gasping closer between bends. I pulled my head forward so as not to look like a drunk, dropout, homeless traveller, or any other menace to society.

The Range Rover steered into view, slowing on approach, the driver and his lovely wife and three children staring from behind ivory windows, in a tidy, glaring, drive-by condescension. In the quickness of our eyes meeting we didn't trust each other, their craning necks struggling to note my vital statistics for transmission to a higher authority.

I finished the cigarette, gave a parting glance to the darkening skies before mounting my bike to peddle away. It had been free and beautiful – as corny as life used to be – and I could have lost myself there but for the anxiety I felt from those questioning eyes.

I flicked on my lights, turning the wheels to commence the creaks, growing more pertinacious in revolutions. They were sharp daggers, harassing from behind, urging me to go faster, then, creak-creak-creak, bleep-bleep-bleep, chasing me.

Above this I became aware of a siren impatiently clawing into my consciousness. I juddered to slow, hugging the kerb to let it pass, only for the thick, psychotic whirr to rest aside me; a uniformed face squashed to the police car's window motioning for me to pull over.

Scything creaks stuttered on my wheels, diminishing to a jolted stop. The police car settled ahead, coughing out a tall, dark figure preceded by a blinding torchlight.

I held hands to my eyes, peeping through the fingers, retreating to find a less bright gap, until eventually just shielding myself from the omnipresence of the light, simultaneous with bold footsteps crunching to a halt.

"What is it?" I asked.

No response from the edging of granite feet, scraping to survey, light enveloping me.

The torch's beam flicked to my feet, a pool of light perfectly forming.

"ID Card," came a demand.

I searched my pocket, still blinded as the afterglow receded. Black, green, yellow shapes squirmed about my vision, shrinking on each blink.

I handed my ID card to the discernible figure: thick, craggy white skin murdered by wet-shaving, blown out, hardened to a square by exercise, withered by late nights. Grey lines cracked his skin, unshifting as he widened his eyes and spoke.

"This is a private road, you are trespassing," he sneered, glee freezing his steadfast features immortally. "Stay there."

He scraped back to the police car, exchanged words over a radio and waited, one eye on me. A garbled voice offered conversation to his monosyllabic indifference. I felt nervous, ensnared in a capitalist autocratic zone, with two policemen. All kinds of scenarios filled my head, every one with an ominous foothold in reality.

The officer returned, his steps less laborious. He was excited.

"Mr Manion, lay down your bike, step over to the car."

"Why?"

"Just do it," he demanded, forcing his huge fist onto the bike's handlebars, fixing the fingers to a grip, pushing it to fall, gesturing for me to lead him to the car.

From behind he accused on each iron boot scrape. "Been in trouble before, Mr Manion? Twenty-seventeen, first arrested, at a riot. Then, illegal raves, riots, vandalism, assault. Pretty colourful aren't we?"

"I was never charged."

"It's all on record. Suspicion is enough. Turn around, keep walking." He prodded me. "Hands on the car, spread your legs."

"You have no right."

"We have every right. Violence against the state is very serious. Just because you've been quiet for four years doesn't mean anything. We know about your type."

"But I was never…"

"Shut up and fuckin' spread 'em!" had nastiness and impatience sewn through its vowels.

I spread my fingers wide on the cold police car's roof, shivering as its unflinching chill spread to my feet. Ahead I could only see varying shades of darkness amid vague shapes of trees. Private road? No questions asked? Nobody sees anything?

Lumpy fingers turned out my pockets, dropped keys, money, cigarettes, matches into the darkness. I didn't argue. That dark field on private land held too many conclusions.

"Turn around."

Blinding torchlight again obliterated his face. I looked down, his body swinging a fist towards me, stopping as I flinched.

"Scared? No more questions? That's right, shut up, be happy. Pick up your shit and get off this fuckin' road. We'll take you in next time, fix you up with something. Huh," he added portentously, jovially pleased with a scenario running through his mind.

He shared the joke with his partner inside the car before reversing over my belongings, into my bike, then driving off.

"Fucking pig bastards," I muttered to myself.

I searched the ground, found my keys, some of the money I'd had, but the cigarettes were ruined. The Cancer Police – here to save you from yourself. Shut up, be happy.

I am a Sinner

"So, fuck 'em".

"Yeh. Fuck 'em".

It was downhill all the way to the riverside and when you've just smoked a few joints you walked like Bill and Ben the Flowerpot Men.

We paced without communication. I was the lead-footed renegade using my boots to steer my mind, eyes darting suspiciously at movements in back streets. Joe moved with more purpose, somehow evident in his short, greased-back black hair, long formal black coat, and the way he took nonchalant drags on his cigarette once every four steps. We were like two dice, tumbling towards snake eyes at Club Independent, our direction clattering off the bodies and motion pulling us through Sector 1, the city centre.

From neon bars the cards hustled in and out and tried their luck. The Jacks played the same card every weekend; loud, brash, obvious, sometimes getting lucky. The Queens were inscrutable, faking it and shaking it, tempting against resistance, parading themselves, beckoning pretenders to take a chance, no guarantees. Frequently, a Queen was flicked from clammy hallways, beneath garish flashing signs, and if you were prepared to gamble with guilt and morality you couldn't lose.

The Kings were the cops. They couldn't lose. Even when you saw one snuffing out their siren in a back street, calling out the ice-cream kids to score, you knew they'd get away with it.

Kings mixed with Aces: pushers, pimps, hustlers, supposed high rollers, beggars and stealers. They were the real gamblers, or they would have been if the period between life and death weren't now treated as a free market. Aces high, aces low.

We entered Club Independent staccato, helplessly drawn. Inside, you couldn't help but be gripped by the grotesque carnival of it all. The bloodshots were out, driving into their drinks and whatever else they were on, every male looking like James Dean had he lived, grown old, had to endure the desertion of fickle fans worshipping a new star. He'd have ended up doing cameos in big budget disaster movies, his moody countenance sagging, contemplating some uncontrollable fire, or flood, or volcano, or earthquake, making ends meet parodying himself in commercials for car brakes. He'd be shooting up on heroin, visiting Club Independent, and on his arm would be one of the bloodshots' women: the ashen-skinned cosmetic surrealists with their misshapen bodies and communal intellect.

On the music machine someone from the 1950s sang about a thing called love. A woman, her face stampeded over countless times by life, and well known to the local hospital, was drunk and dancing, spending the money she'd borrowed to have her stomach pumped. I guess she was happy.

Young and old, men and women, fathers, mothers, sons and daughters all disappeared into the men's toilets with the drug chauffeur. Seconds later they would reappear, ambling off to the other side.

"It's your turn to monkey," I said to Joe.

"Yeh, soon. Quick game of pool first?"

I nodded, Joe calmly slotting coins into the machine as my head rested. Nonchalantly he arranged the balls in a triangle, odd number, even number, towards the eye of the pack.

Once finished he looked at me, caught something of my mood and said, "Don't worry DM. Remember, fuck 'em."

"Yeh, fuck 'em."

I shook it off, necked some alcohol and stood up.

"You wanna break?" asked Joe.

"Yeh, suppose. I'll take the chance."

I made for the table, my final stride interrupted.

"What chance?"

"I take all the risks here don't I?"

Joe screwed up his face, his bright eyes gleaming with dubiety. He didn't care for what I had to say, but curiosity wouldn't let it pass.

"What risk? Why can't you see it as an advantage?"

I chalked the cue precisely, glancing up as Joe impatiently flicked a cigarette loose of ash. He stared to patronise, unable to blink away his contempt.

"Advantages have to be worked for. This is just luck."

I swept dummy shots with the cue before taking aim. A hit, a smash, and nothing potted.

"Y'see," I added as the balls settled.

Joe smirked, crushed his cigarette and took advantage.

Paradise spilled over from the bar into crisp packets and stubby swamps of ashtrays; a glut of resentment drowning with sorrows. The ceaseless music yearned in the background, all thick and lacquered with nostalgia, stuck in another decade. A skiffle beat convulsed the bloodshots into paroxysms, remembering a different generation they wanted to be a part of, where Roy Orbison sang for the lonely.

Joe and I were dragging smoke with the best of them, missing pockets, scattering balls feverishly, until I celebrated a victory by default.

"Wanna monkey now?" asked Joe abruptly, dismissing defeat.

The stunted sound of coin and hand slapped on the pool table broke my reply.

"I'll play one a yaz."

His face had been chiselled away, his eyes drawn into his skull, staring bleakly out from way back in his psychosis.

Indiscriminate luck had been elevated to providence and I replied, "Yeh, OK," turning to Joe with: "One more game, then monkey," before lighting a cigarette.

The challenger jammed change into the table, growling impatiently as the machine spluttered to operate. He set the balls, flicked his face up and said, "You wanna play fa money?"

I smiled, felt hot and hazy, decided to bet on the gods working.

"How much?"

"Twenny on it."

The balls were ready, the triangle tossed aside. His teeth rolled his lip back and forth quickly, repeatedly, escalating to throw out his bottom lip sharply, repeatedly. This evolved until his teeth were jittering all around his mouth, grabbing and chewing flesh inside. The snarls revealed white/yellow clots around his teeth, growing larger, like a plague on his whole craggy face, spreading – in a matter of seconds – to contort his features. Skin shifted like a separating jigsaw before determining on a wet grimace.

I placed a twenty Euro coin on the table. He followed suit.

"You stupid fucker," whispered Joe.

The gods would have their little game and I had to perform.

A crack scattered ahead of Joe's footsteps away. Deranged balls burst open, irrational, unable to find their way into a hole, much to the malevolent figure's annoyance, recorded in a hissed curse.

I surveyed the carnage for an advantage, pacing like I was an expert, like I knew exactly what I was doing. I eyed up a shot, snapped at it and watched a yellow rattle in a pocket and pull out.

My challenger stepped forward, rolling up his jumper sleeves precisely, but with too much haste for it to be nonchalant. Each curl of his sleeve revealed lines to his life, scarred and disused, tattoos for his obituary. I knew whom he loved (or had loved), whom he supported till death, and that his name was inextricably S*T*E*P*H*E*N*.

He chalked his cue, lowered his body and took a shot in one seamless motion. He potted, rushed to where the white rested, took another shot and potted another ball. The cue got a flick of chalk, then he shot again, but missed, just.

"Fuckin' cunt!" cut from his throat.

Chip, chop, crackle rattle drop, I was in. Nudge, hollow, drop, he was sweating.

Joe signified his return to the background by lighting a cigarette.

S*T*E*P*H*E*N* agitated some chalk, seemed to want bury the cue in it before dropping both implements to the floor. Bending down to retrieve, a kitchen knife slipped from inside his jacket. I saw it. Joe saw it. Our eyes twitched over to each other.

S*T*E*P*H*E*N* casually picked up the knife, like it were merely an embarrassment, placing it indifferently back into his jacket. The look stuck between Joe and I, steadfast, elongated, until I re-tapped back into the idea of winning or losing. I didn't want to lose. I was too hot.

I missed, cursed, took a swig of drink as Stephen stabbed a ball home, frustrated, out of position, a firework out of control. His face tightened, suppressing anger as he slammed the cue into the white ball. He potted another, a shot that hustled its way in with a deliberate, swaggering kiss off one of my numbers. But again he was out of position.

He hit a long shot with swerve, the cue ball howling across the table to connect, his target rattling in the pocket's jaws and rebounding out.

"You fuckin' bastard!" he said, accusing the cue ball.

The shot I played missed, but had enough power and arrogance to fluke into another pocket. I had convinced myself of who I was. The next shot again found a pocket fortuitously, and although I had followed with a miss the white edged into a position which precipitated Stephen's response of, "Lucky cunt!"

He couldn't get out of it, did well not to foul, but left me with an easy pot which I exploited superciliously, drawn in to feel my number roll a straight line to the pocket.

Just as the moment absorbed me and I became aware of silence, all I'd blotted out rushed back: Stephen's twitching, the chaos of Club Independent, the indistinguishable music.

"Fuckin' come on!" alarmed Joe, was noted by Stephen, and set me on a path to finish him off.

"Fuckin' cunt!" came from Stephen as cushions bumped my number towards a pocket.

Then a miss. Stephen immediately picked up the cue ball, wiped it on his jumper and placed it back on the table. It seemed some way from where it had been previously. He had taken the shot before I could protest, and in his haste had missed. He thumped the cue's butt on the floor, expelled his familiar catch-phrase.

I walked a pause around the table, drunk on luck, smashing my way to success, intoxicated, inviting hubris, chalking slowly, sizing up an easy black. I didn't want S*T*E*P*H*E*N* to like me. People like that drag you down, so I made him twitch some more before slamming in the black.

"Fuckin' 'ell, ya lucky bastard. An' this fuckin' cue's bent. Double or fuckin' nowt."

"Er, we gotta go."

"Nah, y' fuckin' gorra lemme win ma fuckin' money back. Them's the fuckin' rules."

He stared at me; angry, feral; features dominated by an inscrutability as to how far his madness went. The kitchen knife was talking as he lurched forward the dog's breath proposition.

"One more, that's all."

He snorted an approval, re-racking the balls.

"Monkey soon," I said to Joe. "No messing."

The excitement of scoring, of connecting with that other world was in me, feeding on the deliberate delay. And I couldn't lose.

Colours clattered, numbers locked up, my luck manifesting itself as nonchalance. Another drink, another cigarette and a few more curses from Stephen. I let him in once but he was too agitated, knifing the ball to choke in the jaws. Fortune didn't desert me, trigger-happy as I blew him back to obscurity.

"Fuck! Yer tha luckiest fucker a ever fuckin' played," he said, "Cunt." As an aside. "Well, a 'aven't got no money left. 'Ere." He pushed a packet into my pocket. "No fuckin' arguments."

I knew generically what it was, though the power of the small sample of grey dust was beyond me.

Stephen slunk towards the bar, merging with the bloodshots, still cursing.

I nodded at Joe. "Monkey."

Joe swaggered to the toilets to see the man we could trust.

We didn't know the name of the drug chauffeur: A nod and a show of money were the only forms of communication. The nod was the difficult part. He had a dodgy right eye, one that never moved, so you could end up nodding a few times without reciprocation, believing you'd made contact when his gaze was really elsewhere. He always wore faded blue jeans and shell suit top, always had the same flat greasy side parting of black hair, thinning on top. He'd invariably have the same crowd with him near the men's toilets. One, a younger man, modelling the same clothes, grooming himself for promotion, would usually be skinning up, though he sometimes did the deals, and did them much more jovially. The drug chauffeur's other two companions must've been the heavies: one built to fit barely through the toilet entrance, the other shaven-headed, the stubble on his scalp parted by a deep unhealing scar. They never became our friends but it was always good to see them.

"Successful?" I asked on Joe's re-emergence.

"Yeh. Hey, one more for the road?"

I nodded, feeling the shared anticipation. Joe lit another cigarette as I moved to the bar.

I stared around, took a lifetime to take it all in, assessing each sunken face madly pecking into their drinks. They revolved through clouds of smoke as every now and then a shriek of brittle laughter penetrated my consciousness, demanding my attention above the dull cacophony.

When someone looked back I looked away, but couldn't help feeling I'd stared for too long, and now they were looking at me. Once I took in Stephen's vengeful leer, felt nothing in rolling it back.

"Some scary faces in here," I said returning to an unflinching Joe, crashing the drinks down.

"It's a goddam scary place. Not the environment to bring up your kids."

"But they seem happy enough."

"Do you envy them or something?"

"Huh. I envy the ease with which they disregard society. They live in their own world and they're happy in it. If you don't know how shit your life is, it isn't shit. You're in a coma, you don't know you're in a coma. Yer numb, you don't feel the pain."

"Well they can fuckin' have it," ended Joe.

"Just here on business, eh?"

"Strictly." He took a strong lead in the drinking stakes. "I wonder what that stuff is you got off the crazy."

"We'll research it later."

A modern tune blasted through the speakers, full of bleeps and bams, sending most of the bloodshots into silence, deadened by noise.

Outside, the sirens of another beatbox night; the deep heart of town pulsing. We moved in shadows so as not to be noticed. Anger and love and a pint of life, silence and stares and leers from head to feet.

Thrown from pubs, beneath beckoning neon spotlights, they fight for love and respect. Swanky women flit in and out, clicking careless heels, dancing for the Aces, disappearing up back streets to give advice. A siren saxophone cooled on a corner, hauling in the bleeding, black and blue men. Crowds were dispersed with truncheon gestures. Crowds were a threat.

We were skipping scared for solitude, careful not to get drawn in, passing the guitar man with his toothless twanging and hopeless harking back. He was morals and immorality and he ended begging for a coin. Growls barked lies in the flash of a naked light, a stabbing scream bouncing around inconspicuous space. We had to escape before we became involved. A taxi rescued us.

Kids, the government, it's not like it used to be. The match, the team, bloody disgrace. Winners, losers and constant disappointment.

We nodded enough then paid him to leave.

Joe lived two blocks from me, in the same design of flats, one of about a dozen blocks scattered amid terraced housing in Sector 9.

Joe tapped digits on a box at the entrance door, bleeps preceding my steps clattering behind on the imitation marble floor, passing the fake plastic plants, their tawdriness accentuated by offensively bright sterile lights.

On each level we ascended to, each flat's entry buzzer had the name of Friedland indelibly stamped beneath. It had always seemed sinister and Joe could never offer any explanation as to its origin, but then every creak and moan from the labyrinth of lives inside the block also seemed sinister.

Fourth floor and more bleeps to gain entry. Once inside there was nothing more important to Joe than having a piss. "Do the honours," trailed as he dwindled along the corridor.

The living room, shaped and designed as mine, was cluttered with culture, Joe's collection of books, music and film discs displaying a taste also similar to mine. The decor he employed consisted mainly of empty wine and beer bottles, set against the standard dark blue wallpaper and matching carpets. Its sobriety and blankness served to accentuate the menace of his pictures: Robert De Niro and his array of movie characters.

After pushing two beers into two fat glasses I examined Stevie's dust, fingering some up my nose.

The flush came like a malevolent wave, surfing Joe into the room.

"Let's go to work," he announced.

"I think this is meant to be sniffed."

"Good?"

"Affirmative."

"Well you have to say that young Stevie didn't look the most respectable character, but that's always the mark of a good dealer, and I'm sure he loves his mother."

Joe took a sniff as I took a swig. "Here's to aliens coming to take me away from all this. Cheers."

"Cheers. Here's to meeting two lesbians who want me to save their souls," added Joe, raising his glass.

Each of us waited. Then each of us noticed the other waiting and laughter duly arrived.

"I think our Stevie might just have come up trumps," I said.

"Yeh, we'll have to invite him round one night."

"For coffee and biscuits maybe."

"Smart dress only. What would the neighbours think?"

"Right. We don't want to get a reputation for mixing with drug dealers."

Laughter burst hysterically, seemed to be a second language after the inanity of our words. Conversations followed, led to other brief worlds until the many paths our thoughts took grew knotted and strangled us into laughter again.

"Hey Dano, tell us a story."

"No one calls me Dano, you fucker!" But Joe already knew that. He was just busting my balls. It gave him an exemption from emotion to bust people's balls.

"Hey DM," he said, emphasising the initials, "just shut the fuck up. I'll flip ya for a story."

"You've got a story?"

"Like a fiend."

"Call."

"Heads."

I rattled the one penny coin from my pocket and spun.

Slap. I caught and covered the coin instantly. He looked at me, twitched his lips to grimace. Even something as simple as this could give us a kick. I moved my hand away slowly, anticipating some extreme emotion.

"Heads," I said, tossing the coin to Joe.

A quick snort before getting my accomplice to imagine:

"Picture it. All the clocks have stopped ticking, and on God's little checklist the final species is being crossed off. All the history books are burning. All the laws and acts of parliament are burning, and all our planned futures are dead. As the fires eat all before them the last of their race, Adam and Eve, grunt as they fuck on the bed of a dried-out lake. Adam can't keep it up, turns his attention to the big issue. 'Why did it ever come to this?' he asks. 'Nobody cares,' she replied. But Adam doesn't get it. He wants a simpler answer. He wants A plus B equals C, end of the world wrapped up. Eve just wants to get it over with, drags Adam back on top of her. They fuck and they burn, they fuck and they burn. Flesh sizzles but they never reach a climax, both collapsing unfulfilled into the scorching dust.

"Eve's hand weakly raises itself to pull a cold can to her chapped lips and an omnipotent voice says, 'New eco-friendly coke: when it's the last thing you need, but the thirst thing you want!' And on a nearby advertising hoarding, the aerosol epitaph, 'Adam Loves Eve', glowed a little before flaking.

A pause denoted the end, but Joe didn't stir, his eyes closed, lids quivering. "Joe. Joe. Joe!"

"Wow! Fuck. DM, I was there!" More serious than excited, sweat rolling from his brow. "I watched them." He struggled to put himself upright on the couch, groaning to find a new position he could slouch in to.

"We only imagine there's real life out there," I said, peering through the curtains. "It's all burning. It's just us left Joe, in this little time capsule."

Walking through the rowdy streets and miserable back alleys I pondered why I could only imagine such a bleak and prosaic picture. Why could I not create bright orange houses shaped like loaves of bread and a yellow brick road? It just wouldn't fit in with the inveterate programme established in my head. I had to make do with what everyone else imagines; a kind of consensual aesthetic to reality.

A rolling tin can ignited a twitching curtain throwing light onto a CCTV camera scanning across me. They caught everything these days, from shoplifting to murder to intoxicated blow-jobs and salacious star indiscretions. And, sold most frequently, the bacchanalian ineptitude of the masses, each individual guaranteed celebrity status for fifteen minutes, before the failed law suit and post-celebrity disorder counselling.

A percussion of noises rebounded around Sector 9, anger and addiction with its usual mixture of invective and anguish. Sector 9 festered as a community of terraced housing impaled on five storey blocks of identical flats. The last New Labour government had begun the flat building programme just after the millennium, but after the economic bust took hold in 2002 further plans were scrapped. Of the fifty-one sectors, only those north of the river had flats.

Each sector was noosed by a road, giving congested access to the western and southern motorways, eventually. Northwest of Sector 9, one mucky, impermeable area of uncolonised wilderness, a lump of hills cut off by the motorway. Southwest, the affluent sectors, each named after their sponsor.

East, stretching north and south along the coast, a thick array of chemical plants, plastic plants and factories, only broken by Sector 4 and Sector 3 on either side of the river.

The city centre seethed on our side of the river, over which you crossed to get to Sector 17, Club Independent's home.

Having reminded myself of the geography, I arrived at my flat with perfect symmetry, some natural homing device having guided me through uniform streets.

Strange Days

––––––––––––

Dawn didn't bring with it the sweet chirp of birds but their bleeping imitation of portable technology, urging in the busy conveyor belt of a life needing to be got done.

On the streets, prodigal products, half-enjoyed by half-lives, Friday's Faustian pact finding its nemesis. Litter was where it shouldn't have been, forming a collage of reckless excess to poison wildlife. Birds pecked at each other violently over scraps of wasted food dropped in gutters and overflowing from bins, before flying to shit their contaminated faeces on an unsuspecting public. Peace was not to be found. Cars were clocking up miles, stopping and starting between lights, changing colour, changing shape, going around the circuit again.

Talk blew on the breeze, grew under the feeble sun, seeking to dominate. Groups ghoulishly gabbed; glottal vocals snapping, letting whiny terrors into the atmosphere, dislocated in undiscriminating ears. Lies and rumours were their preoccupation, chewed up and spat out, spiked with maliciousness,

"I see that Lisa's pregnant again…He's a funny 'un though…"

"Well, I said to ah…"

"Like that Mary Dickinson. She's the same…"

"…Oh, he's a bugger…"

"…Never been right…"

"…It's all wrong," said the old woman, hunched by years, rubber-necking in on the conversation.

It wasn't just him, or her, or them. It was everyone. It was one big conspiracy against the institutionalised gossips.

Mr Steal's son is "a bad 'un." He takes drugs, never smiles, always comes in late. He's got some strange friends. "He's not right." She told Mrs Drew to watch her daughter. Helen had heard something. Helen's husband, "Our Alan", was going to go over there. Alan got right proud at the mention of his name and got on his soap box: One nation. One type. One big vision. All in perfect harmony.

A furnace of nods, winks, jerking elbows, raised eyebrows, knowing sneers, ooows, aaahs, blazed away, forming a layer of insidiousness above the city centre.

Off-white clouds filled the sky, of different density and purpose. None from nature's creation. Brooding, looming above the urban cacophony, pillars of smoke from a multitude of factories making products to enhance our lives. Cooling towers and malevolent charcoal conduits peered across estates with their frizzy white wigs, like some docile Santa Claus sleeping off the sherry or sitting in judgement.

Is it really Saturday? Is it really 2020? Are there any real people left or has everything burned away?

A moment's contemplation in bed became a trip around the universe. What is God like? Is He up there, sweeping around infinity, keeping an eye on His many planets? Visited once every two thousand years or so, give or take a little time for complications?

"Ah, there's Earth. Shit! What's happened? What's happened to these monkeys? What's happened to my planet? Where's the air? Where are the fuckin' trees? Shit, they're killing each other! It's a joke, it's got to be a joke! It's a conspiracy against God.

"No, they're serious. What are they doing? Shit, it's free will – that's what's done it. Why did I let them have that?

"That day, I remember so well. I'd been so edgy and tired after creating Earth. I'd started the day by slicing an angel in half, just to see where angels go when their existence has been snuffed out. I didn't learn one thing, other than that there was one less angel in heaven that afternoon. It got me really paranoid. I had to get away from Earth and start on something new, so I threw in a last few things (the orgasm, evolution, whales, marijuana, memory in humans), re-shaped a few things (finely balanced climate, toughening up mother nature, put the human heart in perfect symmetry with the mind), then sent down Adam and Eve. Then, the free-will conundrum. I shouldn't have been in such a hurry. Shit."

I need love. A little bit of love. I need to get out of bed to get love. Love would make everything all right. A man can lose himself in love, lose himself.

Dinner time was over. They were drilling, smashing, lifting, making mechanics the soundtrack. Nothing stayed still for a minute, growing more organised in its pointlessness. Where could life be found amongst this?

A slow motion shower between cigarettes. Mentally dividing the little remaining Stevie-Dust into four more snorts I took a hit and looked forward to later.

In the newsagent's I swiped up two papers and joined a queue which shuffled along after a few bleeps. Invariably the bar-code reader had a few failures, allowing the line to remain at a thickness of six bodies. "Bleep", step, think about all the curious objects on display, glancing at the porno mags lined along the top shelf, "Bleep", step, tapping my foot, exaggerated like some cartoon character. "Bleep", step.

"And twenty red filter please."

"Bleep. Bleep. Bleep."

"Sixty Euros and fifty three."

Separating the sterling from Euros, I got—boom!—the exact amount, the coincidence lost on those grumbling at the back of a lengthened queue.

My "thank-you" went unreciprocated. "Bleep" as I filled the pause with steps, clattering on one more bleep.

Pat O'Thwacke's pub was the perfect place for some knowledge assimilation, an old fashioned pub in that it didn't have any goddam video games, its only concession to modernity being a machine to pay by plastic. I guess that's why it was always so quiet, frequented mainly by old men and Marxists.

I scanned the newspaper columns; their cold, logical slabs of bleak indifference confirming evidence of an impending apocalypse. The words locked on to one another, sentences clicking in my understanding, like digits cracking a code.

Old age pensioner stabbed in the neck for seventy Euros. Bomb blast kills forty people. Global temperatures rise for the thirty-first successive year. There were hermaphrodite fish in the Pacific Ocean where France had carried out nuclear tests some years earlier. A man of multiple identities had been seducing women and infecting them with the old AIDS virus. Dubbed "the Spermicidal Maniac", witnesses reported that he had "a very large member".

In the Science section, the sighting of flashing lights somewhere beyond Pluto: the article quoting a top astronomer who suggested, "If identified it could explain how Earth was created."

Flashing lights beyond Pluto: The Great Welder knocking up another little toy.

Mischief Night

Our clod-hopping boots were once again pacing down to the riverside. Same clothes, same visuals, same routine, thoughts and experiences having nudged our evolutionary paths only subtly.

Neon bars pulsed, throwing out participants for a fight as fire engines, ambulances and police cars slipped into insanity, wailing down streets competing for business.

Two women belched from a pub, entangled in each other, scratching, pulling hair, kicking, slaps with fists. Two men followed, cursing each other, making movements to attack. "Away then!" Hard knuckles hammering skulls. Two more miscreants for the Ark.

Sirens converged to one loud bellowing warning, reverberating around town. Armageddon was coming. Got to score.

The bloodshots were out, the same sterile faces in the same seats, drinking the same drinks, admiring the patterned-with-rips décor.

Sirens inside. Dots and bleeps and loops and stop. Start. Swelling bleeps, sucked up into the vidbox. Bleep. Start again. Crack, balls scatter. We're fifty cups of coffee with excitement, top corner roll up with the gods applauding. We're goddam legends of cool. A nod to the dealer. He takes an emporium of narcotics from the soap dispenser: all shiny happy pills, dusts and natural herbs.

Reeto Dust is all the latest stim. "Big market push," he says. Pot's all dried up. "Pig crackdown. Prices up. Two hundred a quarter." I played my panic like varying degrees of cool, eyed up the bag and staked our money on Reeto.

"Successful?"

"No pot. We didn't have enough." I didn't let Joe unwind his disappointment. "Karma fix baby. A big bag of that Stevie dust. It's called Reeto. It's the big stim in town."

Joe's frown curled to a smile. "Well, we have to keep up with the latest fashions."

On cue, its tip pointed, its body held like a cattle prod – Stevie's right hand choked the neck, his left a full fist around the base, taking off the accumulated germs on each molesting tightening, so it felt thick and greasy and gave the cue's butt a darker tincture.

"Gonna win me fuckin' money back."

Joe and I looked at each other just to see who was the most scared, but the glance galvanised us. We were lucky tonight.

Stevie started off badly, jacking the cue ball off the table, across the floor where it clanked against a chair leg, awakening an old woman who screamed "Aaaargh! It's a snake! Snake! Snake!"

Balls rolled in, silk consummate ease. Excitement pumped nervously, Stevie's brain thinking he was playing at our table, Stevie's hands involved in a game in another dimension. He was thirty Euros down, wanting to hit me.

"Maybe you can join in next time?"

"Fuckin' agen, lucky cunt."

Jaws for coins, crunching metal rammed down its throat, jerks connecting with ambitions, cues chalked like fevered disembowelling.

Looking down the barrel of the cue, coiling the trigger of my shot, dummy runs between finger and thumb: loading up.

Remember everything you see. White ball. Pupils darting. Black ball. A quivering mouth. Blow your brains out, Stevie. Fifty Euros up.

"Fuckin' double or nothing," said Stevie like I'd programmed him.

I got lucky on the break, smacked his ego up as he chalked increasingly impatiently at the cue. Thoughts kept coming through of a kitchen knife with my name on it. I snatched, messed up, but coaxed a ball in. Stevie's tangible sigh felt as thick as a blade in the ribs.

Clattering kisses flung around the table, another ball trickling to the precipe of a pocket before a sound as the ball dropped, like an empty gun chamber in Russian Roulette.

I got apocalypse hot, said, "When I miss, then it's your turn."

I missed.

"Fuckin' bars—stard!" said Stevie, dragged from stomach to lips, a bending posture directing vitriol at the ball which had rattled out of the pocket.

This was it. This was the time to finish him off, to get the money, get the dust, and get the fuck out of Dodge.

Cue ball rolls around in haste, kicks in as I size up the next shot. A clink in a blink, next shot sorted.

"Lucky bastard," didn't put me off, though it preceded an unnerving moment when everything went abruptly and significantly quieter; conversations ending, marooned, unable to kick start; pauses pricking the remaining rumblings, silence asphyxiating them instantly. Mad, bloodshot eyes darted, heads bobbed and twisted, wondering where and why it had started, afraid to speak until they knew. The fear ballooned, time trying to catch up, recover the digits of information and experience, find meaning. They didn't dare speak, growing more insane with each second of incomprehensibility. A bleep on the vidbox. Laughter. Voices relieved, louder then ever.

A crack for the black ball, money times two.

"Lucky fuck," came out hard, boulders of inflexions gnashed through his teeth.

"Being lucky is a skill," felt like quote of the week.

A knife ripped through Stevie's coat on its entrance, gave me time to side step its desperate lunge. Luck flipped on me, flipped out on Joe, his gasp prolonged, thinning before a pain-noise. Three exclamation marks bounced all over Stevie, wrestling him to the ground.

Outside, sirens again, gangs of kids running, battle cries stammering. Smoke filled the air, condensing our space inside the walls of variant tinnitus.

Blood dripped from Joe's arm, half his blue shirt drenched with a darker hue. No answers to my questions before he was working out the time involved in walking to Taff's or hospital. He didn't relay his conclusion, just went.

Think "one", bleep. Think "eight", bleep. Think "nought", bleep. Think "nine", bleep-bleep. Think left, think right. Think left, think right. Think left. Hear voice. I'll remember the last time I was sane and well rested and act like that. Left, right. Left right. A door closes. The buzzer has the name Friedland beneath it. Turn left. Getting closer to escape. Another left. I've been on these stairs for a lifetime. At last, bleep. Bleep. Bleep. Think "four", bleep-bleep.

Type '30.10.2020. In my continuing journey to start the love revolution, I have acquired some more information. People are unhappy, but they've stopped thinking about why they are unhappy. They've decided instead to take the quick fix of a junk culture, where every new shock is something to give your life meaning, something to talk about, to say you were there when it happened. Whether it's communal disbelief or communal grief, it's all communal. The media is there to anaesthetise, not to elucidate. So nobody can really care about the Americans invading Panama again, killing two thousand civilians. There's no time to stop and think about the price of building a fighter aircraft being equal to the cost of providing 1.5 million people in the third world with fresh water for life, because in the blink of an eye "Peace force" on "Humanitarian intervention" numbs the effect, before we're comatose, lapping up the rich millionaire on his round-the-world balloon voyage, or the film star who's been arrested. The scientists at NASA who have experimented with the effects of drugs on spiders finally nail us in our coffins. Those on speed spin their webs enthusiastically yet leave large holes. On marijuana they start with great concentration but make a mess of their webs halfway through. On caffeine they make a complete mess of the web, but it's still better then chloral hydrate, an ingredient in sleeping pills, with which the spiders give up before they even get started. That's the story we'll all remember. Always leave them laughing.

"*Yet I know that the Shellac oil company in Nigeria trains armies to kill local protesters with the help of the country's dictator government. I also know about Rupert C Donald depriving the country in the last ten years of tax on profits of over a billion Euros, through his loopholes and perks, nicely donated by the NRP.*"

A buzz to my consciousness like an electric shock. Joe is distantly contemptuous of the wound, just wants his half. Then he walks away like he's pre-programmed, like he didn't care to stay: it wasn't his mission.

A complaining yowling, a woman's voice shouting, "Now! Fuckin' 'urry up now!" I am awake, exhausted by my sleep. "Gereere now, for a break ya fuckin' neck." I digited myself into the new day, heard a man saying, "Fuckin' listen t'ya muvva when she tells ye somet. And don't start wi' ye fuckin' crying." I heard whimpering. "Fuckin' shurrit, 'urry up," in a tone which suggested the limits of his sympathy. Footsteps took them away.

One quarter of my half-consciousness was asking who I was last night, the other militantly pushing my head into cold water. A coffee, a cigarette, some more coffee and some dust. On top of the world kids.

Anonymity beckoned outside in the freshly chilled air. The sky hung a blank piercing white, cloudless and uniform, cut squarely along the horizon, giving the houses and towers an appearance of being cut and pasted on. An icy piano defined the clarity, a slow plinkety-dropping-frozen-plonk. Whiteness surrounded every tree without deterrent, every home without malice, locking the foreground into the background.

Characters moving about seemed detached from the whiteness, whilst children in Halloween garb seemed more sinister against the colour's autocracy.

A roughly sketched demon appeared from a chemical plant on the horizon, visible as I slumped into town, ignorable as I got amongst the streets.

"Bleep!"

"Fifty-seven Euros and ten."

"Bleep!"

I found a desolated park, the coin machine for swings clogged up with chewing gum and foreign money. No side-flick thrill kill ego-jet quick fix for young DM. Just the paper info.

Manchester Slicer, Rudi Carusso, thirty-two, arrested. No background, fourteen murders over thirteen years. 4,000 million years ago, the origins of life. Triassic, Jurassic, Cretaceous, Palaeocene, Eocene, Oligocene, Miocene, Pliocene, Pleistocene, "Mystery of woman found living in a cave". In Cyprus, woman found, exhausted, traumatised, speaking a language not recognised. Been there over two weeks. Dead male body nearby.

Report says that children of the poor (the underclass, unpeople) are smaller and more malnutritioned than the children of the rich.

An old man had appeared, positioning himself aside me on the bench, gesturing to his wrist to ask me the time. I told him, but he looked dismayed, pointing to his ears and acting out a countenance of puzzlement. He was deaf, so I thrust my watch up to his eyes. It gave me an encore to his bewilderment, his shaking head hinting at frustration. I looked at my watch. It had stopped at just before twelve. I shrugged my shoulder apologetically.

Silence. Just watching from the peripherals. He knew nothing of the pace of modern life: No heels sounding in a hurry, no cars tearing away in the back of his mind. The perennial dreamer, connecting meaning to life with story-lines concocted in his imagination.

He started crying. I had to perform an expression of understanding.

He said, "It's the sea, it sounds so beautiful." It touched, whether by imagining it and missing it or just missing it. Some moment from the memory banks of moments touched him and he was crying either tears of pain or joy, I could not say. At least he was living.

I returned to my paper and – boom! – immediately noticed an advertisement for hearing aids at 'Under E700', which meant six hundred and ninety-nine Euros and ninety-nine cents, because someone above doesn't trust the sales assistant below, because a till must be opened, a sale must be logged. Bleep, here's your one pence change.

I folded my papers, nodded to the deaf man and went to find a payphone that would accept cash; not credit cards or fingerprint charges, but some jangling cash. Not vandalised either, or out of order. It took some finding.

"DM."

"Stranger."

"What about Saturday's game?"

"You're going to be there?"

"Yeah."

"About time," said Dave.

"Where?"

"What eight is to sixty four, at Fellini minus six, being visible."

"Done."

The after tone drill brought no peace. I replaced the handset and looked around. "Neighbourhood Watch" signs observed from walls, from behind hedgerows, tucked in corners of windows.

Thoughts created characters in my universe, philosophers and philanderers, their lives cut short by buzzer interruptions for tricks and treats, the guises for money. I laid in the dark, intercom switched off, detached from their demands, unable to communicate save for spasms rapping imaginary keys; the history of the world from birth to death. Words appeared, an erupting thesaurus of thought-association, lyrically connected by moods and perception. In the dimension where dreams are real, our reality filled their nightmares. Images of a holocaust, its letters on pages, found in a book of mankind's suicide note, found on a moon where no life can inhabit. Click. Gunshots. Knocking on wood.

"Are you dead, DM?" came an imitation of Joe's voice through the letterbox. "Get up ya lazy bastard!" sounded more familiar.

Dusted up, we were on the streets within half an hour.

"Can ya spare a penny for Halloween, mister?"

We laughed as we passed, Joe tossing the figure a penny. Ten yards on the coin whizzed past my ear, tinkering on concrete.

"Fuckin' wanker!" shouted one of the little voices from behind.

Joe affected a wise old tone with, "Whatever happened to find a penny, pick it up, get some goddam luck?" bending down to retrieve the coin. "Spin ya for it?"

"Heads."

"Sure?"

I nodded, he flicked, caught, slapped, tossed it to me without looking. "You're the lucky man tonight, DM."

Added to the usual weekenders, the carnival of adults dressed for Halloween, giving cover to the shifty real monsters. O'Malley's caught us in its net, showed us a real horror show.

"That is beautiful. I could marry her," said Joe like he was deeply burdened. "But she's out of my league."

"Two times."

He hawked around to two more females, observing them whilst lighting a cigarette, dousing himself with panache.

"What about them, DM?"

"Still a few rungs up the ladder. We'd have to be goddam witty and suave to have a chance with them. It would drain me for a week."

"And then there's always the disappointment," added Joe solemnly followed by a dejected pause.

"We are goddam freaks."

We laughed, Joe executing his cigarette swiftly as a prelude to, "Let's do it."

They had sensed our advances long before we'd reached them, halting us with cold stares and one cursory "No".

Alcohol was our salvation, maintaining some dignity whilst quickly finishing our drinks and high-tailing it out of there.

We ventured into spacehead territory where the music was a thunderous techno, urged on by a desultory DJ, "DJ Dictator D". He certainly was a musical fascist.

Men and boys struck vengeful poses in each other's company. With conversation impossible they had to temper this spirit with cocksure posturing when the women and girls passed.

We certainly were freaks here, but took some mental pictures of our unattainable prey for comfort later.

By the time we reached Holden's we were analysing our inadequacies before resting our egos on two chairs.

"You need a good opening line. You need something that's natural, maybe a little bit clever, but not too cocky," I offered.

"No, cocky's good."

"Yeh, but we can't do that kind of cocky."

"If we really believed in it we could. We just have to imagine we are, be like we imagine and we'll be there, like an aplomb bomb baby."

"We've got to get there first, need a rouse. We need fate, we need luck, like an accident or something. If we could just get a drink spilt on us, bump into some women in a gentle, humorous way."

"A light!" was Joe's stab at Archimedes. "We just ask for a light."

"My, you've been rummaging through some pretty dusty vaults in your memory banks."

"Hey, king of fuckin' suave."

We gripped cigarettes in our mouths, scouring the room for smokers. Female smokers. Decent looking female smokers. Not too decent looking and beyond our capabilities though.

Two women, looking late-twenties, caught our attention almost simultaneously. One, mouse-blonde shoulder length hair, pale skin, five foot eight, the other, auburn hair in a bob, slightly tanned skin, about five foot nine.

"Excuse me, have you a light please?" Joe began.

The taller girl gave him a lighter.

"Thanks," and Joe lit his cigarette, passed the baton to me.

"Nice lighter," I said, handing it back.

"Thanks," came a bemused reply.

"Thank you. Without that lighter we would never have met."

They both laughed. That was a good start.

Joe interjected, "But don't get us started on fate."

They laughed again, more curiously.

"I'm Dan."

"Joe."

The girl with the auburn hair said her name was Nicky.

The blonde said, "I'm Nicky too."

We all four laughed because it was expected of us.

Driving home in the taxi Joe said, "That's where we lost it. We had no follow up, nothing to keep it going. It was a lame joke about 'Nicky number two'."

"Hey, I'm sorry, I'll write a script next time."

"Then it was through what's your job, where do you live, what do you do on a weekend? Do you enjoy your job? How long have you known each other? It was like a Spanish Inquisition."

The taxi-driver shrieked, "No one expects the Spanish Inquisition!" briefly alarming us, setting us off the course of our dialogue.

Dusted up, playing cards, thinking of a masterplan.

"Something more imaginative."

"Politics," I suggested.

"Fuck off. No, we want to get into a conversation where we seem to have done lots of exciting things."

"Like what?"

"Erm, holidays, er, great gigs," Joe replied, fading fast. "I can't really remember much."

"Me neither."

"We arrange to do something," returned Joe with renewed vigour, pausing, continuing with amorphous hand gestures. "The day before we go on the pull, we make plans for the day after, so that we can invite whoever we pull along the next day."

"Like playing cards and getting stoned?"

A laugh, "Fuck it, deal 'em."

QUESTIONS

What if you never come down? You've got to phone in sick, get up at noon, ponder all the unanswered questions that gnaw away at you each and every day. Concentrate on them, clear out old rubbish and make space for the come-down.

The surface we stand on travels at around one thousand miles per hour, the earth rotating around the sun at almost sixty-seven thousand miles per hour. Incredible when you think about it.

We need oxygen to live. Trees create oxygen. We chop down trees. It doesn't make any sense when you think about it.

Why did the sky again have that omniscient whiteness, framing the buildings and framing our lives? Had a vast dome been constructed around the town?

A phone call. "Hello?" Wrong number. Perhaps no phone call at all. There is no phone in our time capsule, for there are no outside lines. There's only an imaginary phone to ring up imaginary friends for fake conversations. "How's the weather?" There is no weather, just the elaborately constructed veil of the dome, behind which all is red, arid, motionless. "How's your job?" We have no jobs. Our occupation is imagining that life still goes on after the holocaust. The people aren't real, just barely sketched characters. "How's your love life?" There is no love, there is no life.

What if I never come down?

Going outside convinced me of the plot. We had reached the year 2020 at random and were deteriorating into an ugly, mechanical world. All beauty had gone, life no longer throwing up surprises let alone the epiphanies benevolently bestowed in childhood. There's only this hard, inescapable plod. Even compassion is limited. It takes a hit, a mainline for emotion to function.

I remembered that newspaper photograph of a man, high above

the ground, seated on a branch, his arms in a locked hug around a tree. That's love. So why did they still build the road?

I became entangled in a spider's labour, fine legs drawing out a trap, tapping on gossamer a morse code to allies.

Who knows the damage a spider can really do? I found its lair, crushed its foil body, cut off the government's tracking device.

From my darkness I can just make out the slow bleeps. Every once in a while my imagination fades and I am hanging in reality via a life support machine.

I have to ask myself, "What is Diego Garcia?" to remind myself that it was once a British colony in the Indian Ocean. The British allowed American bombers to be based there, removing the indigenous Ilois people and putting them on Mauritius. That would be important, something to remember.

What if I never come down?

What if this blurred outer perspective stays out of sync forever? Little holes appear in my inner self, allowing the demons of paranoia and fantasy in, eager and indulgent. I wasn't ready to play with this madness yet, I had to clock back in to automatic living.

"So you're better now, Daniel?"

"It wasn't anything serious then?"

"It won't come back then?"

He couldn't ask the questions he wanted to ask, so dressed his curiosity with the pellucid garments of diplomacy.

"No, I'm OK, I'll be back in tomorrow."

Did I Panic? Did I sound abrupt? Would I get through work tomorrow? Like a fiend I would.

THE SHARKS

Thursdays were usually shark nights, a ritual meeting of minds. Taff; stoutly educated, studious features, thickset black hair, bespectacled. Jez; eager eyes, youthful face, a flop of light brown hair. Phil; short cropped black hair, stone features, five o'clock shadow. Joe and I; creased arrogance. A terraced house in Sector 8 commenced ceremony.

Jez and Taff lost the preliminaries and were assigned the dope run, lucky for Joe and I as we had no desire to see Stevie again so soon.

Waiting, we tested our reflexes, Phil busy writing a report upstairs.

"Ya feeling lucky?"

"Maybe."

"Might need some help?"

"Nah."

I took out a penny.

"Don't want a lucky penny?"

"Maybe."

"Call it."

"Tails."

We laughed at my regimented efficiency; spinning, catching, slamming on the table, pocketing.

Joe and I split four victories between us before Jez and Taff's return, windswept and panting, preceding a gradual coming together. A Rolling Stones' disc swaggered in, a haze formed, and cards were dealt. Five bolts of electricity shot out between uniform gasps as each card slurred from the pack and slapped down, whisked around three times without blinking. A final card, face up alongside the pack before hands picked up; Jez, Taff and I ravenously, Phil somewhat circumspectly. Joe waited, because he was enjoying his drink, and he always did so anyway as he thought it good manners.

Exhales, some bluffing. Somebody had a good hand, somebody had the worst hand. Nobody knew who had what or the potency of their own hand. But it could all change after a few rounds of Skat. It just mattered that nobody knocked early.

Jez had to go first, deliberating stylishly over the face up eight of hearts. It was a nice secure card, a little pension and cottage in the country. But if he took it we would know the suit he'd chosen to pursue. Jez liked to play, liked the cloak and dagger, picked from the pack. He put down the six of hearts, gave nothing away in his Machiavellian smile (not the first Machiavellian body language of the night).

Phil considered his move before picking up the card Jez had left, laying down the nine of clubs.

Did he have three sweet hearts, a nice tidy accumulation? Was he going to knock next round, catch some fragile score out?

A mood of desperation came in, Taff picking up the nine, laying down a three of hearts. Joe knew exactly what he wanted, picking up a card from the deck, saying "Fuck!" and laying it back down, face up. Four of diamonds.

I had a healthy twenty-one in diamonds and gratefully scooped up the scraps, giving up a ten of spades. Nothing flashy, but in the early jostling survival was the most important thing. A hybrid murmur – anxiety and wisdom kicking their heels – circled amongst the sharks.

Jez admired the card I'd jettisoned.

"Y'can never pass up a ten," had become a well-rehearsed cliché, always offered by someone in the group at the appropriate moment.

Jez did though, scraping another card from the pack, enthusiastically tucking it into his hand, returning the Jack of Diamonds. My options were limited and everybody knew.

As always Phil contemplated, manumitting a wave of electricity culminating in a joint reaching me, a butt end to toke and kill. Phil picked from the pack, laid six of clubs.

Taff reached for it, swiftly despatching a diamond seven.

Joe knocked at his turn, smiling perniciously at me. "Thought I'd give you a hand."

No doubt what I'd do once the knock had sent out its warning. The diamond three I left in the seven's wake didn't impress Jez, in and out of the pack, turning away the card he'd chosen before it reached his hand. Ace of spades. Phil groaned, took a blind card and raised his eyebrows, fitting it into a place where the three of hearts once resided, almost meeting Taff's darting hand as he withdrew. Taff dismissed the card contemptuously. Nobody cared what it was, attention focused on Joe.

He laid his cards, "Twenty-five," to confirm what we saw.

I laid mine, offered, "Twenty-eight." Then Jez's "Twenty," Phil's "Twenty-three," and Taff's "Twenty-six".

Jez tossed a coin into the centre of the table; one life lost.

The intensity of our involvement was sustained through each round, all encompassing to keep us mute as games progressed.

Joe lost all his lives first, then Jez before I succumbed.

It came down to Phil and Taff in the final, Phil two lives left, Taff none, his so-called "invisible life" between him and defeat. Those not participating watched, fully animated and boggle-eyed, rolling up some joints whilst seeing Taff come from behind – two wins on the bounce – to make the game level; two invisible lives left. Then it was just a question of bottle.

As Taff dealt the cards you sensed it was going to be quick. Taff had that killer look in his eyes. Phil picked from the deck, laid another down. Taff knocked.

Phil took his last chance with the pack. "I don't believe it. Fucker."

Taff laid his cards authoritatively, underlining them with, "Twenty-three."

Phil flung out his cards, muttered, "Eighteen," as Taff glowed in his fulfilment as champion.

Start again.

Something more was being fought out – a mainline of adrenaline, a connection with all around; the music, the air, the one-consciousness, the capacity to manipulate fate. Luck hardly came into it. Through the hours, skill defined character, style maintaining what we were as we summed up:

"It's how you play the game."

"It's how you live your life."

"What do you mean?" asked Taff of me.

"You've got to know when to be cautious, when to dare and when to go for what you believe in."

"We are the masters of our own fate then?"

"No Taff, you are the master of all of us. You are the omnipotent force behind Skat."

Taff laughed, affected being proud.

"You control the game. We just have the illusion of influence. In reality we are all just scrounging at your feet, snapping up the bones of what you transmit."

Joe interjected, "The Rupert C Donald of Skat."

"I take exception, Mr Rogan, at being identified with that cunt."

I defended Taff. "Well, he owns television stations and newspapers, poisons the masses with novelties, gimmicks, lies and distractions. It gives us a quick fix culture based on the lowest common denominator. A sick, unreal world to wipe out all intelligent thought, give him a malleable audience. But you'd miss us if we weren't involved. If you didn't have the chance of defeat you wouldn't want to play."

"He's off," said Joe.

"You really don't have any political ideology, do you, Joe?" questioned Taff somewhat perplexed.

"If I can just quote the late Bill Hicks, and let that be the end of it: 'All governments are lying cocksuckers.' "

"The gospel according to Joseph Rogan," added Jez.

"But you've got to have some interest if these people are fucking us. I mean, it's got to affect you if there's no democracy," pleaded Taff.

"There never has been. Look at your history books. Check out the New Labour government 1997. Big majority, big vote of confidence, big democratic mandate. Didn't do half the things they were going to do. Still sold arms to the world, still stopped benefits, still made people pay for education. Screwed everybody they could screw and gave the big guys a break. You talk about Donald, New Labour helped him build his empire. They were just too stupid to see he was going to take over, and help get in the NRP. And fuck it, that's it."

But Taff was on to something; an intellectual, political and philosophical debate, a kind of warm down before limbering up for the next round of cards.

"I will never understand why the masses don't rise up against Donald, stop buying his shitty papers, stop watching his shitty television."

"That's just about all there is left," added Phil, departing for the kitchen.

"There's some channels left," said Jez, "minority, but they tell the truth."

"Never mind that that's all there is," Taff summarised. "That's no argument. Don't buy it. Switch if off. Think a little."

"People don't know Donald's history, don't know how bad he really is," I said, searching a thick file in my memories for evidence. "Like, nobody knows that thirty-two years ago Donald's Australian tabloid, the *Daily Reflection* published a fourteen year old girl's diary which mentioned a thirteen year old boy and their exploits together. He was expelled from school because of it, then killed himself. They found out later that the diary was all made up. But nobody checked. Donald just wanted a fat, best-selling, titillating story.

"Nobody questions the billions he hasn't paid in tax, money that could help the poor, well, if the NRP were inclined to do that."

"Don't you know that Cocktail Suicide 8, DM?" asked Phil, emerging from the kitchen.

"Yeh, haven't seen them in a while though."

"They've got it in for Donald haven't they? D'ye think they did put that acid in the water supply for the News Channel?"

"It sounded like one of theirs."

"Amazing really that they weren't found guilty?" added Taff. "All the muscle Donald has."

"Haven't you ever thought about joining them?" asked Phil.

"I like 'em n' all, but they ain't gonna bring down the establishment."

"Your aim?" asked Taff like he already knew the answer.

"Oh yes."

"Once he can fit it in," quipped Joe.

Jez went into a long monologue that began, "Just put the revolution on hold while we get stoned and play some cards…" and ended with "…It's all going to happen, but us gods of the cards, our plan's already mapped, so we can play on for a bit."

It drew us all in, let us play with madness.

You Talking to Me?

I tried to remember what Dave had said, easily distracted, seated on a low-level wall in the square, by people, mostly young, hanging out on the grass.

When he'd arrived, he'd started with, "Where've you been lately?"

He'd said something about a chemical plant. Trioxide? Tiloxide? Toxide? He said there'd been five leaks in the past year, said one was deliberate, an experiment. He'd said there were plans and he'd need my help when the time came.

"You know lots of people from the old days," he had said.

That was the gist of it, then some small talk: all wiped out.

"You know lots of people from the old days," I re-ran.

I would get up soon to write them down.

Cocktail Suicide 8. The Earth Tribe. The Anti-Fascist Army. Green Friends. Freedom Coalition. Freedom Network. Hemp World. Peace Movement. Rave Anarchists. Earth Action. The Democratic Marxists. Corporate Watch.

This part of my memory was OK. I burned the lists, crumpled the remains to ash and flushed them down the toilet, twice.

Some more dust. If I could bring these groups together we could bring England to a standstill. We could demand roads be closed, parks be built, people be housed, the sick be treated. We could take all the wasted money that goes to the rich and give it to the needy. We could add a day to the weekend, stop pollution and build a Utopia.

An emptiness needed to be filled. It's been so long, I can't recall what love was like, or youth ripped from me. An emptiness could be filled by television, any television. Cheap trash intellectual hi-jack.

The lottery show.

Chances of winning the jackpot are 1 in 13,983,816.

"Best Dressed Homeless" judged by six fashion designers, discussing aesthetics, "street-smart", "individuality", "colour/environment scheme" and uh, "meaning". Best dressed homeless person won a home. Small print flashed on the bottom of the screen:

"Winning prize is for no more than one year at two star accommodation. The producers reserve the right to film winners and disqualify."

News. Rudi Carusso, suspected of being The Manchester Slicer, has been placed in the vicinity of three of the most recent murders. However, his DNA results have proved inconclusive so far. He was called "shy" by the reporter.

The film world was preparing to commemorate the anniversary of the death of Emily Spencer.

A relationship psychologist exuded a personality as she counselled a couple on a comfy yellow sofa.

A post-pollution disorder specialist offered advice to an audience of malfunctioning freaks.

A neglect psychologist explained to a generation of teenagers how their condition had occurred and how it could be treated.

Filling lives with little pigeon-holes, crammed full of expectations and failures. The post-modern ironist counsellor was on his way.

Flicking through the channels, invariably stumbling on blank screens with "Sport TV", "Erotic Channel", "World News", "Modern Cinema" or "Chat TV" displayed in the corner and "Buy Now" emblazoned in the centre. I could only land on free channels, their quality cloned several times, stretched over a season. The televisual amoebas, the cultural split infinities, more is less and less is more, the lowest of the low for dunderheads who take too long to raise their eyebrows in acknowledgement and surprise.

A game show where contestants put their heads into a vat of maggots before running, semi-clad, backwards, on a path of excrement.

"You sick people!"

The viewers were stupid, were ignorant. They deserved to die. I could not stop the systematic degradation of their outer experiences, systematically denied any alternative culture. Their continual dumbing down by tabloids and TV meant that if any rational, Utopian argument were presented to them, they would by nature regard it with scorn. They were Calibans, subject to subjective vicarious interpretation, all second-hand, all modified and mollified: "New Hope", "New Dream", new bullshit, new lies.

Protruding from a strategically-holed board, body parts on "Sex Date". The challenger ("The Horn", complete with a novelty horn) gets to see the tits or ass of the date, but not the face. Previous horns get to come back and explain their sexual encounters.

Is this what we are? Is this what we have become?

Buy this, it's cheap. Buy this, it's cheaper. Buy this, it's better. Buy this, it's better. Buy this, it's faster. Get up to speed, get in the club, get a new one, get a different one. Look like this, feel better. Buy this, fit in.

The face of friendly fascism – a beckoning finger pulling back the curtains to reveal a catalogue of stuff we can't afford. Credit keeps us paying for the rest of our lives.

I switched off, found difficulty wiping it all from my memory as police surveillance planes murmured overhead.

GODS

They're singing Christmas carols but they don't know the words, drunkenly "la-la-la-ing" until they get to "Sle—eep in he—ven—ly pea—eace" when some unity and application is found.

"Oh my god!" shrieks some woman, vomiting too much laughter.

Jesus writes: "22/12/2020 (snigger). I am most vexed. Not only has my book been re-written again, my ideas and philosophies ignored or manipulated, but I still find that my so-called father's name is the favoured exclamation of mankind. My father's tally far exceeds mine and I have just about had enough. It is time to take some action. I will demand that I am sent back. It's been long enough now."

"Sle—eep in he—ven—ly pea—eace …"

They pass a man in the street pressing a buzzer, shouting through the intercom, "Can I use your toilet?"

The firm's security watch him on a screen from deep inside their employer's building.

"There's a toilet down the street," came through to the man in the street.

Thighs tightening around his groin, he pressed the buzzer to speak again. "I 'aven't gor enough money. C'mon, I won't be long."

"Go in the street," followed with the beginnings of laughter cut short by a bleep.

Buzz. "Wor if a get caught? C'mon."

"Have you got a credit card?"

He checked his pockets, juggling his crotch. "No. C'mon, it's Christmas for god's sake!"

"Sorry, company policy."

He cursed, clod-hopped behind a wall and undid his flies, pissing on his hands before finding the wall. A camera whirred around to film him. He hadn't finished when a police car arrived, officers clasping cuffs on him, taking him away. He was worth a few measly points, which could make all the difference at the end of the season.

The officers race to get back to the station and cash in, passing a gang of boys.

"I'll call it in," said the driver.

"No," said the other officer, looking up from his notebook. "We'll come back for them. Three, five, six. That's gonna be double figures if we collar them."

The boys were going house-to-house, one rapping Christmas carols as the others beat sounds from their bodies. Nobody opened a door to them so they ran down the street hitting cars to set off alarms. It got half the street out, fiddling with controls to "Bleep" snuff out the various sirens.

After a few minutes pause the boys ran back, setting the alarms off again. In blurs they chased the night, distinguished by logos and slogans from all the most famous sportswear manufacturers.

We were waking, trying to make sense of no sense. We were broke, futile, our language slipping into disorder.

"Fuckin' mean," said Joe.

"Did you see that? That unicorn?"

The drugs never seemed to wear off, now one constant in which we had to work for our kicks.

"Jumpin' Jack Flash over the fire."

"It's all burning Joe. It's just us left."

"Good. We got the music, the books, the drugs. It just needs to burn itself out before we need to score again."

"But there'll be no one left to deal."

"Then we'll build a rocket to planet Drug."

"No. I'm gonna stay, use all these books and music discs to educate a new civilisation, one last crack at the human race. I'll teach them how to explore inner and outer space."

"Never work. Humans are bad. You can't change that."

I grunted, resigned, flicking through the local paper and its descriptions of tragedy and loss. They didn't affect me anymore. I'd read it every day for all of my life.

"Story, DM," slurred Joe.

"Uh, OK, yeh. So where do I start?"

"In the beginning."

"In the beginning there was light. Then there were moths."

Somebody laughed.

"It's a prequel. It's how Adam and Eve fucked it up. Well, I guess it was Adam, rutting as Eve painted, their infrequent coming together enough to produce a son throughout the centuries, each one called Adam. And Adam would find his Eve and on and on it went. All was cool until the twentieth century fuck-up. Subsequent Adams got into drugs, got into crime, got into the dying young game.

"Adam moved into a fractured twenty-first century, through three foster families before he fell in love with Eve. He didn't have a permanent job or a permanent family, and he liked that. But he was a manic depressive."

"Screwy Louie," muttered Joe from beneath his REM.

"He took hits from needles, Eve along for the ride. When he had enough energy he'd strum his acoustic guitar outside shopping precincts. He was quite a novelty. Computerised music had established a hegemony in the net charts, death by saturation. Computer games were the new youth medium, controlled by the state. There are no pop stars now, just robots, just faceless pseudonyms behind bleep-bleep music, and none of them ever roar about rebellion, or ever kill themselves for their art.

"Adam's on some street corner now with a needle and a spoon and some idealism mocked and knocked by cynicism. He can't even cut a record deal, sell a couple of hundred discs and get into the top ten, a top ten full of bleeps composed by the same people who write the computer games (and many of them are themes from computer games). These are the new bards. Critics gather around to discuss the symbolism of 'Super Mario Brothers 37'. Music and Adam are out of time and have little time left.

"In the future he's in the out of prison, stealing money for a hit, to get away from reality. He's writing songs for Eve. She's taking hits too. They think they are some kind of panacea, and they would be if anyone had the imagination to listen."

Joe's intense moan distracted me.

"Are you OK, Joe?"

"Stop it, DM," he gargled, clawing his way back from reverie. "Get me out of here."

"Joe, what's up?"

He served up a half-life, one foot in the door of our supposed reality.

"DM, I was there. What's going on?"

Joe flung his body up from the sofa, rushed to the bathroom and wrenched up his guts.

His pale-faced, dumfounded return suggested he had been somewhere he couldn't control.

"Fuck it, Dan, I'm retiring. I was in those stories, man. This dust does something. I'm gone."

He was on automatic as he left. Words could remind him of morality and none were exchanged on his departure.

A group of hundreds, shouting, raging with their fists, placards jutting into the air: "Stop The Cloning", "You Can't Play God", "No More Hitlers".

A teenager asked who Hitler was. Although we ignored it, it disheartened us, the decades of zeitgeist blitzkriegs obliterating our history. We had to get angry, began throwing placards at the police who formed a barrier between protesters and The Institute Of Science.

Gas canisters landed amongst us, the television crew from *Your News* taking orders to turn off their cameras. Our unity of purpose dispersed, the baton charge followed, strikes weighed and paid with malice. State-owned, state-controlled thuggery. Limbs in painful turbulence swung around the peripherals of my vision. Warm glows emanated from the pores, felt the harsh chill, grew sore and demanding. Figures flashed directionless amid the smoke. Larynxes bit the commotion, truncated by violence. Hoarse yells implored, gave voice to subjection, found no reciprocation.

"Get out! Run! Run!"

Legs were scrambling, a sense of self-preservation in the accidental elbows of comrades.

Sanctuary in a field, cuddles up to a hedgerow. Pleas grew dimmer, smoke filtering into the thick heavy omnipresence of pollution.

Television. Everything's gonna be all right. Anarchists protesting at The Institute of Science were dispersed with tear gas after they attacked the police. Pictures from angles; reflecting, reassuring: Opposition thwarted, the status quo reasserted.

English scientists are making breakthroughs which will help cure cancer, AIDS 2, heart disease and any other affliction which will get your vote. RCM Enterprises will continue working for the good of the nation, for the benefit of the individual, for the alleviation of suffering. Here's fifty-two channels of regurgitated cheap shit to watch, shut up, be happy.

A smell of cleanliness pervaded my flat. Seated at my desk, I tried to force out some words to inspire. The wooden chair I'd so often occupied didn't give its recognisable creak, the ritual prelude to a bursting forth from my imagination. I struggled to elicit the noise from it, but found only a semblance, some imitation with less feeling.

I stood up, roamed the room, touching the objects of my existence. None seemed familiar despite appearing identical to those which I had grown accustomed. The desk, the table, the chairs, the bed, into the shower, the kitchen; all gleamed as if new, as if replicas of what I'd once had.

I checked again, checked the carpets, the curtains, the television set, the radio, the music system. I checked the toaster, the oven, the washing machine, the telephone. Suspicions reached a peak, suffocated me, got me to turn out all the lights and sit in silence, listening for static.

Wondering, from inner space to outer space. A man who owns most of the television channels owns most of the newspapers. He owns most of the major world companies. He's Mr Big Business, got a say in everything, can do almost anything, and if you don't make him money or tow the party line, then you're sacked.

I skipped through my files on Rupert C Donald, adding some notes. Know your enemy. Know his connections, his interests and his purpose. Know where he's been, whom he's spoken to, whom he's made deals with. Know what he owns, what he produces, where his money comes from and where it goes to. Know your enemy. Know where he shops, where he eats, where he frequents. Flick through newspapers and know his ideology. Note what he thinks, feels and believes. Note the time he fired a publishing boss for blocking the publication of a writer's opinions (not because he agreed with the writer, but because he disagreed with the writer and the boss didn't make the sacking less public, thus endangering business interests in China). Know your enemy and get into and under his skin.

Rupert C Donald visits England briefly but regularly. He comes to keep an eye on what's going out in *The Shine* newspaper and *The Shine* website, his conduits for the dumbing down of our culture, his little processed news factories. He has meetings with the board of *Your News* to define policy; lots of inconsequential titbits, taking down stars a peg or two, giving the masses some reasons to thank themselves for their humble little existence. Here is the news to reassure you, divert you, dumbfound you. Shut up, be happy.

In passing, the oil tanker disaster and its effects: Two thousand seabirds killed, a coastline ruined. *The Emperor*, owned by Magnet Shipping, a subsidiary of GEC Shipping, whose major shareholder is Heter Pitchens, also head of the German wing of Rupert C Donald's *Your News*. And so on, in passing, a footnote, all insidiously linked, the levers all pulled by one man. Know your enemy and know how to defeat him.

In my dreams I would track him down, follow his movements from brick monolith to brick monolith, wait in the street for the in-between and put a gun to his podgy face, blow his goddam brains out, his goddam life away, send him to hell. I would be the executioner and serve my time in jail. Maybe I wouldn't destroy his empire, but I would destroy him, make him realise what life is all about.

A little more dust and I would be there.

Joe and I had got it sorted. Waking didn't happen until after midday: We'd meet up late afternoon for some drinks, see The Sharks to score some dust, play some cards, take a siesta, then be up for some more of the same as night fell. The hangovers got worse as time stood still (or went past us – we didn't know).

"Another fuckin' year and we're still here, still doing the same shit."

"Yeh, I think I'll get out this year," said Joe, "maybe go to Dublin, meet a nice Irish girl, brown eyes, long dark hair, white teeth. A thinker and a part-time hedonist."

"No more drugs, no more dust. Get straight, get out of this routine."

"Eh?"

"Get clean, tomorrow."

We whirred, scanned simultaneously the scene in the bar. Gestures and movements, ripples of words like waves trying to drown conversation, sighing and grumbling anew. A mass of words and utterances clashing, brushing aside, riding roughshod in search of ears. Words meeting and locking, corroding and clawing for meanings and punch-lines. Laughter like violence, alienating us.

"We've got to be happy, haven't we?" I said. "We've got to pretend to be happy, pretend like we're tapped into the mainstream."

"Fuck 'em. Fuck 'em all. Party on. All I need is cold hard sex right now, love can come later. That Irish girl can wait."

The determination didn't last under the weight of disappointment. We took our drab indifference and misguided hubris around a few more bars, saw out the old year before time rang us into the street, shivering in an abandoned taxi rank.

"We're waiting in the wrong place."

"Hey look," I said pointing to the sky. "There's those lights again, above the hills. It's gotta be Jesus coming back. Big fireworks for the second coming."

Joe didn't look, chewing on a cigarette, face twitching, searching for a vehicle to get us away.

"You've got no control over your imagination DM. Lay off the drugs. Jesus took one look at Earth and fucked off."

"No, look. They're fading," I said, ignoring him as the glory dissipated. "Oh well, gone, gone. Fuck this, I'm walking."

We cut through the town centre, cynically, jealously detached from the pilgrims celebrating. We swayed and avoided, our negative feet on negative ground, finding no comfort or fluency.

Outside Gigi's nightclub we were somehow pulled into the sphere of a young woman propped against the club's urine-drenched exterior. Moving past, about to consign her to a memory dustbin, she let out a hand, attempting to break her fall. Joe caught, her arms flung around his shoulders.

She mumbled sounds indecipherable, her body in a puppet show seeking props. Joe propped her back against the wall, keeping his hands on her hips.

"What's your name baby?" he asked, as close to being suave as being pissed could get.

Her eyes shuddered, snapped shut, then sparked wide unnervingly. She drawled out, "Yaw," in reply.

She had an attractive pale face, smooth and loose beneath dark brown hair flopped above her eyes, dishevelled like the long black dress curving around her languid, slim figure.

"What shall we do with her?"

I shrugged, unwilling to deny the opportunity fermenting in both mine and Joe's heads.

"Where do you live?" I asked.

She summoned energy, a mild current jerking from toes to head, forcing her body dubiously vertical. She said something in a language I hadn't been educated to recognise, then teetered into Joe's arms again.

"What she say?"

"Dunno," replied Joe. "She's foreign."

Her left hand wandered to my crotch, rubbed inarticulately then fell away. It turned me on and was nothing to do with attraction, but everything to do with being a man and having a dick. That's what it's there for, to make us stupid. The inventors will tell you different, but they're just protecting their image. It was meant to be a serious project, "Man" and all that.

"What's your name?" I asked again.

She didn't reply, but swung from Joe to plant a kiss on me. Temptation drove me to comply, desperately, amateurishly, briefly, before she fell back to Joe and did the same to him, grabbing at his crotch now. Nobody from the milling bodies affected the semblance of paying attention such was the Bacchanalian scene all around.

Joe upped the stakes, slipping his hand under the cut in her dress, feeling around her ass.

She broke off, laughing, falling backwards, dressing herself with brick-fragrance again.

"D'ye think she's been sent from the heavens?" I pondered. "To relieve our sexual frustration?"

"Maybe, DM. If so, then I might just have to start believing there is a god."

"Maybe it's a test. Maybe we should sort her out, take her home, be good good double double good."

"Mmmm. Yeh, but what about the opportunity we have?"

"I don't know. I'm somewhere between dithering, doubtful, faltering, hesitating, irresolute, pussyfooting, tentative, uncertain and apathetic, even callous, even cold, cool, detached, impervious, middling."

"You're vacillating, DM."

"She's off it. We should get her sober first."

Then she swung back on to me, started forcing her hand down my trousers, glueing her lips to mine. Animalistic, I delved into the back of her dress, groped a path to her chest, felt the flesh, turned on by the sheer decadence of it.

A claustrophobic multi-storey car park framed the next thirty minutes of our noble and indurated prevarication. A rare thing to witness the work of God and the word of The Devil in slovenly slang-bang debate, punch-drunk soundbites in between gropings.

"Sector 9," I told the taxi-driver.

The madness began. We had no control, yet we should have had it all. She was full on the metre, 'til the glass cracked; we were electrocuting the dial like boy racers.

She kissed me first, let me play with her tits as Joe's hand crawled up her skirt. She changed on a whim: crotch for me, tits for Joe.

The taxi-driver growled to himself. I caught sight of his hands tight on the wheel, his body thrusting back and forth as if he were fucking it. His bloodshot eyeballs fried on the rear-view mirror, red digits on the clock accumulating rapidly, a bleep every time it reached an integer.

At traffic-lights a face, masked by blood – predominantly dripping from his jaws – squashed itself against the taxi's windscreen, cackling aberrantly. S*T*E*P*H*E*N*.

A mutual realisation snapped the plot-line of coincidence. A fist slammed inconclusively against the diaphanous segregator, smearing blood like a drunken pseudo-artist submissive to sleep, collapsing helpless on to canvas, brush in hand like a dagger.

The light turned green and we left him with mute curses.

"Hey, we can go to the Indie!" I blasted at Joe.

He nodded, gurgled, "Club Independent, driver," before locking himself in desire again. He had his priorities.

I felt into my pocket, rummaging past the dying erection.

"Heads," said Joe before I had even had time to spin the coin.

Ritually, he had to take the penny, exchanging it with notes and coins.

"That's all I've got."

It was me to do the run, wink, make a score and no small talk, get back to the taxi, to a scene where the woman's dress was hanging onto her right tit, skirt up to her knickers.

Our driver grunted, coughed up a green one which he launched into his ashtray.

I felt beneath her knickers her moist, warm hairs. I looked, saw the clock taking two more steps before Armageddon.

"Stop!"

All the money had been spent, save for one penny, the car from Pup Taxis pulling away with a heart full of change. We would remember the driver, vaguely, forever, but we would never meet again.

Each one giant step followed the rise and fall of erections, flesh ravished like we were famished. There was no mention or feeling of love.

We entered my flat – the closest – entangled with her before letting her crash on to my bed.

"Good score?" asked Joe as we stared at her, limbs splayed, eyes fluttering.

I took out the package. "Got a little bit of dust, my friend."

"Hey, monkey man."

I divided the dust evenly, one snort each before the debate.

"This is wrong," I said. "She's off her face."

"So we're gonna be saints?" asked Joe disbelievingly, dismissively, all yeah yeah yeah, a cynical twang following the fading of his rhetoric.

"I dunno."

"Don't you wanna fuck her?"

"Does the Pope shit in the woods?"

We laughed a reminder of what we were.

"She's keen."

"She's wired."

"Toss you for it?" asked Joe beneath murky laughter.

One of us was going to speak, and one of us was going to win, or lose. But we were hung by her sudden wailing.

Her chest jerked upright, her head lolopping in recognition, throwing her body onto its legs. She grasped at something invisible, spewing utterances in her native tongue. Her fingers squeezed air, let slip, repeating in roundabouts, ultimately grasping more desperately. She was acting out a drama, walking at pace in bursts, holding her head in fear and confusion, stopping abruptly, statuesque, her countenance filled with horror. She raised her hand, piercing stagnant air, appealing for attention but seemingly unaware of our presence.

Then she crossed her legs, left an X in the floorboards before we engaged hypnotically in watching piss trickle down her thighs. A line flowed to each ankle forming a damp spot on my carpet.

"Shit."

"She's yours, DM," said Joe, picking his share of the dust and making an exit.

She quivered, nailed to the spot as her well of anxiety ran dry. Shaking took over her whole body, her head trembling in disbelief, the incomprehensible words continuing to slurp out.

I held and tried to comfort her. A thousand yard stare seemed to draw me in until a slap came from fear. I got all shook up over the one single defining moment when everything is wiped out; a generation ripped asunder. Everything would be destroyed in the fire raging outside.

Just us, unable to communicate, poisoned with the knowledge that it can all go wrong with a click. We had no control. She began to cry.

I hugged her, as much for myself as anything. Her words grew less volatile, whimpering pleadings submissively. For all I knew she could have been ridiculing me. It's all about perspectives I guess.

Her pain seemed to ease, her figure shrinking into my arms, falling once again onto the bed, intermittently babbling to herself as her eyes closed.

I took a hit, gave a cursory wash to her circle of piss, then got into bed beside her.

She stirred, began kissing me. Desires flickered amid my half-hearted, "You should get some rest."

She didn't understand, pawing the dress from her shoulders to hang below her tits. I couldn't resist, seeing her haphazardly and unsuccessfully push her dress down, feeling her fingers tug at my underwear. She was my toy. She was senseless and I could do whatever.

Her head butted towards my groin, ready to suck. I took her hair, pulled her face up to mine, said, "It's just this life," to God, then kissed her.

It had gone past morality, beyond my control as passion flung off the bed covers, slid off her knickers.

I reached for a drawer, scrambled for condoms, pushing her back as she tried to mount me.

I slipped on the rubber like a desperate virgin. She began fucking me with glazed aplomb, her dopey face lacking the perception of emotion, like it were just a routine.

It didn't last long. It felt great for seconds, then it felt bad for ages. The guilt grew rapidly, all-encompassing. I wanted her gone, wanted not to believe I had become this frail. I wanted rid of the evidence, but she still wanted more, and I was guilty and frail on that count too.

She pawed me, muttering gibberish.

"I'm really sorry. I hope we can remain friends," came two sentences from different bodies, one weak, one cynical.

Some response, her words slow.

"I wonder how you came to be here, who you are. What are your thoughts? Will you remember this moment?"

All the time my musings tripped over the soundtrack of her whiny exhortations.

The buzzer sounded, startled me but didn't pierce her world. I dismembered myself from the bed, pulled on jeans and a T-shirt and went to the intercom.

"DM, it's Joe, let me in."

I hit the door release button before returning to shovel on the woman's clothes. She offered little resistance.

When Joe entered his eyes were as wide as footballs, sweat simmering upon his blushed face.

"What's up?"

"I can't get home! I can't find my way home! There's people out there following me. It's all burning! Fuckin' hell DM, all the streets are the same!" Then he laughed hysterically, slumped down on my sofa. "Good dust though." He laughed again, grew more relaxed. "So have you?"

"Yes."

"You dirty bastard. Is it love?"

"Two star-crossed lovers."

"Any left for me?"

"You dirty old bastard. She'll never love another."

"She's not crazy anymore?"

"Less. Do you want to take her?"

He nodded. I drew him a map of how to get home, all very exact and technical even down to the bus shelters and infrequent bushes. I took him through the route, like some plan for a jail-break or robbery, double-checking that he knew every detail.

Our gal, unsteady on her feet, managed to depart cumbersomely in Joe's arms, going through her groping routine. I kissed her forehead farewell but she pouted an indifferent reply.

Amid the crushing loneliness of my guilt I dwelt on all that I wasn't. Faith seemed to be driving me away, driving me to care less, to go and wreck the temple of the Lord. If there is a god and if there is a heaven then have my chances of entry been ruined? Or were they ruined from day one, from the first sin? And if there's no God, no heaven, no afterlife, then why didn't I take sin so much further?

The drone of surveillance planes overhead breathed in and out, took possession of the skies beneath my ceiling, moths navigating at a constant angle to the moon, furry black wings flapping a line to bounce off the bulb in disappointment. A low blurry fuzz before a tweak, like a bleep. The moth-God was laughing.

Joe told me he'd fucked the woman, twice, and that she was called Kristen, from Denmark. She'd left at six in the morning to board a plane home. She'd been visiting England with a group of friends. When she'd woken she was still wasted, although she'd recovered enough to remember how she'd been pre-programmed with an identity and a flight timetable. That was it. Joe was inside a rush and I was in no state to think about morals.

THE LAST HURRAH

On 1st January 2001 the opera singer, actress and part-time princess, Emily Spencer, killed herself. I'd seen it all.

Emily Spencer had become something of an icon by default. At the age of seventeen she had entered the nation's consciousness through her opera singing and angelic features. Then she became a film star, playing her roles with such charm and vivacity that more aching hearts were captured. Beauty enshrined her; long blonde hair, wide innocent eyes, a fragile figure. She went on to marry a prince, briefly in love with him before it turned sour. It furthered her penetration of the nation's sympathy and affection. She struggled to shine against dogmatism, indulging in charity work to keep her profile high.

After her divorce she flaunted her beauty in the world's most exotic resorts, tempering her apparent hedonism with messages to "give" to those less fortunate.

On the first day of the real new millennium she was part of a charity opera concert, a whole day event, its lighter hours peppered with no names delivering exquisite tones. The event was beamed live on the Opera Channel, and throughout the day no doubt hangovers and disinterest dwindled the viewing figures. There must have been only a few thousand up into the early hours when Emily Spencer came on, slowly ascending an iron tower, a spotlight following her every movement, the camera capturing every fear, every loathing in her face.

Her physiognomy pierced the absolute darkness and silence, her apparition leaning forward against the railings, held in a fluttering white dress, divined by a thin microphone.

From below, from all surrounding space, the opening strains of *"Chi il bel signo di Doretta"* began.

Strings lightly veiling pianos held the air, filled it with importance as she gulped, let out a fragile vocal unrequited yearning which seemed to be killing her. The untinctured vulnerability was symbolised as blossoms broke free from mildly troubled stems, floating on the breeze through the spotlight, casting ephemeral dreamlike shadows across her presence. The most blossomest blossom, ripping up her agony as she soared to the high notes, clawing at them, desperately reaching their peaks exhausted.

In the gentle pauses for instrumentation she seemed ready to break down before lifting herself faultlessly for another effort, her voice tearing the Earth from its moorings, sounds touching anyone who had a heart.

Her head fell forward, her midriff squeezed against the railings, her vocals holding the note, not wanting to come through the catharsis.

Then she seemed to give up, her whole body capitulating, collapsing against, then over the railings, plunging into the darkness.

A camera and spotlight tried to follow the white bones descending majestically, not once touching the structure to interrupt the aesthetics of her fall. Her gracefulness came to a sudden and abrupt end, impaled on spikes, red blood seeping through before transmission ceased. The TV eye, embarrassed, showed an advert for forthcoming attractions. I could never forget it.

1st January 2001, twelve years old, I watched in awe, both shocked and excited. The national grieving which followed took most in, particularly the young, insecure, desperate, confused and vulnerable.

Television saturated emotions, so we all bled together. And those who didn't were heartless and cruel. We had to believe our lives would be irreconcilably changed. People had learned to grieve and not be ashamed, and from this moment forth we would all be sharing and caring. It was an aphrodisiac to cynicism; so fake, so forced, so cloyingly sentimental.

Joe laid a nine of clubs to trap me as the television transmitted a has-been singer waffling a tribute to Emily Spencer's memory.

Late afternoon, wrecked again, not feeling anything of a kick. Ace of hearts; game over.

"I can't face going back to work."

"Thanks for the karma check," Joe laced with sarcasm. "It's not gonna be easy. We haven't been on speaking terms with sobriety all holiday."

"A holiday, been and gone, and I've hardly done anything positive. Maybe it's time to lay off the drugs."

"We've been here before, DM. But once work kicks in, you know and I know that we'll be back. Hey, fuck it, nobody cares."

"That's just it. We're just like the rest of them, wandering through life on auto-pilot, convincing ourselves we're breaking the routine by getting wasted."

"Yeh, but it's still a bang."

"Look at those people," I said, nodding at the television screen where rich and famous amassed in slow procession. "They've convinced themselves that they're full of sympathy and honesty. They can act like they care. We can't even do that."

"Why would we want to do that? Fuck that, the devil has the best tunes."

"I've been feeling a little guilty about what we did with that Danish girl."

"DM, don't sweat on the small stuff. It's done and we all had our fun. That's the way it is and my interest in the subject is now finished. Look, we'll see out this gear, go and have a few drinks tonight, chat to a few beautiful women, then we'll take a break. It's just the comedown you're on. It'll be cool, we'll lay off it, get good good double double good."

"It's not a comedown. Since we started on the dust the days have flown by, and nothing positive stays with me. My thoughts are under surveillance, my dreams consciously constructed. Nothing seems right. It's time I got out."

"No one gets out alive," Joe said conclusively, delivered detached from the world around him, as if not even the actions of those in his immediate sphere touched him. It was an unsettling aloofness, something within Joe's armour which he could effortlessly display.

I picked up a newspaper as Joe left the room, flicked through it, a tabloid rag I'd bought firstly because my usual broadsheet had sold out, and secondly to see what the masses were being fed.

To my surprise there was a piece on a new digi-image of The Manchester Slicer, the story having moved on at speed since I'd last absorbed the news. Another killing, described in lurid detail, the woman from Leeds, her body found just outside Manchester. Amid the gore-fest, a brief by-line referring to Rudi Carusso, "the impostor obsessed with the real killer, who'd followed the murders, dressed up in clothes reproduced from digi-images of possible sightings of the real killer, who'd visited the scenes of the crimes and acted pervertedly to attract attention…"

Later, after poring over cold, isolated pinpricks of news websites, I found some comment from the police responsible for mistakenly charging Rudi Carusso as The Manchester Slicer. The official statement was that the DNA tests had been handled wrongly.

Joe returned to my exasperation.

"I haven't even followed what's going on in England! I didn't even know that they hadn't caught The Manchester Slicer! Who knows what else I've missed? Icebergs floating from the polar ice caps? Rain forests burning? Genocide in third world countries?"

"Look, the only thing you need to know about the world is that people don't care and there's no tomorrow. End of story. Now, let's put on a good disc, take an heroic snort and put some polish on our chat up lines."

"The voice of reason. Amon nino."

Twelve

It was raining again, coming down in blinding sheets, cold and impenetrable yet able to fill you with all the emotion in the world, pulling all the feelings wrapped in memories from your body, leaving you sad as hell.

I took another drag on my cigarette, had one last dream from the wonderful rain, then let the blinds clank shut. Period three, Tuesday morning. Statistics and league tables measured success and failure around walls, a pile of exercise books neatly piled on the table demanding the English jury's marks.

Cigarette killed, I picked up a sighing pen and opened the first book. Title, craggily underlined as an afterthought, "My Dreamworld":

> In my dreamworld nobody would get killed and there would be no crime. If you committed a crime, you would go to a prison where they would teach you how to be nice. There would be no pollution. All the factories would be shut down and destroyed and they would plant trees and flowers and make lots of rides for people to go on. In my dreamworld there would be no weapons because everyone would have to have peace. We would spend all the money from not having weapons on feeding starving people. We could also have rockets to take us to the moon, and Saturn, and other planets...

On it went, perfect spelling, all copied from a computer printout.

A knock at the door.

"Come in."

She breezed through, dripping blonde hair hanging heavy on her shoulders, untouched by the rain.

"Hello, Mr Manion?"

"Yes."

"They told me to go where the smoke came from." She curled a knowing smile. "I'm Mrs Godfrey, Kelly's mother."

She spoke slowly, easing off her barely damp coat, shaking then tossing it onto a hanger, placing an umbrella precisely underneath. She looked like she'd been chauffeured through the last ten years, let alone the rain outside. Her presence absorbed the air, filling it with pauses in which she could seduce her audience. She looked too young to be Kelly's mother, yet her smile betrayed a sagaciousness only deliberately, subtly obvious on her smooth, unblemished features.

She looked maybe thirty-five tops. If she were older she looked damn good for it, damn better than any forty something I'd ever seen.

Kelly Godfrey was in my form class, now at year eleven, their final year, though I hadn't seen Kelly since her father's death over a year ago.

Mrs Godfrey seated herself before I could offer, her movements suggesting for me to pull myself closer to the desk which separated us.

"How is Kelly?" I asked.

"Well, that's why I came to see you," she said, scraping the wooden chair as she pushed it back from the desk, unwilling to let it confine her. I liked that, it meant I could see her gorgeous long legs covered sparingly by a short pale blue skirt, crossing them extravagantly yet coyly before offering a cigarette, as if she had just finished screwing me.

"Thanks."

I got a light and drew.

"Kelly's taken a long time to adjust to her father's death, but she's been doing the coursework on the net. In fact that and reading books is all she's done really. She hasn't much time for anybody. It's that teenage thing I suppose."

"I see. Well Kelly always was a good pupil."

"Yes," she said dismissively. "It's certainly time she returned to school, associated with other people, got back to a normal life," adding, "especially with her exams coming up," as a well-rehearsed conclusion just remembered in an afterthought.

"Good."

"I believe she would be having Mr Patton for English, but it seems to me that you would be a more appropriate teacher to help her back, having known her for those first three years. I know she used to talk about you to Stephen." I raised my eyebrows. "My ex-husband."

She paused. "English is so very important. All very interesting, analysing, thinking, connecting ideas. Kelly really needs your guidance." She leaned back, put a swagger on her inhaling, the cigarette loose between two restless fingers in a little naked puppet show.

"Well Mrs Godfrey, you'll have to talk to the head first, but if you have a problem with Mr Patton then maybe you should see him first."

"No Mr Manion, you don't understand, it's you I want. Or rather, it's you that Kelly needs."

"Right. I'd be delighted, but as I say, the head will need to know. I hope we can work something out. Kelly had a lot of potential when she was last here. I remember she was the only one in the class who took home a copy of my favourite book."

"And what would that be?" she asked, leaning forward to tap out some ash, a cleavage hinted behind the smoke.

"*The Catcher in The Rye.*"

"Isn't that banned?"

"Yes, in schools, unfortunately."

"Hmmm," she purred, "please save us from puritans."

Mrs Godfrey still had half a cigarette left to talk with. I'd sucked mine to the filter. I guess she felt no stress, ever. Too cool, casual and confident for that, her mannerisms evoking a sense that she had some great master-plan for the rest of her life and everything was going smoothly. As I did with every woman these days I sized her up for love and sex. Love needed a nuance of naiveté and innocence, something Mrs Godfrey's manner didn't embrace. No, such things were a weakness. Sex appeal on the other hand gushed from her. Yet even this didn't persuade me to contemplate being with her. Too much effort and expectation, and ultimately probably too many complications.

I sniffed too that Mrs Godfrey's interests were not solely with her daughter's education, confirmed when she changed the subject brusquely.

"I think Kelly had a bit of a crush on you, Mr Manion. You must be the star of many a schoolgirl's diaries."

"I don't see it."

"You don't look like many other teachers, all uptight and starchy."

I laughed, staccato, unsure.

She finished the smoke signals, parting with a handshake which required only my participation to prelude her encore.

The bell sounded abruptly. Time to get out there, to mix with the innocent and addicted. The rain continued.

"Your attention please." The year elevens settled gradually. "Last week we went through two Philip Larkin poems. Who can remember what they were?"

At least half the class stared blankly whilst some flicked through exercise books to find the answer. No more than six raised their hands immediately.

"Paul."

"Essential Beauty and Sunny, er, Preston."

"Prestatyn. Good."

"With the cock and balls," shouted Andrew Smithee from the back row, provoking some laughter.

This I didn't need, hamming up an expression of exasperation, all exaggerated and condescending, as I strode over to him.

"How interesting that you should remember only the cock and balls. Why, you seem to have cock and balls on the brain today, Mr Smithee. We could almost call you a dickhead."

Now the class were laughing at him.

"At least I'm not a wanker!" he shouted back.

"Get out of my classroom!" I snapped back.

He grated his chair abruptly across the floor, cursed under his breath and stormed out.

It was going to be one of those days, like all the other days, trying to teach children who cared little about their education, whose parents cared little about them, who saw no future in the world outside or who didn't even appreciate there was a world outside their four walls and iniquitous streets. Their petty crimes got them by and school was just something to do to stop their parents hitting them, for being bothered with a social worker when *Porn Squad* was on.

But I had to go on, had to give the half dozen who were interested a chance.

"In these poems we discussed how Larkin is criticising the world of advertising for being false, for telling lies. These lies are everywhere. Look at your copies of the poems and see if you can pick out a word or phrase which shows that these lies are everywhere."

Papers shuffled, about seven hands going up; a careless brave first followed by intermittent admissions, each subsequent one preceded by wary glances to see who existed above them in the care less class structure. A certain kind of cool found expression and subtle appreciation, its evolution found in silly stupid sit-com kids and comically contumacious cartoon flicks.

"I've lost mine, sir."

"Me too."

A chorus followed, the same grief.

I handed out some spare copies, kept one of each poem to photocopy the next time it happened.

"OK, one word or phrase. Anthony."

"Dominate, sir, in 'Essential Beauty'."

"Excellent Anthony. And what does it do to the people who look at these advertisements? How does it make them feel?"

"They feel like they've got to be like the people in the adverts," replied Anthony.

"Correct, well done. So they buy the products and they feel cheated."

Just then, Peter Gratten, a hopeless daydreamer and part-time thug, put his hand up.

"Yes ,Peter."

"It's like this basketball I bought once. The advert said it was what they used in the NBA burrit wasn't, it was what they used in practice. They ripped me off."

"That's what adverts do Peter. It's a good point. There are many adverts around today which tell lies."

Hands were shooting up like little sparks of inspiration, each one with a gripe about something they had bought. I heard them all, got them involved, got them angry.

"And of course Larkin also shows us how adverts make us feel inferior, by using beautiful people, like the girl in 'Sunny Prestatyn'."

Again, the willingness to share thoughts, complaining about beautiful people.

"We are all made to feel like we have to be the best, have to try to be the best, or we are failures," I interjected.

Anthony eagerly raised his hand. "That's to do with Capitalism sir."

"Yes, excellent. The advertisers want us to spend our money on their products. They don't care what it does to us, if it cheats us or makes up feel bad. Capitalism is just about making money. The government in this country likes capitalism. It gives it control of our lives and we can't do anything about it, we just have to buy and accept it."

"What if we didn't accept it?" asked Jenny Simpson.

"What do you mean?"

"What if we went on strike or something?"

"A strike? I haven't heard that word for a long time. I suppose if everyone who felt cheated joined together then they'd have to take notice." (And I noted the point.)

"Yeh, that's what we should do," she said.

"So who should start the strike?" I asked.

"Everybody," Laura Marlott burst in.

"But who is going to be the most effective? Who are people going to take the most notice of?"

"Us!" threw in Peter Gratten, his enthusiasm implicating him, pathos suddenly casting its shadow on his abruptly lowered brow.

"No, it's a good idea, but why would they take notice of school children?"

I didn't let the fermenting conversation develop an answer, engage in a hearing, exploding in their rumination the hand grenade of a question:

"Which group of strikers would do the most damage to the running of our lives? Which group of people could mess things up the most? Teachers? Nurses? MPs?"

We got though television presenters, footballers and movie starts before electricians, shop workers, train and bus drivers, pilots and net operators.

"What about those at the end of the chain, the tiniest cogs on the wheel of what keeps the world ticking?"

"They can't afford to strike," offered Ronnie Blesham from the peripherals, rousing himself from his stupor.

"Why?"

"They need the money. They can be sacked 'cos there's so many want a job they can easily get others to do the job."

Remarkable to hear it, from Ronnie Blesham of all people, but it led to a connection, to another connection, to a way to bring up the exploitation of third world countries. So they got to know about who made the replica Premiership footballs they bought or wanted to buy: India's young and poor working twelve to sixteen hours a day stitching footballs just for a meal, working in dangerous conditions with no rights. The balls were bought cheaply by a conglomerate which Rupert C Donald had his paws in.

Many of the class had ignored the advancing clock and were intent on discussing the ideas. When the bell came I concluded with, "A reminder that Larkin is not in the exam, but this exercise was to sharpen up your questioning skills and your ability to come to your own conclusions, both of which you have done very well. Thank you, you may go." They rushed to pack up and depart leaving a shell of ecstasy inside me, inside the room.

Andrew Smithee remained sullen as I directed him back to the classroom. I tried to explain but he kept protesting at me calling him "dickhead". He had all the rights and protection so I tried to diffuse him by explaining how much trouble he could be in if I took the matter further. I could only hope he knew not of the trouble I could be in if he took the matter further.

Inside the staff room, run-down faces, venting their stress with complaints and cynicism.

Clive Patton entered, a worn out "Huh" marking his appearance, joining a circle in which I had become unwittingly trapped.

"That fuckin' year nine class is full of nutters..."

I shut off his words, knew exactly what was coming. All words were blurred, the volume lowered to a muffle as I watched his thinning bubble hair hiccup when he emphasised his grievance.

I'd been here before, a thousand times in my four and a half years at East Tyneside Comprehensive. I needed to get out, the feeling accentuated by a lack of drugs for an after work crutch. I'd be out of the profession soon anyway. There were too many children raging dissatisfaction, a purposeless dissatisfaction against the rules, the meagre future and the general neglect in their evolution. It came inveterately, handed down with fists, nurtured with lies and scams defined by disappointment and disaffection.

In addition my parental contracts were dwindling as the grinding down skinned the concern and sympathy from my body.

Talk turned to the forthcoming general election so I tuned in. John Cogburn, with senior management aspirations and a suit to match, chimed in. He had perfected the philosophy of Automatic Living to equate with his own life:

"You have to work hard, be the part, be everything your boss expects. Play by the rules because they'll help you cope, and just get on with it. The reason people are so unhappy with the NRP is because they've stopped people being scroungers. Life is hard, you've just got to switch off and get through it. Live for the pay cheque, keep climbing the ladder. There's no point in thinking about Utopia." Other staff were exasperated, waiting to argue, but he carried on. "Ideology is only important if it's linked to economics. Anything else is just spitting in the wind."

I thought, "I'll direct his lips to somewhere secluded."

An argument raged, but he was smugly indifferent to it. He'd perfected this pseudo-ballsy character as a gimmick originally, but through playing it so many times he'd become it and actually believed what he said. Hard to believe he'd joined the school at the same time as Joe and myself, that he'd had drinks with us, shared even a splice of our hedonism (albeit free of illegal drugs).

Surprisingly he found some support for his belligerence. Clive Patton told us all whom he wanted locking up (most of the pupils in his classes).

I stayed silent, waiting for a pause, formulating my ideas, waiting for, click:

"Who are you voting for, Daniel?"

"It's simple. I believe all right-wingers should be hounded from their homes, charged through the streets, accused and ridiculed, and prodded with sharp objects, then be thrown onto a bonfire."

A divide opened, from blank, stony faces to unbridled laughter. I noted their faces and names, deposited them in memory boxes, made my excuses and left.

I could barely feel the break, half of me dreading the afternoon session, heading for the smokers' room to kill myself slowly.

Not long lit up and Joe breezed in, playing cards already in his hand.

"Hey DM, quick game for some currency?"

"Deal."

Fifty three months ago I made contact with Joe as we were being given a school tour. When he asked the secretary where he could smoke I immediately befriended him.

Joe taught maths, one of the "old subjects" like mine, English. He hated the routine as much as I did, but seemed to cope more admirably than myself. In the staff league tables, based on contracts and exam passes, he was somewhere around the middle whilst I hovered above the relegation zone. Since NRP legislation any teachers at the bottom had to go on probation again for a year.

In all the time we'd been mixing it neither Joe nor I knew much about our respective pasts. Perhaps we could have, but we were generally stoned and never could remember anything we might want to confide. Our energies had focused on a determined drive to live a little, trip round the universe, get tense with The Sharks, try to make the make.

We flipped some cards, passed coins between us, ended up about evens before the bell choked us back onto the production line.

The afternoon clicked rustily into place. I taught the first years some poetry about animals, using Ted Hughes' 'The Jaguar' to get them to condemn zoos and vivisection.

With the third years I discussed sharing without mentioning socialism. I had the feeling it hadn't been such a bad day as it drew to a close, until a message came to see the headmaster, Randolph Hillier.

He patronised me into a corner, some venom in his beady eyes as he ticked me off for using the word, "dickhead", producing a list of crimes from his file and giving "a final warning", reiterating my need for more league points.

The train's shimmying shook fragments from Joe and I, seated at either side of a graffitied table, staring through grey-tinted windows. The machine crawled into town, halting just outside for some reason which would never be explained.

I formed a pistol with my left hand, aimed it outside the carriage and pulled the thumb-trigger.

"He goes," I said, directing Joe's attention to a middle-aged man in a smart suit, laptop chained to his arm. Contentedly I withdrew to savour the satisfaction of the kill.

"Why?"

"Looks like he doesn't care. Looks too successful without having any morals."

Joe peered through smudges, pointed to a fat man in jeans and T-shirt, a long ponytail and roughed-up stubble.

"He dies."

"Why?"

"He thinks he looks cool, and he thinks about it all the time. Look at the way he pauses to look in shop windows. He's checking himself out."

"Good choice. Those two," I urged.

Two women, in avid conversation, using their hands to express exasperation, curling their lips sanctimoniously.

"Why?"

"Gossips, defiling someone because their own lives are so empty. They eat meat pies too, probably watch game shows."

"Him. He's old. But, ah, maybe not, they'll be going soon anyway. I'll save my bullets. That bloke, he looks dodgy, looks like he's up to something, probably robs houses, probably wants to rob my things, rummaging around the peripherals making no contribution to anybody's happiness."

"The lad with his arm around that girl, laughing brashly, laughing long and hard and forcing her to laugh. And she's beautiful and deserves better. But she'd never want to love me, so she can die too."

"You're a harsh man, DM, but I respect it. Him there, he can go."

"Yeh, no questions."

It was a policeman.

"What about that man?" asked Joe pointing to an oldish man stood with his dog, smoking a pipe. "He looks a likely candidate."

I felt such excitement with the megalomania that the power engendered a benevolence in me, like it was my duty. I could see some charisma in the caricature, back to an old England.

"No. Salt of the Earth. A wise man who doesn't suffer fools gladly."

"Yer getting soft."

"Him there, reading *The Shine*! NRP motherfucker!"

"Just kill 'em all DM. Bottom line is that none of them really care."

"Wanna destroy passers-by."

The train shunted into darkness, flinched at the station before halting.

"Wanna monkey tonight?" asked Joe. "One of The Sharks could get down for us."

"Nah, I don't think so. I thought we were laying off?"

"We have haven't we? Two solid days."

It made us laugh, but the conversation never got started again, our wearied frames parting with grunts.

There we were, trying to part reality and fantasy, getting our lines crossed and mired in both, merging their combined globule of existence. We were broke, futile, our language disorderly.

"Fuckin' mean!" said Joe.

"Hm," my mumbled response, hypnotised by the television news.

"The building was completely destroyed..." over pictures of smouldering, demolished buildings in the desert. "US military sources said it was part of an estimated collateral revision and that communication lines had been disengaged.

"With only a week left until polling, the pre-election war of words is reaching boiling point. Opposition leader, Anthony Breff, hoping New Labour can end nearly seventeen years of NRP rule, called the government, 'Uncaring, undemocratic and dangerously unhinged'. Prime Minister, Mitchell Portman said, 'England under New Labour would return to a crime ridden society, with scroungers and focus groups conniving to sponge off the public.' Expect meltdown next week with polls putting New Labour just ahead."

The voice-over emphatically paused, delivered a solemn, transparently sympathetic tone for the next item:

"In Leeds, nineteen year old Louise Woodling, The Manchester Slicer's fifteenth victim, was buried today." Pictures of ordinary people in black huddled around a coffin. "In an empty space in the church Louise attended every week, just simple yet striking white bows, a poignant reminder of the innocence ripped from this community."

Friends and family were cut up to offer soundbites of Louise's life. As it always seems, ordinary people whose death is newsworthy, are always wonderful people. They're always selfless, caring, usually young and pretty, usually sensible and unremarkable. That sells vicarious pain to the public. For once I'd like a real character to die and get his obituary:

> "Yeh, Phil wasn't a bad bloke. He was a bit of a bastard about letting you use his tools though. I didn't trust him with money, but it's a shame anyway. I mean, I didn't see him much, but he wasn't bad. Couldn't take his drink like. He was bit dodgy about that, a bit of a nutter. I think it was because of his cock..."

"After the break, lottery winners who never get bored with luxury and extravagance. Hey big spenders."

Coki Coli beamed out, fresh and clear, "The get up and go drink." Young and old found comfort with it, spliced together as a series of vignettes charting the history of the drink. Expensive lush graphics reminded why the drink was needed, now. The advert, as with the ones that followed, lasted longer than most news items.

After a sharply edited, visually bludgeoning re-cap of the news over imposing technobeat, "...Lottery winners on the other hand might not be too concerned, especially the ones who've decided to spend, spend, spend..."

I could bare no more, activating the release button. The glorious beneficiaries of the Tax On The Poor, smiling and patronising, would make me want to kill. This was news as a TV dinner, served as an enema, slick and tendentious; repetitive information shorn of real human emotion or suffering. And indeed, shorn of real people. Truth only came into it as a neatly conceived marketing tool, all neatly finished off with an item to reassure the world that everything is all right; a less subtle reaffirmation of that found in previous items. Go back to bed England, everything is gonna be fine. Pituitary retards will be along shortly to entertain you.

"...Extinction is part of the process. It wouldn't be the first time in Earth's history. No great tragedy."

"But you wouldn't be just a little bit sad?"

"Hey, no one wept for the dinosaurs. All evidence points to them being untamed, with pea-sized brains and a primitive existence. Don't tell me most of us aren't the same way. So I won't weep."

"But what about what there is of intelligent life, capable of ultimately ridding the world of want and disease, of exploring outer space? How tragic if all that were wiped out."

"Just because we have the capacity to think doesn't make us important. If you look at some of the complex regeneration and lifecycles of plants you'll see a much more advanced and durable species. Human life is not more sacred than plant life," Joe said, dispassionately, his expression unmoved by such a bold cold statement.

"So nudge mankind from the stage and usher on the next species?"

"Or nothing at all. It might all go. No return ticket, all torched to dust. Hell on Earth. I suppose they'll be some satellite drifting about which might reach some far-off universe, serve as a warning. It doesn't have to add up to more than that."

"No. If the satellite's filled with the right books, music, films, art, news, it could be a tragic epitaph."

We started looking around the shelves of Joe's room, selecting most of the books and discs there for inclusion in the satellite.

It struck me as to why the association between Joe and I had become permanent: Joe, the closet intellectual, with a love of literature and higher thought. His tastes mostly replicated my own, in books, music and film. A few odd exceptions were noted.

"The Bible would have to go in as well," I added.

"Why?"

"Just in case The Ultimate Being happens upon the satellite. With the right explanations it'd get a good laugh. But I guess if The Ultimate Being is our God then it'll make kind of sad reading, you know, if he was on his way back to save the planet, and just missed the apocalypse."

"Eight minutes delay, points failure at Saturn."

"Stopped off at Jupiter for a snack."

"Woke up late, smoked a joint the night before."

"Like Stax."

"Late for his own funeral."

"And it's a long way back to wherever God hangs out. Maybe he'll start work on another planet whilst he's in the area: Spit on Mars, a bit of light sprinkling, bosh-bosh, Civilisation."

"Still time to get home for Blind Deity, where omnipotent beings are matched up for a weekend in another dimension."

"Though they always argue, coming back to tell the audience how they didn't get on. She says he was always bragging about the things he'd created. He says she was a nice goddess, but not the type he usually dates."

"Vivid, DM."

"Yeh! Did you see that God?"

"Fuckin' yeh! Dusted."

"It's burning outside, Joe. There's nothing left."

"Then there'll be no more politics for you to talk about," said Joe slyly.

"We'll just have to talk about the existence of God."

"And if he'll come and bring some gear."

"Hoping the big G makes it on time."

"Gets to bed early the night before."

"Sets the alarm clock."

"A quick wank before sleeping."

"Shower in the morning."

"A quick trip to the inter-universal drug dealer."

"Sneaks a joint before setting off."

"Thinks fuck Earth, I'm going nowhere."

"I'll sit around and wonder who created me."

"God's god."

I remembered the night before whilst pondering Joe's absence from the seat opposite. God's god. I couldn't remember coming back from the train toilet, sitting back down, but I remembered before going, Joe saying God's god, the night before, then realising the dust was still in my pocket. That took me to the toilets, but coming back?

The train's predictable slowness sent me into reverie, creaks of wheels on steel levitating through the floor. Like bleeps, information moving between bar-codes in my brain.

The day had passed by in a blink. Was I dusted in school? Did I fuck up? Search.

Bleep. Kelly Godfrey returning, hot to trot, swaggering through the maze of desks, smiling at me. Her simmering beauty had flowered in the intervening nineteen months since she had last been in my classroom. A quiet confidence pervaded her manner. I felt heartened to have her back.

Bleep. Reading *Stoned News* at dinner time in the smokers' room. A story about Frederick Marquand, hypnotist, his act so good he was considered too dangerous for television. He'd grown bitter at his lack of exposure, decided he would show the world his genius, hypnotising his agent into believing he had been in a car crash leaving him brain dead, in a coma. Marquand had arranged that his agent would only emerge from the hypnotic state when he heard the words, "Turn the machine off." Doctors puzzled over the condition for months, believing it to be a brain haemorrhage, although there was no discernible evidence to support this theory.

Over the following year Marquand fell in love with his agent's wife. He said he'd intended to bring the agent out of his state after a month, and was only delaying it whilst in love.

The wife decided to tell the doctors to stop feeding her husband, and he began to fade away, until the next day when a cleaner was hoovering his room, listening to a Walkman. A nurse entered, lectured her about being unprofessional, shouting at her to, "Turn the machine off."

Well, they both thought it a miracle when this dying guy flickered his eyes and grunted for air.

Doctors rushed in to attend to him and within a week he was recalling his story.

The police arrested Marquand, made him wear sunglasses so he couldn't hypnotise anybody else. He got sent down for ten years. And the wife? She divorced her husband, stuck by Marquand. Some believed she had been hypnotised too. Bleep.

In the 'Red' section of *Stoned News* an item about a two hundred per cent increase in mental illness amongst twenty-five to forty-five year olds. A report had pointed the finger at the drug culture which had proliferated in the last decade of the last millennium, and continued at speed, unabated, ever since. Titled 'The Big Comedown' it warned of the social consequences with asylums in England housing some four million people, not including those in Community Care, or those with less severe conditions who go about their daily lives undiagnosed, always ready to fall over the edge. Bleep. Bleep. Bleep.

The train picked up. It felt like I had been on it for hours, a feeling accentuated by gathering dusk, held off by the whiteness which again froze in the sky, re-creating heaven.

Bleep. I remembered Kelly again.

Bleep. Kate Flowers unexpectedly entered the smokers' room. Kate Flowers, science teacher, immense beauty coyly focused behind thick black glasses. Long dark brown hair, an engagingly honest and upbeat manner.

"Hello Dan, want to come for a few drinks with us?"

"Who's going?" I'd asked.

"Peter, Mike, Heather, Jane, Liz, a few others maybe."

"No thanks. Hey, seen anything in the skies lately?"

"A lot of impenetrable mist."

Four months ago I'd been to Kate's house when she'd just started at the school, looking through her telescope at the universe and talking about space into the early hours. We'd never been as close since, due mainly to...

Being like this.

A screech and the train stopped. Bleep "Mind the gap". Got to get it straight, make sure I don't fall down the gap. Don't want to get into an altercation with it. Gangs of gaps roaming the streets to be mindful of. Better make sure too that I can stay on the escalator, not have a loose bit of clothing get caught, pulling me into its metal teeth. It could happen, like anything could happen. *Mors certa, hora uncerta.*

The possibility of not concentrating as I crossed the road left me contemplating getting splattered by a bus, dithering to look both ways, repeatedly.

The lighter in my pocket could be filled with some cheap, highly flammable fuel, warming to ignite and burn me in the streets.

Any one of the people moving around could suddenly snap and attack me. A loose tile could fall from a building and crack my head in two. A policeman could see me looking furtive, search me, find the dust, finish me off. The bus taking me home could contain someone unknowingly carrying a contagious and deadly disease. One of the criminals on Pourische Road could be robbing my flat, taking my culture with them, beating me with a baseball bat when I interrupted.

But hey, I'm the luckiest person alive, so I don't have to worry. I crossed the road.

Joe buzzed just after I'd arrived home. I guessed we were going to start early.

"Hey Joe, good day off?"

He didn't answer. When I drew closer I could see sleeplessness in his eyes.

"What's up?"

He pulled a newspaper from his jacket, a tacky tabloid I had little time for. He flicked the pages before pointing.

"Look, that girl we had. She's been missing since New Year's Eve."

I read the article about Kristen Ingersson from Denmark, just seventeen and over in England with her college friends.

"Shit Joe."

"We must have been the last people to see her."

"Do you think we should go to the pigs?"

"Christ no! They'll have us. They'll frame anybody these days just to get some points. And if this gets out we'd lose our jobs."

"No great shame," I added, not impressing Joe who was unusually stressed.

"Fuck you, I need what I need to keep this life interesting."

"I don't know about that but you're right about the pigs. She got a taxi home from yours didn't she?"

"I walked her to the end of the street, flagged one down for her. At least, I think so. That was a heavy weekend. I can't remember much after leaving yours."

"The first or second time?"

"What d'ye mean?"

"The first or second time you left."

"I only left once, when you drew me a map."

"Shit Joe, with our alibis we'd better go on the run now."

"No, I reckon just keep quiet, and if they come to us we say we've never seen her before."

"I don't know about that."

"But if we tell the truth we'll be stitched up, no questions asked."

"Yeh, I guess, but I'm gonna have to work this one out."

I'd never seen Joe so agitated, only easing as some of it transferred to me.

"She might just have tripped our somewhere," I said to convince and reassure.

"Maybe."

Argument done and dusted, winding up somewhere in our consciousness.

The NRP

"It's all wrong," said the old man.

"Thur all the same," said the old woman.

"Am not even gonna bother this time," added a middle-aged woman. "They do nowt for ya."

"Aye, it doesn't change a thing. All the same. It's all wrong ya know," came again the old man.

A younger voice said, "I don't trust them New Labour cunts."

"Well, tha no different to the rest. Ar remember that last time they gorrin. Did fuck all."

"It durrent matter who ya vote for, nothing changes."

"They do nowt."

"Aye."

The secret machinations of big business and the economic collapse of 2001 managed to break up the New Labour government in 2003. The New Right Party, supported by *The Shine* newspaper, grew in support on the back of prejudice against European integration. It formed a coalition with the old Conservative Party, a link severed in 2004 when the NRP won outright for the first time.

Soundbites kept the masses happy as acts of parliament toughened the criminal justice system, increased police powers, deported immigrants, punished those in poverty and generally lowered expectations.

Big business called the shots, didn't pay their taxes, and gave their influence to the NRP. Nothing could bring them down. Scandals were brushed over, hypocrisy filed under the censorship of omission, delivered through a malleable national press. And yet, millions still supported them, and those who didn't had little concept of an alternative.

Under the NRP people have a lot of material possessions; all but the underclass have at least a TV, all the digital channels, a video recorder and a Net Surfer, all the technologies to spoon-feed their entertainment and ideologies. But they weren't happy. Their purpose had gone and nothing could fill its commercially saturated void. Their machines frequently broke down. And then the repair men came in to bug the machines.

Despite Joe's political cynicism he too wanted them to lose the election. We were in high spirits, having a drink after a shark feeding in which we'd snapped up some more dust.

The pub buzzed with grumblings, but we were celebrating the new dawn early, running down a list of which ministers we hated and how we wanted to see them die.

Our high spirits were enhanced further when they shrugged off a little gnawing burden. An article from the disk-news Joe had bought said a foreign girl had been found under a tree in the Lake District and that police believed her to be Kristen Ingersson. It was reported that the girl couldn't remember anything.

Waiting at the bar I was next to a man supping his pint, eyes stuck to the television screen above, mind merely visually placated by the election coverage.

"Bloody election," he uttered like it was a flash of inspiration to him. "Dunno why they 'ave to 'ave it on all night. There in't even any results yeh."

Jovially I said, "It's gonna be worth watching when they do, seeing those bastards kicked out."

He seemed the type who had gained nothing from a party who showed no interest in the lower middle-class, let along the working or underclass, either of which category he would neatly fit into.

"I don't care. A didn't vote. There's no point."

"Whom would you have voted for if you had?"

"Ah dunno. It doesn't marra worah think."

"So you won't? Everybody should have a point of view."

"Yeh, well ah do. Nowt to do wiv those politicians though."

"But everything is political in some way."

"Yer, ah suppose, but they do fuckin' nowt fer us."

"But the NRP are doing things against you, only you don't see it. They influence the media, make the laws, control what you become as a person..."

"Yeh."

"The NRP isn't looking after our rights. Worse still, they're ignoring the negative effect it has on people and our society."

"Yeh."

"That's why you've got to think..."

His yeahs came at intervals, not following the argument but pretending that he was.

"Yeh, well, am not really interested in politics," he said; a guillotine of euphemism for his intellectual deficiencies to snuff out my ideology.

I realised that they were people in the world who had hit their heads on an education ceiling years before maturity and had made little progress since. The cultural pollution had anaesthetised them, left them unable to understand certain words and sentence structures, so that point of view was a carrot on a stick, held by the media; never able to grasp it, or get passed or through the impatient hands of zeitgeist junkies.

I was speaking nonsense to the man at the bar. He didn't even get my gist, so I stopped talking abruptly and made to leave.

He said in parting, somewhat bewildered by my abruptness, "Mind you, the new right has kept taxes low. But they're still all fuckin' rubbish."

His words came back to me as television technology baffled us with ifs and buts and swingometers of mind-boggling graphics. It was a virtual reality election where you didn't even really need an election, the results forecasted before the final count. Computers could do it all for us.

Just before midnight we took some dust.

The first result was a bad one. The NRP had held onto a seat they needed to lose.

"Ah, fuck 'em. Of course they're gonna vote for them down there. That's where all the right-wingers go to die."

"I bet crime is a novelty there," added Joe. "Nice houses and luxury though, all full on the meter. I wouldn't say no."

"They'd hang you, or castrate you."

We took laughter, let in some more beers and waited.

By 1.30 a.m. we were comatose, disbelief clouded by drugs and drink. The realisation that the NRP were going to get back in. Words failed us; intermittent expletives keeping us living. It felt like the purest disappointment, making me lose faith in my fellow citizens. For Joe it confirmed what he already felt.

I didn't care to look anymore, taking some dust before looking from the window. The world outside was burning. We were only pretending to live after the holocaust.

The modern consciousness is filled with images of the holocaust, the ultimate gory titillation flashing across television screens, zooming around information superhighways. Scorched earth, paving the way for the ravenous march of Capitalism consuming all before it. This is the first day of the end of the world.

Joe had passed out on the couch. On the other television channels nothing to inform, explain or describe, just junk, screaming dissimulation, the lowest common denominator conditioning the masses to accept it. Patronising trash dressed up as fun. We must laugh, and buy, and come back for seconds because it's newer and faster and better, until it leaves us living automatically.

The numb and psychopathic had voted the NRP back in.

"Hey Joe, I'm going, fuck this, I can't take any more. I'm going to build a rocket to take me to outer space."

Joe mumbled, "Fuck the world, let it rot," gesturing with his arm before sagging back into the coma.

Nothing moved in the night. Nothing stirred but a low-lying discontentment. I had never known the streets so quiet. I wanted to kill somebody, to get it out of my system, get on the news and tell them why I did it.

As I followed a natural homing device over my brain's own preoccupation and the identical streets, I became aware of footsteps behind me. I picked up speed, had the idea it was Stevie behind me, or maybe the police, or maybe just some regular psychopath. Paranoia diluted with fear propelled me to a trot, only to hear the steps follow a similar pattern to mine.

"DM! DM! Stop!"

As the hand grasped I gasped, turning to a face full of intent. A long-haired, bearded madman, his gnarled face somewhere beyond torture. Only his eyes shone life, and in them I saw some recognition, some warmth, determination, and a passion for life you rarely see these days.

"DM, it's me, Ted."

"No way! Shit! I'm wrecked."

"I told you to just stay on the herbal."

"You're out!"

"Last week. They've been keeping me under surveillance in London, but all the intelligence services are busy tonight."

"You know the result?"

"I knew it weeks ago."

"What about the opinion polls?"

"Never believed them. That was just a device to get the old faithfuls worried, get them out to vote."

"Shit Ted, you're out."

I hugged him, renewed a part of myself. Ted Kandinsky was out of jail.

"How are you man?"

"Battered, but the spirit's still there."

"Good. Hey, we'd better get somewhere safe, there's cameras up there."

"All on holiday for a while, no problem."

"Where are you at then?"

"The hills."

"Do you want to come to my flat, it's just a block away?"

"No. I just wanted to let you know I was out. I've been in touch with some of the organisations and told them to dust off their plans. We need you though, DM. Are you still in?"

"More than ever Ted. Shit, let's blow the whole lot of them up."

"Have you been keeping in touch with the good people?"

"Some," I replied unconvincingly.

"Still carrying out the plans?"

"Yeh, most of them. It's hard work Ted, I get busy."

"Don't sweat on it. Contingency plans were made. I didn't expect everything to keep moving while I was away."

"How come they let you out?"

"Served my sentence, they had no choice. Some protests were organised to remind the public. Pity we can't do that for the others. Of course, the NRP turned it into a show of their benevolence. Didn't you see the news?"

"Must've missed it. But what if they let you out for a reason?" I looked suspiciously behind Ted, then to the sides.

"Don't get paranoid on me. We need you. Look, I'll get back in touch once I've got sussed and laid low for a while. I might go abroad then secretly re-enter the country. You need to make sure everything's ticking along. You know most of our good people." He knocked his knuckles on my head playfully. "You still got all the plans up there?"

"They're a little fucked up and hazy, but still filed away neatly."

"Good. Well, peace for now."

"Peace."

He was gone, shifting in shadows before being submerged by nightfall.

Ted Kandinsky's life story followed the steps up to my flat. He'd been jailed after the last revolution five years previously; the failed revolution. But they couldn't pin that on him so they trumped up some charges. Sure, he'd written pamphlets about blowing up the House of Commons and deposing the monarchy, but they were just stories, his Art. They'd jailed him because he was raising awareness of the NRP selling weapons to oppressive regimes that persecuted their nationals.

I flicked on my television to see the disappointment in gleaming smart-suited smiles and soundbites.

"Yeh, but Ted Kandinsky's back now."

I would have to alter my programme for the weekend. They'd be no escape on Friday. That would have to be moved to Saturday, which was on the agenda for that night anyway.

7.00 a.m. Another alarm call bleep, rousing an awareness of my sweating. I reached for the snooze button-bleep – and slipped back into a coma.

7.02 a.m. The alarm of a well-monitored heart attack. I could never pick myself out of this, lacking the strength, making to press snooze again.

A shock went through my hand, scared open my eyes. Wires at the back of the clock had frayed. And boy was I awake. I touched the wires again, felt the same jerk in my hand before pulling away. An excellent device had been found I thought.

Leaving the sheets unwillingly behind, I lit a cigarette, poked a hole in time to remember: FIVE MORE YEARS.

My spirit picked itself up, conventionally, shruggishly; they won't give a fuck, take the thy fair hour way.

My bicycle would have to be fixed, but some other time. I did an automatic approximation of my morning routine:

Cornflakes fell into the bowl, onto the floor, crackled underfoot as I searched for some milk. A car I could win sublimated the box. Me and the rest of the suckers. Or, wrapped around the coffee jar, the enticement of a holiday. Every bite and gulp, beckoning open the curtain for desires gleaming on a conveyor belt, a chance. From cradle to grave a series of competitions, just winners and losers and don't get caught on the wrong side.

7.50 a.m., under white skies, the number ten bus sniffs up to stop. A card. Bleep. The faces are deranged, dazed, insecure, anxious, an endless list of commodities, bleeped awake, set on the bus, extras to a scene.

Something had changed. You could see it in the faces of those rocking wearily through the underground. Blurry eyes from staring too much; at numbers, blinking, flashing; living by numbers. From zero to nine, a choice of catalysts and epiphanies, and you will soon be next in the queue.

8.20 a.m. Train arrives, three minutes late.

8.45 a.m., sweating and shaking through the school gates.

Lessons passed in shifts; words, phrases, sentences and precepts ejected, trying to pierce the impenetrable bubble that is youth culture, a virtually autonomous state that adults don't know how to and daren't enter, preferring to leave it to its own devices.

Their minds were elsewhere. Whatever I said didn't go as deep or stay as long as that which flickered on their television the previous night, very late judging by some of their sullen, sunken eyes.

3.50 p.m. Talking to Kelly Godfrey about all the books she'd been reading whilst absent. Without the audience of friends she came across as quiet, temperate and contemplative, her shyness balanced by a revealing enthusiasm for literature. She talked to me for twenty minutes. A spark of energy went through me.

5.10 p.m. I became a ghost, sneaking through the town centre, spying on the masses. Queues waited for buses stuck behind buses with endless lines of numbers offering a destination for escape. Bleeps coughed out from shop doorways, mingled with chattering asking for the time until life became like a speaking clock. Language was obsolete, merely a fanciful means to help us get by. All that mattered was one zero three, to Sector 9. Eyes searching and urging, and searching and checking, felt the agony of sight, blurred by hypnotic glances at car plates denoting identities.

When you look deeply into people's eyes, penetrate every contour of their cadaverous faces, you can see a madness trying to get out. Normality keeps them sane, its mask a mask to conceal disenchantment. But nobody's normal, deep down, when the door shuts, the lock bleeps conclusively, the curtains are closed, the machines turned off; when only a pulse keeps them from slipping into Automated Death.

In the brain the wires are fusing, the soul's eyelids quivering to blink, the body's eyelids like shut steel doors. Vision is propelled at a million miles a second, over the darkened landscape.

Behind the façade they just want to scream, to be woken up from the modern nightmare.

And I waited with them for my shot of news, for some truth. I waited in a queue to be told The *Guardian* newspaper and disk had not been delivered. I opted for the most left-wing alternative, a middling paper more at the centre of an all-encompassing political spectrum.

I spoke in numbers; for a purchase, for the bus, journeying without communication, photocopying the ink which might explain it all. I alighted with others, dispersed to a solitary existence where they couldn't touch me.

11.05 p.m. A puddle ripples back and forth from my DM boots, creased in a crouch. Zeke, Barney and Aisha adopt the same position. Chuckie E arrives, nods, gives me a small package which I stuff under my cross of St George T-shirt. Words would trip us, so nods and glances, twitches and nudges set our plan, triggered the synchronising of watches.

11.15 p.m. Moving towards the hubbub, a shaven-headed gut on the door, propped up on a stool, looked me up and down. I nodded, he nodded back, and I was in.

The sound of thrashed guitar grew louder, through tunnels from whence it came: to a small, cramped room, sweat dripping off bodies, off the ceiling, splashes of harmless thumps touching bodies in time with the pounding music. A few nods, a quick beer, head-butting the air as if I understood the sound having heard it before. Grown men and adolescent males pogoed on a wooden dance floor, vibrating the soles of my feet, sloshing the pint in my hand. Merging in the overlapping shadows of their secret lives, Neanderthal Man slouched under the weight of ignorant pride, pumping fists on flesh as some kind of homo-erotic ballet, just waiting for one of the pudgy skinheads to lift a partner above their head.

"White race! White race! White race!" *et cetera* seemed to be the chorus.

When one "song" finished another began, indistinguishable from the last, the same thrashy guitars, the same gravel vocals, urging those punching each other to, "Burn all black, burn all trace! Send them back to Africa and their own fuckin' race!"

11.40 p.m. A cubicle in the toilets, avoiding the temptation of a snort, but feeling like I was tripping.

I returned to the bar, bought another drink, lit another cigarette. Just entering, a fat grey oil named David Smithson, a right-wing publisher and owner of a sportswear chain. Boom! Indeed. This was our lucky night.

11.55 p.m. Back with Chuckie E, crouched down, exactly the same feeling as before, about to move away when a figure left the pub.

11.58 p.m. Following the figure. The blast stops his progress, makes him turn to see the club in flames, smoke billowing toxically. He quickens his pace, sirens and alarms going off all around, a cacophonous symphony of chaotic bleeps.

To a back alley, disappearing around corners before I could move, pausing to send messages over to Chuckie E under the hushed bleep of walkie-talkies.

The figure entered a bar. Our forces re-grouped and waited.

When he emerged I followed. He took a bus, sat upstairs. I took downstairs, radioed in his destination.

12.45 a.m. He was crossing through a children's play area in a park, the sort of park children never go in.

I was too close. He stopped suddenly, turning to me.

Ignore. Walk straight past. Think of a new plan.

"All right?" I said as I approached.

He put his hand out to halt me.

Fate stepped in. Plan A was here and now.

"Are you following me?"

"Ya wah in the club weren't ya?"

"Ya what? What the fuck's going on? What's happened?" he demanded without trust.

"Dunno. A fuckin' bomb a think. How come you gorrout?"

He twigged to my suspicious tone, was all I needed him to be.

"How come you fuckin' did?"

"Calm the fuck down. We gorra get t'the bottom of this. It was probably the fuckin' coons."

"Fuckin' coons, yeh," he added.

"Fuckin' niggers!" I added with a thick dose of irony he couldn't detect.

"Ya mean niggers like us?" asked Chuckie E, into the scene, the others closing.

"Fu—" was all he could manage, my foot hitting his groin, taking meagre language from him. All the words he had to offer hung in that moment, rubbed out as I struck his face. Eight legs and eight feet rained down on him, into him, flicking blood around his sculpture.

Chuckie E stepped back, took out a gun and shot him in the head.

"Fun's over. Get your asses outta here. W-Two."

Two vans had come to pick us up. I had such an ache for the dust I felt ill.

We slipped into lives with ease; these careless lives; stoned voyeurs of mankind's history.

"I think we're being watched, Joe. I think we're just in this big bubble, being watched by some almighty force. They are mocking us from somewhere, laughing at our giant steps for mankind. They are rolling dice on our future as they lose their minds. There's a big party outside this universe and planet Earth is the entertainment. It's a game and we always think we can win. It's all about odds, long shots and thinking 'surely this time life will come out good'. Roll 'em and the thunder drums to a conclusion. And then we pray and roll 'em again."

"What are you on about? What do you mean?"

"I don't know, it just came out. What do you mean?"

"I mean I want to know what you mean."

"I mean, do the cards play God, or do the gods play cards?"

I enticed him with a pack, dealt at speed.

We thrived on the tension. Just to hold a few cards in our hands, to think we knew our own destiny and could determine it.

Games, coins, butts and matches piled up; numbers logged in our brains until we became almost telepathic with anticipation. A snort before revelation, the adrenaline rush peaking as numbers were added up.

God shook the dice, warming them to get them lucky in his palms.

"A seven says there'll never be another holocaust."

"Don't fix them, big G."

"I'm not going to, and don't call me that. How many times do I have to tell you? Father!"

The dice rattled.

"Twelve. Bad luck. I told you they were all evil."

"It doesn't definitely mean there will be a holocaust, it just means it's not certain there won't be one."

"OK. Eight says there already has been."

"What? I would have heard."

"You've been busy. You'd really have to look at the fine print to be sure, and you haven't, have you?"

"You're bluffing son."

"Eight?"

"Roll them."

Jesus rolled two fours.

"But when? Where?"

"Try Burma, try Sierra Leone, try Bosnia, try Tibet, East Timor, Nigeria. Or if you want a more subtle form of genocide, try the capitalist countries. Fuckin' Romans!"

"Son!"

A siren. A siren coming. A loud, blaring tidal wave of a siren to tip up the table, scatter our money and numbers, mingle our coins. It was flashing red, orange, blue lights on our consciousness, inside our unconsciousness, waking us from the burning future.

"Wake up!" screamed the voice of a burly figure crashing into the room. Behind it another, equally weighted, both bursting from a background of seemingly painted figures of their ilk. All were in tight grey uniforms, shiny buttons straining to hold in the unaccommodating flesh. A glaring into my vision, a sparkling badge to denote their authority.

"Get up! Now!" screamed the first man, a laser gun pointing straight at my temple, its warm glow fixed. The second figure trained his beam on Joe. The other figures squeezed into the doorway, for as far back as the eye could see, but did not move.

I stood up, then Joe copied.

"You assholes!" he raged, his large round face flapping ripples from him mouth, ejaculating words turning him in stages into a pig. "Wake up now! Reality Police! You are breaking the law! Reference number two three four one five. Wake up, now!"

His chunky, inflexible baseball bat hand took a swing, clouted my left cheek. In co-ordination, briefly delayed, his partner administered the same to Joe.

"Wake up! Repeat after me: This is twenty-twenty-one."

"This is twenty-twenty-one," Joe and I replied in unison.

"The New Right Party are in government."
"The New Right Party are in government."
"We live in a democracy."
"We live in—"
"We work, we must work, we enjoy work!"
"We work, we must work, we enjoy work!"
"We are all right!"
"We are all right!" said Joe.

The blubbery figure served me another whack across the cheek and boomed, "Now get back to reality, stop thinking and lose your imagination! Or we'll be back!"

The figures were sucked from the room. The TV bleeped on to Rupert C Donald's Lifestyle Channel. We slumped into our comas.

Slow motion, our words were unpunctuated attempts to fathom the moment, winding down to merely receive images. We were shadows of another life, acting out like puppets, like some drunken Pinocchios, the meaninglessness of our existence.

When time stands still you go through the motions; bus number eleven, twelve, thirteen, twenty-three or a hundred and three will do. Slow motion; brain off, six point nine six-debit-bleep. The skies are white, nothing to comprehend but motion, automatic motion without passion, without any real human input.

The bus's jolting progress seemed like bullets lowly hitting my flesh, peppering me at intervals, just enough to surreptitiously drain me before I emerged from its confines.

Little shifted, except for the things we rely on. Buses and cars moved staccato interspersed with pedestrians consuming. Everything steady, nice and neat and unthreatening; so it would seem if God were to cast his eye over Earth, making a quick check. But I can see behind their frozen eyes and colourless faces. Through a long process of erosion they have stopped knowing how to act like real people, fear and greed draining them, hoping to hate that no one can see the madness in their eyes, the wonder that it's all not worth it, that something is wrong and we can't do anything about it. Bodies are taut through living the lie, all semi-conscious at the execution of their lives.

Each step made me feel more ill, more scared to vomit in the street. I was sweating then shivering, unable to map my progress accurately.

The skies were white, always white; a permanence that kept us stuck forever in this life, this vile unimaginative life.

Again neither the *Guardian* newspaper or news disk had been delivered. I took a replacement to Tinman Square, an area of grassland amid the shopping centres where students lazed about, where the next generation was formulating its plans for revolution. They swigged from cider bottles and cheap cans of lager. They smoked to look cool, ersatz poor, shunning when convenient the wealth of their parents. Each one, a Conservative, because it was cool and ironic. They wore T-shirts designed with slogans to register their individuality. The T-shirt revolution was well on course, big business rubbing its hands gleefully. Safe sex, designer drugs and manufactured beats 'n loops.

I observed: Laughter, bodies briefly jerking to some incessant musical beat, then crumbling back down to slug some more cool. Could I massacre these students for their apathy? Would the world care as my tanks came to oppress and crush? Bullets would spray into the scattering pack, killing and maiming the students. The Tinman Square massacre would have known names, slotted into the history books, superseded by my shaking hands with presidents and prime ministers.

As drizzle came from the blank canvass, their incomplete sketches moved home to watch some really trendy game-show, so tacky as to be the coolest thing they could imitate all year, until something tackier came along next year.

3.30 p.m. Dave was there on time.

"DM. How's life?"

"I feel shit. You tried this dust that's out?"

"Reeto Dust? No. I've heard it's dodgy."

"Don't tell me it's a government drug?"

"I don't know where it's from."

Dave looked to the CCTV cameras. "I think they're just business ones."

"They're all in it together."

"Yeh, but they just want money so we don't mean shit. They want pop stars and actors taking coke and getting blow-jobs so they can sell it on. Or a good fight, car chase or murder."

"Thank God for being without fatal fame."

"You heard about the *Guardian*?"

"Only that it hasn't been in for the last two days."

"The NRP have closed it down, and their website."

"No."

"Oh yeh, and that's on the back of twenty-five per cent of the vote, not including those made ineligible. You have only forty per cent of the population voting and only a quarter of them voting for the NRP. It's all getting really fucked up in the capital. And this is just the winding up; we ain't seen nothing yet. We won't know what's hit us. It'll be like an asteroid hitting England."

"And none of the opposition are doing anything?"

"New Labour aren't doing anything, but Adam Benn's getting The Labour Party's message across as best he can, through what media's left."

"Pissing in the wind?"

Dave got to the bone quickly: "So we're getting things tight again, getting everyone organised."

"Have you seen Ted?"

"Kandinsky?"

I nodded. "Yeh. He's telling everyone to get ready for the day. It's all back on from him too. He'll be what's behind the re-organisation."

"And now you're back. What's going on? I've seen you twice in a month."

"I told you, I've got a busy life."

"Busy tripping?" Dave joked.

"Busy trying to stay in work."

"Quit. I've told you, you don't need it."

"Whatever." My stomach cramped, my pain audible.

"You OK?"

"Yeh, just the excess of getting over the agony of work."

"Are you coming to the demo tomorrow?"

"Maybe." Dave noticed another pain kick me. "It's all right, I just need some food, it'll pass."

But it continued all day.

Each morning I left my hand a little longer on the exposed wire at the back of my alarm clock.

Each day I did the routine. Kelly Godfrey gave me a reason.

Each night, the dust, until it was all gone, and it was Thursday, and The Sharks could make the trip Joe and I didn't dare to.

I arrived late, The Sharks already circling.

"DM."

"Mr Manion."

"Hey, sit down."

"Evening Daniel."

"Who's winning?" I asked of the figures huddled round a small rectangular wooden coffee table: Two armchairs for ears, one sofa for pouted lips. Playing cards found perfect space amidst the ripped Rizla papers, half-empty beer cans, converted ashtray beer cans, scattered tobacco and lumps of cannabis. It told a tale.

"Taff," replied Joe.

Taff grinned; one of the beneficial effects of pot.

Phil, "The Master", played the game with style and grace and a detached nonchalance, lacking flamboyance but imbuing his game with an old fashioned deliberation, a sense that he came from another more nostalgic era. It made him a fascinating character to us, all stoned, all in awe of his intense seriousness, until he lucked out. "Fuck," brought him back to us.

Jez was as flashy as ever, always so close to victory yet rarely able to win.

Joe and I mirrored each other; enjoying the beer; moments snatching a hit; expecting to win. We would, though inconsistently.

For consistency you had to look to Taff. He was having another good night: He never finished empty-handed in Shithead or Black Mariah, and in Skat, well, he was almost untouchable.

Minds were winding up, sending out charges, taking in re-charges in silent pauses between songs. Eyes could not blink: photographic evidence for some alien race. Cards twitched, waited for a decision to be sent to the sweaty palms and fingers.

Taff had to lay a card. We were all still in it, but with the right cards he could wipe us all out. If he had two pictures and an ace we were gone unless we could match it. Taff put down the queen of hearts, but Jez couldn't use it.

Joe had twenty-five, I had twenty-six, Phil had a nice thirty but he knew it wasn't safe, a smile curling to a frown, revealing darker despairs.

Taff's delighted eyes gave it away first, his arm levering down to reveal Skat, our eyes withdrawing back into craning heads as the cards descended.

Taff's narcotic laughter infected us all. Comments came in the pause for joint rolling.

Taff and Phil weren't into the dust so we stuck to pot and its fiendish avenues.

Designs of numbers, corners browned and curled, some sticky with tobacco-clingers, came our way. Face down, face up amid the debris, burdened by the weight of expectation.

The thick suffocation kept us mesmerised. Time could have gone forwards or backwards and we would not have noticed. We were intent to hold that thrill of superiority, or at least that moment of being part of the race.

Numbers were subtracted until I was alone in the darkened shadows of a.m.

It felt almost safe, almost peaceful. A tight chill wrapped itself around my jacket, incisively cutting through to flesh spoilt on stuffy warmth. I shivered, sucked in my skin, ambled on like a robot.

A black cat hung tensely in an alley, waited on its nerves for me to pass. A car alarm invaded the surveillance plane's whirring, rang echoes of anguish around the houses, chiselled its monotonous plea to materialism.

Is this what I am? Is this until the end? Thirty-two years have passed and what have I done? I can't even remember a childhood, something that might give this life a reason and purpose. What have I done with my life?

Why can't I be more intelligent? Why can't I know everything that ever happened? Why can't I know every word? Why can't I absorb the history of mankind and find a solution?

Why can't I remember an England that used to exist? My parents were somewhere, with all my memories, with all my good memories.

It was here, calling early, the worthlessness and despair, the self-loathing and doubt.

Nobody loves me. I am wasting my life. I deconstruct myself. I am all these parts, each one flawed.

I cannot sleep and I mutilate my consciousness with the negative, until it bleeds reciprocation.

The electric shock to focus me.

Thick short pieces of metal, rigidly moving backwards, forwards on the force of wheels bolted to their joints. The incessant chug, morning never getting to day under an omnipotent whiteness masking all but noise, so we did our best to imagine what the sight could be. Metal corroding metal, pumping away to shit out an object of utter fascination for consumers. Loose change wasn't enough. This was a gratification only achieved through the swish bleep of a credit card.

Swish bleep. And in every swish another life came into view, experienced with vitality before "market focused" atrophying. Then the bleep to start all over again: each plastic debit noted on their souls, until they were up to a limit and had no room for appreciation and aesthetics.

They unravel a dark grey mask, twitch at it to ask questions briefly, then submit, pulling it on again to walk around day after day, free, believing in immortality. They can live like this for ever: basic fatty food stuffs, alcohol, cigarettes, ejaculation, titillation, gossip, spurious news, belonging to a group, going about their rituals. Blank faces for work, for the routine, fear and mistrust for strangers.

A thirty-minute lunch break, crammed with going to the bank, standing in a queue, getting "bleep", dashing for bite-sized food, all the time worrying. Is there a meeting I have missed? Are there bills I haven't paid? Is my job secure? When will I fit in that appointment with the doctor? When is that report due in? Why did I stay up late and give myself a hangover? I need to get back in touch with those friends I haven't spoken to for months. I need to get my body and mind fit. I need to get through this more easily.

And, soon, they are automatic living, just to get by. And I am automatic living to get to work, to feel safe from my depression.

Into the whiteness a shred of smoke, rustily oozing, like relief, like all but the character pulling the release lever would die, simultaneously executing and igniting lives. Before the end though, you have time to purchase an epitaph. Here is what we left behind: ideas, ideologies, philosophies, spirits of dead poets, authors, artists and thinkers; all choking above the crackling flames.

Everything looked pitiful, meaning more to fatality than originality, hanging like an overwhelming question about spires and brick living quarters, throwing off exclamation marks against high neon signs. It drifted and belched filthily across the horizon, scratching its indenture into the dividing line.

A soft yet dense "fog" hung in nooks and crannies, enveloping the masses, absorbing their functions, seeping into the daily routine. It made the tawdry acceptable, the corrupt amenable.

Democracy dealt out. Characters played and swept aside. Our shuffle amounted to no more than a few soundbites in history, our anonymity saved by great artists and psychopaths. Transient shock. Whom do you most fear, the man who organised the callous and clinical death of millions or the mass murderer who's compulsively tortured and butchered fifteen victims face to face, frantically deranged? Transient shock, severed at birth. Contentment serves the automatic machine working millennia ahead of the first dead. We are dead meat on the wheel of progress. Bleeeeeep!

The masses would stay in their armchairs, let it go in, content in their crammed homes, fuelled by all the easiest television, most vacuous films and deceitful newspapers. Staying indoors, watching video recordings they'd made of their greatest participations in computer games. And somebody was filming them for a television show about how ordinary people are uneducated, bigoted, rather immoral, prone to violence and lacking in taste and decorum. And there's a zany, crazy host telling us to have fun, to shut up, be happy. These are the people who led us into the holocaust.

My misanthropy had to turn to philanthropy, arriving at work drained, sick, unbearably paranoid. Story-lines were tailing off into the distance, growing feet, moving on their own, tangled in the developments of other imagined plots. I beat an exhausted retreat, the effort of making myself act correctly and believing it sapping me of energy. I had to get fixed for work, find a corner of the memory that would remind me how I behaved last time.

"Are you all right Daniel?" asked the secretary.

Memories dealt me luck. "I think it's the same illness as before coming back." It was moments like this, when a lie could be turned into a truth, when luck seemed to guide me, that I lived for.

"Shouldn't you go home?" she enquired.

I played the martyr: "I'll be all right."

"Did you hear about Kate Flowers?" she was excited to ask me.

"Knocked over."

I felt the sharp needle of feeling, storing the information before a kick of spiteful pain.

The secretary told me to go home, make an appointment with my doctor.

I had to stop eating crap, drinking, taking dust, smoking, slouching about. God must give me one more chance.

Soundbites

'Wanted: Cliché-machine for thriving office devoid of personality.'

☐ ☐ ☐

"Good evening. Ten years ago after you the people voted my party back into office, we set out a radical programme to improve people's lives; make them feel safe, give them dignity. As part of that programme we have invested in science and health projects." PM Mitchell Portman paused, steadied his head and looked directly into the camera. "And we were determined."

He walked again, to stand by a man – balding – aged about fifty, who stood next to a man in a white coat, presumably to denote a doctor.

"This man was diagnosed six years ago as having cancer. He is now completely cured. Our investment in science has created history. Finally a breakthrough in the treatment of one of the most deadly diseases of the last hundred years. The new drug, Panamera, can treat and prevent cancer." Again the prime minister looked hard into the camera. "We intend to share this with you, the people, for this is a government for its citizens. Just as fluoride was introduced into the water supply to help prevent tooth decay, so we intend to add this miracle medicine. This notorious disease will be confined to history.

"And after our recent election success we can promise that the work won't stop there. The NRP will fight disease and want, fight crime, fight for the people. Thank-you."

"That was a public service broadcast from the government. Next up tonight crazy prankster Jeremy Bedelem talks to Susie Baster on *The Susie Baster Show.*"

"…Now Jeremy, one of the things you haven't tried to hide is your low sperm count."

"Well yes. There are people out there who want to hear about this…"

The patronising "out there", so egotistical, like there's just a mass of emptiness out there soaking up the shite. It makes him real, gives him an identity beyond the milking of fun.

"We will leave our imprint in the history books."

"Just like Hitler and the holocaust."

"The right honourable member will have to apologise or leave the chamber."

The clamour of voices chugging "Aye, aye", waving their fists.

First editions land, splattered with "Actor arrested in toilets", "Star in sex scandal", "Grants down", "Grant out of control".

The next day, after the analysis, Michael Grant was in hiding, speculation mounting that drugs were involved.

The next day, Grant revealed that he was bisexual. His girlfriend was going to stand by him. "I still love him and I'm sure we can work this out."

The next day, police ruled out drugs. Grant had been masturbating in a cubicle whose door was half-open.

The next day a man who had had sex with Grant three years previously sold his story.

By the week's end Panamera was in most water supplies.

"…And the message we shall send out is that the evil hand of crime will be manacled by punishment. Crime does not pay."

"What free-thinking society would deem violence to be the only way we can think of punishing? What about treatment, education and rehabilitation?"

"Our investment in correctional facilities has been phenomenal, but we must accept that some crimes are too abhorrent to deserve treatment. We have allowed murderers, rapists, terrorists, and paedophiles to proliferate. Prison does not deter them. This bill will make it quite clear that we are a law abiding society."

"Capital punishment belongs to the dark ages, and its re-introduction shows the NRP have run out of ideas."

"Try telling that to the parents of Louise Woodling, or the parents of Jamie Bones, or the family of David Smithson."

DR TUMBLETY

The traffic barely slowed, only red lights leaving impatient motorists to slam on their brakes.

In Sector 4 everybody's in a hurry; to get out, to get away from the law, to get away from an assailant, to be in an important place for a meeting, a deal, a robbery, a killing, a score. The overspill from Sector 3 had transformed a once (mainly medical) student area into a community living in fear; dangerous, unpredictable knots of intense, unchecked violence lurking amid streets of addicted apathy. Too unstable to have easy targets for police, and certainly bad enough not to be safe. Criminals seeking a new market brought about the change, flooding the area with cheap new drugs, exploiting people who had nothing to look forward to, who received them as some kind of panacea. In their intoxicated homes televisions never were turned off.

The medics who didn't flee after taking a beating stayed around and decided to create some new drugs. They had a code where they were all tested and all came with safety instructions. The Medikals kept a lookout for each other and made enough money to get them by. When they'd finished their courses most decided to take up drug-dealing full time. Then the gangsters, notably Fuck Mob, started bumping them off and most of them got out or lowered their profile. Some even went back into the medical profession. Taff was one of those people.

The asylum in Sector 3 had been completed in 2000, after research had revealed a potential market in mental illness, identified as probably beginning after the disappointment and depression of the new millennium had set in. They were about a year early with that analysis but the asylum had thrived since, a fact not reflected in the tainted hue of its once white exterior, coloured with pollution blown down the coast. It now merged with the dreary landscape of terraced houses, terraced flats and cut-price supermarkets.

Within the radius of a mile around the asylum, certified crazies dominated the population, set up in Community Care streets, patrolled sparsely by a private police force of the asylum, advertised in most sectors as "Suharto Protection Inc". "If we can keep safe the streets in our sector then we can tackle the crime in any sector. Normal Street Protection rates apply." They kept the government police quiet with back-handers of good point-scoring collars.

So it was the criminals and crazies, the odd genius and artist, and the downright scared who inhabited most of Sector 3. Throw in a few private and consumer police, a dash of well-protected "responsible businessmen" fleetingly, and you see it's not an area one would wish to frequent. In many ways it was more daunting than Sector 4 where death came in only a limited and unimaginative number of guises. In Sector 3 it had been "Clergyman's daughter skinned alive", "Family slain at dinner table", "Psycho slays bus queue with scissors", and "Mad, crack-addicted pitbull tears twins apart".

Dr Tumblety had practised in and around Sector 3 anonymously for a number of years before moving his operations permanently to the asylum three years ago. I hadn't seen him since he'd moved. He wasn't a character you really wanted to see, a rather shady persona projecting from him, always skulking behind an aristocratic manner with an aloofness bordering on detachment. I was just too lazy though to bother with all the paperwork and opening up of one's files to get a new doctor. So I saw him as infrequently as possible.

A guard looked over my ID card, bleeped it into his belly computer before bleeping me through the gates.

Through the basic entrance hemmed in by wire fencing emblazoned with sponsors, I moved along the twisting path.

Wails echoed from inside the walls, swirled stretched monosyllables around the cold corridors.

The receptionist had his arm in a sling, a somewhat docile look on his face.

"I've got an appointment with Dr Tumblety."

"Name."

"Daniel Manion."

"Health number?"

"Six seven two six nine."

He bleeped information onto a computer screen, his eyes quivering from side to side. "Right." He bleeped again. "Floor 3, Room 4B."

I shuffled on the spot, casting my vision in semi-circles to decide a route.

"Take the elevator then keep walking when you get out. Take your first right and keep walking, then you'll come to a sign for corridor B. Follow that. All the doors are marked."

Boom! Perfect timing on the elevator part. I entered alone, smelt the pungent aroma of medicine and fear, medicines for fear, fear of medicine, medicine that could nullify fear.

At Floor 3 a jolt, then into the piss-coloured corridors sparsely decorated with beautiful portraits of the countryside. Twyford Down was one of three landscapes which had disappeared since being experienced and interpreted.

A knock on 4B and a woman's voice: "Enter." A fixed smile snapped at me. "Name?"

"Daniel Manion."

She bleeped the computer. "Do you know your number?"

"Six." Bleep. "Seven." Bleep. "Two." Bleep. "Six." Bleep. "Nine." Bleep.

Her fingers dangled expectantly over the keypad, gave some more bleeps, then paused, her face working to address me.

"Correct. Dr Tumblety will be with you shortly."

So I waited, let my eyes travel around the room, information posters feeding my paranoia, briefly making me want to get a check up for all the recommended illnesses displayed.

A bleep alerted the secretary to alert me.

"Mr Manion. Six seven two six nine," Tumblety began, not looking up from his computer screen, talking like he was speaking into a dictaphone. "What is the problem?" he asked, his unkempt white beard lifting from his tie as he pushed out his lips and squinted at me.

"I've been having these stomach pains."

Dr Tumblety isn't on anyone's wavelength, drifting in and out of his own thoughts, only able to answer you after a pause, like he was waiting to dismiss something curious in his brain. It's like:

"I see," as he consults his computer, "yes," as he quickly does a pulse, blood pressure and heartbeat check. "Mmm, no problems there."

"You're here permanently now?" I ask to break the imposing silence.

His gaze rolls away from the computer screen, surveys me. He gathers breath, leading into dialogue with an "Er…" as the final solution. "Many people seem unable to control their minds. My attention is required incessantly." Another check on the computer screen, segments of his mind paying attention to two concerns. "Hmmm." Eyes rolling to the ceiling. "I try to show them reality. It's brutal, but that's what they need to face. People are so thoughtless as to kill at random these days, with alarming regularity. Nobody's safe from themselves. It can infect anyone. One day you can be baking beans, the next you are pulling out some prostitute's internal organs, and you don't know why."

He picks up the stethobeam. "Lift up your shirt again please."

The blue laser, infamously cold, focuses on parts of my chest and stomach.

"Well," he begins, putting away the stethobeam, referring back to his computer. "You don't seem to have any previous complaints of this nature. How long have you been feeling these pains?"

"About ten days."

"And, well, what are they like?" he asked, each comma weighted with indifference.

"Sharp, then spreading, like lightning. Then they go away."

"Do you do any exercise?" he asked belligerently.

"I cycle a bit, do walking."

"Do you still smoke?" was prompted by the on-screen display.

"Yeh."

"How many?"

"Fifteen, twenty a day."

"And what about drinking?"

"No more than most."

"Any illegal drugs?"

"No."

He made an audible exhale through his nose, like I'd wasted his time. "Er, well there doesn't seem to be that much wrong. It's probably just a stomach bug. Take these pills, rest for a few days, come back if it's no better," he added dismissively. "Eat the right foods, keep exercising, cut down on smoking, alcohol and whatever else."

"Oh, right."

I expected something more substantial in the summary, but it was clear when he tapped his computer and bleeped in the next patient that none would be forthcoming.

Moving out, my progress was stopped by Kelly Godfrey's mother.

"Mr Manion. School driving you mad?"

"Not quite."

"Dr Tumblety is a specialist in mental disorders, you'll be in good hands." She left the sentence hanging, flirtatious though seemingly exclusive.

"No, he's my doctor that's all."

I was weaker than the future tense.

"Ah, that's what you tell me."

"Yeh," gave me time to find the banter and get in and play. "He's done wonders for you," was a bit risky in case she was a patient, so I went with, "Have you grown up to be a psychologist?" which didn't make much sense, but then I thought I said it like Humphrey Bogart, and maybe I did.

"No, just business," she said, concluding the game. "See you around, Mr Manion," began and finished the actions which followed: the door drawn to a click.

It wasn't so easy negotiating re-tracing my steps, turning into one corridor with a voice bleating, "I'm trying to save you! Don't you see?

They've raped the Earth! I'm telling you, I'm telling you! Just join us! Be free! You can be free! You don't need that car! That house! You don't need it. Hey! I'm a fuckin' political prisoner!"

I retreated, got all sort of mixed up as I took another route: the wrong route. At its end, echoing about the confines, unattached letters to the god who looks down on them. Mad barks to save the world or be saved. They wanted an audience for their ideas. This was important. This had to be heard, from disparate characters calling for an ideal, with punches on walls, uncontrollable spasms in their bodies. This was their act.

"You have taken me!" retreating behind loud footsteps, squeals veering away under a jab from the modern world.

I turned, down a blind alley of rushing white spooks preaching restraint. Not that corridor. I had to just follow the signs, the numbers, the letters and levels.

This way. Not quite. I peered into a rectangular window, to the self we keep in check. My attention was drawn, grew gluttonous until I pressed a red light bleep for sound through an intercom.

Patient No 1

With his head in his hands he can no longer view the bland white room filled with cocaine memories.

Two figures stand each side of him, urging.

"…What about why you are here?"

He claws up a weary head, his splayed hands resting at his chin, palms holding a position, out of time, out of place.

"Why are you here?" again comes the questioner.

He lets slip his palms, rubbing over skin for fingers to clasp his forehead, half hide each eye.

"How do you feel?"

"Low." A grasp at life as he breathes in slowly, lets air out perfunctorily. "Sometimes, ah, sometimes. Sometimes I see houses lit up, curtains closed, and it can hurt. Sometimes I can get this low."

"Why does what you see upset you Adrian?"

"Quiet footsteps lead away taking life with them."

The pause seemed to bring his life to a standstill, where it had been slowly heading for a long time.

"Sometimes I can't express the pain, nonsensical stinging. Unrelenting, driving against my mind, sucking all passion from my heart. Sometimes I am so empty I want to die. The days are too still, the nights fractured. Sometimes you just can't tell anybody."

"So you did what you did to get attention?"

"Sometimes I can taste suicide, taste its bitterness before eternal peace. Sometimes I want to touch it, be comforted by it. Sometimes I am too crazy low to deny its possibilities."

A twitch at his eyebrows seemed to take a pinprick of an epiphany.

"I hear cars outside my room, a welcome killing me from across the road. I daren't look out, to see those warm curtains. Sometimes they are my unknowing assailants. When life kicks in and passion bursts I am still here, resting the days with a wreath of long-lost memories. Sometimes I am broken glass, destroyed and haunted by the memories of youthful passion."

It's a strange thing when fate impinges on reality, when what you imagined you'd done is startled to the conclusion that you have done: the words jolted me back seventeen years, to a poem I'd written for school.

"What is it that hurts you so much?"

"I've been in love."

"Sex?"

"No."

The pause ached, storm clouds gathering in his thoughts.

"I can't cry, I can't laugh, I can only stare the nights away, beg sleep to be long and loaded, beg and plead for some brilliance in my imagination."

"Punching four walls to bleed for sleep," I thought.

"I've punched these four walls until I've bled and slept, just to escape. I've enjoyed the pain, it's been a release from my thoughts. Sometimes I get this low."

"It could be you in that house, you with that car. Don't you think about good things? Good things that you want?"

"No," he replied to another world. "Can you ever understand this low? Have you ever been this far down? Can you be motionless for hours, agitated to live but gagged by emptiness? Sometimes I am this low."

"You need to think of something good. Think of something you've owned that has made you feel good."

Adrian was oblivious, addressing his words to a spider's web at a corner of the ceiling, incongruously articulate, weaving his words for artistic expression.

"I've heard said it will pass. Cry, and there'll be a hand to soothe this anguish. You'll forget it all by the next moment of joy, but where is that moment? The waiting kills me. I will still be here, staring, crazy, laughing, loving, funny, brilliantly dead. Imagine being a genius artist but having artistic self-destructiveness and failing and dying before you'd even got your foot in the door of recognition. Crazy, eh?"

He laughed without restraint, laughed to scare. And, as I tried to find an exit, his laughter stayed with me. I snooped in on other lives like some sick voyeur. I watched them with concentrated avidness, babbling something significant to them, talking in symbols and violent gestures.

Walking felt like drowning, walls suffocating, supporting a hissing ceiling. Each corner held another story, philosophies screamed into the air, breathless and barbed, insanely incomplete. I registered all, kept turning them over in my mind, repeating and repeating until some sentence could be found:

"They told...Me...The Lord...Betrayed! The Truth...Know ...More ...God can save us...Money..."

Delirium pumped my heart as I turned corners with increasing pessimism. I was trapped here.

"Where am I?" I involuntarily blurted.

A large man approached, his proportions satiating the corridor, his clothes tight as skin, in white garb creased by muscles. Furrows on his brow grew deeper on each stride towards me.

"Number?" he demanded, gripping my arm.

"I'm not an inmate. I've been to see Dr Tumblety."

His grip lessened, although its thickness and potential remained to remind me of his doubt.

"You got ID?"

I scrambled at an inner pocket, produced a laser-disc membership card.

His grip fell away. He laughed like he was slugging me, like it was all my fault. I was the clown.

"You wanna rent a movie?" began a litany of derivative gags. He laughed again, laughing all the way to the exit, each guffaw punctuated by a movie title suggestion.

Most of the news websites I frequented had been closed down and it took a while to log onto one I was familiar with.

In the new parliament the prime minister set out his plans to tighten further the laws on night-clubs, allowing their permanent closure if any drugs were found on their premises, or even if their owners or patrons had ever had any connection with drugs, or belonged to any drug supporting organisations, or if their mother's Aunt Fanny's son's dog had ever taken drugs. Coki Coli was to open night-clubs where people could go without any threat of drugs being around.

The last Indian Tigers had failed to mate. Scientists were working on artificial fertilisation in the hope of saving the species, but initial results had been disappointing. However, "all is not lost as an Indian Tiger has been successfully genetically engineered in Idaho."

The Manchester Slicer had killed again. An unidentified body had been found in York carrying all the trademarks of the now not-so-Manchester-only Slicer. The name stuck though. It had already created an image and a mood, and changing it to The Northern Slicer might conjure up images of a cloth-capped working class hero cheekily doing the rounds.

I paid little attention to it. It was just one of those things, initially shocking and gruesome until gradually sinking into memory banks filled with all the other shocking and gruesome stories of modern life.

When I read about the "success" of the Government Water Scheme I realised the site could no longer be trusted. I had to break down codes, clues and passwords for some truth.

An Intergovernmental Panel on Climate Change report had been hushed up by the NRP. The IPCC report produced new evidence to suggest notable human influence on global climate. Continued emissions of carbon dioxide and other "greenhouse gasses" such as methane and nitrous oxide have accelerated global warming. The result has seen the end of a ten-thousand-year period of relative stability in climate, a period in which humans have been allowed to flourish.

The report also showed that tropical diseases such as malaria, yellow fever and dengue fever had moved out of traditional regions and were affecting parts of southern Europe and southern England. Cases of malaria and river blindness had doubled in the last ten years in these regions.

A rise in sea levels had seen the number of floodings triple, whilst arid parts of the world had grown even drier.

Because climate warming occurs faster than natural vegetation can adapt, forests, alpine areas and coral reefs have disappeared.

Northern areas of England and Europe would get notably colder due to the effect of climate change on the Gulf Stream.

Outside on Pourische Road, the dwellers would have no interest in the information I'd digested. Oncoming, the pitiful hedonism of an underclass deprived of truth and reality. Here cars moved from early morning, dodgy deals in the frequent comings and goings. Voices were always loud, always full of their own perceived remarkable behaviour. There was each day the same careless bang of some object against another, armies of toddlers trying to find something to break.

"You can fuck right off!" A coarse female voice.

"Ah, ga'an fuck y'self ya cunt. Y'fuckin' slag!" Another woman's sandpaper voice.

"Y'fat fucker. Y'll fuck owt you."

"C'mon bitch."

A male voice: "Shut the fuck up you!"

Another male voice: "Fuckin' cunt. Fu—"

This was the daily vileness of life on Pourische Road, characters cut from society with no awareness of responsibility. They never let up, even at night and into the early hours when stolen cars screech, people curse and crash into arguments, smashing windows and thundering anger around the block. The police rarely showed up; no points in domestics rarely prosecuted, invariably patched up in transient sobriety.

I wished to kill one of them; for being ignorant, for lacking a goddam vocabulary; a language of disappointment saturated with anger, a knowledge-less underclass who could only receive a cheap, obvious culture.

POURISCHE ROAD

Little John was a sullen child, eleven years old and trusting no one, his head shaved by his father to save money on shampoo. John thought it looked "hard as fuck".

He came home late in the evening after a day of smashing up vidphone booths. He hadn't been to school, but his father didn't care much about that.

He entered the house timidly, diminished by vandalism and his father's likely bad temper. Here was the place of his constriction, his nurturing more a vicarious upbringing, absorbing experiences for survival. Reading, writing and arithmetic were anathema to him. He could swear, could fight, could fill his time and could keep himself alive. A little deal, a little threat and a little gamble could keep him solvent. Aspirations were limited: He could only ever be king of his cage, but that was something.

"W'tha fuck've you been?" his father demanded, putting down his can of cheap lager, whose taste he didn't care for, but twenty-four cans at "cost-price" from a mate down the street made it last longer.

"Round Mackie's."

His father lifted himself from the armchair, cigarette burns where his arm had rested. His forehead jutted forward to within a sniff of his son's, pre-empting a familiar tirade.

"Worrabout the fuckin' shopping? Y'wa meant t'get the fuckin' shopping after school! Ya fuckin' dickhead." His stiff greasy palm gave a firm whack to his son's head, catching the top, leaving John cowering.

"S'av gorra g'ta work n' come back t'fuckin nowt. Gorra g'ta the shops and fuckin' buy me own fuckin' dinner coz 'av gorra lazy fuckin' bastard son!" He grabbed John's collar, turned him round, kicked his backside, following through to force him out of the room. "Ger upstairs! I don't wanna see ya fuckin' face."

Upstairs John wasn't the leader of the gang, kicking in bus shelters, smashing vidphone boxes. He punched out the soft baby flesh of his flat pillow, whispered darkly, "fuckin' bastard!" as his fist sank in.

He heard his mother screaming, "Where's the fuckin' ticket? Where's the fuckin' ticket?"

Five doors along at number seventeen, Shelley Morgan and her boyfriend Pete were watching a game show, trying to chip in when they thought they knew the answer, "ooh" ing and "aah" ing and "fuckin' 'ell"ing as they lived the contestants' lives.

Their hypnotism was broken as a door breezed open and in wobbled Shelley's seven year old son, Steven. For Steven it was a beautiful feeling, to come downstairs crying and find somebody in.

His young body grew vague, engulfed by smoke barrelling thickly past him through the room. It was like a magical place, through which he could see the natural inveterate warmth of his mother.

Steven moved towards her, stopping at Pete's knees as his mother fired out a pointing finger.

"Stop there y'bugger!"

Pete was getting restless, infuriated at having to sit up to look over Steven's head at the television.

"You get back to bed now," said Shelley sternly, before being briefly wounded by her child's eyes: "For mummy."

Steven stood staring at his mother, unsure. He wanted her to pick him up, comfort him, tell him everything was going to be all right. But his mother's impatient face grew taut, and this time didn't break as she pointed to the door.

"Go on, gerrupstairs."

Steven began to cry.

"Ah fuckin' 'ell Shell."

Shelley took the hint.

"You get back to bed now, ya little bastad."

"Don't wanna."

"Do as yer fuckin' told!" shouted his mother.

Steven shuffled, timid to move, little fearful edging towards his mother stopped as Pete straightened up and leaned over to the boy.

"Ya do as ya fuckin' told 'fore a belt ya!"

Steven ran out, wailing, kicking over a can of lager deliberately as he did. He scampered and struggled to negotiate the stairs, crying himself some more bad memories.

Shelley and Pete started arguing.

"Ee's ma fuckin' son, a'll do the beltin'."

"A wuz only tryin' ta fuckin' 'elp."

"Well keep fuckin' quiet in fewtcha! I'm 'is fuckin' muvva!"

"Oright, oright, shurrup Shell, the fuckin' numbers're on in a minute."

At number twenty-three the Brandles were discussing culture:

"Y'want somet wiv action. Them's the best movies. Some fuckin' excitement, a few laughs. That movie last night was fuckin' shite. The whole fuckin' channel's shite. All bloody talkin'. Bored shitless I was. I'm not gonna 'ave the fuckin' BBC anymore. For that price we can get the Dangerzone Channel and the fuckin' Laughterzone."

"Well I don't care," replied Mr Brandle's wife. "The kids'd rarver watch them anyroad."

"Orrh yeh!" said Brian excitedly. "Coxsy! The Iron Fist is on Dangerzone!"

"Ee smashes baddies 'eads off!" added his brother, Ryan.

"Oright," said Mr Brandle, "shurrup now, the lorrery's on."

Mr Brandle held his ticket in front of him, his wife beside eagerly holding hers.

The balls were rolling. Keith Hammond and his young wife Cindy were both gripping their ticket, for the luck that love might bring.

They needed the money for their three kids. It was a hunger they felt every week, twice a week, sometimes more if they did one of the European countries' lotteries. Yet they'd only started playing a year ago when a relative told them how to fill in the ticket.

They had chosen sixteen because that's how old they were when they got married. They'd chosen three because they had three children, thirty because it was the number of their house, and six and seventeen for each of their birth dates. The last number, thirty-seven, equated to the money they received each week to cover the cost of bringing up their children (spent wisely on nutritional pills and food substitutes).

Hope and disappointment have never followed so closely behind each other. A life of extremes.

The minutes leading up to the draw are always quiet on Pourische Road. It's kind of like a delinquency cease-fire, like they're all in their houses, pausing, practising decorum for the moment when they leave their disenfranchised lives.

Then, thirty seconds after the draw it all starts up again: sirens going off, cars skidding, stereos blasting, people arguing, shouting. A symphony for the tourettes.

A boy of nine threw mud and rocks at a lamp-post. His nine-year-old friend went to collect the re-useable debris, bringing it back for him.

"Fuckin' coxsy wunnit. Comin'. Bang. Tops."

"My go Robbie. Bastad slave nuh. Nuh swatsa."

"Fuckin' peeze. Der mizza one, swatsa."

"Peedo."

As the second boy retrieved another stone a lump of mud hit him on the neck. His friend laughed.

"Swatsa! Swatsa! Peedo peedo swatsa!" chimed out lyrically to interrupt his laughter.

The boy began to cry, feeling the pain at his neck. Immediately his assailant saw danger, headed it off by blocking the crying boy's attempts to run away.

"Soz. Soz."

The boy tried to see through his tears, negotiate a way around, but his opponent blocked every move.

"Soz drug-bud. You go." He picked up a stone for the boy. "We ant peedoze r swatsaz."

He urged the boy to throw, feigning excitement to help the tears subside. The did, compelled as he was to feel the thrill of pain against imagined enemies.

Three girls were hanging about on the corner of Pourische Road, none of them more than fourteen, a routine going between them with two cigarettes and a bottle of Alkoka, so that none were without one or the other: Drag, gulp, drag, drag, gulp.

A football growing louder, belted against walls, signposts, doors, metal shutters, each sound a percussion of aggression preceding the arrival of a group of young boys shouting obscenities.

"J'wanna fuck me?" asked one of the boys, the one with the ball, with that symbolic representation of captaincy, leadership, inspiring blind faith from the others.

"Fuck off!" one girl replied.

"Can't ya fuckin' 'andle me or what?"

"Ah, fuck off. Go 'n' 'ave a wank."

"Lesbo!" came another boy's voice.

"Peedo. A only fuck cock."

"'Ave mine, it's coxsy."

All the boys laughed.

The girl's friends got involved, spewing obscenities, playing hard to get.

A car cranked itself from death, tyres screeching as they burned rubber before speeding to a speed hump, clattering a coughed pause, then taking off again, sirens aching in the distance.

Shouts poisoned the contaminated air, burning with hatred, raging against the machine.

A siren came like censorship, smothered language, reverberated around the street, then faded, doors banging, mad screams resurfacing.

Pourische Road wailed itself through the night, into the early hours, trying to find a reason for living.

STONED NEWS

Stoned News started in Newcastle seven years ago, growing to have publications now in most parts of the country, despite being banned. They printed it on hemp so you could smoke it after reading. It mixed real political, environmental and social stories with completely absurd articles. The rationale was that it showed how insane we are as a race, that the true stories were often more unbelievable than those which were apocryphal.

The government used the police to close down branches, but they always sprung up again somewhere else.

The "Red" section came inside selected copies: A means of passing on information and a revealing insight into some important truths. No stories in the "Red" section were made up.

The Coffee Pot was a small café in Sector 7, just outside the town centre, down by the river. It opened Tuesday, Thursdays, Saturdays (late), and Sundays, always smelling very strongly of coffee to mask the aroma of pot.

They were only two characters in, sitting separately, eyes ringed by lost sleep. I asked the waitress Molly Simms for a coffee. Her body moved sluggishly (she could also act senile for anyone) but her face acknowledged my presence.

"Are you growing your coffee beans deep down?" I asked.

She shook her head disapprovingly before the skin on her face sighed, and – "bleep" – she pressed a button underneath the counter.

I took my coffee, moved through the kitchen to a door made for a midget and pulled away the fake board at the back of a cupboard. Stone steps twisted to below to another small door and wine racks that slid aside. A few feet to another door before entering the brilliant white headquarters of *Stoned News.*

Greetings warmed me, from six characters huddled around computer screens, Phil amongst them.

It felt comforting after the depression, felt like the first real warmth for decades. And when Theresa Yates came over to hug me it felt like love.

Theresa had founded *Stoned News*. A dynamite hack, Theresa ran the whole show, donating her profits to the Decriminalise Marijuana movement. She always looked on the money, for forty-two, and more so to me recently: short, dark black hair, a tall slim figure, emerald eyes.

With an office full of writers suffering strange mood swings she was the one who kept the product infiltrating the machine, made sure everything got written and sorted. When she smoked a joint it organised her mind so she knew exactly what she had to do before she could relax and have another. And she never got paranoid. That she still brought imagination and determination to *Stoned News* was testament to her powers and self-belief.

"DM! Long time no see. Got any stories?" she asked before a swig of coffee.

"Bits. So how are things here?"

"Good. Where've you been? I didn't see you at the People Power rally."

"Work keeps me busy."

"Quit. Roll with it," she said lavishly. "What've you been up to?"

"Ill mainly, but just starting to get politicised again after watching too much dreadful TV."

"Good. Don't let it slip away. The NRP is a fascist government. Panamera may or may not help prevent cancer, but for sure we've heard it's got other properties and can reduce the thinking process, leave people susceptible to subliminal messages. We're putting together a report for the Red section. Don't drink the water unless it's been boiled first. Buy bottled if you can afford it. It's getting scary. They've closed papers in the capital, they're tightening the laws with draconian measures. Portman is an airbrushed Hitler."

"Is the *Guardian* finished?"

"Some copies are getting out." She moved to a drawer, took out a newspaper. "Here's today's if you want it."

"Thanks."

"I've heard things are starting to happen?"

"Yeh, it looks like it's back on. You know Ted's out?" She nodded a reply. "He seems to think we can go with The Plan still."

"Why not? We certainly need something. People just aren't aware though. The underclass have no idea or concern about what's going on. Too busy getting by. The working class are controlled by the routine, really just want to get pissed afterwards. The middle-class have the carrot and stick, and the omission of important news and playing to their prejudices seems to keep them happy. If you look at the stats we have more working class supporters than middle-class; they're just paying lip service to liberalism; it makes them cool around the dinner table."

"Any word on the Essex bomb?"

"The police have no leads, but they'll get somebody. A nice hit though. Fifty-five dead and David Smithson is a good tally. No names have been given out but there were thirteen survivors. We've got the names of seven. I'll fax you over the list when we've got them all."

"Thanks."

"Are you coming to the capital punishment protest tomorrow?"

"I don't know."

"Come along, we need support."

"Yeh, OK."

I kicked it around before leaving. Evening's early cloak hung around the day's body as I re-entered the solitary greyness now hanging over town.

I thought walking home would clean me out in time for the last bit of Reeto, so it would be effective and not just a continuation.

Once again the sky suffocated reality as I wandered past cardboard houses, one dimensional, silent. I looked into the deadness of humans' eyes, saw no trust, no sense of them being in control, just going through their routine, fists jerking in spasms in case a fight came as a catharsis, to ejaculate their hate and disappointment.

I caught sight of faces like faces in the asylum, inscrutable and fearful, like pauses before an explosion. I imagined their lives and homes, bursts of noises disturbing my reverie, stopping me falling off the end of the Earth.

Despair was coming on again. I needed to take evasive action.

The nurse's uniform should have identified someone who cared, but a ten-inch baton strapped to her side said only "Don't fuck with me".

She asked to see my card, tapped its details into a computer, then gave me directions.

Through small glass circles I glimpsed families around beds, hands being held, people crying, people laughing, people being bored by the necessity of showing they cared. And those all alone just slept, or stared, their heads lopsided, blankly catching my look as they focused on the glass hole hopefully.

Kate was sat up in bed, drawing a picture. Great concentration tautened and slackened on her face, eyes lighting up as she considered her next application of art.

"Hello Kate."

"Dan! How nice of you to come."

"How are you?"

"Not bad." She put aside the pen and drawing pad. I noticed some formulae amid etchings of a coastline on fire.

She pushed herself further up, the neckline of her white pyjamas hanging down to her cleavage. I took a peak as I darted my eyes around the room. It was wrong, but something jarred my control. I concealed my glance well enough though.

"What happened?"

"I can't remember much, just my legs being taken away."

"What about the driver?"

"No word."

"Anything broken?"

"Two ribs, but other than that just a few cuts and a badly bruised ankle. The boss said he needed me back in tomorrow."

"Even the dead need a doctor's note for him."

"Well I've got one."

She kicked aside the bed covers to reveal her right leg, bandaged to above her knee, toes poking through. She wore white silk shorts. Her left leg looked beautifully smooth.

"Bruises here, here, here…"

As Kate pointed I pretended to look, instead tracing a path up to her thighs, focusing back in time for the covers being replaced.

"Have you seen those lights in the sky?" I asked, to erase my immediate past.

"Yeh, I've been studying them. I've heard through my astronomy group that it shows life elsewhere in another galaxy. I've even heard it suggests another big bang."

"So what's all this 'electrical storm' the papers are saying?"

"Cover-up. There's too much to lose in admitting other life-forms exist."

I wanted to tell Kate I loved her. I felt so much for her beauty, her sensitivity, the honesty she maintained under a weight of social cynicism. Just talking to her gave me the sense of hope I needed.

I could go home running story-lines through my head of how I would find a time and mood to fall in love with Kate.

Just Got Lucky

A dream about letters; iron letters being shovelled up, pushing towards a compressing machine, crushed into tiny squares then fashioned into little vehicles, silent and deadly. I'm in one and I can't drive, and it's out of control, swerving to avoid the other little boxes. The sights are familiar, speeded up as I go round the block, passing my house, unable to stop and get out, to answer the phone ringing loudly inside. On one lap a postman is delivering a letter, but I can't get out of my machine as it whizzes round and round. Something explodes and I am thrown from my machine. My whole body jumps. I am awake.

Too late to go to the protest. The stomach pains and being off had fucked up my sleep pattern.

A letter from Ted had been delivered. It gave orders to get a message to The Redskins by logging onto a particular website on Wednesday. I guessed they were getting the web address from elsewhere.

A printout from my computer produced something I hadn't remembered typing the previous night. I could only recall the stars and the dust taking me to them:

> "DM18703.INUTHUA NEEE Y LIFE IS BREAJING. CLEAROGG THE DRITGS."

It certainly fitted in with being mind-altered, but found only a place in the bin, discarded by my memory.

I had to go into town, pass on the word to someone who could pass on the word to The Redskins. Then I had to return to put out some information on the net. It felt like work, persuading me to visit Joe for one last hit before giving up. He was either not in or not answering, and with Joe you often favoured the latter.

I scanned the *Guardian*, its pictureless front cover filled with "OUR FREEDOM IS THREATENED" above bullet-points of information.

Inside, between lines exposing truths about the NRP, a sense of pleading, trying to encourage and force the issue. I recorded every word and sentence, every dot and comma strategically placed.

Other news was reduced to short articles:

> The situation in the USA had worsened. White supremacists who supported the jailed racist governor of Texas were in shooting battles with the army.

> The Middle East war entered its sixth week with an estimated four hundred thousand civilians already killed.

> Ten people from a religious sect had committed suicide after seeing lights in the sky.

> Men all over the country were coming forward to admit to being "The Spermicidal Maniac", but none so far matched police evidence. A group of women had set up a fan club and were "pining to meet the mysterious, deadly lover". Never mind good humour and intellect, these women wanted to tell their friends about the psychopathic idol and his unique party tricks.

> The Manchester Slicer had been caught. This time the police "…had definite evidence to link the man with six murders". His identity was not revealed though information had been leaked quoting him saying, "I had to kill twenty-seven, put them out of their misery. My work will go on."

News too that Kristen Ingersson's body had been located. The missing seventeen-year-old had been found in the Hendon Sector in Sunderland. I could not breathe, could not connect the words of the next sentence. I was Catholic with guilt, reading about her parents flying in from Denmark to identify the body, mutilated and headless.

Messages on wires sparked in my brain, trying to find a thread to understand the plot, trying to rationalise, to calm, to finish the article.

Police said that Kristen had been dead for almost four weeks and that she was probably killed on the night she'd disappeared.

Should I go forward? Should I try to help them catch the killer? Would that arouse suspicions? Could I tell them the whole truth? I would lose my job. I'd be subjected to attacks from neighbours who'd followed my story through the tabloids, where I'd be represented as a kinky sexual deviant. They'd probably charge me anyway. Murder raps get you eighteen points; a nice monetary boost at the month's end.

Joe still wasn't answering the intercom.

Maybe the killer might fuck up, do it again. I might get lucky. Or maybe even the Manchester Slicer could have done it.

Scurrying home, the eyes in the heads of the bodies I passed stared impassively. Each one of them could have been the killer, or just any old killer.

Joe wasn't in at hourly intervals and sleep only came when a bottle laid empty.

So hard to get back into the routine, to get out of bed. Electric shocks from the frayed wires at the back of my alarm clock were no longer as effective. Then the same bus, to the same train, to the same job, to feel the same strains and pining from my spirit that my life is meaningless, that I have fucked up.

Joe wasn't in school. I found out from the secretary that he'd phoned in sick yesterday. Why hadn't he answered the intercom?

I had to temporarily forget the implications. The police hadn't been near us since Kristen's disappearance. Nothing would ever lead to us.

What about the taxi-driver who took us home?

He was wasted. He hadn't remembered anything after three weeks, he wasn't going to have a flashback. He was paranoid enough without getting involved with the police.

School's sober mood was broken by Kelly Godfrey asking me what I though of Emily Dickinson. Her eagerness, effervescence and innocence rubbed off on me, her whole a part of me: Some distant, other era and some sanctuary of the present.

At lunch-time her mother called, all restrained excitement with a job offer she wouldn't discuss over the phone. She wanted me to visit her, said she'd pay for the petrol. I told her I had no car, she said she'd pay for my travel and later would drive me home.

On the positive side it might take my mind off Kristen, maybe even get me out of this job. There was also Mrs Godfrey's body. She was too wise and experienced for me to love, but sex would be good. I agreed.

A bus and train got me to the affluent Egdon Sector, south-west, over the river, clear of the motorway, nestled beneath the picturesque hills.

A gravel path twisted to a large detached house, a CCTV camera scanning above the grand oak doorway finding space beneath two front bedroom windows, and astride two smaller windows.

Kelly answered the door.

"Hi, Mr Manion," she greeted me, politely, her domestic character suppressing excitement. She wore tight, faded beige jeans and a loose dark red sweater, her blonde hair cute in its impish pigtail freshness.

"Hello Kelly."

"Come in. She told me to fix you a drink," came with incisive neutrality.

"Thanks. Small vodka please."

Kelly took my coat, showed me into a vast living room, at the back of which a staircase twisted once around a marble pillar as it wound itself upstairs. At its peak two deep balconies positioned on two sides of high walls, four doors peeking above railings. Heaving ornaments and expensive art sought to tone down the bareness of two uncrowned and overbearing walls. At ground level, comfort and elegance mixed with technological innovation, positioned around a fake real fire whose virtual flames licked with sound.

Kelly and I played together for fifteen minutes, her frivolous questioning opening her out more than I'd seen in the classroom, evoking a sense of carelessness in her youthful spirit. I flirted merrily, practising self-restraint between glances to the stair's pinnacle, waiting for an entrance.

A shadow came first, flung onto the walls, sending back a spotlight of red, preceding the flourish of a long, low cut dress straining back the apparent pink of Mrs Godfrey's skin.

Her slow disciplined descent deliberately built up some tangible expectation. When she met the twist in the stairs her head moved slightly so her eyes were only a blink's absence from us; a lasting impression left as she briefly disappeared behind the pillar. In several heartbeats she re-appeared, re-gained our immediate attention.

"Good evening, Mr Manion," she said upon gracing our level.

"Hello."

"Has Kelly been keeping you entertained?"

"Yes thanks."

"Good. Run along now Kelly," Mrs Godfrey said without looking at her daughter.

Kelly's movements were only paused as she said, "Goodnight Mr Manion," before making an exit.

"Bye."

She closed the door with a fervent bang, Mrs Godfrey's eyes flickering knowingly.

"Well, let me fill that up," she said, taking the glass from my hand, pouring two very full glasses of brandy for each of us.

"So why's this job offer so secretive you couldn't talk about it over the phone?"

"I am aware that the lines are nearly always tapped these days, especially if you've got some status, criminal or otherwise."

"Is it legal?"

"Oh yes. In fact it is a thriving and well supported industry. It is also very well paid for the little time it involves."

"Less work-time is the motto of my panacea," I affirmed, deadpan, something of Joe's technique in it. "What I'm doing now is taking up too much time."

"You'll certainly have spare time to do whatever. What do you do with your free hours Mr Manion?"

"Er, things, writing sometimes."

"Really? I write a little myself."

"Anything published?"

"Not quite yet."

"Times two." I raised a glass. "Good luck with it."

She copied me in finishing the drink, though slower so I had to watch before she poured us both another glass full.

She wasn't going to be able to take me home, the thought breeding excitement: the thrill of the chase, caught in her web.

"Well, I have plenty of ideas, it's just making sure I get the plans right. Beginning, middle and end. I don't need to tell you that though." She took a timid sip, then a hard gulp, never letting her eyes drift from me, daring me to blink. "This appointment, Mr Manion: I hope you will see it as a challenge. It involves your teaching skills, but is more flexible."

She bent the words with empathy, awaiting a reply. I swigged, signalling her to continue.

"The reason I was at the asylum last week was because I am a shareholder. We have big plans to modernise treatment of the insane. We are undergoing a programme which suggests there will be a ninety per cent success with rehabilitation. We have commercial sectors interested, offering sponsorship and jobs to those who are cured. It's just a question of having the right apparatus in place."

She paused, saw my glass was nearly empty, promptly fixed me another and offered it ahead of a creeping smile seducing her face's contours.

"That's where you come in, Mr Manion. We feel it is important that patients get the proper education, both in language skills, and, the, what you might call enlightening effects of literature. So, they become better people through their understanding. Your wage will be tripled and you will work half the time you now endure. You may find the hours occasionally peculiar, but I'm sure you will agree the free time will give you more opportunity to indulge in the pleasures of life."

The last words twisted with her cigarette smoke, curling to my most base need; leisure.

"It sounds interesting."

"Of course you would have to leave your present job." She stage-managed the humbling of her features. "I really want Kelly to do well in English. She likes it and I feel it would help her full recovery from her father's death. I need you to tutor her after you have left your current job. For Kelly more than anything. In fact, it would be helpful if you began immediately, so Kelly can get used to it, really make an effort to pass those exams." This was all gloss, but well played and persuasive. "It would help us lay foundations for the asylum appointment, and you would also feel the financial benefit."

"I'll think about it. Can you give me until the end of the week? I have to organise things."

"Fine. No problem there, whatever pleases you. How about I take us for a meal on Friday and we can finalise it them?"

The fait accompli rested, left me to murmur, "Hmmm, OK."

She kept me in various conversations, teasing me with drinks over the next few hours: Chinking like bleeps between our celebratory inquisitiveness. We played it in defensive acts, withdrawals only occurring with Kelly's friends' arrival and departure.

The midnight hour had crept upon us, sounding from a haughty doom-laden grandfather clock in another room. I shook myself to a partial life, arose to leave.

"Oh, I'm sorry, Mr Manion, I'd forgotten that you needed taking home."

She'd forgotten too about travel reimbursement: well forgotten, perhaps not even considered since the idea had darted across the machinations of her brain.

"You must stay here. We have a spare room and I will not take a refusal. I can run you and Kelly into school in the morning."

It made life just that little bit easier; still difficult, but just that little bit easier, so I accepted.

We flung back some more drinks before I followed and she waved me to a closed door at the far end of the corridor running along one balcony.

I had difficulty sleeping, troubled by a constant thought of how I needed a fix, a snort, a hit of that dust which would make me feel special. In its absence, thoughts of Kristen Ingersson, the girl I'd seen naked, now logged as "Dead". It didn't matter whether I did or didn't kill her, it just mattered that the trail might lead back to me. One connection and the desperate law would have me. Records could be made to match up. It wouldn't be difficult: A word from the anonymous and case solved, conscience cleared, eighteen points and everybody's happy.

Insomnia lasted long enough to give my bladder an urge. I crept along the darkened corridor, passed the door to Mrs Godfrey's room, turning the corner to pass Kelly's, noticing flashing lights underneath the door, in that little speck of space between privacy and public display. I presumed it to be an indulgence of late night television.

A swallowing flush subsided as I faced me, out of time, out of place, growing older, being ground down. Deconstruction in soundbites: the person I could have been, the life I could have led; all segmented, analysed, traced back to a black hole of memory.

Passing Kelly's door again I paused, feeling acute embarrassment as she opened it – boom! – simultaneously, her face flushed, glowing, beads of perspiration matting her hair, carving it on her forehead.

"Oh, sorry Kelly, did I wake you?"

"Uh, no, Mr Manion," she replied, trying to order her confusion.

Anxiety inhabited her personality. From behind, lights continued to flash until she fingered the doorknob, pulling it to, diminishing the flashing, her gaze never lifting from me.

In convulsions the light exhibited her body, a white T-shirt clinging to curve around her breasts, perspiration accentuating them. The stereotypical fantasy infiltrated my mind-set, kept me hooked, my will subordinated.

"Well, er, you'd better get back to sleep or you'll never be right for school tomorrow," came my feeble response.

"Yes."

I moved away, aware that Kelly didn't move until I'd reached the spare room, hearing her click shut a door before steps took her to the bathroom.

The next morning Kelly seemed subdued, exhausted, indifferent to her mother's presence. I myself said little, nursing a precarious hangover. It was only when Mrs Godfrey had dropped us both at school and driven away that Kelly returned to something like her normal self, or the self I had come to regard as normal.

"Mother wants you to teach me, doesn't she?"

"Yes, and other things."

"Do you want to do it?"

"I don't know yet."

"As long as you know what's going on," she said, making for the school building, hedging her opinion, a slant in her dialogue hinting mistrust.

I didn't have time to question as her friends moved over, teasing her about walking in with me.

The day in work: same shit.

I picked up a paper on the way home, scanned the sanctioned information to distract me from the train journey's monotony. A local paper, it had news of a factory closing down to reduce overheads, robots replacing flesh and blood.

There were no new leads in the Kristen Ingersson murder, but the paper managed to devote four pages to titillation and speculation, interspersed with graphic descriptions of the past. They loved the fact that the head still hadn't been found.

Churned out from the low commotion, a whiteness consumed my vision, kept me suspended in a kind of conscious sleep. And when the chair on which I sat overbalanced and flung me onto the typewriter keys I didn't wake immediately.

Keys whirring, echoing my thoughts, yet somehow displaced and distanced. These words were not mine, but they found me, somewhere alone, facing the man with his head in his hands.

Patient No 2

His hair strung in matted tufts: Some bumpkin. A glob of dribble enslaved to his lips: Pathetic. A sudden look up, aware of the eye spying him through the peep hole: Showtime.

His performance had a dilated madness, an internal twisting, a carving away of flesh to reveal the one true self, decayed and abandoned.

"Who am I?"

He stared at the peephole, so intensely that he absorbed the viewer; a voyeur of the enchantment his predicament created. His gaze never flinched, never said or revealed anything obvious, his upper body in gradual movement, slightly nodding his head to some internal rhythm.

"Who am I when no one acknowledges me?"

A shivering threatened to spread to full shakes, yet never reached that nirvana. He ceased suddenly, cast his head slowly to his right, as if some macabre act of his lay there and he were directing the spyer to watch and feel his glee.

"Who was I? Is that the person I am?" There is no natural progression; a jolting numerical stab at infancy, grasps at air, wants to breathe, and maybe even live.

"This is my life from now on. Here are my complexes, my fatal flaws, created, for me to perform. Eat this, drink this, be this. Cut to the chase. Bang. Bang! Bang! Bang! The only noise I hear. It stabs me forward, gets me through, quickly, so so quickly. Game over, thank you very much. I say more than you ever will."

Spit. An achievement in a movement.

TWENTY-ONE

Joe halted on my second call, his eyes in ever decreasing circles of paranoia, a man without a hit who mirrored me in exaggeration.

"Where've you been?" I asked.

"Away," came dismissively. "What're we gonna do?" was added robotically.

"We have nothing to fear," was toned as a question but still had more calm than any of Joe's mannerisms.

"Yeh yeh. I dunno."

Joe had never had this level of panic, and consequently I had never had this level of calm in interactions with him.

"Nothing's gone wrong yet," I stressed.

"But they'll have us for a sniff."

"No, no, we're innocent. It's gonna pass, we're too lucky. We don't exist in their sphere."

"They can drag us into it anytime. Don't be so sure of the future. History is decided on the flip of a coin. We're nothing. We can wind up dead if the wind changes direction." Joe fired words as bullets.

Joe's eyes, more bloodshot on each guilty blink, looked around the room.

"What?" I asked.

"Sure could use a hit. You got any?"

"No. I haven't been in contact with our friend either. What about The Sharks?"

"They'll be all closed up. It'll have to wait until Thursday. Shit, DM."

I'd never seen him like this, so uncharacteristically agitated, concerned about something outside himself. He made his excuses and left, absent from work again the following day.

□ □ □

There was a pocket in my mind I could retreat to, a flashily constructed fantasy whose drawn lines were easily visible on close inspection. Thoughts there were preoccupied with Kelly Godfrey whom I had become more than a little enamoured with of late; her dignified innocence coloured by a passion for something indefinable. Her enthusiasm in lessons made a connection between us. She seemed some purity, some hope when all else was tainted and forlorn. I was a vessel, drained, going through motions with thoughts of Kelly as some salvation and escape. She was inside that little pocket, that little bubble, a semblance of the world so long ago blown away.

Leaving work I headed for Will Correca's place in Sector 16, west of town centre, and became immediately aware of the other life I could be living.

Will perched on a stool in his back garden, propped against a low-lying wall, smoking a pipe, painting a picture of the bleak skyline, a canvass for his fluttering pigeons.

"Will!"

"Hey DM! How're y'doing?"

"Twenty per cent."

"Too bad. Want a smoke?" he asked, laying aside his picture, offering his pipe.

"Cheers. It's been a while since I've had some pot." I inhaled. Nice and smooth.

"I got it from Amsterdam. The stuff round here's too expensive. So where've you been, DM?"

"Working. It's back on now though. You need to start making up the numbers."

"Yeh? I heard Ted was out. D'ye think it's gonna happen this time?"

"There are enough militants, but we're way short of the majority. All the middles who've stayed afloat won't risk their prosperity for equality. The lowers and underclass are mere proles, easily amused and contented and too ignorant to know they're being fucked."

"That's a bit patronising, a bit of a generalisation."

"I can't help it. If I could broadcast invective at them to get them motivated I would."

I pulled a paper from my pocket which I handed to Will.

"Can you get this to Ted? He's on the hills and he's bound to get in touch with you. You know him and his pigeons."

"Yeh. I've still got about twenty of his. Amazing really how long they've kept going. Old Cassie's still there."

"Cassie? Wow. The old bird."

Against the white sky pigeons fluttered like ornaments held on the world's living room wall: beakless, cold, off-white plaster stubbs, injured plummeting to the carpet during dusting spells, replaced with care, ordered in an artistically ascending line to the sun. Yellow nicotine clouds breathe in perfect symmetry.

Two small sofas have ash burns, waiting and wasting away the surface gloss. Three characters are placed; an abhorrence creating the abhorred.

"Fuckin' shurrup, it's on!"

"I 'aven't goh mi fuckin' ticket Kez! Fuckin' where is it?"

"In tha fuckin' bill drawer ya dickhead. Danny, go 'n' geh ya dickhead dad's lorrery ticket."

I stayed with it, knew what was coming: A few minutes to digest failure, then the screaming starts and all of Pourische Road is stealing cars, breaking windows and finding solace.

Twenty-four destructive hours passed before Will got back to me with a note from Ted showing compass directions for the weekend.

Too many dead days to get through. The alarm clock shocks didn't get me up so I had to put my mini hi-fi on the bedside table, defiling its wires to take an extra, fairly painful charge to wake me in the mornings.

By Friday I was convinced.

Waiting with Kelly at the school gates we chatted about her progress in English but somehow managed to get on to the subject of her mother.

"Are you going to take the job, Mr Manion?"

"Probably."

"I don't trust her y'know."

"Why?"

"She's only interested in herself. All she wants is more money so she can buy her nineteenth pair of shoes. She didn't even want me. She only had me so she could keep dad."

"I'm sure that's not true, Kelly. You've both had a difficult time and you shouldn't look to blame your mother."

Kelly, coiled, was about to say more when her mother arrived with carefully crafted warmth, directed more at me than Kelly.

She drove out west to a restaurant in the country, where each crony manufactured affection when greeting her, exposing cheeks to feverish pecks, so you could catch in the light both sides of their faces.

An obsequious waiter fawned over Mrs Godfrey's dress before taking our order. Moments later his plastered-on smile was back in our space, leaning forth from behind each side of a champagne bottle, nodding forward expectantly, waiting for approval.

Mrs Godfrey presented the contract to me, nicely computer-printed, sparse hours projecting from the mass of jargon about methods and responsibilities.

"Are we ready to pour to your new job, Mr Manion?" she asked, fingering the stem of her champagne glass.

"It's a very attractive offer, Mrs Godfrey."

Her eyes were all *femme fatale*, inviting yet exclusive, the kind of image us mortals never touch.

"Well?"

"Yes."

"Wonderful! Perfect!"

Kelly's lips received a charge, quivered doubtfully.

"It would be good if you could get a feel for the job as soon as possible. Maybe Friday?"

"I'll have to get back to you."

"Just fine."

Kelly said very little during the meal, only engaged after prompting from her mother. I tried to fill the gaps with ropy anecdotes about school. Mrs Godfrey seemed to love it all, playing something out that I could only brush an essence of, and which seemed to stifle Kelly.

Finishing off, Mrs Godfrey lit a cigarette dispassionately, flicked on neutral for us, growing bored and casting her eyes around the room, homing in on the bar.

"Ah, Mr Manion, there's Dr Tumblety now. Please excuse me whilst I have a word. Kelly, keep Mr Manion entertained."

She positioned herself beside him at the bar, flicked acknowledgement back to us with her cigarette.

As she talked I saw Tumblety stare over to our table. Without the deceptive omnipotence and sagaciousness of a white coat, and the accentuating backdrop of sedated cream walls he had an even less trustworthy presence. An ill-fitting black suit squeezed him, compressed contours on his face, skin piled like sludge above and around his ballpoint eyes. The lights made his flesh an unnatural bronze, glistening as if basted. Neon gimmicks and signs scattered behind drew attention to him, and the words being spelt out weren't "Clean, fresh, elegant. Fountain wine", but "Clever, furtive, elegant. Found out why", parading some answer or insidious alternative, dismissed by his seedy, disquieting countenance.

"Won't you be a bit sad about leaving school, Mr Manion?" asked Kelly, a breezy tone contrasting with her mood throughout the meal.

"Yes, a bit, but it takes up too much of my time, until there is no quality left to it."

"At least I'll still see you."

"Yes," I said, caught up in that fantasy which lay in a pocket somewhere inside of me. "But that'll mostly be work. I don't want to be like a teacher, but your mother has hired me to get you good grades."

"Yeh, but you'll have breaks."

I smiled at her at length before thumbing through the characters at tables, resting my vision on Tumblety and Mrs Godfrey, his hand on her hip, hanging there as if drawn by magnetic forces. She had her back to us, apparently doing most of the talking; Tumblety merely nodding, opening his mouth for brief periods only. At times she would laugh, though the closest Tumblety ever came to being humoured was a flinched smile which he quickly arrested with a tightness suppressing loathing.

"Look at her chatting that old man up," said Kelly with some distaste.

"No, I think he's a business colleague, Kelly. He works at the asylum."

"So did her last boyfriend."

I turned back to Kelly. "You don't seem to like your mother very much."

"She's no mother to me. She doesn't care. That became obvious after dad died. She used him that's all. She was glad when he died."

My shock didn't have time to register. Tumblety overshadowed, his "Mr Manion" forced out; menacing black nebulae of disinterest.

Then Mrs Godfrey was in like syrup, "Dr Tumblety has kindly offered to drive us home."

The "offered" sat uneasily, squirming sheepishly in discomfort on an oozing couch of compulsion.

Kelly and I followed them to the car, a flashed credit card dismissing the bill as we left.

Mrs Godfrey sat up front with Tumblety, flipping on the radio. They were involved in short covert dialogue, snapping up ultimatums and information, sentences tangled with the radio's droning. Forced politeness kept their bodies positioned as their half-mouths ate each other's words then spat them back.

Kelly and I played hand signals, a game I'd introduced to her in lessons where we communicated without words, using facial expressions and hand gestures, giving some fun.

We screeched around corners, bumping into secrets and threats as conversations got distracted, heads turning away to tyres facing death, neglecting the rub and hub of what Tumblety and Mrs Godfrey hinted. We were excited young fools upon the backseat, whispering silly gossip.

Arriving back at the Godfrey's home, Dr Tumblety remained in the car, impassive as we sauntered out, our collective spirits stressing his dourness and agitation.

"Nine-thirty," he said to Mrs Godfrey.

"Ten-thirty, Dr Tumblety," she purred immovably back at him. "And take good care of the car."

He nodded and departed. We were indoors before he disappeared completely. Kelly said her goodnight as soon as we entered. All Mrs

Godfrey's supporting cast had taken their places. She poured a whisky for herself, then one for me, proposing a toast:

"Here's to the insane!" and she knocked back the drink in one, laughing devilishly. "Mr Manion, thank-you." She kissed my cheek. "I need to sleep, I have an important day tomorrow. You have another drink, make yourself at home."

I took a sip at the whisky, watching her ascend the stairs, a feeling that she was somehow watching and judging my masculinity driving me to knock it back in one. Wince.

I poured another, took out a pen and jotted some names to contact. I saw that Mrs Godfrey's chosen newspaper was *The Briton,* a superficially sophisticated right-wing broadsheet, one of Rupert C Donald's respectable toys. Some information was worth keeping:

The unemployed were being forced to pass tests to meet new job descriptors, or else face losing their benefit. The paper quoted government ministers extensively, the soft sell being people would be impressively equipped for success in given jobs. The hard sell incited long-established prejudices: The scheme would force "state scroungers", "community parasites" and "professional criminals" to take work.

The Briton ghoulishly roused the dead to influence its readership on the NRP's plan to re-introduce capital punishment. Recent murders, terrorist bombings, serial killer extravaganzas and paedophilic predilections were disgorged, their angelic victims rising from their graves to weep plaintive tears.

A second headless corpse found in the north-east interested *The Briton* enough for a column. Kristen Ingersson's death returned to haunt me. Lurid details were reiterated and I could add them to the facts and descriptions I already knew. A precise reconstruction could now run through my mind's eye, from Kristen's last sighting inside Gigi's to her murder. I knew indelibly her appearance and clothes, the way her skin felt, the curves of her body. I knew the way her flesh was butchered with a kitchen knife, internal organs pulled out, her head incongruously cleanly cut off. The missing scenes of Kristen's last hours I could imagine, imposing in my imagination a dark silhouette for the killer, which I could replace with Joe or myself for reality, or A N Other barely sketched character.

As I made my way upstairs I saw again the flashing lights under Kelly's bedroom door. Drawn closer, a moaning became audible, brought to an anti-climax by gasping. I thought she might be ill, though contemplation let in the thought of her having sex. Weighing up that embarrassment was less than my concern for her well-being, I knocked gently at the door. No response. I knocked again, a little louder. Fumblings followed, preceding the flashing lights ceasing. A long pause winched up my arm to knock again, stuck in time as she swept back the door to unerringly halt me, all my actions and thoughts juddering into a tight, potent coil.

"Sorry Kelly, I just heard you moaning. Are you all right?"

The scales tipped over to embarrassment. I made to move away immediately, to get away from the moment, but Kelly grabbed my arm.

Perspiration emanated from a red mark banded across her forehead.

"Thank-you. It's just a stomach-ache. Probably something at that meal."

She rubbed the white T-shirt covering her belly to illustrate the point.

We stood facing each other in silence, as if waiting for the other to spark a conversation. It made my embarrassment more acute. Where were the ad-libs and cute quotes now? I could only think of "Human kind/Cannot bear very much reality" (T S Eliot, "East Coker").

"Well, er, better get some sleep then. Goodnight."

"Goodnight sir."

Something of her mother's laconicism rolled in her intonation. She slunk back into her room, the angle opening out to measure the curves of her body. I watched her door yawning shut before moving away, Kristen Ingersson's dismembered body back in focus.

Dr Tumblety arrived early, and waited. He offered sounds as response to Mrs Godfrey's excitement, dropping me off in town, grumbling under her dismissive farewell.

On the front of the local paper S*T*E*P*H*E*N*'s tormented face drew me in. He had been sentenced to thirty years in prison for stabbing to death a young man, his weapon, a kitchen knife. Apparently Stevie had attacked the victim after losing a bet on a game of pool. Boom! Indeed. Inverted boom.

I thought of the victim, who'd died instead of me, wondered if Stevie had still been so pissed with me for beating him at pool that he'd snapped, let it all come out at this other guy. I noted my luck, times two, as it now meant Joe and I could resume business with Club Independent. That's if Joe ever turned up.

Tomorrow People

Joe didn't want to talk about Kristen's headless corpse or where he'd been for the past week. He didn't want to discuss what the police might do or what we might do. The second headless corpse got all yeah yeah yeah from him, and there was no point in even engaging him with the state of the nation or the poisoning of the public.

"One word: monkey."

In an exchanged stare we established that we were all right.

"One reply: monkey."

We sat tight against the hard red plastic seating, riddled with holes from burns, knives and graffitists' over-enthusiastic pens. Perpetual smoke circled overhead, hung heavy at the ceiling, dimming the lights and dulling the music. We were in stop-start motion, a never-ending elaborate technobeat pounding away in the background, somniferous loops taking us away, becoming bloated with vibrating circles of noise before implosion: Then some brief return to awareness in Joe and I as the whirlpool retreated to grow again, louder and more insidious, the circles of sound swelling to omnipotence.

We awaited the signal. Our man with the wonky eye and shell suit wasn't there, but his head shaved henchmen with visible scar parting where hair once flourished was. He eagle-eyed all who entered Club Independent, sending the visuals to a place in his brain where a file determined whether they were regulars or not. Outsiders had their facsimiles sent to an underground laboratory of his paranoia, some identified as newly addicted novices, some matched up with images of undercover cops he'd remembered from hacking into police files. He nodded to an obesely brooding man at the far corner of the room who nodded back. His job for one hour was to keep both single-minded eyes on the undercover cop and press a buzzer in his pocket if the law moved in for some points. Shaven-head would get the buzz, as would a muscular man at the toilet's entrance. With that they could buy enough time, pause the cops' biographies, get innocent.

After one hour Mr Far Corner and Mr Toilet Guard swapped roles; the former peaking at the precipice of efficiency, ready for a fix; the latter, fifty cups of coffee concentrated, pre-programmed for his task, loaded up on stimples.

They crossed paths at the room's diametrical centre, Toilet slipping tablets into Corner's pocket.

For novelty in the whole operation, any unlabelled persons were stung: an elaborate plot executed in which the suspicious figure would get into a fight and either (a) be thrown from the pub under protests, or (b) pull out his badge and arrest his opponent.

A red herring sponsored (b), for the opponent would buck the charge having been specifically chosen as a police informant, all protected and cosy with the law, all fearfully and fiercely loyal to certain criminals. He did more for them than he did for the law and subsequently had more freedom to do what he wanted than most. So he took a few beatings; everyone takes a whack once in a while. It never lasted long because once his employers had twigged there was no cop, they sent out troops to beat what they thought to be a cop like he really was a cop. Then Red Herring was back in position, his eyes a little redder.

The bloodshots were packed in, their long slow motions and drawled words infrequently cutting through the din. Snatches of conversations staggered forth, blind epithets, slavering and fumbling, bumping in to meaningless dictates to find a scrubbed down theory of evolution.

We loved this: the sense of being part of a reality we only skirted around. It was a mad, mad, mad world, inhabited by the throat-cuttingly desperate and the almost dead. We were in, among, living out this egocentrically hip fantasy, all quick cut, impatiently edited. Having to rely on The Sharks for a score, having to go some days without: this didn't cause our recent direction-less gloom. We needed to be the ones to score, to be temporarily witnessing and participating in the chase. We needed the fuel of illegality, the match of danger. We needed to live it, reach a climax, exit with the thrill of anticipation.

Joe was full of himself; a new person, not a sniff of murder on his mind or in his conscience. We tossed a coin for business: my deal.

A nod, a number, a fix; no bleeps, no bills, no money back guarantees. Paving stones rolled under our feet like escalator steps.

The King's Arms enhanced our route home as a place to celebrate "The Return of the Two" as dubbed by Joe.

We were on our second cigarette when both pints of Guinness neared settling. Joe sipped first, before the drink had become full bodied, something I had never seen him do before.

I took a hearty gulp to counter, somewhat lagging to his strenuous downing. The pints didn't leave our lips until Joe slammed his down, froth slipping back to its base. Mine followed: runner-up; second; last.

Then we were racing with our cigarettes, contentment growing to arrogance with each draw, until a dead heat was declared and I moved for another round.

Propped at the bar, a bearded figure bent over his pint, scribbling on a notepad. As I waited my turn he caught my stare, sending it back inquisitively.

"All right?" I muttered before turning back to the bar.

"Not really. This music, y'know, it has bad messages. Can you hear them?"

"It ain't beautiful," I replied, dismissively flicking my view back to him, then back to the bar staff.

"Don't you just know – have a sort of gut feeling – that these sounds are bad?"

"I suppose. It would be nice to hear a guitar or a real drum sound sometime."

"No, listen," he began anew, beckoning me closer. I obliged, missing my turn. He pointed to his notepad filled with incomprehensible writing and doodles. "See, I know morse code, and I know what all those bleeps mean. Those, noises, they're full of messages, telling people who to vote for, what to buy, how to behave, what to think."

I turned away to order the drinks. This guy was strictly Club Independent part-timer I thought.

"Here, I'll get them," he said to the barmaid. "And a pint of scotch too."

"Cheers, but—"

"They've researched the effect of sound patterns on the subconscious mind. The result is they can create sound patterns which subtly encourage people to buy this or think that. With all the record companies owned by big corporations now, they can say what kind of music people listen to. The top ten discs are all in their own way passing on messages. You gotta believe it."

Memory threw up a newspaper report from two years ago about research into the effect of sound patterns on human moods. Months of intense experimentation paved the way for "The Angel Liquid Experience": wash your dishes, inhale the scents of aromatherapy and send off for a free disc to take you into that fresh, clean world our rivers have died for.

"Yeh, I remember reading about something like that a few years ago."

"And with this Panamera too—" He broke off, pushed his face closer still, lowering his voice: "It's the systematic brainwashing of the masses.

There's no free thought anymore. The word democracy is just a rhetorical device." He pulled his face away, sipped his beer. "I've seen you, heard what you've been talking about. You know what I mean."

There was not much time in being taken aback when an idea prodded me upright: "Can you be hired?"

"No. No way. I don't sell. Fuck corporations. They've asked me. Fuck 'em, I've got you wrong."

"No, not like that, I mean hired to fuck the corporations."

"Go on."

I gave him a rough cut and he took the gist. He asked my name and got the truth. I asked his and got "Morse" cagily, his whereabouts somewhere on a journey that would lead from The King's Arms.

Joe had a complaint about having to wait for his drink, and I told him about the slow service, the time in settling and the frivolous need for a build-up of expectation. He talked up an equation which evidently proved me wrong.

"Give details on this new job, DM. What's the bones?"

"Kelly Godfrey's mother has offered me a job. You remember Kelly? Dad got killed."

"Yeh."

"Her mother wants me to teach at the asylum in Sector 3."

"Teaching who?"

"The patients."

His uproarious laughter infected me.

"And I'm teaching Kelly too. I'm getting paid more and I'm working less. I'll have free time like a prisoner."

"To do what?"

"Enjoy this short life."

"With your crazy friends?" was contrived out of jealousy; sent to my ears, then my brain before he continued: "I saw one of them today, outside your house. A guy with dreadlocks. He was white though. He had his eyebrows, nose and ear pierced. It's gotta be low self-esteem. Who was he?"

I replied, "Don't know," as a matter of course.

"He looked like one of your lot. I see that Ted Kandinsky is out of prison. Have you heard from him?"

"No."

Joe was asking too many questions. He had a natural talent for arrogance and condescension, so I figured it was just part of a technique to bust my balls.

I joined in the verbal inspection, forcing Joe out of his character with, "Lazy, worthless slob, tool of the government and corporate puppet. Tow the party line, Joe."

128

"Fuck you. I hate this government as much as anyone. Get Utopia finished and I'll sign up for it. But all your tree protestors and Marxists aren't gonna do it. This government will piss all over everybody. And it's not just them, it's anybody with power. Karma check it out. The whole world's fucked." Joe let the resignation in his voice get the better of him and quickly arrested it. "We might as well enjoy getting fucked. Speaking of which, how about we go looking for some Scandinavian gals tonight?"

"Shut up man."

"Don't worry about that, DM. Nobody's come to us about it, have they? Just one more murder in the naked city. Get blissed man." His exaltation received my misgivings, forced him to change tack. "What are you so worried about?" he asked accusingly, thrown behind the wait of a suspicious pause.

"What are you so confident about?" came out exasperated. "The pigs are paid on how many points they get. We're a bonus waiting to happen. Think of all the CCTVs we must have passed through that night. Anyway, whatever happens, our part in the whole matter isn't exactly savoury."

"She encouraged it."

"And therefore we should have had a higher degree of morality and risen above it."

"You haven't found God have you?"

"Hey fuck you." A laugh. "I found God years ago riding around on a unicorn."

"Amon nino. Monkey. Let's find God."

"On."

I felt like the sole survivor on Earth, walking on the expanse of hills, drizzle and fog obscuring vision, all around seeming like a white room, the pale sky indecipherable from the space defining a circumference six feet all around me.

Frosty markings were scattered on the grass, where it was thicker and greener. The yellow brick path gleamed.

My com-pass machine showed I had strayed off course and needed to adjust. I stepped left, watched its LCD arrow and minus digits heading back to neutrality.

From the mists a dark shadowed scared, then reassured, assimilating into Ted's body and features.

"You were close, Dan," he said, placing his left hand on my shoulder, the other supporting a branch he had fashioned into a walking stick.

With Ted's air of wisdom and experience it more resembled a staff.

"Life should never be exact."

Ted laughed. "I see you are in the mood."

His arm urged me to walk, to nowhere, just to keep moving.

"Have you been in touch with all the groups?" he asked prosaically, like he expected only one answer.

"Most, but I thought we'd have had a date for them by now."

"We will have, soon, but this has to be done properly, and everything has to be in place. Sixteen can't be repeated. This is our last chance, we can't fail again. The consequences would be unthinkable."

"Yes, but you must know the date."

"I do, but it can't be definite until just before the day. We can't take those risks."

"You can tell me though, Ted."

"But I'm not going to," he said heartily, a dash of laughter dismissing it without malice.

"You can trust me."

I'd had the chance to take his compromise, but my persistence injected impatience into Ted's tone:

"I know, Daniel, believe me I do, but it's not necessary to tell you now. No risks. A sure thing can be cultivated but you have to take care of every little detail and there can be no divergence from the plan. To veer away now would risk the sanity and very existence of the human race! Shit, they have a law now which allows what they call Reasonable Force in interrogating an accused. They fuckin' torture people! If the psycho-violence of their words doesn't break you the electric shocks will! You know what I'm saying?" he finished demandingly.

"Yes, right, you're right, impale me."

"Good." We began to move again. "Now Daniel, I need to ask you about one thing; the kids. Is all that gonna be OK? I don't want any problems, any leaks."

"Nothing much is on at the moment. I've just been laying the foundations. It can happen within about three days."

"We won't have that. If you want that thing to go ahead you'll need someone who can trigger it at short notice, maybe one of the kids. I like the idea, if it can capture the mood of the thing, but it makes no difference to The Plan if it comes off or doesn't. I just want to know that it's not going to trip us up."

"No. Anyway, it might not happen. I'm starting a new job soon."

"What job?"

"It seems to be more like social work, educating patients at the local asylum."

Disinterested, Ted merely added, "Well, at least you'll still be in the area." He again placed his free hand on my shoulder. "It's going to work, Daniel," he stressed. "A new world, imagine it. Sharing will be our currency, our epitaph when that big rock eventually comes and blasts us out of existence."

In the pause, a faint jangling sound, like bells animated by a slight breeze. In some other direction, what sounded like a cello.

"What's that? You got a band up here Ted?"

"The hills have been full of sweet airs lately. They have no ill-intent. Make plans, DM."

With that Ted moved away at angles, staff in hand, back into the cocoon of whiteness.

Leaving the shopping area in town I was halted by arguing at a bus stop. I immediately saw that one of three girls was Kelly Godfrey, in furious exchanges with the other two, both apparently older, neither known to me as pupils.

Kelly faced more of their wrath than she gave out, taking accusing fingers which cornered her.

One of Kelly's acquaintants looked pale, addicted to something in her mind as she psycho-babbled "We need thirty, we told 'ya! Not fuckin' twenny! What's up wiv ya? Can't ya fuckin' count or somet?"

My "Hello Kelly," was greeted by the other two with gratuitous expressions of contempt.

Kelly, pleased and relieved, said, "Hello."

"Anything wrong?"

"Nothing. I was just saying goodbye."

The pale girl's sidekick, slapped up one day, all make-up and heaving bust, glared at her; a glare that ran out of ideas with, "Bye then, and fuck off. Don't bovver us agen."

Kelly looked forlorn as they walked away.

"What's their problem?" I asked.

"They're idiots, they can't help it."

"Best rid of them then. Are you going home now?"

"Dunno."

"What about school tomorrow? It's getting darker too."

"I can't go home. I told her I was staying out. She's gone away, locked up. She said she was gonna send someone out to pick me up in the morning. I'll have to go and make up with Tiana and Phoebe."

I wanted to tell her she could stay at my flat, but that seemed immoral, inviting rumour and offering temptation. But then there she was before me, diminished by her dismissal, alone, and willing to enslave herself to her two bullying friends in order to find a bed. I didn't like to think of her wandering around to find them, being with them, tucked up in some stranger's bed.

"Isn't there anywhere else you can go?"

"It doesn't matter. We've fallen out before."

"Are you sure?"

She paused, made to speak but withdrew, merely nodding and offering an obviously faked smile.

"See you tomorrow sir," she said before trudging away.

The walk was more lonely without Kelly; up that long road with minimal bends: twocer's paradise. Thoughts of Kelly recurred, faltering when a boy racer burned rubber, screamed after by a siren.

Outside my flat block two men stood talking to a neighbour, a police car nearby.

I tried to play it cool on approach. Passing their drawn attention I heard the neighbour mutter something: an affirmation.

"Mr Manion."

I hadn't got indoors, turning to my neighbour's eyes, eagerly transfixed, egging on the two figures who emerged from his sides and obliterated him.

A grey-haired man, his stringently dour face poised cracking for a reply, took the foreground. Following, meticulously, a baby-faced bald man, his cranium and fifty per cent of his crystal ball eyes looking over the shoulder of his partner.

"Inspector Howard," announced the man I wholly faced. "This is Inspector Collins. Could we have a few words with you?"

"What about?"

"Can we go inside?"

"What's this all about?"

Not a reply, just a gesture to lead the way.

Their footsteps were a slow echo of mine, more permanent, a whip-cracking ricochet around the staircase.

Entering my time capsule, their heads twitched to look at every aspect of my flat, Collins noting details on his handcom, his fingers going through strenuous exercise in bursts as he noted something significant.

"Mr Manion," began Howard, leading us all to a standstill in my living room. "This is just routine, nothing to worry about."

Excerpts from the final hours in the life of Kristen Ingersson had been flashing into my mind as soon as I'd seen the police car. Presently, they were a coherently imagined narrative, and I was expectant that they would ask about her. I felt my guilt, felt it slowly; needing it, then strangling it, so that when Inspector Howard said, "You must have heard about the murder of Kristen Ingersson?" I had it in submission. No sign of recognition twitched on my face; I'd arranged that trick minutes previously and was planning the lies for the alibi as the law played catch-up.

"Uh, oh yeh, the Danish girl?"

"Yes. We have been checking up on everyone who was at the nightclub she was last seen in, and now we've turned our attention to those in the nightclub's vicinity on that night."

Inspector Howard's eyes rolled back and he had no means to suppress a sigh: images of the boredom of the borders he'd have to cross crossing his mind; ever-increasing circles of decreasing influence which might just lead him back to the killer.

As Howard recycled his emotions to retrace the character who thought quickly, intuitively, Inspector Collins typed information into his handcom. He was fixing up the beginnings and endings of crime, tying their unconnected threads together through committing to the memory of a file bits of facts which could be used to implicate.

Collins just wanted to get it over and done so he could go back to the sadistic thug he enjoyed.

They were partners in competition, and it had to bring the bastard out in Howard.

"You must have seen our requests for information on the web, in the papers, on the TV?"

Inspector Howard's voice changed slightly, its tone pouring onto an already mannered, learnt one, imbuing it with greater artifice, inflected with such plainness that it seeded irony, became a leading question.

"Yes, but I didn't think I had anything to tell."

"Well, yes, you weren't the only one. And you're not the first we've had to remind, that we did emphasise through the media that anyone who was in the area at the time should come forward. And we did stress that those people should come forward no matter how little they thought they knew."

A pause left that festering. In truth I had missed those police pleas but I'd imagined them, trained for them. I shrugged my shoulders.

But Howard sensed blood, recalled the facts that he had at his disposal, ordered them into his dénouement:

"We looked at the film from a camera positioned in a square adjacent to Gigi's. It captured yourself and Mr Joseph Rogan passing by."

A fifty-fifty was thrown down by God. If, or when they had spoken to Joe, did he lie? And what would be the plot of his lies? Had we seen Kristen?

Collins and Howard both saw the chink of an opening, felt a unity of purpose in their pursuit of me they had never felt before. I had to think quick, think like Joe.

"Did you go in Gigi's that night?" asked Howard.

"No."

"Did you and Mr Rogan stay together all night?"

"What do you mean?"

"When you were out, did you ever get separated?"

"Oh, no."

Inspector Collins' bald head caught the light, face down, tapping figures into his handcom.

Inspector Howard took a photograph from his pocket, took an eternity to show it to me. "Look hard, papers and sites don't always give an accurate likeness. At any time on New Year's Eve did you see this girl?"

It was barely the girl we had taken home, my recollections of her seeming vague against the image handed to me. At the time, as a feeling, an experience, I had only thinly recorded her features. Now she had a smile, beaming from a healthy, bronzed face; all neat and tidy in the last days of her school uniform.

"No."

He took the picture back, placed the life into his pocket.

"Did you see or hear anything remotely suspicious that night?"

I took a while to think, deliberately evoking that I might have an alternative answer other than "No".

"Are you sure? Something which might have seemed insignificant at the time? I know it's hard."

His words offered some sympathy, but the heavy, measured monotone which eased them out was always holding back unwillingly from the edge of condescension.

"No, sorry. I'll have another think tonight, but I must now get on with some work for tomorrow."

"Of course. You couldn't tell us the whereabouts of Mr Rogan could you? We've been unable to get hold of him."

"I haven't seen him for a while."

"Well, when you do, ask him to get in touch. We can't cross his name off until he does."

"Yeh, sure."

I ushered the pair out, Inspector Howard continuing to be overly jocose with small talk designed to lower my guard.

In their wake I became aware of sweat dripping from my forehead, clinging the shirt to my body. Had I been sweating in their presence? Fear and relief mixed. Maybe it was over with. Joe would be as reticent as myself, but I had to get to him first.

First thing was to take a hit of Reeto, overload on paranoia so I could work out a convincing alibi which covered everything.

The buzzer went. First thought was Joe (the dust hadn't yet kicked in to make me worry about the police unexpectedly returning).

I hit a bleep on the intercom.

"Yeh?"

"Mr Manion, it's Kelly."

"What? What's happened?"

An inarticulate fumbling of anguish followed.

I bleeped her in. "It's the fifth floor."

I watched from above as she skipped upwards, slowing upon reaching me.

She looked vulnerable, forlorn; a garish sweater and name logo incongruous to my style tastes, a shoulder-bag dragging at her feet.

"I didn't want to go back to them Mr Manion. They're shits, they just use me. I'm sorry, but I followed you home. I waited for those police to go. Sorry."

"OK, come in. Can't we ring your mother?"

"No."

"Any relatives?"

"No."

"I'm not sure about this, but I guess you can stay here if there's nowhere else to go."

"Thanks."

She smiled, wide and overpowering, her confidence returning immediately.

We were seated in the living room, speechlessly trying to adopt new characters. I had no idea of her thoughts, why she wasn't speaking, why I wasn't speaking. Plans to offer her my bed as I slept on the sofa — emphasizing I wasn't interested in anything else – were delayed. Silence enticed an idea between us, nervousness hinting at the attraction I felt.

"Look Kelly, I'm tired, I'll take the couch. You can have my bed."

"OK sir, thank-you." I made to depart, but her sentence hadn't missed a beat when she asked, "What did the police want?"

"Nothing, just routine."

It didn't easily satisfy her, but reluctantly she departed with an alert "goodnight sir".

Not that I got much sleep, the idea of kissing Kelly erecting itself in my head long into the early hours. No sooner had sleep come than Kelly was before me in her school uniform.

"I have to go in half an hour," she said, sitting on the sofa at my waist. "She's sending someone to pick me up at eight in town."

I felt myself drawn to her, adolescently aroused, propping myself up to retreat.

"Thank you for helping me last night," she said before leaning forward to kiss my cheek, her face hovering about mine.

"It's OK," I said, placing my hand on her shoulder.

The moment was already out of control. Waves of emotion poured forth, then were held in check by the intensity of our reflecting stares. All implications were obscured beneath a dense temptation to feel what could be taking over.

She closed her eyes, put her lips to mine and we were locked, bringing an embrace to the kiss, excitement and relief comforting us against the danger of a barrier broken.

A break resumed our eye-contact, sparkles mirroring the release in our bodies. It felt original and we needed more; passion clamouring to take more, get a fix of this emotion. An inseparable, defining episode, when at last love did mean more than anything.

Within the soundwaves of pleasure the voice of reason kept repeating itself, challenging me until I complied.

"Kelly, I'm sorry, I shouldn't have done that."

"It's OK, I wanted to," she replied, the trail of her words evaporating as her actions drew me in once again.

It felt more real with the emotions going deeper, taking shape, formed by impulsiveness and risk.

The prolonged devouring pulled us closer, her chest tight against mine. Reason fed more information to my brain.

"Kelly, this is wrong."

"Why? Nobody's getting hurt. Everyone here's intelligent enough to think for themselves, unless you think I'm just a silly schoolgirl."

Her hurt expression underscored the validity of her argument, forced me to apologise with a kiss. I felt that electric surge anew, took enough before breaking away.

"No more Kelly, this is illegal. We must stop. This should never have happened."

She nodded, reluctantly concurring. "I'm not going to tell anyone. I won't get obsessed. I'm not a character in some teen mag."

"I know you aren't. You are very special. Let's just forget it please. I've done wrong here."

But the previous passion was still in our bloodstream and it invisibly influenced the sense we now professed. Kelly's sharp, unruffled exit concluded her demonstration of maturity, but managed to leave me yearning.

Throughout the day I tried to distance myself from love. But the incident kept being replayed in my head, and with it returned a unique tingle to my whole system.

When I crossed Joe's path it seemed incidental to tell him about the police visit. Fear and guilt were occupied elsewhere and I couldn't suggest to him the desperation I really felt inside. Our conversation was brief, calm, just enough to get our stories straight.

My afternoon's upper school teaching concentrated on discussing society and how people could change things. We played a game where the pupils had to offer what they would change. Kelly didn't put a foot wrong, made no intimation of what had occurred between us as she contributed enthusiastically to the discussion.

After handing in my notice to little disappointment from the head, I met Kate Flowers.

"How are you?"

"A little stiff, and more than a little worn out with the kids asking questions."

"Any word on the driver?"

"Nothing. If that wasn't scary enough I had my house broken into on Saturday night."

"Shit."

"They didn't take anything either. I'm staying with a friend until it gets sorted out."

We indulged in conspiracy theories which grew progressively more absurd and light-hearted.

I enjoyed talking to Kate, and was touched by her sadness when I told her I had handed in my notice. Here was the woman I should be kissing, but experience had left my love hermetic. I could not go through the acts with people who knew the acts as well as I did. You grow up, you learn the parts, you get bored with the same character you have to be.

MORSE

A techno machine turned them out; smouldering backbeats inside a mass consciousness lulled into passivity by liquor. The sound and motion repeated itself with subtle changes of direction whilst a chant, "Black Rock Jeeza", circled, ensnaring a rogue "bleep, bleep".

"This number, it's pretty inoffensive," said Morse. "It's just persuading people to buy peanuts at the bar. It's a dry kind of beat, slow grooves punctuated by demanding slabs of ethereal metal riffs, elongated 'til they fade, arid. The echoing chant in the background hypnotises. It's just the tip of the iceberg."

Sector 11 was the most northerly of those in East Tyneside, encroaching the factories and chemical plants there. With that it was the most sparsely populated, row upon row of empty houses testifying that reports of high death rates in the area might be true.

Morse guided me to a run-down cemetery, at the centre of which we reached a dilapidated, boarded up church. He pulled up a segment of earth from a gravestone's garden, ordering me to jump into a dark hole, landing four feet below.

"Feel the walls to guide you."

I did this only to be told several times, "Stop, not that way."

After five long minutes he moved past me, lifting wood from above and letting in dim light. We climbed steps up to a room whose walls were dark, no external gleams piercing. But scattered about this were many small lights; assorted reds, greens, whites and blues; some flashing, some with additional smothered bleeps.

A lamp lit by Morse cast up machines and monitors, hi-fi and radio equipment, giving purpose to the bulbs.

Morse silently led me through into a small church hall. Ashen gloom filtered from holes in the roof and cracks where thoroughly boarded-up windows were.

Deteriorated hymn books, forlorn and unused, gathered dust amid various effigies of Jesus Christ.

Morse told me that the person who'd owned the church had gone bust, unable to compete with the MacChurch down the road, where relatives could get burgers as well as grieve. "This place got repossessed and boarded up. Because it's a historical building they have to put it on the market for three years before they can do anything with it. It's supposed to give time for heritage groups to buy it up. But they don't advertise. They've already got a buyer who owns all the works round here."

He paused, said, "Some say they use the meat from dead bodies down at the MacChurch."

"No!"

"There aren't many cows left."

If it was a joke, he deadpanned it to perfection.

"I sometimes pray here," he said, looking around solemnly. "It feels like the only peaceful place in the whole world, a place where mortals don't watch."

We returned to the first room, Morse flicking on a table lamp, pushing a wooden chair towards me, seating himself on one opposite.

"What does all this equipment do?" I asked.

"Some helps me decode technobeats, some is for radio contact with like-minded people. There's stuff to help hack into computers and equipment which helps me avoid detection. It's a bit of a hobby. I put together some of my own tracks for the underground scene."

"Really?"

"Yeh, I used to be a DJ until the clubs started telling me what to play."

"So you'd be able to put together a sound which might influence people?"

"Like I said last time, I've never done it, but it shouldn't be a problem. I don't think it'll bring down the system though."

"Have you ever heard of Ted?" I asked guardedly.

"Ted K?" he asked, equally cautious.

"Yeh."

"Never met him, but I know some of his people. I know that he had some big plans once, back in sixteen."

"And were you down with them?"

"For sure. The Man and I have had nothing to do with each other since I learned to think for myself."

"So what about if we create a sound which will inspire revolution? One that would lift people, get them angry and give them hope. It needs to make people act, do something, and feel it is right what they are doing."

"Subliminal messages in the sound?"

"Well, yes, but that sounds so manipulative."

"That's how it works. It's about judging how to get into a mood, then create a mood within that."

"Can it be done quickly?"

"Yes, and I know a lot of DJs who could push it."

"Perfect."

"It would start with a slow, monotone, industrial beat linked to the idea that we are all chained to miserable lives," he began to envisage. "Then there would be some chaos, using artificial feedback with wah-wah, building up gradually with looped sirens and a phat bass line. It takes over their senses, giving way to a more melodic guitar copy, chugging in to wake people up. Various different noises and sounds would be scattered, their beats spinning, ideas germinating; vast globes, walls of sound growing more powerful, combining into one all encompassing resonance. I'd use some chants, some excerpts from revolutionary speeches."

He was possessed, breaking off to look excitedly at his machines, hinting he wanted to start.

I signalled to move, aware that I was cut from his world. Hurriedly he escorted me out, but I parted with his trust (and some chaotic directions).

"Keep walking south," I remembered him saying.

Keep walking south, keep walking south. Try to get out, feet over ground. Waves of bass rock, resounding loud, merging with ethereal loops. From all directions, disparate sounds converge to a positive whole; the choked drum repeating before climax, the underlying glitter of earth vibrations, the spools of fevered rapping. Hectic beats per minute guide my sole-on-stone steps, all funked up, mixed up stax on tracks.

A copy of the sound of vinyl cut back, scratched to a hyper speed blur, mimicked my pause, lost in Sector 11.

"Keep walking south."

The sounds repeat, remind me "Keep walking south", put me on automatic to return me home.

ALL THE GOOD PEOPLE

All week I had been surprised by Kelly's behaviour. She behaved like nothing had happened between us, controlled by a strength I lacked. I felt myself ready to crumble each time I saw her, wanting to hold her, feel love. It gave my conscience an excuse to stay off work.

The days of absence could have served me a better hand; Ted's frequent messages through Will Correca invariably wanting me to find and fit pieces into his jigsaw. My dusted bliss had no fluency.

Jim Hickston from Reclaim The Streets met me in The Coffee Pot. His hair still had that permanent electric shock look, his face long and weathered, permanently hale and hearty.

"Long time no see, DM."

"I've been hibernating."

"Stoned more like."

"Hey, it's nature."

"As long as it's not that dust I've heard about."

"Reeto?"

"Yeh. I've heard it fucks you up."

"Sounds perfect. So, are you ready for it?"

"Thirty-five motorways for definite. We can put them out of action within an hour."

"Good person, Mr H."

"Wayback Mac", as usual, was leafleting for Anti-Mac outside of MacDolland's fast food joint. I took one of the newsletters with a grunted, "Scream."

I read it as I moved away, taking in the bullet-points between brief glances up to check my progress.

MacDolland's staff had worked amongst sewage on at least two occasions at an outlet in Colchester. It had resulted from management's cost-cutting and refusing to replace special equipment which would have allowed the cleaning and re-using of fat. Instead, fat was poured down drains, solidifying and blocking them. The sewage rose up from floor vents in the kitchen. Staff continued working though, handling food whilst stepping on bun trays which elevated them above the sewage.

An ex-employee of MacDolland's was quoted as saying the outlet had been also ordered "to water down drinks, syrups, ketchup, mustard, milk shake mix". To keep up profits staff were forced to keep food for longer than the recommended ten minutes, sometimes as long as twenty.

After being in Primal Scream half an hour "Wayback Mac" arrived. He had the neat innocuous features of a desk clerk, and the short black hair and average facial features had changed little over the fifteen years he'd been campaigning.

As was his manner, he busily took mental note of the information I gave him, digesting and sorting and offering only affirmative "Hmmm"s in between.

"I'll get on to it. Now, I've got to do Sector 6 and 7. I'll see you soon, DM."

"Good person, Mac."

I slipped into Primal Scream's underground level to find Kath and Grassy, wading through the hazy nowheres of a mid-afternoon bliss-out.

We shared some beers, some spliffs, catching-up banter before the bones.

They had groups in most of the sectors, and they knew linchpins in other areas throughout the north, who in turn could find connections with groups all over England. Their plans centred on marching through city centres towards wherever major industry was.

"You wanna come down here tonight, DM. They've got a real band on," said Kath.

"They've got drums and guitars. They write songs and even sing," added Grassy enthusiastically, pointing to a poster promoting The Pointless Fanatics.

"Sounds good. I haven't heard a proper band live in years."

"Be there."

"Yeh, but I've got to make a few more contacts yet today."

"No worries, come later. Have you heard anything from the CK Eight?" asked Grassy.

"No."

"I hear they're planning something."

"Oh."

"Oh yeh," added Kath. "Dangerous motherfuckers."

"They get a bad press but I know what you mean. Look, gotta shoot, I'll be in touch. Is this band on tonight in with The Plan?"

"Don't think so. I'll find out tonight."

"Yeh, do, but make sure they're OK." I gave hugs. "Good person, Mr G, Miss K."

Just to break the monotony of my labours, and with Club Independent in the vicinity, I made to make a score.

Mid-afternoon it was all four of clubs, three of diamonds; all slumped, comatose in an alcoholic hibernation, nondescripts flaking as a ray of sunlight caught the smoke in freeze frame. Now wasn't the time for talking or dancing. It was the comedown before the comeback, a little space to be depressed and drink a bridge over the vacuity of daylight.

Straight in, straight out, a bag of fresh Reeto in my pocket. Surreptitiously, walking back to town, I took a hit, then I was good for some more plotting.

The people milling about were only imagined. All was burning. They were ghosts, fading in and out of my consciousness. It became a pub crawl to escape, to people I knew if I got lucky, and in between there were more hits from the dust.

When darkness ruled the feeling became magnetic: another beatbox night winding up, a wind whipping up, trash and cash slinking from neon spot to pick up joint. A range of substances got them high, from the glue-sniffers looking to pick pockets to the neo-big rollers and their cocaine fetish.

The women flirted with their chosen dirt; bright pinks, whites and yellows pretending it was summer and their love was on every corner. Sex brushed against the night with the busyness of business.

I'd seen almost enough people before returning to Primal Scream to meet Zeke and Aisha.

"You sure full on the meter, DM," said Aisha, the whites of her eyes glowing from her smooth brown skin, bright against the bar's dark interior. "What's the tune?"

"Reeto Dust."

"I heard it's bad," said Zeke.

"I've heard that too, but y'gotta try these things out f'y'self. Y'want some?"

"Maybe some other time, DM. Right now I've got myself spliffed up to Bob Marley heaven."

"Praise the Lord."

And we were all silent, content, evaporating under the heavy bass ascending into the air, off into the distance, mellowing and fading and taking us with it.

We returned to contemplate a route downstairs, the noise from above coalescing with that below, the transition smoothly pounded, then abruptly halted. At the back of Primal Scream's underground a stage was being cleared, figures coming on to assemble the band's equipment.

"My god, look at that, what a beautiful sight," I said. "A microphone, a drum kit, guitars!"

The instruments' cacophonous tuning was something of a manna. I hadn't seen a live band since 2011 and they were arrested mid-set for apparently inciting a riot. That's what music can do, or what it used to be able to do when it meant something.

The Pointless Fanatics had drawn a good crowd, arriving on stage to rapturous applause, although most people I asked had never heard of them before. Like me they were just there to see a band who played instruments.

The lead singer, bleached blonde hair, ambled to the mike nervously, looking down at it as he flicked guitar strings, eyes not addressing the audience.

"Thanks, people of one-consciousness."

The guitar motored, spare strikes at chords leading into a fevered crashing, drums joining like re-started heartbeats, bass thumping as the crown began to move. First, a small number at the front jumped steadily, their movement spreading out until bodies were clashing, returning the flailing ripples back inwards.

The mike drew an echo effect from the voice, forcing out details of first-person pain. The bass player bounced at intervals, as if the music which was saturating him had to burst out spasmodically. The drummer went crash-boom-bang, his head swaying to a hypnotic beat, as if enacting the show being imagined behind the rhythm guitarist's closed eyes. In the crowd we shared their involvement. This wasn't some faceless machine churning out beats, this was from them to us and us to them.

An even louder second song spat out lyrics above demented guitars, pushing in one direction then changing to another; more angry, antagonistic and uncontrollable.

I spotted Kath and Grassy, pushing through the jostling to reach them.

"We gotta get these involved!" I shouted in Grassy's ear.

"They're tuned in!" Grassy shouted back. "I've spoken to them!"

I kept looking over my shoulder waiting for police to kick down the doors. Paranoia now stood beside me, began to detach me. Something slow was being conveyed through a chiming guitar:

"And we'll burn their houses down, we'll raze them to the ground!"

I saw it all burning; all the goddam factories, all the fat cats, all the politicians…

Temperature rising, fever breaking. It was time to step to or step back.

"All right, DM?" Aisha's face, almost her voice.

"Let's go and burn some right-wingers," I said.

"Watch it."

A Crash. Bleeding. Step off. An arm around my waist.

"Come on Dan, I'll get you a taxi."

Keep it going, going on and on, even when you are unable to communicate with the world.

Aisha kissed me. I loved her.

"Pourische Road, Sector 9," she said.

Hands on the car, faces screaming in: and the mad, bad taxi-driver with the white, emaciated goat's face.

"Y'fucked ur-y? Good fuckin' night then? Anyowt y'want? Somet extra? I can get ya owt. I'm the minstrel man." He laughed, his laugh thin and sonic. He was the taxi-driver driving me to hell. "Some nice girls at Sector 6 if y'want a detour. Do owt for ya. No problem. Har har." His laughter squealed. "You got the crazy shit. Oh I fuckin' know that. Fuckin' sorted creeda. A-fuckin' juz been t'that fuckin' loony tune zone. Fuckin' mad bitch going home for some drugs. Fuckin' crazy crack."

I had an erection for Sector 6, but I hadn't the words to reply to anything he said, just dreaming into a coil.

Kristen Ingersson, smiling. Kristen Ingersson, headless corpse. Joe and I the last to see her. God's making notes, but he's got a good sense of humour. He'll be OK, he knows I'm good at heart.

"Wake up!" I screamed at the taxi-driver.

He slammed on the brakes: two tyres over the red light line.

"Y'gorrra fuckin' talk ta me ta keep me a-fuckin'-wake."

"If? When? Why? I got blisters on my fingers. I got trees in my feet. I am the resurrection and the light. Scientists say the Indian Tiger died out due to man's encroachment on its natural terrain. By 2038 the world's resources will have reached breaking point – Environmental Commission Report 2005…"

I recalled being at school, using a train of thought to stay alive, only now I had more compartments of knowledge to ransack.

"…Every day fifty thousand people die of hunger-related diseases. Chemical International Corporation has been responsible for two hundred unauthorised pollution incidents in East Tyneside over the last eighteen months. Of these, fifty-eight were considered serious and eight very serious – Friends of the Earth Report 2020. Just here is fine."

"You got dollars or pounds?"
A lump of cash from my pocket was presented for him to pick.

Lights flitted across the hills, entrancing me enough not to sleep. When they faded I faded.
My mind didn't rest, putting dreams through its shredder.

PATIENT No 3

She squirmed around cell walls, pushing her body against the padded prison, fucking it with her imagination. She shook her wild, long dark hair, whipping its sweat-soaked straggles onto her face.

"I have met them. I am a messenger in your subconscious, delivering the ideal. If you try, you can. You can!" Laughter, like all laughter to me these days, stuttered out insidiously. "Try to picture it, I am the ruler of all that is beautiful." She ripped down her shirt, pushed her bare breasts against the wall. "I have met them!" The cackle she spoke with grew more affected, like some dreadful Shakespearean witch. "Oh, I have met them, and you can release me. That's why there was that earthquake in Japan, that cyclone in Bangladesh, that flood in Argentina, that fire in China. Nature bites back to save itself." She barked, bit in to the rubber walls, drooling as she pulled her mouth away. "Motherfucking nature. It's in your motherfucking nature. I am your mother nature, fuck me. Breed me. Fuck me." She bit into the wall again, took a lump of artificial stuffing out and started chewing.

"Tumblety pressed a button in his pocket and two great rocks of white bounded into view to tranquillise her.

"You can imagine what she used to do with plants," he said with some glee about the woman only identified as "Christine" from a long list of untraceable names in her past.

Signed Up

Mrs Godfrey used variable smiles when telling Dr Tumblety how many hours I would work, saying I needed spare time to write and to teach Kelly.

A list of duties, numbers, faxes, websites, rules, consequences and liabilities was laid before me in ever decreasing print.

"It's all like we discussed, Mr Manion," she exuded.

I signed, shook hands convivially with Mrs Godfrey and formally with Tumblety. She kissed my cheek, he averted his eyes, withdrew his hand quickly. Then we were all whisky and expectation, Tumblety muted in his participation, perhaps aware that Mrs Godfrey would expect a lift home, which he grudgingly supplied.

Drinks flowed back at Mrs Godfrey's. Kelly was nowhere to be seen, although grumbling upstairs placed her occupying her bedroom.

"Kelly tells me you've been absent from school?"

"Yes, a little illness."

"A little illness always needs taking care of, so it doesn't become a big illness. When I worked I had to take time off, felt much better afterwards."

"Where did you work?"

"I was assistant manager on a small cable TV station for a while. It wasn't much fun to be honest, but there were some interesting people."

"And now you are working with more interesting people."

"Oh yes, the crazies are fascinating, but that's more Dr Tumblety's area. I just take care of business."

"How did you get into it in the first place?"

"Through one of Stephen's associates. After Kelly's father died I needed something to supplement my income."

"If you don't mind me asking, Mrs Godfrey, how do you think Kelly has coped after your husband's death?"

"You've seen her, Mr Manion, she's got through it. Oh, she'll play the girl with the weight of the world on her shoulders, but that's just like any other teenager isn't it? The only thing that I can see is unusual is the books she's always reading, politics and philosophy. But it keeps her quiet, and she certainly isn't complaining about all those bits I've bought for her computer. Don't be fooled by her little-girl-hard-done-by routine, Mr Manion."

We drank into the early hours, her flirtatiousness held on a leash, insisting I call her Laura, but only because she'd bestowed the indulgence. I had quickly twigged that she was just toying, that there was no sex on offer, so I played it blank, elusive. I trusted her little, mistrust fermenting the more we communicated.

Unwisely I took a snort of dust before trying to sleep, inviting in several dreams, the tangents of which were lost when another abstraction snuck up, dominated, then took me off on its flight of fancy. I had had no sense of sleeping, resting, shutting down, when a knock interrupted my unconsciousness.

"Mother's gone out," Kelly said standing at the door's entrance. "She left a note. It said you should wait until this afternoon and get a lift home from her," she added, sitting beside me on the bed, damp hair clinging to her face, steaming skin revealed below her white shorts matched with sweater.

Our eyes shared a yearning, missing something that had happened in the past. She led, kissing, minimally at first to gauge my reaction. Liberated delight in my lineaments prompted her to kiss again, passionately and confidently.

Her pressure took me with her on to the bed, forcing my arms to embrace. We were unshackled, attempting to writhe, all juvenile and ingenuous. It was something I had never felt, an excitement denied me in youth.

"Are we going to be sorry again?" she asked, pausing to catch air.

"Yes. But I've missed this with you."

"Is it still wrong?"

"Yes. I'm hooked though. Whenever I was teaching you I kept expecting you to behave differently, like you couldn't control yourself. To be honest, I felt hurt that you'd detached yourself so easily."

"I don't want to make you do anything you don't want to. I don't want to stop this, but I can."

She'd sucker-punched me. Reeling, I kissed her incautiously, ran her damp hair through my fingers, abandoned and honest and pure.

She broke away, contented us both with a smile, then said, "I'll make coffee," like a robot. The adept personality switch had echoes of her mother.

Kelly's busy humming from downstairs persuaded me to get dressed and do the bathroom duty.

Kelly's bedroom door was ajar and I couldn't resist peering in, noticing the technology and lights on a table beside her bed, wires connecting it to an extravagant array of computer equipment across the floor.

Curious steps inside allowed me to read the lettering on a headset: "Virtual Sex" in thin red lights. An empty cartridge box jammed between bed and table had the same title, with a teasingly inexplicit picture and enticing words to sell it. I'd heard about the system before, banned in some of the more puritanical sectors, and certainly not available to under-eighteens.

"You WILL believe it's real. You WON'T be able to resist…" was as far as I got on the box.

"Oh!" drew my attention to Kelly, two cups wavering in her hands.

"I'm sorry, Kelly," I began.

"Yor not ashamed of me, are you?"

I took a cup from her, watching the permutations of her face as she circled round me to sit on the bed, taking the cartridge from the headset, putting it into its box and into a drawer.

"I shouldn't have been looking."

"Do you think I'm bad?"

"No, of course not. I've only ever heard about this Virtch, never seen one before. I suppose it's harmless."

She looked coy, said, "I've seen it all in my headset. It's exciting. I know what to do."

"Just from that?"

"Yes." Her mood had changed subtly after the crushing of my attempts at penitence. "I've never done it for real, but the VR's quite real, I suppose." Her desire seemed sudden, but only because I had not noticed the gradual deletion of her embarrassment, replaced with a realisation that fortune had placed her in a situation she could manipulate. "I want to do it for real."

I almost dropped my cup as she pulled off her sweater. My muscle-less arm laid the cup down – spilling – my fingers not loosened from its handle.

"Kelly, no," and I was going to say more, give reasons, fathom out a balanced explanation, but all I could do was stare at the pert breasts and the white bra which eroticised them.

She moved closer, pulled my body next to hers, pulled the back of my head so our lips could meet.

A line had been crossed already, but past this point would change a five-year stretch in jail to life. This had to be love, officially, forever, signed and sealed. That would be my plea. I would only be able to defend true and utterly indefinable love.

We were on the bed, kissing and kicking away the shreds of that other life. Her hand eased off my shirt, purred over my back: my uneven skin against her taut adolescence, our *venae cavae* to the same resolution: one God, one love. I felt the thud of my heart all through my corpuscles, delivered to her like blows, reciprocated as I kissed her neck, following an artery to her breasts.

My fingers nervously found a method which severed the connections on her bra, its shoulder strap breathing out, her heaving pushing up her nipples to peer over the cups.

She unbuttoned my trousers impatiently, one button flung up and onto her belly. She laughed, shot her hand down my trousers ravenously.

She knew all the moves as I paraded my well-crafted technique, seeming somewhat old-fashioned against her anarchic desire.

Her arms strained to push my trousers half off my ass. She determinedly continued the task, offering kisses to my lips at intervals to appease coyness. After each, some gigantic erotic gesture swept off clothing until we were naked and gnawing.

An entangled foreplay of pushing, guessing, retreating and repeating was enacted as our tongues lashed. Her potent skin blossomed, imposed itself against me, coiled and enticed me, till she wrestled me over, reddening my chest with playful bites.

I pulled her body down to touch mine, feeling the tension mirroring my own at the back of her neck. I tasted her dry lips, cut her throat with my tongue, sucked at her nipple tenderly. The curves of her body coasted under my fingertips, waves of her flesh drawing in my palms to feel the full flesh of her buttocks.

It ached to wonder when the moment would come, but something held us back; each motion of our groins floundering, wanting further enticement before point break.

She commanded, had the moment of connection formulated; rising above, crashing down, then retreating, saving me from drowning then pushing me back under the water.

Our physical and spiritual consanguinity combined, concentrated blood transfused through pores opening and bleeding. Temptation reached an audible ache, our veins all consumed by the body injected to keep us alive.

Kelly swiftly reached into a drawer, picked out and ripped open a condom packet with her teeth.

She thrust forward arrogantly, pain and pleasure taking our breath away. We were between heaven and hell and only words could absolve us.

"I think I love you," came from me.

"I love you too, sir."

We hit a rhythm, a hot sticky latino rhythm with an encircling back beat, narrow and hard to master, pounding out sweat. I tasted, swallowed, returned for more; my senses devoured, the motions coming quicker, forcing me to grip her for safety. Her body came and went in flashes, my eyes closing to shake her away, to envisage two paths crossing, having walked from eternity to reach each other.

She wanted something she'd seen in virtual reality. A whirring, like sucking my conscience into a vortex. A whirring, turning us in motions, finding us exhausted, having to look upon each other's nakedness to generate a renewed fever in the excitement.

She pounded down like I were a part being added to on a production line. We were weak and drained and desperate for a culmination; flesh slapping, crashing, Kelly laughing: to a shrill, fading away, then collapsing. She tightened, her domination completed as I came, less dramatically. We slumped, fell into pools to drift.

An embrace froze over us, kept us static for what seemed like hours.

We were at opposite sides of the television, posing with cups of coffee when Mrs Godfrey returned. Kelly even managed some semblance of politeness towards her mother.

Mrs Godfrey barely acknowledged us as she berated the price of clothes (and shoes, which gave Kelly a snigger I couldn't resist). Mrs Godfrey was too wrapped up in her own world to notice anything untoward.

Kelly and I were all coy looks and forced farewells as Mrs Godfrey drove me away. Her performance in the car suggested she had returned to her wavelength. Although her language and tone lacked the flirtatiousness that had previously been an integral part of my dealings with her, she had resumed self-control.

Coldly, she confirmed what would be my future lessons with Kelly; plainly and simply and smoothly indifferent now that I was signed up. Things had moved on.

She said Dr Tumblety would sign a certificate of illness if ever I needed any more time off work. I accepted that and it threw me off thinking about her motives.

She let me out in town, bestowing a showbiz kiss to brand me. I wandered, somewhat dazed, found a quiet spot to take a snort, then continued to unravel the plot with Kelly:

There was no guilt, although my mind did keep slapping up tabloid headlines for society's reaction.

But fuck society. Society buys *The Shine*, society allows pollution. Society suffers knee-jerk reactions to horrors and tragedies, offering short-term solutions which find a home in right-wing pragmatism. The result is that all those horrors and tragedies (from ethnic cleansing to child abuse) get forgotten as society glows in its own vengeful short-term responses. No, it wasn't society's reactions that dogged me, it was the exposé which would alter perceptions of me. To be branded immoral meant I would be opinion-less, unimaginative, negative, and my backing wouldn't be sought for any cause.

Stop. What about Kelly?

I had work to do for Ted, but an exhaustion closed me down, kept me locked indoors, hitting the dust, typing out the features of some characters, locking them in a part of my computer.

Jumpin' Joe Rogan

"The sky's bluer now."

"It's the night coming through."

That only meant one thing: time to get out there with our hip shit now that night had thrown down its cloak and all crimes could be ours.

"I can't feel the goddam pavement."

Joe shadow boxed with irony and deadpanned, "I float like a butterfly, sting like a bee."

"Ali, booma yaye."

He was in his not-giving-a-shit mood, all wrapped up inside himself, given out at intervals nonchalantly, dismissively.

"It's a make the make night, DM. You game?"

I wasn't. Kelly surfaced in my thoughts, but I knew I couldn't tell Joe about it.

"Your host, Joe. A little gaming first, mind."

"I'm tuned in, DM. Got ma predatory instincts sharpened. Casino Bob's?"

"Whatever."

Casino Bob's lay on the outskirts of the town centre, to the east, bordering Sector 4. Number 1's drunken expectation met 4's resentful, drug-dependent violence.

This usually meant trouble, invariably death. But tonight was different: the criminals had all booked their holidays and the addicts had stocked up; this was Championship Decider Weekend.

At the end of the police season, the winner of the northern forces' league went head to head with the winner of the southern league. From five o'clock on Friday until six o'clock on Saturday the two finalists would compete to see who could pick up the most "Crime Doesn't Pay points".

East Tyneside had reached the final against Brixton. And East Tyneside, like every force around the country, had made plans for being there. Firstly there was a list, added to throughout the year, of big point-scorers they could arrest at anytime. Murderers, rapists, drug dealers and paedophiles had been allowed to continue their practices just so they could be caught and counted on Championship Decider Weekend. Their second trick was to pick up the usual suspects, perennial petty criminals, hookers and dodgy dealers. It got a tidy few points, especially if your force had a king snitch.

"Insecure points" came from people picked at random and fitted to crimes.

They weren't many police out on routine patrols, but where they were they were concentrated. Sectors 1 and 4 got this distinction, through their notoriety and opportunities to score points.

Normally Casino Bob's wouldn't be a place you'd travel to on foot; and at the end of the night you wouldn't hang around either. Winners were robbed and killed; losers killed more savagely for not being winners. With Championship Decider Weekend the area held fewer fears.

'Bob's' had two levels: ground floor for the cheap tricks, top floor for the high-rollers.

We spent a half-hour downstairs sharking it with the deadbeats. A few card games got us the pocket money to go upstairs.

All faces were stern, watching somebody else. A plethora of muscular men stood by structural supports, eyeing up their patrons and their enemies, noting the movements of any undercover cops they'd recognised. Joe and I only passed through their gazes: we hadn't the expensive dress or manner of people who were going to make a big killing.

Slick speculators breezed between tables and virtual machines, posturing obviously to attract a mate. Whores who'd saved enough money hung around men who were making enough to pay for their re-invention. They stayed until losing became a habit, then slunk over to a new benefactor.

There were also more classy women, almost static beacons seated at expensive tables, playing a little, smouldering a little, wanting to give the impression they had everything under control; no asides to fears or fatal flaws.

Joe and I sat at either side of one of them; a slim brunette with pale red lips. We got dealt into a game of Black Mariah.

"What are the stakes?" Joe asked the brunette.

"A quarter," she said back without biting.

Joe and I took different routes and manners to lay two hundred and fifty on the table.

There were two others in the game; a middle-aged man in crumpled white suit, his downbeat expression suggesting an upgrade from the floor below. He was the one to watch.

The other was a bronzed meathead, his head shaved, his broad body moulded by an expensive-looking suit. He had some other purpose, the game just a distraction. Some metres to his right, the eyes of his minder. He was the house rep. House always took forty per cent of all card games' stakes, but they would often throw in a player to make it a hundred.

Nobody spoke during the game. Eyes rarely met, focused as they were on the cards on the table. Joe and I couldn't look at each other. We'd take a beating from someone if they knew we were actively conspiring. But we knew each other's game well enough from the cards being laid that we could help each other out and make sure one of us won.

Round one went to Joe. The woman, who'd come second, lit a cigarette. I'd got third, just ahead of Crumplesuit.

"Can I have a light?" Joe asked the woman.

She handed him the lighter without looking into his eyes. I knew that he knew that she thought he was small time, not quite good enough for her. I also knew that Joe loved the challenge this presented to him. He handed the lighter back, without looking at her, not quite into her hand so she had to break her pose to retrieve it.

Round two was sweet for me early on. I had some big, nasty cards after the initial deal. I kept them, passing on only a black jack, an afro jack and a piddling eight of diamonds to the brunette. I accepted her knowledge of the game and didn't want to arouse her suspicions. Then I took Crumplesuit's three most bastard cards (which he must have thought would kill me) and I began to aim for The Moon.

Joe quickly realised what was going on and helped me to shoot the moon, playing me into scores and out of trouble.

For the round I doubled all my opponents' totals. That didn't harm Joe, his score only seven from the first round. It boosted his chances of winning, placing everyone's accumulations well ahead of his.

Now I lit up and asked the brunette for a light. She sensed a piss-take but was too staged and toothless to bite. It would let her guard down, so she contemptuously threw the lighter across the table to me.

I lit up, leaned over to place the lighter precisely back in her hand.

Round three saw Meathead trying to shoot the moon to halve and claw back his score. But he was too obvious too early, and it took one card from me to break him, passing points on to the brunette and kicking him out of the game, his score going past the two hundred and one limit.

He stayed to watch, possibly ready to step in at the end, having hustled us into believing him inept at Mariah.

The drinks kept coming – the alcoholic killer – but dust depravation had reached critical point and a refuel was necessary; the expectation of getting it sending out an adrenaline rush. Crumplesuit won the next game, only just ahead of Joe and I. The lighter lady was in trouble.

When she went out in the next round it was left to either Joe or myself to win. Crumplesuit was too close to two hundred and one and would need two hits on The Moon to pull it out of the fire.

He went for it in the next round but Joe, deliberately picking up a nine of hearts, suckered him.

With only two left the game was over. House rules were that there could be only one winner, no matter if one competitor had scored two hundred and the other zero. All gambling joints had that rule, although nobody played it in their homes. It was about getting as much profit as possible, and there was a nice little twist too: the two remaining could either forfeit twenty per cent of the sixty worth of winnings and split the difference, or allow a house rep in to play a new game and find an outright winner. Things went on in that twilight zone of clauses which usually ended with the house winning.

Meathead didn't look quick-witted enough to beat us, but Joe and I needed a hit so we took the forty per cent and split it to split.

First I did a cubicle whilst Joe kept look out at the sinks, then we swapped.

"Hot to trot Joe!"

"Apocalypse hot!"

We re-emerged, finer people for having taken a trip around the universe in our time capsule, refuelling on alcohol's imagined bliss.

Black Mariah called us to another table where I played Joe into a winning position against a classy looking black man. Joe cleared up, blew away all competitors.

We split the money downstairs. A fight had broken out. A young man got a broken glass in his face. Plain-clothes cops were holding themselves back, willing on a murder when three bouncers intervened to throw the two lovers out. The man threw wild punches at the air, unable to see through blood streaming from his eyes and forehead. The woman had no sympathy, her arms flailing at objects to pick up and throw at her boyfriend as she was carried out.

A minute passed before the plain-clothes uncrossed their fingers and moved outside to score some points.

We put money down at the pool table's cushion, two skunks rubbing their stubble and agreeing to doubles. Winning's ease bored us, but we had to appease them with a re-match, then took twice their money.

Joe wanted to go back upstairs, but I had other plans and we split.

I stood in the neon light of Casino Bob's entrance, within sight of two bouncers, caught between the splatter of cash from inside and the sirens converging on yells in Sector 4. Burnt rubber found a layer in the thick air. I needed a taxi. Boom!

In Primal Scream I met up with Aisha and two of her girlfriends whom I only knew by sight.

"This is Selina and Dhali. This is Dan," Aisha announced.

"Hi," I offered.

"You look like you are again, DM," teased Aisha. "Are you sure yor up for this?"

"Sure," I drawled out. "I couldn't be more lucky."

"Zeke's meeting us there. We were hoping we could do this on the day. Any word yet?"

"Soon."

"It's gotta be," interrupted Dhali. "There's people I know who've been drinking the water, and they're fucked. All they do is watch TV and go to the shops. They think it's great. They think they're gonna live forever."

The world was burning, creeping up around houses as occupants indoors watched "Criminal Violence" and its taped, edited real-life footage.

"DM. DM! You ready?"

"Uh, oh yeh, let's go."

Aisha left her van at a motorway diner, a safe and pretty pointless meeting of minds for lorry drivers working for CIC and other chemical plants.

We moved on foot for about half an hour, over grassland intermittently covered with the frost and lush green grass, similar to that I'd seen on the hills.

Aisha led with her com-pass to wire fencing which ran all around The Institute of Science. A hole had already been cut.

Within five minutes Zeke was there.

"DM. Didn't expect to see you again so soon. It's good, we can do one more. You take this, Dan." He handed me a device I knew to be an incendiary bomb. "There's molotovs at every hole I've cut. Spread the petrol out to cover as wide an area as possible. Place the bomb a few feet away, then retreat. We all light up at one-thirty then run. There'll be five fires going which should take hold before they're spotted. One minute after you light up the bombs'll go off.

"Manny and Jake have put bombs in some of the trucks as well. The whole place should be out of action for a while after all that. OK good people, be good."

Watches synchronised, the other four set off and I pushed through the wire to begin pouring petrol. Lights scanned leisurely at regular intervals, but none caught me during my clockwork retreating and returning.

I loved the smell, the sense of anticipation: the world burning, Joe and I zooming off in our time capsule, loaded with drugs, good music and literature. I laughed, caught myself, checked my watch.

Then I couldn't help thinking of Kelly, felt an urge to be with her, replaying in my mind the sex we'd shared.

A smell of burning in the air focused attention on my watch. I was two minutes over starting my fire.

Nature scratched my arms and face as I made my way back to the van. Petrol saturated the air, sirens squeezing it. Four explosions came in quick succession, lighting the sky with flames.

Running further, losing concentration several times, I heard one more explosion. Fear heated my body, made me feel like I was slowing down. A succession of further explosions, distinctly louder than the previous five, threw a ball of flames high into the air. When I got back to the van Aisha, Selina and Dhali were already there, their clothes caked in mud. They, like myself, smelt of petrol. We were the guilty parts in the right place at the right time.

Sirens preceded flashing lights rushing up the motorway: four police cars, their occupants disgruntled at being sent on a pointless job; eight coppers who had heard there was a fire and knew their prospects of being the weekend's Most Valuable Officer would be hindered by this apparently routine mission.

Dhali anxiously waited for a break to enter the motorway, taking the van some distance along, crossing to the other motorway which took us to the hills.

We followed a rickety dirt road, under cover of trees, to park beside a small pond.

The three women knew the drill, getting bags from the back of the van and beginning to undress.

"I got spare shorts, DM," said Aisha, laughing as she beckoned me into the water with them.

"What a buzz!" said Dhali, throwing her head under the water.

The excitement caught us all, like we were drunks celebrating a new year.

As they dried and quickly changed into fresh clothes I observed their bodies surreptitiously, felt the sex drive in me. Sure was buzzing.

I needed a piss, meandering into the woods for release, searching my dirty pockets for a sniff of dust.

The three girls were completing their re-clothing beside the van when two dark figures emerged from the woods, guns at the ready, police uniforms apparent when my senses came to.

"Against the van, black bitches!" one officer shouted.

They all complied, placing their arms against the van as the second officer tucked his gun away and began to feel them. They were half-dressed and little could be hidden, but the officer took his time, fingering down each of their bodies.

For some reason my smashed up bike came to mind.

The first officer counted with the nodding barrel of his gun: "Forty, eighty, a hundred and twenny. Brixton won't have terrorists."

I had to act, for any connection broken in our group would be fatal to me and the whole organisation.

I found a rock, sneaking under the phonics of the officers' gloating. Feel lucky, feel dead fucking lucky.

I whacked the first officer on the side of his head, his body erring sideways as his gun went off, a bullet smashing the van's right rear view mirror.

Aisha kicked back at the officer frisking her; a full force boot in the balls. The three women were on him in an instant, booting and punching ferociously.

I raged some more stone blows down on the dazed officer, blood splattering my face as his skull cracked. He looked dead when I'd stopped.

Dhali held a gun on the living officer, pinning him down with her legs.

"Wha—" was all I could get out: a hyphened click and a full stop bullet parenthesised a concentrated explosion.

Dhali took no pause for emotion, coolly striding to my dead officer and shooting him.

"If yor not part of the solution, yor part of the problem," she said.

Automatic Living

The streets were pouring, the ugly side of bleak; grim reapers of consumerism, coiled animation as they bumped along the gutter.

A greyness had infected the sky, shovelled out like some PoW in a WW2 movie, dispersing debris from his escape tunnel. Dirty trails led back to the factories, genocidal fumes from experimenting with beauty.

A suffocating fog infiltrated my view, breathing out bulbous, insipid characters to pass me by. Blank, pale faces, still with concentration, betrayed bodies functioning from memory.

Bleeps were heard from every shop doorway, accredited fulfilment in the figures leaving; back to their homes with a deep madness in their eyes.

A man crawled along the pavement, his back hunched, his movements ceasing at rubbish bins where his eyes and fingers searched for something to eat or sell. His job was getting by and he'd ran out of dreams. And when he found a two-pound coin he bought a lottery ticket and lost.

They were all looking at me. They could see I was scruffy, they knew I was a drug addict needing a fix. They could link me to any one of the crimes they'd seen reconstructed on television. I was the type. They'd be handing in descriptions to the police as soon as they'd made a purchase, got a "Bleep!"

I had to stay off the dust for a bit. Last night's heroic finishing off and making plans to keep clean had to be obeyed. Stay off the dust, stay sharp, start the revolution. Get back to the dust after it.

"Bleep!"

Read the newspapers.

A local newspaper had "East Tyneside Win" emblazoned on its front cover. The police had gained more points than Brixton and would now go into the European knock-out competition. The paper carried details of the force's arrests over the weekend and how their points total was accumulated.

Page two celebrated East Tyneside's year, with a top ten of high points-scorers.

Page three told of three murders that had occurred on Sunday night: one in Sector 4: a drug dealer; and one in Sector 3 where an inmate from the asylum, let out for the day, had set fire to an artist. There was also a body found at the foot of the hills, that of a waitress from Casino Bob's. The police were asking for all people there on Friday night to come forward.

Here was the catch. To come forward would put me in the vicinity where a murder victim was last seen, for a second time. That might be all the police needed. Not to come forward, and then to be found to have been there would seem more suspicious. I had to report my presence, but only when the dust had cleared from my system and the paranoia lifted.

Unproportional to its importance, an article about The Institute of Science bombing appeared on page eight. Its details were limited and digi-images of "the suspects" identified nobody I knew. It made me feel lucky, briefly, until I logged that the two dead policemen had not been mentioned.

Joe was unavailable all day to aid my cold turkey. I had to listen to a clicking clock echoing about my room, detonating the anger and vexation out on Pourische Road.

I remembered bloody memories, thought I was going crazy.

I turned on the television, irritable that cigarettes weren't doing anything for me.

"Oh yes, give us some shite TV with wankers with grins and cuddly beards. We'll laugh at anything." Flick. "Give us game shows where morons win prizes. And get this, they're ordinary morons just like us. Let us claw and aspire desperately to win the lottery. Every week you find the money to buy into the dream. And you spend and you lose and you spend and you lose, and the conveyor belt of riches passes by, each week with bigger prizes you could have won, or could've bought if only you hadn't spent all that money throughout your life; buying tickets, buying those fags, buying that beer. If only you didn't need everything else to get by. Fuck us, eh?" Flick. "Gossip; about soulless, ball-less, corporate cocksuckers in the entertainment business. Make us all into leering, voyeuristic beasts, drooling as we devolve back to Neanderthals. We are mere animals, prodded and given concoctions to kill us." Flick the fucker off.

Time hadn't moved on enough to sleep. I put out some coded messages to organisations over the net before surfing for a new addiction: pornography.

A black-haired woman thrust her basque-defined body against a chair and said she'd do anything I asked. She did too, but after half an hour she was just repeating herself.

I needed to make a list of groups I hadn't yet contacted for Ted, but pen to paper demanded some level of concentration and I was too agitated.

I downloaded some faxes, memorised then burnt all but one. One message from Kate Flowers I kept to re-read and ruminate over. She used a code from *Cracking Codes for Kids*, a book she'd had from childhood. I'd noticed it once when visiting her house and could re-call it as a part of my distant childhood. She'd photocopied and bound a version of it for me, and we'd had some fun passing notes during staff meetings.

I deciphered that she had returned to her house briefly, and whilst there had taken some fingerprints. She'd matched them to a criminal the police had not even mentioned to her as a suspect: Leonardo M Smith, whose records showed a life of petty crime and burglary, in and out of prison and untraceable since a spell at the asylum. "Coki smile get 9-14-6-15-18-13-1-20-9-15-14," she requested at the end of the fax.

Trying to create silence I create chaos, in my head; so demanding, seeking to smother sounds, to hushes and whispers, until it is almost like the last drop on Earth of pure, nourishing silence. And I want to enjoy it, but all the silence does is highlight noises which choke the ambience. From distance, muffled yells and motors grow in my head, taking me over.

A slight breeze curls through the window, causing a shudder to briefly animate the blinds, their hollow metal base clanking. Am I not alone after all?

Fear takes hold and I daren't go to sleep.

Patient No 4

He thinks he's a genius. He thinks he can rock and roll. He thinks he can write a sequel to The Bible. He thinks his art can change the world.

When not straitjacketed, when the drugs are wearing off, he cuts himself and smears blood on the walls. He finger-paints globules, from out of which come explosions, and he sprinkles dots with wrist-flicks, like stars in the universe. He pisses to dilute his palate.

His head is shaved, his face scarred. His arms have ridges where knives have gone in, crossing over the tracks of injections. His eyes, hollowed into his face, broadcast psychosis, cleaved above cheekbones protruding through thin skin.

He has changed his appearance every year for seventeen years so now no one from his past knows him.

He says he has his best ideas when he sleeps, but never gets them written down: too involved with his own imagination.

"It was my idea, I thought of it!" he says, and he'll give you a list of artists who've committed his ideas to copyright before him.

"I dream, they get the waves, they write them down. All the writers in the world have received my ideas. All those fuckers owe it to me, and when they die, then they'll know."

"A predictable sense of his own importance, Mr Manion. We can work with that. You'll see that when he imagines, he lives, and if he doesn't imagine he just stays motionless. This usually leads to him cutting himself."

He knows the guards will come when he begins to draw blood, so he slices open bigger wounds to give him more raw material. So they give him higher doses of drugs and keep him bound for longer, until he is tortured by always thinking yet being unable to write.

"I need to write! I need to get it down you fuckers!" he screams wildly, screams turning to pleas, desperately genuine and honest. "I won't hurt myself."

Everything must be committed to paper.

"This is mine. Once it's down it's mine."

"My head is spinning and I am looking at four walls. This is the story of a man who looks at four walls. He thinks and he makes people do things outside these four walls. My fingers grip the pen. It makes an impression on my skin. I take the pen away and the skin can't puff out into its original shape. They are watching me. I am writing, with a pen, making ink. I want imperfection. I want the blood and guts of art; that's all there is. When I picture a head being blown off, thousands round the world imagine it too. Thousands around the galaxies witness it. One day I will bleed to get through and get back. But they are trying to get me. They are watching me, waiting for me. Here it is world, time to make you characters move. People get stabbing."

He rips at his arm with the pen, gets in several punctures before they wrestle it from him, forcing a needle into a vacant vein. His defiant words are left bloodied.

THIRTY

An electric shock starts the morning routine, all sound smothered in cotton wool, all actions slowed and delayed, every observation magnified a hundred times, autopsied and sterilised.

I can't get bad thoughts out of my head. Sleep has not drained it of them. In these visions, a Grand Guignol of real life crimes was illuminated, waking a part of my conscious mind to allow them in, placing me at the centre of the action. Patients' blood ran through a list of crimes, wailing questions being asked of me. Who killed Kristen Ingersson? After all, it was you and me.

Day two of a dustless existence hadn't started well.

In the school staff room I waited for Kate, despite feeling hemmed in by strangers I acknowledged only as colleagues.

They were a microcosm of the world; people I couldn't connect with. The key is to find the good people and unlock them. But they're not eager to let you in because they know the score, they know the game. Trust is hard to come by and there are so many keys. Keys to lock yourself out, lock yourself in, when really what you want to do is kick down the doors and be free: paint yourself green, stuff soil in your pockets and scream, "I am a cannibal!"

There were only Joe and Kate who engaged me in any meaningful way, the rest received an approximation of courtesy, day in day out.

"The only thing I can get from the asylum's computer files is that Leonardo Smith was admitted in June 2018 and released in November last year," said Kate quietly. "There are a couple of other patients like that, but most have an extensive list of why they were admitted, their psychiatric history, their families and what treatment they underwent."

"Strange. I'm going there tonight. If I get a chance I'll try to snoop. Have you been OK?"

"Yeh. My brother's coming down next week to stay with me for a bit so I can move back home. I'm not that worried though. It was just the ransacking coming so soon after the hit and run. I placed too much importance on coincidence. Coincidences happen all the time and we always get spooked when we notice them."

"Have you told the police about this Leonardo Smith?"

"Yeh. They had a secret conference before telling me they had already put a warrant out on him. Don't trust those bastards though." Concluded, she moved on to tell me something even more cagily. "I got something else you might be interested in, DM. Those lights in the sky, they create readings on my air frequency monitor. It's primitive, my decoder, but I got a message. Well, most of the words were unintelligible, but some are discernible as language. It's a little crazy I know, but I'm working on sending a message back."

"Tuned. Say hello from me." I noticed Joe pass the staff room on his way to a smoke. "Oh, I gotta see Joe before next lesson. I'll get back to you on this, see what I can do tonight."

I cut down Joe's ebullience immediately on entering the smokers' room.

"Did you hear about that waitress from Casino Bob's getting murdered?"

"Yeh," he replied.

"And we were there the night she was last seen."

"So?" he asked, already bothered by this conversation's continuation.

"The police have asked everybody who was there that night to come forward."

"We never even seen her."

"But we were there. Those fuckin' cops busted our asses about not coming forward over Kristen."

"So we hand ourselves over to them? At the scene of two murder victims' last sightings?"

"Yeh, I know, Catch Twenty-two. But I've thought about it and they're bound to have cameras inside the casino. If we don't go then we're gonna look even more guilty."

"You're right. Suppose I'll go down tonight."

"I can't make it tonight, how about tomorrow?"

Joe shrugged. "It doesn't matter if we go down separately. I'll just tell them you'll be down tomorrow. Anyway, going together might look a bit shady, a bit pre-planned."

"Hmmm," I contemplated. "At least we can tell the truth this time."

With that Joe stubbed his cigarette out and left.

Standing at the school gates with Kelly, waiting for her late mother, we resisted the urge to kiss, though language incriminated us.

"I've missed you, sir."

"I've missed you, Kelly. We've got to be careful though."

"I know, but I'll be finished this year, and I'll be sixteen in three months, then we can do whatever we want."

"What about your mother?"

"She won't care."

"Well, let's just be careful. We can't do any of that stuff again until you're sixteen and have left school."

She changed track completely, dismissing our love easily. "Do you drink the water, now it's got that Panamera in it?"

"No, why?"

"I didn't think you would. I've heard over the net that the government is using it to brainwash people. We've never drunk tap water in our house anyway. She thinks she's better than that. But d'ye think they're really brainwashing people?"

"It wouldn't surprise me. You must have access to some pretty obscure and illegal sites to get that information."

"I don't like the NRP. I've been following all the bad things they do. I bet you hate them, don't you?"

"Well, yes."

"I thought so, from your lessons. I bet you're what they used to call a socialist aren't you?"

"I suppose I am."

"I read lots of books while I was off school. I know all about politics. She doesn't care, doesn't even know I joined the Eco Warriors. I can't wait to go on some demos. Capitalism is parasitic, don't you think?"

I had to affect shock, standing aback. "Wow, Kelly, you're clued up. It's good to see."

I couldn't help feeling a little suspicious, such was the curious mix of comedown and fearful roller-coaster excitement coursing through my system. In the absence of drugs I was rewinding at a thousand seconds a minute, the brutal progress of expulsion relayed to me at a thousand minutes a second. At points it gave me a psychological high, followed invariably by quickening paranoia.

We had no chance to discuss further when Mrs Godfrey arrived, fifteen minutes late.

We took our cue, Mrs Godfrey directing Kelly to the back seat.

"It's nice to see you two getting along," she said.

She carried on this theme throughout the drive, grew bored with it only after dropping Kelly off and arriving at the asylum. I remained reticent to her insinuations; even the jokey ones suggesting she knew the bones about Kelly and me.

Tumblety gave me pamphlets I had barely time to read. A quick thumb-flick through noted a section titled "Objectives": "...to create people who can give something back to society...no threat to the public…" I took in scant details from each fifteen page section of the pamphlet: "…physical and mental tests…and ability to construct ideas through writing and speech…"

Tumblety served another business-like pamphlet which he called, "The education pack". It surprised me to see I would be teaching poetry. Teaching the insane poetry! I had not heard of the poet, Geoffrey Durkins-Spear, but there were plenty of examples of his work; each one supported by "Working notes" which detailed themes and ideas that could be found.

There were other books listed too, mostly the work of authors and poets I did not know. I recognised the formulaic thriller writer, Frederick Foswith, whom I didn't think appropriate, but again they were teaching-notes for his work.

I glanced through the pages, noticing at the bottom of each a sponsor's logo: Coki Coli. It disturbed me but Tumblety resumed audible domination and pushed the misgivings to the back of my mind.

"I suggest you take them home to study in more detail, Mr Manion. Our predictions suggest we can aim for a ninety per cent pass rate. Your experience in education will help with the process we have already started. It's very important we get started soon. As you may have read, we had an unfortunate incident recently with one of our inmates on day release."

Tumblety's sentences mixed words I couldn't define with methods and regulations as we twisted around wailing walls.

A dishevelled young man, seated at the edge of his bed, stared at nothing in particular; his eyes merely fixed on adjacent walls; his face perverted with a strange babyishness.

"We're not sure if this man can be helped. He's due to leave next week into community care. He's no longer dangerous, but he's not— erm—focused. We think he can be improved. If you look at page sixteen tonight you'll see the section we have allocated for him."

"What's wrong with him?" I asked, watching as the patient's head moved in little gestures, as if involved somewhere else.

He was living in a permanently constructed fantasy. Each day he moved through actions like a routine, his body there but not his mind. His cell was his world. Once, his bed was a confessional, once a cinema seat, once a phone box, and he'd behaved like he was really in that world. Everything his body does is imagined. He even imagines where a toilet is and goes there.

"As it is generally the same corner we put a bin there."

His pet topic is tape head cleaners. He thinks they should be banned because they carry satanic messages.

"…Whisperings from The Devil."

The man in the cell got up, moved across to his table, seemed to pick something up, handing it to an invisible person opposite who dropped it to the floor.

He smiled and began to talk, pausing for replies, his face looking diligent and serious before further communication.

"Want to listen?" asked Mrs Godfrey, pressing a button to "Bleep" open the lines of communication before I could reply.

His words grated through the wire meshing:

"…But that's impossible Mr Hutton, that's far too idealistic, and it's an idealism based on economics, progress and development. It's admirable that you want to share the wealth of society." He paused, nodding at the response he imagined. "But you want people to want what you want. A Utopia with a high standard of living and material possessions is just another example of the middle-classes purging their guilt with token gestures. It's got no reality—"

He broke off, nodding in a very affected way as his debating partner countered with a point about the middle-classes trying to change themselves and then change society.

"Yes, agreed, but the change has got to mean a whole new way of thinking. It's a lateral revolution. You just can't share wealth. Wealth isn't pure! You'd have to share ideas, philosophies. You have to share culture; otherwise it serves no purpose. Culture does not belong to the individual. We need to be collectively aware so that our appreciation can have some relevance."

Tumblety muted the voice with a bleep. "Anyone would think he was highly intelligent, and indeed he is, but it is not connected in any way with the world in which you and I function. He has made progress since being here. We've used drugs to realign his perspective and are hopeful these doses will recede as he adopts a proper perspective permanently. Your work will be to try to make him more productive. Page sixteen, tonight, Mr Manion."

"I'd like to see his records first."

"Not necessary. He's safe. Just look at page sixteen."

"I need to know his background, what he's done in his life. I need to know where I shouldn't go and where I should when I try to get into the way his mind works. Every personality is different. I need to be able to flesh out the character to understand the character."

"Mr Manion, the treatment does not require you to form a relationship with the patient. Page sixteen—"

"Mr Manion is right," weighed in Mrs Godfrey. "He is a writer, and he knows that all things require fine detail. What you want this lunatic to be will not be reached unless Mr Manion can thread all the plot parts together to lead us there." She contented herself with the brilliant speech, made a mental note of it for a later cocktail party. "Rest on it, Tumblety. You know it's right."

Tumblety had been thrown from his pragmatic, scientific path, now leading us through corridors and downstairs to a room on the ground floor.

A zombie-like dimwit male receptionist was too in awe of Dr Tumblety to greet him, cowering under orders to print out "File six nine three zero two".

I needed to be back in here, alone. The deadwit wasn't a problem. So I pretended to read the extensive details of the patient I was to be treating. Got to get back in when Tumblety's gone. I turned a page. Be friendly with the receptionist on the way out, get my face known and trusted. When I come back on a pretext it'll all be smiles and no suspicions. I turned a page. The pretext? Tumblety would clear back to his office quickly. He hadn't the mood for walking Mrs Godfrey to her car. So we sign out, I do a quick chat like I'm making the make, then we meander to exit. Turn page. I'll slow Mrs Godfrey down with some conversation. It'll need to be about four minutes after bye-bye Tumblety before I stop, fumble in my pocket and realise I've left keys behind. Turn page. Last page. Not keys. Why would I get them out?

"Right. Well, that helps." I handed the papers back to Deadwit who immediately put them through a ravenous shredder. Tumblety's disapproving eyes met his and he cowered. "I think I know how to help him."

"Page sixteen," reiterated Tumblety.

I took out my pen, asked for a piece of paper to write down the page number, then did some wind-bagging to divert everyone from where my pen ended up.

Deadwit's fingers were morbidly conscientiously tapping out bleeps on computer keys when I next saw him. My presence had rested a while before he noticed it.

"I need another file for Dr Tumblety. Leonardo Smith."

He bleeped obediently for a print-out.

The sheet only had a name and a date of admittance.

"How come there's no background on this one?" I asked, handing the sheet back to him.

"I don't know," he replied and I believed him.

"Are there any other records kept anywhere?"

"I don't know."

"Are you sure?" I pressurised him out of desperation. "Think. Think hard. It's very important for Dr Tumblety."

"It might be on one of the ones he's downloaded."

"Where does he keep them?"

"I don't know."

His ignorance unwittingly halted my progress, probably doing Dr Tumblety a favour.

Wails guided me out, and this time I'd forgotten to be pally with the receptionist.

"Did you find your pen?"

"Oh yeh, yes thanks."

The wails followed my steps, like anarchy exploding all over the building; an anarchy which could barely be quelled. But syringes hit their spot and the eyes and heart sagged back and slept. All quiet on the crazy front.

So hard to get them out of my head, like they inhabited me. The desire to score remained, and with it some permanent high that couldn't be expelled. The clock continued to swish its ticks. The air continued to breathe heavily upon me. Nothing felt normal.

THIRTY-ONE

The electric shock surged through me, a razorblade whiplash waking every nerve in my body, leaving my right palm smouldering. The ghost of a sensation passed through me, closed me back down. I took another shock, gripping the wires for longer, until I jarred myself awake.

Morse's tape had arrived, with a note saying he was distributing the track to DJs through the net.

Ted's faxes took up space in my faxbox, compelling me to act to get up to date.

The Donga Tribe was all set to storm Rupert C Donald's *Shine* offices. I had to put them in contact with Radical Youth who were going to take care of all access roads in the area.

I had to work out the logistics for distributing leaflets showing what CIC Manchester had pumped into the air, then give "Manchester Ef" the details of who to get in contact with and when to act.

I had to see Will Correca, get him to send a pigeon to take a message to "Workers Against Nasty Killers Especially Revolutionaries". ("We don't use faxes, sites or telephones as they represent capitalism.") They were going to help "Phone Bug" infiltrate lines of communication in Kent, play recorded messages explaining The Plan.

I sorted the list of all the Shellac oil company's "Loyalty card" customers. I typed up a letter explaining that Shellac had paid the military government in Nigeria to suppress, arrest and kill those nationals who opposed its operations in the country. A few bullet-points followed of all that Shellac had done: turning one area of Nigeria into an uninhabitable tar pit, having plundered its natural resources, displaced its people and left without clearing up or making safe.

The letter ended with a quote from a memorandum sent by a military general to Shellac's boss, Robert Parsons. General Ocuntemo listed recommendations for the continued prosperity of Shellac's oil production. One "strategy" advised was "Wasting targets, cutting across communities and leadership cadres, especially vocal individuals" and "wasting operations coupled with psychological tactics of displacement/ wasting as noted above".

I set a timer on the "invisible" faxbox to send the letter out to each Shellac customer.

I had cleared my mind sufficiently. I deserved a score.

It all went smoothly at Club Independent: in and nod and out. I was the man. The kid was back, all blissed, all ready to trip my wires.

At the top of the stairs in my flat block, a reminder of plans not carried out: Inspectors Howard and Collins waiting.

"Mr Manion, you must be feeling better," said Howard. "We called the school. They told us you were ill." Guilt had been assumed.

"I've just been to get some fresh air," I replied, the path to my door blocked.

"Must have been a long walk. I hope it did you good."

"Yeh. Is this about Casino Bob's?"

"Yes. We were waiting for you to report in. Mr Rogan was rather late himself, but at least he came to see us."

"I was going to come down today. I've been too ill."

"Of course."

Inside, we adopted similar positions to their previous visit, but strangely, despite being less complicit in this murder, I felt more ill at ease. It might have had something to do with the stash next to my burning heart. It might have had something to do with only having the truth to cling to this time.

"You were at Casino Bob's last Friday?" I nodded. "And you know about the waitress being murdered?" I nodded as Howard presented a photo to me. "Do you remember seeing this woman?"

"No."

He put the photo away. Collins typed information into his handcom.

"Mr Rogan said you left early. Where did you go after the casino?"

"A few pubs, Primal Scream."

"Other names?"

"Pat O'Thwacke's."

"Just those two?"

"Yeh."

"Where did you go to last of all?"

"Scream."

"And then?"

"I went home."

"At what time?"

"I can't remember."

"Approximately."

"One, two. I was pretty drunk."

"Like last time?"

Howard let the words grow monstrous tentacles, idling away, browsing around my room. Collins looked up from his handcom and stepped forward, his eyes red and grisly.

"Who was with you at Primal Scream?" he snapped, his voice whiny, each word enunciated like the dead bleep on a heart monitor.

"No one."

"You have a history Mr Manion," he said, moving closer to me, taking the air into his nostrils. "You've been involved with subversives."

"That was years ago, before I became a teacher."

"And you don't involve yourself with it anymore?"

I shook my head, smelt the strong mint of someone trying to hide bad breath. He rubbed his thumb and finger together, let me concentrate on his playing of the world's smallest violin, then darted his hand to my scalp, tugging out a bunch of hairs.

"Hey!"

Howard stepped back in: "It's routine, Mr Manion, just a sample to clear your name."

Collins ground his teeth, after something more, reluctant to step back after Howard flicked his head.

"Did you meet anyone or talk to anyone in Primal Scream?"

"A few hellos."

"Who?"

"I can't remember. I just went to see a band."

"Just a few names so we can check your story."

"I don't like this. You sound like you're accusing me of something."

Neither man replied, Collins slipping my hairs into a small polythene bag, Howard looking coldly at me, all fake bonhomie gone.

"We have a job to do. We need the public's help. If you aren't part of the solution, you are part of the problem." He smiled dirtily. "We'll check Primal Scream, and O'Thwacke's. I'm sure we'll be back in touch." He turned and left, followed sluggishly by Collins.

"Fuck."

A greater fear and sense of isolation I had not experienced before. Even the dust didn't help. I needed to plan how long I would have, how long I could keep them at bay. The revolution would take care of them, but I needed it to come before they had enough to nail me.

I didn't dare go out, using the net to warn Aisha of what was unfolding, my mind ahead of fate, outrunning it to lay a new path. Investigations could lead to the Institute of Science bombing.

Kelly, from memory, came back to reassure some small part of me. I needed her. I needed her love.

COCKTAIL SUICIDE 8

The yellow brick road's surface has an unnatural hue in the dark open night. All around, a mysterious foreboding lurks in the darkness of nature. The yellow gleaming path is more sinister, with its sense of isolation. The illuminated bricks showed where the easy prey was for demons prowling in the silent wilderness.

Kate diverted me off the path, walking through undergrowth for ten minutes before stopping at the foot of a small hill.

"It's over there. Keep low and keep back. They've got a laser fence up."

It was difficult to make much out in the thick, white fog which hung inside the sprinkling criss-crossing laser lights. Figures moved about at the place where Kate had identified the strange lights above the hills being most predominant. They wore protective uniforms over their whole bodies, nothing of facial features visible behind the visors.

According to Kate, helicopters came and went, most only going as far as The Institute of Science. She'd taken frequency readings from there and here and they had matched up.

I noticed the strange frost on the grass, remembered it from previous journeys up the hills, and from that night at the Institute.

"What's this?" I asked.

"I took a sample. I can't identify it, but it has a curious effect on vegetation. It gives protein to plant life, extracts impurities."

"What do you think they're up to?"

"Maybe experiments, but that doesn't explain the lights."

"Aliens?" I offered.

She laughed, but her laughter was anything but dismissive of the suggestion.

"I know it's not 1999, but you never know. We have proof of activity in other galaxies now. Sure, the government plays it down, selects the strict scientific version to put out: twenty million light years away a star is created, condensing out of a disc of hot gas and dust; from the star 70 Virginis radio signals are reported, repetitive sounds which suggest a language. It all gets cloaked in technicalities and made difficult to swallow or appreciate. They are out there, but whether they can get in touch with us remains to be seen."

"Or if they'd want to."

"Indeed."

Our return along the yellow brick road consisted of happy childhood memories recalled. We remembered 1999 and all the comics, films, TV programmes and news reports about aliens landing and the end of the world. I worked well with Kate's prompts, found some semblance of what I had been.

On reaching Kate's car she pointed south. "Cocktail Suicide Eight live over there. Do you know them?"

"You do too?" raced out.

"Some of them are in The Astros, my astronomy group."

"Shit, they're a dangerous lot."

"Now you're believing their press."

"I know, They're OK. I haven't seen them for a while."

"Wanna call over? I'd like to know what they think about all this."

"OK."

In the rich and expensive Sheadle Sector, four blocks away from Mrs Godfrey's sector, all buildings were luxurious and sparsely populated, separated by quiet country lanes and greenery. Here was where the filthy rich resided, mostly Americans who'd fled their own country.

The Cocktail Suicide Eight also resided here, in a mansion they'd bought from the National Trust. They'd saved their money from selling their art, and they'd bought a run-down mansion. They'd done their research, knew the mansion's grounds were once the site of a medieval monastery. So they dug up treasures which paid for the house's upkeep. Since then they'd survived on their wits and their imagination.

I'd gotten to know them in the early-teens when our paths crossed at festivals and demos. We'd gotten on fine, but their ideology was more to do with art than politics, and most of the organisations I worked with looked on them as loose cannons. I hadn't seen them for over a year.

Green was on the roof with his telescope as we walked up the twisting pebble driveway.

"Hey it's Kate!" he shouted out. "And good person DM!" he added quickly to clear his senses of surprise.

"Sound the alarms, it's the DM!"

Shortly afterwards the grand front doors were swung back to reveal Maggie.

"Hiya Kate," she said, greeting her with a hug before turning to me. "And our man from the town." She kissed me full on the lips. "To what do we owe this pleasure?"

"To lock you bad people up," I joked as she linked arms between Kate and myself and guided us into the house.

"Orders from Mr Ted?" she sauntered back. "And how are you, Kate? Any word on this Leonardo Smith?"

"No. Dan's had a look in the asylum but there's nothing on him. I'm not too worried though. My brother's been staying with me. Any news on what's happening on the hills?"

"Lots of unsponsored lorries and trucks with police escorts on the motorway. A few more chemical leak warnings than usual."

"You still get them?"

"Sure, DM. This is where the money's at. They don't want dead babies here," Maggie replied. "Visitors!" she shouted at the walls.

Green trotted down the staircase first, ahead of Tina, the little luscious pixie who moulded clay. From out of a side door came Lal and Red, both naked, covered in paints of many colours.

"You should have your own TV show," I said to them, affectionately ironic.

All five of them sat down, cross-legged in a circle, two opposite spaces for Kate and I to sit in.

"Come for a paint, DM?" Lal teased, catching me gazing at her body. "Gotta get naked baby."

She and Red laughed, sending out ripples of mirth, felicitous in their infection of others.

Maggie had a quirk to add, capriciously interrupting: "I think DM's come with orders from Ted to tell us to stop messing around."

I acted to hush them, but Red spotted this: "It's OK, DM. Kate knows about The Plan."

And I couldn't stir up my exasperation before Kate added, "I didn't know you were involved, Dan. I'm not against it, don't worry."

It only took a few seconds to begin thoughts about Kate being the perfect woman for me, about her being whom I was meant to end up with, not Kelly; and then end such thoughts.

"Good, good. I should've guessed really. All the clues were there for me."

"So is Ted concerned about us?" asked Maggie.

"Nothing big. Have you got plans?"

"Oh yes. Roget, Moz and X are out now doing some preparations," said Maggie. "I've heard it's Sunday."

"I don't know. What're your plans?"

Green produced some pills from his pocket. "Only if you take these with us." He threw one at me, one at everyone in the circle except Kate, whom he passed a joint to.

"What is it?"

"It's OK. All grown naturally. It gives you about an hour or so."

They were all ready to pop them into their mouths, waiting for me.

"And you'll tell me your plans?"

They all nodded and smiled in unison.

We popped the pills and Kate lit her joint.

Nice and easy was the slow ascent to nirvana. This was a silly world where all roads were made with pebbles. This was a progressive world where people worked four-day weeks. In this world, every small village or town cared for its own community. The people in these communities helped each other with bills, traded with their own skills and incurred no debts. Somewhere in the world this system was happening.

"We call it Wantok. We made it ourselves. It's completely harmless, except to some of the psych—" Green couldn't get his tongue around the words. "—Ssss psychologically disturbed."

"Plans," I urged pathetically.

"Deeee Emmm," began Green. "Here's the de—al. We gonna put acid in the water system agen. Fud that Pan-nim-nim-pan-nim-err-a. We gonna get everybody wasted so's you can gerron wiv tha revolution."

We all laughed.

"Or," began Maggie, "we might be planning to broadcast where everyone has to go for safety when the revolution's started, then cover them with paint."

We all laughed, for longer, before my making to speak got interrupted by Red: "We're gonna take over the chemical plant near Sector 4 and pump out tons of marijuana fumes. All across the town. Big clouds of hash relief."

The laughter formed as words, changing "ha-ha"s.

Tina followed quickly. "No, it's the plan we have to take over a plane and drop paint all over government buildings. Then we have our troops on the ground painting every monument, every sign, every blank canvas. And we hand out paints to the kids to join us. It's wicked. 'Ellish."

"Yor lying to him," said Lal. "It's the one with the molten lava. Y'see, DM, we've been brewing a volcano deep inside the hills. We're just gonna blow it, let the lava pour into the town and see what gets moulded."

Laughter drowned out my half-hearted protests, drawn along with the mood. The disturbing thing was that all scenarios were possible with the Cocktail Suicide Eight.

Some three hours later they still wouldn't tell which plan it would be, but assured me it wouldn't interfere with anything that was going to happen with The Plan.

Love was shared before we parted.

START CHISELLING

I'd finished my story and added it to my web library. I surveyed proudly the graphics which produced a bookshelf of my "novels", their binders titled for someone to click onto. From *There Are No Saints In The City* to *Infinite Wisdom*, a biography of my dreamed life. And there, on the shelf below, *AL*, shadowed, to click on for unfinished parts of a novel that's been in progress sine Day One.

AL got three more chapters:

Tip of the Iceberg

Between 2,780 and 2,870 metres below the Greenland ice-sheet a terrible secret lies. Deep into the ice-sheet there is a record of the world's past climate, contained in tiny bubbles of air that get trapped as each year's sleepy snowfall lays down a new layer of ice. Two different isotopes of oxygen, varying in temperature, hold climatic details from thousands of years ago. Between 135,000 and 115,000 years ago, the earth's climate would move wildly between hot and cold, until a period of stability which began some 10,000 years ago and began to end in 2000. With global warming the earth was returning to this hectic period.

Professor J C W White was quoted as saying, "It seems that Mother Nature had developed a carefully balanced infrastructure which could choose to set the temperature at any level it wished in order to survive. It chose the system for optimum comfort, for itself and mankind. We turned up the dials and ruined that. In normal circumstances, nature would rebuild itself, but now we are in the equation, and we are pretty desperate and selfish when push comes to shove."

An iceberg, two thousand square miles in size, shifts its moorings, begins to move…

Ultraviolet Skies

Ultraviolet B streams down on England, its rays causing non-melanoma skin cancer, damaging plants, crop plants and plankton. The essential base of the food chain is being eroded. Industrial compounds have damaged the ozone layer irrevocably. People are dying, but they are not running about screaming. Nobody is. They don't understand the facts, so they have to ignore them...

It's You

I take a man in the street by his lapels and shake him: "Listen up!" I say. "These are the facts and you need to tell everyone you know. Warn everyone. Tell them to warn others. Tell everybody you meet! The factories are polluting the air. Don't believe what they tell you about safety! They pollute the air, they make the air you breathe poisonous. Yes, that's your air. The air is becoming thinner and the ozone hole is getting bigger. Don't you see? Don't you see? Life on this planet is going to end. Don't you see? You are going to die. This planet is going to die! Human life will come to an end! Warn everyone, tell everyone. Make sure they know. The poles are melting, the seas are rising. Don't you see that the seasons barely conform to traditional patterns anymore?"

I drink and smoke and take drugs to get away from there and get to here, but here is so transient, and when I've reached it, there is always another here, and my fear is that when I finally get to a permanent here the hedonism will catch up, and I'll never get the adulation of being there; on top of the world. Just a memorable corpse, fulfilled and satisfied.

The words on my computer screen are a nonsense:

'CONTS KATED FGFLOWTS.NED HEHR TOP DROP THE IDNVESTYSHDIAGATSUON.'

I couldn't even remember typing it. I couldn't remember anything. Automatic.

Nothing could get passed recollections of the man in his padded cell. I called him "Nick". Dr Tumblety told me that was his name. I could barely get a word in through his constant yabbering. "1900, one hundred thousand tigers. 1996, five thousand. 2021, none. Dinosaurs are abstract to us, distant relics only ever experienced through clever CGI movies. In the future, children will wonder at the beast that was the tiger, the lion, the panther, the elephant…"

Within the within of within, I charted my standing there: mental footage of myself; my bluffing Dr Tumblety, my owning up that I had not read page sixteen.

Then I am walking with Joe to Club Independent. Than I am here and I'm looking at:

'ALEYETR PERCEPTIDON DMD…'

beamed from the screen in coldly shaped green flashing letters.

I'm trying to remember who I was, but then I'm in the future and the world is burning.

A shotgun blasts and there's a bleep.

Dying, bleeding, he'd said, "Why not?" But he hadn't said it like I'd experienced. I could not get under the memory's skin, couldn't feel the gurgled words "Why not?" within. I replayed it, emotionally edited, strict visuals and economically summative.

He directs me to take the note from his pocket, its title 'Ars Moriendi'. It says this is a transition, a reunion. He's drawn a gravestone, his name on it with the dates 1968-2003. At the gravestone's base, there's a chisel and some rubble from where the words were carved out.

He'd spoken to me.

But I couldn't get passed him, couldn't get beyond December 2003. Only when I thought of Kate Flowers could I get back some second-hand and selective recollections.

This is the madness I play with. This is the addiction I have. I just need to control it, because I can't leave it.

Opposite, seated, Mr Jacobs, unkempt, balding head, puffed out eyes exasperated by a thin face. A rubber suit grips him, one from the 300 range which could absorb waste and clean for up to forty-eight hours.

"You've read the curriculum, Mr Manion?" asked Tumblety over my shoulder.

I nodded a lie.

"Then please teach Mr Jacobs."

I positioned myself to draw level with him. Mrs Godfrey left impatiently, lighting a cigarette on the way out despite the "No Smoking" signs.

"Mr Jacobs, hello," I began unsurely. "I'm Mr Manion."

His head had an angle to stare at my feet, but he raised his eyes' glare to look above the vision of mine, offering it as some sort of acknowledgement.

"I'm here to teach you. Is that OK with you?"

Tumblety made an audible sigh, signalling his disapproval. Jacobs smirked, levelling his face with mine. He felt superior.

"Teacher? Teachers are lunatics and we know it, don't we, Manion?"

"As long as we have something in common then we can make a start."

That seemed to melt an anger solidifying inside, and he had no comeback, his brain hypnotised into thinking through the implications of what I'd said and the way I'd said it.

"You have the choice to learn," I began, fired up. "It will benefit you. It will help you, believe me. You might even enjoy it. You will learn to think for yourself, question what you are told, channel whatever's inside of you into something positive, maybe even change—"

"Mr Manion, a word," interrupted Tumblety, beckoning me aside. "You must follow the curriculum. It's been specifically worked out and it goes hand in hand with the medication. We can't afford these big ideas, we haven't got time. We just want to be able to make these patients function in the outside world. We haven't got time for this educational ideology, and more than that, it's a danger. These people cannot be allowed to think for themselves, yet. That's what got them here in the first place. Stay focused."

I nodded, faced Mr Jacobs again.

"Do you know the alphabet, Mr Jacobs?" I asked.

"A, B, C..." He went on, pausing at points but clearing each hurdle eventually.

"Has knowing the alphabet been helpful to you in the past?"

He didn't answer.

"What I'm saying is that without the alphabet you wouldn't have been able to get through life, and that's education. That's where education starts."

He made no comment.

"How would you describe yourself, Mr Jacobs?"

He slapped his tongue around in his mouth, ruminating before speaking: "Life is dangerous. Yor either scared or yor dangerous. If yor scared you've gotta kill them before they kill you. I do that and they put me in here! But it's not my fault. There's nothing wrong with me. I've had the danger. They wanted to kill me because they were scared and they couldn't be dangerous."

I felt Tumblety's impatience breathing heavily; prompted to flick through the work-pack for one of the poems: one of Geoffrey Spear's, handing a copy to Jacobs, reading its lines.

"Beautiful rain washes it all away. I don't mind the rain, it washes everything away. I want to make it rain every day, wash away the diluted colours, make them fresh and vibrant again, for a long sunny day. I want to wash away those who can't picture this, picture this for us, just us. If they can't see then wash them away. Only we enjoy the rain, its wetness, its catharsis. We'll run to the rain, we'll be drenched, and those who aren't pure can burn in the sun. Let it rain, make it rain."

Mr Jacobs nodded some approval.

"What do you think of it?"

"It's about rain being nice," he replied, unmoved.

With nowhere to go and Tumblety beginning to fidget I hastily looked for notes on the poem, reading points from them in between making eye contact with Mr Jacobs.

"It's about a fresh start, what you can have. It's about having anything you want if you can wash away all the bad thoughts," I read without conviction.

"Or blow them away."

He looked dead at me, as if he knew something.

"What do you mean?"

"Shoot the bad thoughts from your head. You know, don't you?"

I did, but how did he?

"You know Manion. Kill or be killed, or kill yourself. You might as well do that to me, that's the only way you'll get rid of the bad thoughts."

"Why?"

"Don't you know? To be better than those in power give you credit for. To be put amongst people who are not as clever as you, so they can drag you down to their level. And people, like you, don't even know who I am."

I referred clumsily back to the work-pack: "Imagine you have washed everything away, and then, and then you can start again, and you can have—" What was this about? "You can have a nice car, a house—" I read with bewilderment.

"Blow your brains out, Manion. You know how to do it."

"Who are you? Do you know me?"

Tumblety had seen enough. "That's enough Mr Manion, come."

My eyes were locked on Mr Jacobs and vice versa. He never let the stare break, continuing to focus on me from behind the meshed wire glass peephole. He knew something.

"I need to see his files."

Tumblety ignored me. "You must be more in touch with the curriculum, Mr Manion, or this isn't going to work. Do you really want this job?"

"I need to see his files."

"It didn't seem to do much good last time," he countered disdainfully. "No, what you must do is read the curriculum in detail."

He wasn't happy, leading me back to his office without further communication. Passing, I heard from some cells the mellow beats of electronic bleeps deliberately elongated. Very chilled.

Mrs Godfrey showed little interest as Tumblety explained what I hadn't done and needed to do. She had an appointment to make, whisking me back to her house where a taxi waited with her luggage.

She half opened the door to let me in, shouting Kelly from upstairs, not staying to see her appearance.

Kelly's bright face at once lifted my spirits and distracted me from suspicions. We hugged and kissed, like two teenagers excited that parents have left them the house for a night. It was a feeling I'd only dreamt about experiencing.

We were close, sharing a sense that we had been apart for too long.

I stroked her hair, let in contemplation. She had become the centre of my universe; something I could cling to; something worth cleaning myself up over.

"Whatever happens Kelly, I love you."

"Nothing's going to go wrong, Dan, don't look so worried." She kissed me tenderly, withdrawing from my taut lips abruptly. She saw my fearful countenance, saw behind it the images of me losing her. "I want to make love."

As she showered it occurred to me that this might be the last time. Maybe I was too high all the time, maybe unable to come down, but events seemed to be catching up with me.

Ascending the stairs, I felt a sense of foreboding.

Kelly's dimly lit bedroom had disks and cartridges strewn all over the bed and floor. Much was made up of left-wing literature, philosophy and politics. Her VR headset lay on her bed. Pattering water kept Kelly busy and gave me a picked lock to temptation.

The "Virtual Sex" cartridge was in the back. I put on the headset and pressed "PLAY".

The picture quality was very good. Before me, a clear and astonishingly accurate likeness of Kelly, laid on her bed, reading a book. As I moved to sit upright on the bed so Kelly moved in the same manner. When I gestured to turn the page, so did Kelly.

This reading was interrupted as I heard footsteps climbing stairs. I took off the headset to check reality. Just the pitter-patter of water.

The footsteps grew louder before a knock on the bedroom door. Kelly put the book down. Another knock at the door. Nothing happened. The knock came again. I had to gesture an entry with my hand before the door opened. The figure who entered was me.

I began moving towards Kelly, smiling, stopping to stand at the edge of the bed. Kelly waited on the bed, unable to move until I did in reality. But this disk evidently had a back-up system for certain points of its actions, beginning independently when no instructions were given by the user. In the picture I began unbuttoning my shirt.

This was a very strange thing to view, yet also highly compelling. I lifted off the headset briefly to hear the shower still running.

My image continued unpeeling until completely naked. I couldn't say that the body was or wasn't an exact replica of mine as I haven't studied my body that much in seventeen years, but the champion cock hanging between my legs certainly made me blush.

There followed another pause in which I reached out to touch my image. The cock started to grow to something beyond my wildest dreams. Then another pause followed.

I gestured to take off Kelly's skirt and she did. When I lifted off the headset the shower had ceased.

I laid the headset down, stood up to catch a plot. My curiosity wanted to confront Kelly about it, but I'd played the spy once and my guilt had been credited. I couldn't admit to doing it again. I had to think of a way to broach the subject, manipulate fate. First, pretend to have just entered the bedroom, to be undressing.

Kelly entered, her hair pinned back, a white towel fastened under her right shoulder.

She locked me in a kiss, manoeuvring my body onto the bed.

"Have you seen my new Virtch?" she asked teasingly with a nod to the headset. "You have, haven't you?" She laughed, absolving me of guilt for a second time. "It's good, isn't it?"

"But how come I'm on it?"

"I got you from the security camera in the main room. When I first got the Virtual Sex cartridge it had an Italian hunk in the picture. He was OK for a few months, but he could only do the basics because the programme was cheap. Then I got an updater and programmed in Tom Creaney from a film he was in. But I got bored with him and loads of other actors 'cos they weren't real enough, 'cos I knew I could never be with them. I realised I could get you so I programmed you in and it got much better. You can do everything. I couldn't resist you after seeing that."

"This was before we—?"

"Yes. It was sort of being with you in virtual sex that made me love you."

"I'm not sure I'm flattered."

She smiled to reassure, kissed to emphasise, "I love you more in reality."

As we entwined I felt nervous, uncomfortable. She either had the tact of a child or an arch-manipulator. That realisation worried me on both counts.

"It's a bit risky to have though, Kelly. You should wipe it really."

"Oh OK, I will, in the morning."

The sex was delirious, out of this world, and she slept soundly shortly after it, unlike myself, who stared at the ceiling, watching shadows for most of the night.

Admiring Kelly peacefully sleeping as daylight threw colour through the curtains, I felt in love, her white fresh skin quivering as she breathed, the covers easing off her nipples with each inhale.

Alarms shocked us both into wide-eyed awakening. I scrambled my clothes from the floor, Mrs Godfrey's impatient shouting piercing the sirens, finally extinguishing them, her complaints receding.

The clink of keys from below held us captive, doors opening and closing, switches being flicked, footsteps coming upstairs, entering the bathroom.

I kissed Kelly's cheek and made a sharp exit, naked, clutching what might be my clothes, scurrying along the corridor into the spare room.

I was settling into position when Mrs Godfrey knocked at the door. I groaned like waking and she entered.

"I'm sorry Mr Manion. Got back early. Just checking to see if you'd left." She looked at my pile of clothes briefly, received some pleasure from seeing them, then looked back at me. "What a night. The bastards have taken my credit card on some stupid misunderstanding. So I couldn't do much in Paris."

"That's a shame," was all I could muster.

"For them it will be. If you want to get ready I'll take you back."

After she'd gone I noticed one of Kelly's socks caught in the pile of my clothes. I was sure Mrs Godfrey must have seen it. With no opportunity to return I stuffed it into my pocket.

Mrs Godfrey complained for most of the drive, seeking to test her arguments on me, to convince me she had the money in her account. For once she did not allude to Kelly.

Stopping at The Coffee Pot, Theresa set about a train of events with a message from Ted: "It's Sunday."

I needed to make some contacts urgently, but more pressing was the desire to visit Club Independent to stock up on Reeto.

The young apprentice was dealing; Shaven-head and the fat man by his side. He was ebullient, giving me a "Top fuckin' deal". I emerged from the toilets with Shaven-head's eyes trained on me, a mistrust in them I had only ever seen exercised on strangers.

In the confines of my time capsule I took a few snorts and listened to Morse's tape whilst making contacts via the net.

My faxbox was overloaded and I had to be selective to find time for a trip around the universe. I would make the final contacts tomorrow morning.

One fax was from Kate: "I've made contact with the aliens, get in touch!"

I wasn't going to answer the buzzer that interrupted my thoughts. I was going to ride it out until they went away. I could only think of cops, tuning in my television to the surveillance channel to confirm as the buzzer insistently persisted. Kelly's image came up in black and white, her finger glued to a button.

She cried into my arms, saying that she loved me.

"She's been horrible all day just because they wouldn't give her any money." The tears were subsiding as I squeezed her to comfort. "Then this man came round and she was just being horrible, trying to get rid of me, so I left. Can I stay here? I've got nowhere else to go."

"Of course, Kelly, but just for tonight. You'll need to make up with her tomorrow."

"Yor getting ready for Sunday?" My disbelief answered her. "That thing you were on about with the pupils, is that part of your plan?" She saw my mouth forming to affirm and continued: "I can help you, I can do it."

"I don't know, Kelly, it has to be right."

"Don't you trust me?"

"Yes." I replied, exhausted. "Look, we'll have to talk about this, make sure everything's right."

She nodded, her face burying into my chest.

It tempered my anxieties at having her there, allayed my fears regarding the police. We smoked some grass she had, planned a way for her to be part of the revolution, and chose comfort over sex at night. Final contacts would be made tomorrow.

CARDS FACE UP

The red laser beam smouldered. I traced a path to the figure holding a weapon, its thin light catching dust to swirl like blood in its cylindrical ray. I searched my brain for the comfort of dreams, but words confirmed the waking nightmare:

"Do not move Daniel Manion, you are under arrest."

The lights came on. Five figures in combat outfits stood around the bed, each with a variety of weapons all trained on me.

Kelly screamed, gripped my body, digging her nails into my flesh as the covers were pulled from both of us.

"Get y'fucking clothes on!"

But Kelly couldn't prize herself away, her wails and half-completed words growing more hysterical. A figure pulled her from me, handed clothes from the floor which she struggled to put on.

"Now you too. Slowly."

Clothes were thrown at me and I finished dressing before Kelly, moving to help her but held in position by the thrust of a gun barrel.

"Daniel Manion, you are under arrest for murder, sex with a minor, drug-dealing, terrorism, incitement to violence and treason. You have the right to remain silent, but your silence can be used against you in a court of law…"

In the maze of my predicament plots were running through my brain thick and fast, but panic led them to dead ends.

My arms were jerked to the small of my back, two cold handcuffs snapped tight then bleeped locked. Kelly's crying submerged everything, re-establishing the guilt I'd been exempted from in the past. I tried to face her, to answer her desperate pleas, but each time a thud came to my ribs.

"Be fuckin' still!"

"Leave her alone, she's done nothing."

They bundled me out of the room, doors clicking shut as they pushed down stairs lined with police and peering neighbours, at the foot of which stood Inspectors Howard and Collins.

"Guilty," drooled Collins.

Outside, the partial daylight came and went as I scraped flesh into the back of the police van.

For a brief time Kelly's crying and screaming came back to me; somewhere outside, helpless. I had tears to roll, ready to savour their therapy when the van violently pulled away, crashing my bones against its piss-stinking panels, head against a wooden bench.

The driving grew more frantic, my body battered into semi-consciousness.

Everything I had experienced came back to me in flashes of dénouements, all gone wrong, all bruised and exposed.

The vehicle's motion ceased abruptly, its back doors opening at some area in the countryside. Howard and Collins were there with two uniformed officers who dragged me out, stood me up and held my arms to keep me erect.

"Do you recognise this place, Mr Manion?" Howard asked bluntly.

I looked around as best I could, shook my head in denial.

Collins put two fingers into a small bag of powder, shoved them precisely up my nose, a bone cracking as my eyes popped out and watered.

Like knives were lacerating my brain, like acid into my eyes. I threw up violently, choked, threw up again, felt the pain again, my body jarring and juddering until it receded like a tortuous echo.

"Wrong." From Howard. "This is the place where two of our officers were shot after a terrorist attack on the Institute of Science. Your hair samples match up with those found here. Also, Dhali Bakharta's hair samples. Do you know her?"

I didn't answer.

Collins squirted a liquid into my mouth.

A claw fist stretched its fingers down my throat, sent shrapnel into my lungs. I had to work to breathe; could not balance it with efforts to quell the pain, and fainted abruptly.

In this dimension only agony existed, vision coming in brief moments of intense clarity when more questions I didn't answer were asked.

"Where is Kristen Ingersson's head?"

"Where is Ted Kandinksy?"

Other substances were used. This was it, the end, for ever.

Darkness had come when I could reach back into my consciousness and find the strength for clarity. I'm the luckiest man alive. But Howard and Collins were still there; inside some dismal wooden shack.

Howard said, "You see, Mr Manion, we don't need to leave any marks on you. We've got all sorts of terrible concoctions, and we'll keep messing you up with them until you give us some information."

A police car had arrived and was driving me back into town. We passed a house where some activists lived. A car blazed outside, a crowd held back as police picked off people to take away.

Into the town centre we were halted by debris strewn across the streets, figures charging around with molotov cocktails, fires burning. The city was not sleeping, kept awake by the swirling bass of Morse's tune. The revolution had started. I had a chance if I could stay alive.

Bricks bounced off the police car, cracked a break in the booming pockets of chaos.

Accents were strange inside the police station, a laconic and clearly pronounced foreign tongue. Howard and Collins ignored the bewildered figures who loitered in ill-fitting uniforms, taking me to a room at the end of a cob-webbed corridor.

They charged me, though I was barely responsive. They bleeped a scanner across my fingers, injected a needle to take blood.

In a dusky cell only partially brightened by fires which lit up the night outside a barred window, I slipped into sleep briefly. Each departure never ascended to take me away, interrupted by the busy comings and goings inside the police station's structure. Feet were rushing, perplexed voices in clipped English were shouting (and laughing), whilst sirens tried to dominate the endless loop of Morse's anthem, corroding the night and eventually snuffing out the opposition as cells filled.

The first person in the cell I occupied was a plain looking young man who offered a muted "Hi" before sitting on the floor, his back propped against the cell wall. He buried his head in his legs, apparently searching for sleep's escape.

Another man was pushed in, his head bleeding, his eyes bruised. He aimed a retaliatory kick at the door when it closed him in.

"Fuckin' bastards!" He uttered before addressing myself and the plain man. "Hey, either of you with the revolution?" he asked, eyes darting between our faces.

The young man on the floor looked up. "Yeh, I was doing the radio station when they broke in and took me."

"Something went wrong," said our new comrade. "What about you?" he asked me.

"They got me before it got started," I replied reticently.

More people were being brought in, forced into the cell. Some faces I knew, and they knew me, but the disconsolate mood kept us from talking. The third man grew more agitated, continually looking through bars to relay what he could see burning, whom he recognised being brought in.

As the cell filled to bursting, anger and recriminations surfaced. I knew one occupant well, and he knew I was important to the revolution, but he wisely never brought it up, save for a nod.

Through the early hours, the smell of marijuana floating on the air, into the cell, permeating everything. The atmosphere changed, from invective to hazy yearning, from remonstration about the injustice of a capitalist state to demands for chocolate. I thought of the Cocktail Suicide Eight, found myself laughing at what they'd achieved, a laughter which spread throughout the cell.

Gradually, as people were taken and replaced in the confines, news filtered through that the army had been deployed, many dressed in uniforms, posing as police, similar to a tactic used in the 1984 Miners' Strike.

When daylight came I was once again alone in the cell. Sirens continued outside as smoky daylight emerged, though the crash-boom-bang that had run along with them throughout the night was now sporadic and muffled. Ash filled the air, embers of a dream fading away.

A man in precision square black suit, short-cropped matching hair and briefcase, entered the cell accompanied by two armed officers.

"Follow," he said with a European twang.

He led me to a cramped room with pine desk and chairs occupying the space between whitewashed walls and two-way mirror.

He set up a tape recorder and video monitor, sat opposite me, the two policemen fixed at either side of him.

He bleeped the digits into his briefcase, an efficient click opening it ahead of my vision.

He took out a bundle of papers and files, placing them beside the briefcase before moving it at an angle which let him view both its inside and my face.

He set the tape recorder playing, the camera playing, then bleeped keys inside the briefcase. He composed his thoughts and spoke:

"The date is the first of February, 2021. Detective Villems, Amsterdam East, with Daniel Manion, born the thirteenth of November 1988. Confirm," he said looking at me.

"Yes."

He handed me a photograph of Kristen Ingersson and said, "Have you ever met this girl?"

"I want a lawyer."

"So you refuse to answer the question?"

"The state squeezing the balls it holds. I want a lawyer."

"I'll take that as a negative," he said, typing bleeps inside his briefcase. "The photograph is Kristen Ingersson, a Danish exchange student who was visiting Newcastle between December the twenty-ninth and January the first, 2021. She was murdered early on the first, her body butchered and decapitated. On December the thirty-first, the last day she was seen alive, she had been in Gigi's nightclub. Later, she was caught on security camera in an underground car park with two men. This is footage taken from the security film, digitally enhanced." He placed another photograph in front of me, a still of me snogging Kristen, my hand under her skirt. Joe's image blurred on the peripherals. "Is this you?"

"Yes."

"With Mr Joseph Rogan?"

"Yes."

"Why did you lie to the police when you were questioned about this?"

"Because I'd have been framed, like what you are doing now."

"Tell me what happened that night."

"I want a lawyer."

"So you won't answer any questions about Kristen Ingersson?"

"No."

"That has been recorded." He picked out another photograph, of a woman I didn't recognise at first, scrambling my memories to realise it was the woman from Casino Bob's whose picture I'd seen in the paper. "Helen Freestone, aged twenty-five, found brutally mutilated on the fifth of February 2021. You were at a place called Casino Bob's the night she was last seen?"

"Yeh, but I never spoke to her. I didn't even know her face until I saw it in the papers."

"You told the police that you left the casino early and went to a number of bars. Yet, there has been no one who can verify this statement. Security cameras have you returning to your residence at three zero eight in the morning. Where were you until then?"

I didn't reply. Villems let the silence grow, take on the form of an accusation and verdict before continuing:

"Your hair samples were matched with those found at the scene where two police officers were beaten then shot dead." He was reading from a computer screen inside his briefcase. "Your hair samples also matched with those found on Kristen Ingersson's body. Blood samples were also matched with those found on Helen Freestone's body. Can you tell us why?"

"Because you say so."

"No answer again," he said into the recorder. "I don't need to show you a picture of Kelly Godfrey, fifteen, do I?" Again the pause was filled with subliminal subconscious dialogue, filtering through the tape's murky whirring. I recalled the patient at the asylum with his devil's messages on tape head cleaners.

I shook my head disconsolately.

"Her mother has testified to you having a relationship with her, brainwashing her, supplying her with drugs, banned VR cartridges and banned literature. Interviews with pupils at your school tell of how you tried to brainwash them and incite rebellion. Just one look at their exercise books is enough." He tapped in bleeps, waited for a print-out which he surveyed. "An essay on the banned book, *Animal Farm*, has one pupil writing about 'All those in power are just using the public. We should not be like the sheep, we should speak out and rise up if we don't agree with the NRP.'"

"I want a lawyer," I said slowly into the recorder.

"Did you have sex with Kelly Godfrey?"

"I want a lawyer."

"No reply to accusation," he directed at the machine. "You are also charged with treason, inciting anarchy and armed rebellion, and plotting to overthrow the democratically elected government. When was the last time you saw Ted Kandinsky?"

"Whenever you say I saw him."

"Mr Manion, you are not helping yourself. You have the right to make your case now. You would be advised to take that right."

"So you can work out a way to frame me?"

"Look, I have always prided myself on my integrity and those of my fellow officers. We didn't come over here to win, but to show how a police force can be an integral part of the community. Whatever you might think, the evidence against you is compelling, and I'm basing my assumptions on truth."

"Truth! Rights! What about the right not to be tortured? Will you bring that up in your report? Or will you erase my fucking words?"

"All these words will remain on file. Are you prepared to answer any of the accusations I have put before you today?"

"Fuck it."

"I conclude the interview at eighteen twenty-six hours. Duration ten minutes, sixteen seconds."

Bleep and the tape was off. Bleep and the camera was off. Bleeps in his briefcase before shutting and locking it with bleeps.

"Fuckin' cop killer scum," said one of the cops, delaying himself until Villems had left to add in a threatening whisper, "We'll fuckin' show ya torture."

Through the evening, sirens were intermittent, the cell once again filling with revolutionaries, each one complaining of police brutality. They spent little time in my company, taken out and charged and transported to maximum security.

I didn't expect any colleagues to visit me, certainly none active in the uprising. If not in prison, they were probably lying low, blaming me for the revolution's failure. Early afternoon on what I'd worked out to be Monday, I was escorted to a room where Taff and Phil waited behind grimy meshed windows.

"How are you doing, DM?" asked Taff.

"Bad. But thanks for coming. What do you know?"

"You've been in the papers. Kelly's mother's story is across most front covers, most sites. She's got a book deal sorted already. Is it true?"

"Probably not her version."

"But you did do this Kelly?" asked Taff, cheekily but not maliciously, more in an attempt to lighten my spirit.

"You're up for murder too?" asked Phil, to the bone.

"They've been looking at their list of unsolved crimes. Have you seen Joe?"

"No," replied Phil. "There's a curfew from nine until eight. Have they questioned him?"

"I think so. He must be inside somewhere."

"We haven't heard about it if he is. We heard about you over a site, but there's nothing on him."

"He hasn't got the contacts. He must be inside. But if you see him, tell him to get down here. I need to know what he's said."

"What about all these murders though? Why've they got you down for four?"

I didn't answer, aware of technology functioning beneath the apparatus of our scene. I let two fingers out from my fist and grunted like a pig, pausing long enough to separate it from the cough which followed.

"They've fixed me up for those two women. Joe can help me though. You've got to find him, tell him."

"Sure," said Taff. "At least East Tyneside didn't win the European round—"

"Of course, yeh, European round one."

"The Dutch won by miles. There was so much going on Saturday night and Sunday that they were over two hundred points ahead at the finish."

"I guess the people didn't take power then?" I asked.

"Alas no," said Taff. "They were riots all over England and in parts of the British Isles and Europe. They called the army in. They've arrested hundreds of thousands. The NRP said it was about fifty thousand altogether. That's way off. They blamed it on left-wing anarchists, did a TV broadcast talking about the threat to people's livelihood and communities and all that bullshit."

"So they're not taking any responsibility? They don't want to listen."

"It's terrible," concluded Phil. "They're using it for their own benefit too, saying it shows they need to crack down even harder on crime."

"They're untouchable," added Taff. "Not enough people did anything. Where were the working classes, the middle-classes? The underclass were probably sat at home watching shite television. Most of them probably didn't even notice it until a newsbite followed their favourite advert."

"Did you hear about the kids from your school?" asked Phil.

"No, just that the police had talked to them, got them to say I'd been brainwashing them."

Phil continued: "A couple of hundred of them took over your school roof on Sunday. The papers made out Kelly Godfrey was the ring leader, and obviously put that down to you."

"What's happened to her?"

"They've taken her in, that's all I know."

"Shit."

At that moment a karma check tipped me into depression: the worst since "time" began; since last seeing Kelly. The torture didn't compare. I could only imagine Kelly, in a cell, all alone. The guilt weighed heavily, so much so that I couldn't work up much more for continued conversation.

Taff and Phil had to go, get back indoors before curfew. They said they'd try to find out more and get back to me. They suggested starting a campaign, but I doubted I would have much public support.

Within minutes of meeting my appointed lawyer and hearing the jargon he spun, I told him I didn't want him and would defend myself.

I only had the afterlife left. There was my only hope. There was where everything would come together and make sense.

Inspector Howard and Inspector Collins were gnashing their teeth, pacing about the cell, trying to stoke up fear; an emotion I had lost long ago.

"You're in the shit now, Manion. You'll go down for two murders, rape of a minor, incitement. You need to help yourself," said Howard. "Your little revolution is over. Crushed. Your idealistic dream is dead. You failed them. You fucked it up. Don't think they won't be after you either. They'll be enough of them in prison with you. You've been discredited, you have no allies. All the liberals have disowned you. You're little more than a joke. Help yourself, win something back. Tell us where Ted Kandinsky is, what part he played in the uprising. Who else was involved? You know the protagonists. Drop them in it because they aren't doing anything to help you. We can help you out when it comes to sentencing. You might as well, we'll get them anyway."

"Or you'll torture me some more?"

Collins curled his lip, a black-death look creeping into his smile at the back of Howard's head.

"Who planted the bombs? Who was in the stock exchange? I know you know."

They were fishing. They hadn't enough to frame me totally. However Howard cloaked his suggestions, I wasn't going to reveal anything. I was fucked already and all the talk of leniency wouldn't be bought by a blood hungry public who viewed me as a sex offender.

They rattled off questions, occasionally exchanged cold stares, but could get nothing out of me, arguing with each other as they left.

THE TRIAL

All the Sharks were there, Joe seated away from them as one of the witnesses. He never looked at me, and I became uneasy at what he might say.

Around the courtroom, monitors and television cameras kept whirring expectation below the hush. In a sound-proof booth at the back, Bob Furlong and Sylvia Driscoll mouthed words into a microphone for *Court In The Act.*

"Word is that Daniel Manion doesn't stand a chance, that with four counts of murder, treason, drug-dealing and rape he will be lucky to get life. How do you see it, Bob?"

"Well, y'know Sylvia, the country's still reeling after Sunday's riots. There's no doubt about it, this is a big trial. We are in for one helluva session. My sources tell me that the police have all the forensic and video evidence to convict Daniel Manion, no problem. What I'm looking for is what he tells us about the other characters involved. Ted Kandinsky is still at large and you've gotta be looking at Daniel Manion to unlock some doors. It's going to be gripping whatever happens. I know I wouldn't wanna miss it."

Sylvia faces the camera, a studied seriousness encroaching on her gleaming teeth: "And *Court In The Act* viewers won't miss a thing. We'll be back after this short break for trial time."

Fade out for a sponsor's sketch; a man in an armchair opening a copy of *The Shine* newspaper. His armchair shoots back carrying him with it, a fixed expression of shock on his face as he comes to an abrupt halt. The caption reads; "The truth might hurt, but we'll give it to you."

A grey landscape is shown: a street coming into view; a car burning, yells and screams and anguish played over the visuals. An old man is being beaten, a long-haired youth leaving him bleeding, running off with a wallet. A clean-cut woman is entering her driveway, pausing as she notices her front door is open, entering slowly and breaking down in tears when she sees her house has been vandalised. The television reflection stops at five second intervals on the space where her computer was (a mouse mat denotes), where her disc collection no longer stands (a cracked case left behind) and where her television once entertained (a vacant table at the centre of sofas). Her tears are faded as the authoritative vocals lament:

"Pain, loss, heartbreak, your life turned upside down and inside out. If you've ever been the victim of crime you'll know that it doesn't just happen to other people."

The visuals are bleeding with pastel colours, a climax in the making.

"Do you live in fear? Do you wonder what it would be like to have a peaceful sector? Is this just a dream?"

The colours form around cars first; shiny, fast automobiles cruising up avenues. Then there is rouge in the cheeks of pedestrians, strolling past luscious greens; in the grass, in the trees.

"Suharto Protection has won the Northern Private Security League in four of the last six seasons. It has made sectors safe, let people live without fear. It's not a dream. It can happen."

A Suharto officer, complete with this season's uniform, is chatting to an old woman. Then there's another, female, pointing directions to a young girl. The following officers all look professional, but graphically enhanced to look human. They're helping, they're aiding, they're sharing a joke.

"You can live like this. You can walk the streets without fear. You don't have to imagine."

A lengthy pause, to indulge some more officers. But the colours are fading to black and white. An unshaven, greasy looking youth is selling packages to unblemished adolescents. There's needles scattered around him.

"Say no to crime. Get protection, get security and get your life back. Don't say crime won't happen to me, because one day it could be you."

"Suharto Protection Inc" is in bold letters, towering over small print, contrasted with emollient replicated handwriting, beaming from the foot of the screen: "Your life in YOUR hands".

A beam of light hits the screen, then a succession of newspaper headlines and computer print-outs, each one uncovering a crime: those people with long hair and tatty clothes are shown being arrested; the reconstruction of a thin man in an infants' playground is shown, then his figure in handcuffs. *The Shine* matches headlines with arrests, concluding with a computer screen; "Buy It Tomorrow, And Learn Something".

Bob and Sylvia are back and I'm delayed by five minutes.

I've just gotten in my "Innocent" when they were replaying a grainy video of my embrace with Kristen Ingerson, carefully edited and paused as my hand went under her dress, fingered her ass.

I'm an animal, groping her, desperately propping her up when she wavered. I'm feeling her tits, pushing the dress down to reveal her right nipple, rubbing it violently.

"Well Bob, that certainly doesn't show Daniel Manion in a good light. He's gonna have difficulty explaining that."

"And that's even before the bones."

"Is this the kind of behaviour we should expect from a teacher?" asked the prosecution lawyer.

He's *Court In The Act's* star lawyer, all slick and theatrical, all shocked and indignant, all afflicted and sympathetic. He's whatever he's cast and he's perfected his performances for an Oscar.

"We were just drunk, just messing around."

"And then you took her home?"

"We'd decided it wasn't right and we would help her out. We took her back to mine."

"Where you had sex with her?"

"Yes."

"Yet you told the police you'd never met her. Can you explain this?"

My face filled the visual box; focused on the sweat dripping from my forehead.

"That's a sign," said Bob.

The globule of perspiration is replayed, in slow motion, then circled with a green marker and analysed by an expert, Professor Nicholas Monroe: "It's an obvious sign of guilt. It's a very early significant moment in this trial. It possibly lays the pattern for the whole programme. We are witnessing here a man fighting for his life, up against it. He's guilty, no doubt."

Subscribe to *The Universal*, the only channel that shows everything: an American comedy loaded with sarcasm and irony, an exclusive montage of sports events, a pair of jiggling breasts for a documentary on table dancers.

A re-run of the Suharto advertisement, an opportunity to win a million, a cascade of sounds for "Balance" – the drug to restore your body and mind's natural balance.

"You left Kirsten Ingersson with Mr Manion?" asked the prosecution lawyer.

"Yes," replied Joe.

"Did you see Kristen Ingersson again?"

"No."

"He's a fuckin' liar!"

"He's a…" Bleeping "liar!" replayed over and over again.

"Is that guilt or innocence, Professor Monroe?" asked Sylvia.

"If there was doubt about the evidence, it might suggest innocence. But with Daniel Manion's record it is guilt, without doubt. This is his primal scream. His real inner self desperately clutching at straws…"

"Why did you lie, Joe? Don't you know what they are trying to do to me?"

But Joe's uniform steps ignored my questions, taking him into a private room out of the picture.

"Now it's your turn, *Court In The Act* viewers," began Sylvia. "You haven't been wrong before, so get voting now. Is Daniel Manion guilty of murdering seventeen-year-old Danish student Kristen Ingersson? Did he mutilate her body and cut off her still not yet found head? You can vote on our site at www.court.com. Give your verdict now."

Suharto Protection, MacDolland's burgers, *The Shine* website, "Razorblade Whiplash" now on at local cinemas.

"It's ninety per cent for a guilty verdict Sylvia. I've never seen any criminal come back from that…"

The Helen Freestone case was so full of holes it should have been in Blackburn, Lancashire. Forensic and psychological experts gave their opinions and eighty-five per cent of *Court In The Act* viewers found me guilty.

The two dead cops got "Videographies" during the boring bits of the trial. Each cop was a young and idealistic man. Each had worked for the force with honesty and commitment, and each had relatives ready to grieve for the cameras.

"Mr Manion, you have no witnesses as to your whereabouts, and your claims to have been at home between one o'clock and three o'clock have been disproved by numerous security cameras…"

"It's an amazing ninety-six per cent. Sylvia. That's a *Court In The Act* record. He isn't going to come back from this…"

"We have to really look at what type of character Daniel Manion is. It could be argued that he is suffering from schizophrenia, paranoid delusions. But it could be that he's just plain evil…"

A video compilation of "Evil", from Adolf Hitler to The Manchester Slicer and including serial killers of all denominations.

The Shine newspaper with Laura Godfrey's exclusive story, Suharto Protection, The Universal TV, MacDolland's fast food, "Foxcar Five" with its power-steering and numerous gadgets.

Laura Godfrey would have her day in court, all restrained glamour and graceful solemnity. She played it at the edge of a breakdown, steadying pauses holding back her lumps of tears.

"Due to the sensitive and explicit nature of the following footage, *Court In The Act* viewers are asked to use their discretion. Use your Evidence Card now if you wish to watch."

Kelly laid on her bed, reading a book. I knocked at the door, entered and undressed. We were naked, writhing in virtual sex.

Porn Squad, Lifestyle Channel, Suharto Protection, a female judge undressing with a phone in her hand, urging viewers to dial for Miss Judge, live one-to-one.

"I'm getting a ninety-eight per cent reading on this one, Sylvia. That's amazing, unprecedented. *Court In The Act* viewers are known for their sense of justice, and this is a pretty damning indictment of Daniel Manion's credibility…"

"This is a farce, and television viewers should know that. This government is corrupt—" I broke off to see a TV monitor showing adverts. "I did not kill Kristen Ingersson. I did not kill Helen Freestone. I was and am in love with Kelly Godfrey. The reason a revolution took place was because people in this country have realised we are now living in a fascist dictatorship. George Orwell wrote about censorship in a supposedly free society being infinitely more sophisticated than an obvious dictatorship, because 'unpopular ideas can be silenced, and inconvenient facts kept dark, without any need for official bans'. The NRP is poisoning the people with Panamera, the police force and army are corrupt, and accountability is non-existent. The revolution was about creating a sharing society with everyone having a say. It was a vision of Utopia, and it could have happened. It could still happen, if we only could have the vision…"

Suharto Protection, MacDolland's, Coki Coli, *The Shine*, "Balance", "For stress relief and easy sleep, get the balance right."

"Guilty." The judge's long hard stare.

"Guilty." The prosecutor's knowing expression, his curled and curtailed smile suppressing jubilation.

"Guilty." Laura Godfrey's appropriate tears.

"Guilty." The jury's reconstructed, self-congratulatory faces.

"Guilty." Cheers from the balcony.

"Guilty." My hollow eyes.

"Guilty." The advert break.

Coki Coli, naked women wrestling, power tools, Suharto Protection, health insurance.

"Guilty."

"This is live," whispers Sylvia over the visuals of the judge's return.

"One wonders where Judge Drayson can begin." Sylvia makes sure the audience know she is hushing expectantly.

"Mr Manion, the crimes of which you have been found guilty were unthinkably appalling, made more so by your apparent intelligence. That you have been a role model with such responsibility defies belief. Not only have you murdered innocent girls for apparent excitement, but your subsequent actions, masquerading under the banner of social justice, have caused the deaths of hundreds around the country. It is only due to some excellent work by the police and military that a greater catastrophe was avoided. Your unwillingness to answer questions, your constant and transparent lies, and your refusal to help the law arrest the main agitators suggest to me that all your distasteful acts were pre-meditated. This nation is a democracy. We have elections. The public are given a choice on whom they want to govern them. Attempts to change things through terrorism merely show how flawed and undemocratic your idealism is. Mr Manion, it is more than obvious that you want to be the dictator, you want to force people to think like you, live the life you have chosen. Indeed, you have dictated when life should end.

"You clearly require psychiatric help, but this is not going to get any sympathy from me. You will learn from your mistakes, but you do not deserve to do so in this life. Justice must be done and I am compelled to recommend that, pending government legislation, you should be sentenced to death…"

"My god, Sylvia, this is history in the making…"

Astonishment fills the faces of those who fill the camera.

"What does this mean for England?"

"That the NRP's get tough on crime pledge isn't just an empty promise…"

In my cell, shaking, unable to eat or sleep. This cold turkey was forever. Liberties I had taken with drugs had sustained me with little ill-effect over many years. Now I had to absorb reality, let it coagulate around my system. Hallucinations came and went and came back again, distorted and unfamiliar.

I found no silence, not even in sleep; vicious voices piercing the gloom; characters checked off from my past, all life-forms accounted for. All I had now was time to think. I imagined Dr Tumblety coming to me in the night. The spooks were loud, cacophonous, riddled with inaccuracies. Evil was pouring from me, consciousness fading away. Cold sweat seeped continuously. Mortality had gone.

I heard the clubbers from a street somewhere outside my cell, outside the prison walls; the silly clubbers laughing in staggers. The revolution had come and gone and life was going on, on its fateful path to self-destruction. Everything would be burning. This was my new time capsule. Joe had stepped out and was burning too.

I am trying to imagine what will become of me after death. I have deconstructed the pain and been comforted by its impermanence and now I am looking to the future.

I'm thinking about what legacy I will have left behind as steps take me along a narrow corridor. Have I left anything of substance or is the life I am exiting merely a burning page in a burning history book?

I feel out of body already, as if I am watching myself being strapped into the chair. I can feel fingers around my arms and legs, tying me down, then a metal crown lowered onto my head. I am beamed live on *The Justice Channel*, my image looking back at me from a monitor.

Words are being spoken but I am oblivious, until there is a pause and I recognise the fear in the eyes of those looking on from behind clear windows.

A current coursed through my veins and bones annihilating my physical self easily.

My brain was short circuiting, randomly fusing together past experiences, giving my inner sight a glimpse before wiping them out. Mother, father, came back to me for the first time in years, then Mr Marx's disfigured face.

Electricity absorbed my emotions, concentrated the mind on staying alive. I travelled passed boundaries, through the cosmic explosion and over the raging fires of hell.

I was in the blackest spot of all infinity, a small star, bleeping in flashes. The pain came back, shaking my body, breaking my bones, my nose bleeding, my eyes bulging. Screaming, clawing demons were chasing me, space and time crushing me. I had lost control of all but primal files in an underground cavern of my consciousness. There, the repetitive image of me in my bed, waking to get up for work.

I held on to the electric current until closedown came with the flick of a switch.

Daniel Manion's body was naked, pale, tagged at the toe, laid on a cold metal table. All was still save for a slow pulse bleeping vague signals at the centre of his memory.

Focus on the bleep, follow its signals around the circuit. On each lap of the lifecycle, note any forms of life and remember them for the next turn. Pick up on them and try to construct some narrative around them. When you have an image, make a word, then make a sentence. Try to define so you can attach yourself to the experience. Piece together bit by bit why you are here, then try to break out from the other side.

It's all black. I have enough brain activity to remember I am Daniel Manion. Then I can see myself, strapped in a chair, shaking and frying. I realise I am either still alive or I've begun a spiritual journey to enlightenment.

Fantastic fascination swells in my thoughts, renewing emotions, in excited anticipation of the odyssey that might lay before me.

But I can flicker my eyelids, and as gloomy outer vision comes to me I can recognise a room. My head is at such an angle that I can just trace a path down the far wall, to a naked body, dormant on a table. I can just make out the nose, stomach and toes of another body near it. These are undoubtedly dead bodies.

I cannot move any limbs, any muscles, anything but my eyeballs and their lids. At the corner of my perception, light is bursting through a square. Fuzzy circles merge, grow into one large glow, obscuring all else in my vision. White pours into the room, splashing on walls, warming my flesh.

I was compelled not to look away, though my retina burned slowly. A bright shape formed from the light, converging into the features of a figure, a contourless body with a jaggedly shaped head.

I had no fear or sense of panic as the figure drew its left arm up above its head, a gleaming machete held in a vaguely formed hand. In the blink of an eye it had swooped down to my neck to disconnect the body no longer able to function.

TRIPPIN' OFF EARTH

All colours of lights were bouncing off each other in some fantastic laser show beneath my eyelids. An intense heat, then a cooling, then my eyes open.

Stars speckled the darkness all around outer space. I could hear a whirring in my ear, though there was no feeling below my throat. My head seemed to be moving judging by the visions guiding my eyes to extreme left and right.

It soon became obvious from my education that I was heading away from Earth, passed all the planets I'd been taught. Saturn and Jupiter looked particularly magnificent, way beyond what I could have imagined.

Pluto's cold focused my attention. It had taken no longer than half an hour to reach the edge of Earth's galaxy, as though all the planets were just miniature toys.

New, colourful planets, one glowing purple, one yellow with hundreds of tiny moons surrounding it sending back violet beams; all passed out of view in minutes, my head manoeuvring to perfection every time debris approached.

At times the blackness was covered by colourful mists millions of miles long: with speed estimates came distance estimates, relying on some kind of uniformity but based on averages to calculate my position in the scheme of things.

On the template, ideas could be moulded. My head, brain intact, was moving through space. Why?

But ideas and questions were easily distracted by the flow of amazing spectacles, like a conveyor belt of possibility: another planet, fires raging from its surface; three smaller, green planets, all connected; strange craft flitting in between like flies. One hazy area, its colours and shape changing, reverberated with soundwaves.

The sounds "Zshrr" whizzed passed my ears as I roughly calculated a journey comparable in length to about twenty times the distance between Earth and Pluto.

I passed a vast, expansive, colossal, illimitable, astronomical, limitless, monumental, immeasurable ball of burning gas, somewhat similar to Earth's sun, only this had four red rings of debris circling its burning matter.

Many smaller planets followed before a sense of slowing. Ahead, growing fuller, a planet with blue and predominantly green hues, similar to Earth's. Becoming visible, towering above and dwarfing it, a planet from which sprouted a tree-like object of inexpressible size.

The slowing continued, an apparent landing imminent as vision contracted; closing out the second planet, levelling off on lush green grass.

THE PLANET INUTHUA

The landscape of the Plant Inuthua is completely green, its vegetation carefully cultivated by underground oceans and sea-life and the inhabitants overground, Inuthuans and Prouls. Inuthuans are the dominant species, and although hermaphrodite there exist two emotional types, Finuthuans and Hinuthuans.

The only Inuthuan balanced with both types was The Immortal, their visible creator, having always existed for as long as all living Inuthuans could remember. For millions of years Inuthuans have visited different galaxies and dimensions throughout infinity, returning to download the data into The Immortal.

Inuthuans are sustained through their plant-like bodies and the power of their brains. They communicate through extrasensory perception; sending out an image, an evolved idea, in seconds able to relay a book's worth of knowledge. They can communicate with the cells in any living life-form, and have recently made breakthroughs in controlling the molecules in inanimate objects.

Essentially blind, they use small worm-like creatures, Prouls, as their eyes, keeping the creature chained in close proximity to their brains. Because their brains are so well developed they can imagine the environment surrounding them exactly, but use the Prouls to save energy with immediate vision.

There has been no need for technological development on Inuthua, for the species' brain is so powerful it can do almost anything.

Inhabitants of the Planet Inuthua became interested in Earth some two thousand years ago upon realising that humans had the same brain capacity as them. Although aware that humans lived some two hundred years less than Inuthuans, they were puzzled that the humans never exploited the brain's full potential. Despite finding much life on their intergalactic travels – some stupid, some intelligent, some hostile, some wonderfully bizarre – none came as close to their own species as humans.

Probes were created to be sent to Earth, to gather and relay information. The early models were imperfect; they took many years to return, if they returned at all, and the information was often limited.

The Inuthuan Mind Revolution of (Earth's) 1900 began a period of great development in the understanding of Earth and Inuthuans' own capacity. It was realised that Earth evolved in dimensional shifts, roughly every thirty-two years, that probes could enter dimensional shifts and rewind time. At the end of each dimensional shift Earth's fate would be reconstructed based on the evolutionary karma of the previous thirty-two years. This was a cut-off point and the template could not be altered.

Along with this awareness came the Inuthuans' ability to develop more sophisticated probes, catching the souls of dead humans and using them to give the probes a more emotional capacity. They created androids which could send delayed live images back of life on Earth. Inuthuans had to use considerable energy to receive these images so Prouls were brainwashed as conduits for transmissions, displaying visuals for Inuthuans to view. Invariably the Prouls burned out and died after six months and needed replacing.

Inuthuans were fascinated by the horror show on Earth, its path to self-destruction. Bewilderment overrode any concern at the time, until the 1968 Inuthua Conference.

In an unprecedented move The Immortal drew all Inuthuans together to pass on information he had discovered. Having sent probes to research Earth's moon – a long-considered preliterate planet – he had discovered, buried deep below the surface, a book. Titled *AL*, it described how Earth would end. Further research into Earth's cosmic vibrations and one-consciousness experiences suggested its karma was affecting life on Inuthua. The Immortal had connected the book with these findings, informing Inuthuans that something needed to be done about Earth.

The Immortal put a balanced argument forward for and against Earth: if Earth's fate could be changed and life was to continue, then maybe Inuthua's evolution would progress positively. In a similar way, Earth's destruction would end the bad cosmic vibrations being received by Inuthuans. Earth could either be changed to a better place or helped towards self-destruction.

The Immortal had a preference but would not divulge it, wanting Inuthuans to make up their own minds. The Immortal proclaimed that all probes would have to be made with a mission, to help save Earth either directly or indirectly, or help destroy it. The Immortal had created a probe as a sperm which would be sent down with a mission, a male whose mindwaves could influence the world around him. Whether for or against Earth, The Immortal would not relay.

Hundreds of groups formed to create probes in human form, each with a mission based on the ideologies of its creators, the ideologies assembled from what had been viewed through Proul-visuals, apparently objective accounts of life on Earth, transmitted from human-probes already in existence.

A lot of these groups created inferior probes whose transmissions burnt out after a number of years, the human form continuing to exist on Earth on automatic thereafter. The more advanced groups invested time in observing the lives of humans whose death they knew would be before the age of thirty-two. These groups created human-probes who could be reclaimed once and returned for a second chance.

Since the 1968 Conference The Immortal has grown dramatically in size, to such an extent as to threaten the Planet Inuthua's existence. Increasingly Earth's karma vibrations are affecting life on Inuthua.

Hooldoon looked on at Leenen as he worked on DM45's head, admiration somewhat tempered by real fears. All of the Marchous had put such effort into DM45 that its failure had disappointed them almost to the point of abandonment of the project. Hooldoon knew that some of the group would be against a return to Earth, that it was conceivable that all their hard work would amount to nothing.

The Marchous' work had begun in 1988, observing DM45's life. Thodol, their leader, had gotten them all together – Hooldoon, Peelah, Leenen, Cantoon, Reemo, Beeel, Lahro – to assemble a probe integral to the saving of Earth.

Thodol drew up the plans, brought in Leenen to put the brain together and Peelah to help work with him on DM45's soul. Beeel and Lahro travelled through time to intercept a time capsule which had been spotted flitting through dimensions, launched from the 2020 era. Useful cultural guides were found inside the capsules, helping the Marchous create a background for DM45. Cantoon retrieved the soul that the Marchous had been tracking since 1988 when it was finally released in 2003, after an inevitable suicide.

Cantoon wired DM45's system before the almost complete project came to Beeel again.

Beeel liked the mind-altering properties of the marijuana plants and magic mushrooms he had learned to grow from studying an ancient Earth probe's findings. Although he had by far the best knowledge of the English language of any Inuthua bar The Immortal, it was somewhat limited by the data found in the time capsule, a pocket dictionary, a middling disk-thesaurus and a collection of no more than fifty books and disk-novels. Through this he inputted DM45's knowledge of words. As he grew bored with the task, his mind raced and he put in words more than once, got adventurous and threw in some phrases and philosophies, often slumbering into subconscious before they were finished.

He passed DM45 onto Lahro to add a solid understanding of maths.

"How did it go?" Lahro sent to Beeel.

"It would have been very dull if I hadn't been a bit imaginative."

"You wasted?"

"Monkey."

Lahro reverberated a mood of questioning.

"I made up some words of my own man: monkey – got to get high man."

"Thodol won't like it. You know he wants Hooldoon to do the imagination."

Beeel released waves of reassurance.

"What about this Lahro; 'the face of friendly fascism?' Do you like the sound of that?"

Lahro nudged on time for Beeel to be summarising: "I just put a bit of jive into him. If you don't have the words you can't be the cool. He needs the charisma, the catchphrases, the soundbites, and he's gotta have fun. I know all that learning from Earth, saving Earth idea is good, but if we get Inuthuans to tune into our transmissions then we can influence more, and DM45's gotta be cool for that."

Lahro's waves jarred with disbelief. Beeel sent an elaborate consciousness back: "You gotta get high and squeedgy your third eye. You know why people on Earth make magic mushrooms and pot illegal? Because when I took them I laid in a field of green grass for four hours going, my God, I love everything. The heavens parted, God looked down and rained gifts of forgiveness onto my being, healing me on every level; psychically, physically, emotionally. And I realised our true nature is spirit not body, that we are eternal beings, and that God's love is unconditional and there's nothing we can do to change that. It is only our illusion that we are alone, the reality is we are one-consciousness capable of universal love. Now if that isn't a threat to the world then I don't know what is. Those in power would certainly be worried if people realised we are all one-consciousness. Geez, what would happen to the arms race and the economy then? I can see why the governments of the world are cracking down on the idea of experiencing unconditional love.

"It's interesting that two drugs that are legal, alcohol and tobacco, are drugs that ruin your health, and do absolutely nothing positive for you. Yet drugs that grow naturally upon the planet, drugs that open your eyes up to make you realise you are being FUCKED every day of your life are illegal. Coincidence? I don't know."

Lahro reflected Beeel's contentment.

"You wanna monkey, Lahro?"

"Yeh, once I've done the basics for DM."

From Lahro, DM45 went to Reemo whose unenviable task it was to input knowledge of world history from bits and pieces of books, disks and many ancient probes which had collected scraps of information.

Cynicism allowed him a release from the pressures he was under and he passed DM45 onto Hooldoon on schedule.

The youngest of the Marchous, Hooldoon had been personally chosen by Thodol to create DM45's imagination, add some lateral philosophies and link them up to the original existing soul, leaving unfinished connections for Thodol and Peelah to connect to the soul they had created.

During Hooldoon's work on DM45 his one-time associate, Nooosh, had absorbed the system's structure, workings and psychology. Hooldoon had no idea Nooosh was a Foulah, whose group was indifferent to Earth, and who were working on their own probe, JUDD101.

The Foulahs had worked closely with the Marchous for many years. They had helped Thodol during the early stages of DM45's development, but because Thodol wouldn't include some of their idiosyncrasies in the creation, they decided to create their own probe. DM45's creation at the time had barely begun and Thodol could adjust the plans easily.

The two parties had been acquainted over the subsequent years, occasionally exchanging basic ideas and plans between periods of cold relations.

Communication was severed after Noosh's theft, but Thodol didn't blame Hooldoon when DM45 returned to Thodol with a vibrant and expressive imagination and well-crafted loose ends easy for Thodol and Peelah to connect.

As Leenen finished work on DM45, Hooldoon recalled the fantastic feeling all the Marchous shared when they rewound time to place DM45 on Earth, 1999. Hooldoon led the memory back to the experiences so Hooldoon could feel it again: the expectation, the appreciation that a planet could be saved; the pride and togetherness, the sense of achievement, the joyously imagined fate. They could feel that again thought Hooldoon, they just needed belief. The Marchous' disappointment couldn't be left to fester and take hold. They could still save the world and Hooldoon had to convince them.

I

I existed in a very green landscape. For as far as my eyes could scan was green and mostly flat, unobstructed by any form of building, the black night and scattered stars laying cosily on the surface.

Green shapes scattered about seemed to be moving, though I couldn't be sure. Eyeing downwards I noticed a green square fed as a vision from apparent laser beams constructing a screen. From this, branch-like connections ran to my head, like I was hooked up to an electroencephalogram.

A figure emerged into my vision, a blurry hovering body of about seven feet high, its shape shifting. A roundness at its top suggested a head, supported by almost shoulders, on the left of which squirmed a worm-like creature with a rectangular light beam emitting from the tip of its body; a body kept relatively still by some kind of chain. The approaching main shape had approximate arms, connected to the body by wings. Two points supporting the body floated over ground to reach me.

I felt movement, lifted up, placed on some higher point, then one, two, three…seven other creatures moved into my vision, similar in appearance to the first, though of varying heights, each also with the worm-like creature bound to their shoulders.

I heard a voice in my head say, "Welcome, you are on the Planet Inuthua. My name is Thodol." The first creature made a bowing gesture to identify it.

I moved my mouth but no words came out, miming instead the thoughts in my head: "What is going—?" before realising the futility of my actions.

"Carry on," came the voice in my head, another of the creatures gesturing with its wing.

I put in my thoughts, "What am I doing here? What is going on? Who are you? What—?" The enormity of what I had to comprehend silenced me, dumbstruck.

Again the ESP communicated back: "You have a lot of questions, naturally. Be patient, You are twenty million light years from Earth."

Bleep. The grey screen formed an image, focusing on a fiery, red ball in space.

"This is Earth now, burning away. Very little exists save for a few sea creatures in the vast chasms of the Atlantic Ocean, and they will have a tough fight to survive. The only survivors of the human species are in space stations, but they don't know where to go. They will die."

Bleep. The screen went dead again.

"Humans caused the destruction of Earth. The signs were there but were ignored by those in power. The destruction of natural resources such as rainforests and coral reefs, the tons of pollution spewed into the atmosphere and the expanding population allied to global capitalism brought about the end. The air grew thinner, the planet heated up, began burning, sometime around what you would call 2040. It became an irretrievable process sometime around 2035 when several fates crossed and took an irreversible route."

A different tone in the mental dictation indicated a change of communicator.

"The higher state of awareness of our species means we have no wars, the whole of our planet governed by a consensus handed down through The Immortal."

I can hear a whirring at the back of my head as the information is taken in. One of the creatures then moved forward to turn my vision to see the unimaginably large creature towering from its own planet, its features similar to those of Inuthuans.

"The Immortal has been visible forever. From as far back as our history has been recorded The Immortal has been present. The Immortal's creation of Inuthua and our evolution are chronicled in The Koubah, a more factual version of what you would call The Bible. The Koubah has guided us throughout eternity—"

Another tone interrupted: "Not even The Immortal knows the meaning of our existence. Much has been made of a higher force controlling everything, but few can deny The Immortal's near omniscience. Our function as Inuthuans is to explore what lies in the vast infinity of space. We have cultivated many planets, found a variety of life-forms which we have helped develop. Nothing has occupied us as much as Earth's evolution.

"It has followed some similar paths as our own, though whilst Inuthuans explored the mind, humans concentrated on technology, machines and the pursuit of power. We grew apart as planets but some traits remained and it was inevitable our fates would cross again."

Another "voice": "Thoughts and experiences throughout space create soundwaves. Those from Earth have been affecting Inuthua, adversely. We are a strong race because of the power of our minds. We don't need weapons because collectively we create forcefields or make the weaker minds of those that enter our galaxy do what we wish. Nobody can destroy Inuthua or take it over, but recently we have become worried about the way our planet is going, with some parallels to Earth.

"We created human probes to send to Earth, to gather information at first, but then, when The Immortal told us of the danger Earth posed to Inuthua's existence, we began sending probes on a mission. Some wanted to destroy Earth by accelerating its demise. Some, like us, wanted to save Earth. The Immortal would not be biased in guiding us, we just had to have faith that good would always triumph, and that that didn't necessarily mean the survival of the species, it just meant that the laws of physics and matter kept the universe together in the search for an answer."

Something sprang into my thoughts: "It's like we need a map and a plan of all creation before we can start living for today."

Some of the group moved, seemingly to focus on one of their number. A sensation like laughter echoed.

"Indeed. That's why we chose you D—Mr Manion, for what flourishes in your soul. Your revolution was meant to save the Earth. We haven't got long, but we can send you back before the Earth's next dimensional shift. If we decide it can be done we will attempt to save Earth. You may yet have a second and final chance Mr Manion…Rewind…dimensional change …time…distance…"

What was all this? Some absolutely fantastic trip on Reeto or the afterlife? Whatever, I needed to get off the drugs, get back to reality. But when had I lost my grip on reality? I must have just dreamt I survived the electric chair, and if I'd imagined that, then maybe I'd imagined conviction, arrest, murder.

This was a coma, that was it. I'd be OK if any of The Sharks remembered what I'd told them; "If ever I'm in a coma, feed me marijuana." That was it, give up the Reeto, get back on the pot.

"DM, you are here, this is the reality. The bones is we are giving you this information so you can answer our questions. We need to know why the revolution failed so we can rewind and change things;" came as accelerated bleeps injecting my brain from all angles.

A fuzzy vibe, "Hoooold", came through.

"You made mistakes DM45. You—"

A loud, prolonged gong reverberated inside my skull.

"Why did you take drugs Mr Manion?"

"You sound like the police," I sent back.

My thoughts tripped.

"No Mr Manion, this is your reality. If you want to get back to Earth, get living and get out of this you have to answer our questions and persuade us you are worth sending back."

"Just answer the questions," came gently to ease a cacophonous headache of sounds. "Now, your drug use. You must realise it caused the revolution's failure, directly and indirectly. We just want to know what you didn't have and needed drugs to give you."

"To speed up my evolution. To open my consciousness, to get me the hell out of automatic living."

"But wasn't the revolution the most important thing in your life?"

Bleep. "Yes." Bleep.

"Why did you have a relationship with Kelly Godfrey when you knew it was illegal?"

"Love."

"What about Kate Flowers? What about Aisha Hussein? What about Kristen?"

"Just love, right time, right place, just love."

"But wasn't the revolution the most important thing in your life?"

Bleep. "Yes." Bleep.

"What about getting involved with Mrs Godfrey?"

My answer had passed before I recognised "Bleep. Yes. Bleep."

"…Dr Tumblety…"

"Bleep. Yes. Bleep."

"…Joseph Rogan."

"Bleep."

Bleep, bleep, bleep-bleep-bleep-bleep-bleep bleep bleep bleep bleep bleep.

"…Declan Marx."

A shotgun. I was alive for a brief period, a matter of seconds only. Eight creatures surrounded me, green in colour, changing in shape, distinct from the fertile grass and space-night background. From sperm to shotgun, Ars Moriendi.

"Still transmitting, Peelah."

Bleeeeeeeeeeeeeeeeeeeep

DOWNLOAD

Bleep. Images flashing, edited in blinks, words changing shape at the foot of the screen.

Bleep. 1256192: "Gunshot".

Bleep. 1355879: "Disappearance". "*I WANT MAM AND DAD*", "*Bad Luck Boy*" headlines on a notice-board. "Fatal fame". "Suicide".

Bleep. DM119764: "Millennium chaos".

Bleep. DM1256192: "Gunshot. My Last View Of Life. Ars Moriendi".

Bleep. DM1355879: "Disappearance". "*I WANT MAM AND DAD*", "*Bad Luck Boy*" headlines on a notice-board.

Bleep. DM1499731: "Shuttle launches release 75 tonnes of hydrogen chloride into the atmosphere and tonnes of pollutant waste from rocket fuel burned during lift-off. This causes more damage to the ozone than a year's worth of CFC emissions from fridges."

Bleep.

"NASA kept this quiet, but it got through to some publications. Why didn't the humans take notice?" sent out Peelah with a catalogue of bleeping incidents that involved bleeping NASA preparing to leave the planet.

Bleep. DM1829943: "Government Environmental Agency report 1996: GE Aircraft Engines in Cardiff has released 27 tonnes of carcinogens into the air; Bush Boake Allen (Widnes) 30 tonnes of carcinogens; Shellac (South Wirral) 37 tonnes; BASF (Redcar) 48 tonnes; Ciba Leigy (Cambridge) 50 tonnes; Rhone-Poulenc (Dagenham) 57 tonnes; CIC (Thornton-Cleveleys) 85 tonnes; Montell (Manchester) 87 tonnes; Recticel Manufacturing (Derby) 233 tonnes; CIC (Redcar) 361 tonnes; CIC (Middlesbrough) 1,650 tonnes; CIC (Runcorn) 2,150 tonnes."

"Two thousand one hundred and fifty tonnes! Shouldn't that worry the island, let alone Runcorn?"

Bleep. DM2076388: "When a tree dies it becomes a natural home for many creatures and is also subject to rotting agents, insects, fungi and bacteria. They all break down the wood which becomes part of the soil again."

"Fantastic. The eco-system was so beautifully balanced, so perfectly developed. We've got to try again," pleaded Hooldoon.

"It reminds me of the fish who feed off other fish and clean them, of the jellyfish who feed on the sun's rays. Hey, boom—" delivered Beeel.

Bleep. DM2303429: "Coral reefs, 'the rainforests of the sea' face destruction. They shelter more than 25 per cent of all know fish species; more than 25,000 have been destroyed along with 2,400 species of reef building corals. Causes – the growth of coastal cities and towns, outright destruction from the building of airports and harbours, dredging to keep shipping channels open, mining for construction material, sewage and agricultural pollution producing algae that blocks out the sunlight corals need to survive."

"But they don't notice because it isn't human, it hasn't got their brain power. Corals dying don't affect them," released Reemo.

"It goes on," directed Leenen. "Seahorses extinct, mole cricket extinct, the adabra tortoise extinct, on and on."

Bleep. DM2510713: "Shellac ruining the waters of the Cashiriari river in Peru, turning it black."

Bleep. DM2720200: "The sturgeon, one of the oldest known animals, dating back 250 million years, has declined by 70 per cent: World Wildlife Fund report 1997."

"Look at it, 30 million people killed by automobiles, 8 million a year; 200 million Americans believe they will go to heaven; the 1996 meningitis epidemic in Nigeria kills 3,889 people, affects 22,545 others. Humans had the capacity to contain that. Why didn't they? What's wrong with this fuckin' planet? I'm gone." Beeel sloped off, to squeedgy his third eye.

Bleep. DM2750002: "China uses US machine tools to build missiles."

"I know it looks bad," began Thodol, "but it's the truth, and the truth shall set them free."

Bleep. DM2955501: "United Nations statistics in a report on human rights abuses. Out of 10 China gets a 10 for extra-judicial killings, a 9 for denial of freedom of speech, a 4 for denial of free movement. Out of 30 it gets a 23 for torture. Indonesia scores high in all categories, particularly "Disappearances". Burma, Algeria, North Korea all figure highly."

"The worst abusers are countries with huge natural resources who deal with western businessmen. Rewind."

Bleep.

"Rupert C Donald, CIC, Shellac, ABT, MacDolland's, Reeback, all the western governments, all the US governments. They're all in on it. DM45 came so close to destroying them. He can do it next time."

Bleep. DM3154153: "Freedom Network, Cocktail Suicide 8, the Earth Tribe—"

Bleep. DM3196225: "Ted Kandinsky".

Bleep. DM3200156: "Ernestine Kiersling sentenced to five years by a Viennese court for locking her mentally handicapped daughter in a coffin-shaped box at night for six years, between the ages of fifteen and twenty-one. The mother said it was to help her daughter grow."

"Why's that in?" questioned Reemo.

"The madness of humans. It's what Inuthuans tuned in for," returned Lahro.

Bleep. DM33611002: "Revolution fails."

Bleep: DM33800131: "200 tonnes of explosive naphtha spilled from a pipeline at CIC Newcastle."

Bleep: DM34342884: "Begin Automatic Living."

Bleep: DM35538991: "Potted history of Earth: 1990, Washington's 'Worldwatch' unit gave Earth forty years for transition to an 'environmentally stable society'. 'If we have not succeeded by then, environmental deterioration and economic decline are likely to be feeding on each other, putting us into a downward spiral of social disintegration.' Desertification, rising human population, political instability, famine, deforestation, pollution, loss of topsoils, rising carbon dioxide levels, falling per capita agricultural production, eroding genetic diversity, dying lakes and reefs and rivers: these will all result in Earth's self-destruction."

"Why should we save this species?" Reemo interjected.

Bleep. DM35538990: "Morris Strong at 1992 Earth Summit predicted, 'If we continue along this path of development and destruction, we will destroy civilisation…if we do not act decisively and soon nature will, and in a much more brutal manner.' "

"It's there, it's there for them to see," administered Reemo.

Beeel returned, psychically challenged: "So they're stupid. As superior beings in the universe isn't it our responsibility to protect the weak?"

Beeel owed Hooldoon that and Hooldoon acknowledged it with good vibrations.

Bleep. DM3599287: "Chlorinated hydrocarbons, particularly DDT are disrupting natural processes and mimicking reproductive hormones, causing breast cancer; yet they are still produced in third world countries."

"RCM Enterprises again," confirmed Leenen.

Bleep. DM3895349: "Graffiti on wall: 'Revolution allows the revolutionary to sublimate his sado-masochistic, neurotic, anal tendencies into concern for the working classes.' "

"Significant in DM45's change," amplified Leenen.

Bleep. DM4000005: " 'Occasionally I wished I could walk through a picture window and have the sharp, broken shards slash me to ribbons so I would finally look like I felt': Prozac Nation, Elizabeth Wurtzel."

"Beeel. You crazy bastard," sent out Hooldoon on a low frequency. The Marchous felt something but were too distracted to disapprove.

Bleep. DM4399533: "Kristen". Bleep. "Cock-eye". Bleep. "Godfrey". Bleep. "Tumblety". Bleep. "Love".

Bleep. DM5438172: "Love".

"It's beautiful," coloured Hooldoon.

"Fascinating, precious," brightened Peelah.

"It's in his emotions," let Leenen balance the mood. "It must go back to something in DM45's inveterate soul. We'll never get into the centre of it, but we can understand it."

Bleep. DM5782993: "Caught In The Act".

Bleep. DM5800021: "A gleaming machete held in a vaguely formed hand. In the blink of an eye it had swooped down to my neck to disconnect the body no longer able to function."

THE MARCHOUS

"Any comments?" asked Thodol.

"I think he did quite well," sent Hooldoon.

"He failed. He didn't save Earth," sent Reemo.

"But he came close, and we can still save it," countered Hooldoon.

"Friends, please," interjected Cantoon. "We've seen the results, we can't argue with them. We must be constructive. The system retrieved information well, that's all we could ask for. We've got all the information we need. I don't see much point in sending DM45 back."

"To some extent I agree," layered Leenen. "The brain, the system; both fulfilled their purpose. There's something in the soul we can't get to. We haven't got time, but I exist to be convinced."

"But we can send him back one more time, it is our duty!" came from Hooldoon in desperate, passionate persuasiveness. "It's what we stand for. We just need to make a few adjustments."

"There's only a few things we can do. We can't get too deep inside of it," Leenen sent out, a distorted echo response to Hooldoon.

"I know, but things can be done. We know where he went wrong, we can change it."

"I agree with Hooldoon," Peelah absorbed everything. "Our idealism has got to be backed up with action. We have to show fellow Inuthuans that our way can succeed. We are not in it to entertain, we have convictions."

"What about KRIST2000?" had Lahro changing the mood.

"That was sex, that's all they're interested in," stunned Reemo coldly.

"I think you underestimate the Brouvahs," sent Thodol sagely. "When the time comes they'll be with us. I think they were trying to help DM45 with what they created. But I do agree KRIST2000 caused us problems."

"I thought he was cool," breezed in Beeel. "It's like we need a map and a plan of all creation before we can start living. Take thy fair hour. There was nothing wrong with his soul."

Leenen ignored: "If we are to send DM45 back I don't think we need to alter the technical specifications too much. Information retrieval showed no problems."

Hooldoon added an upbeat: "He made the right connections most of the time."

"Except for connections with JUDD101, TUM3—" started and faded from Cantoon.

"The drugs didn't help," sent Peelah. "Love too if we look at it that closely. We cannot change what lies deep inside DM45's soul, but we can make sure it is more focused on the mission."

With finality before a change, Thodol's "Agree" shifted perception. "He needs love, otherwise we might just have sent out an old probe. We can confer with the Brouvahs and get some help and we can certainly re-tune some of the threads of DM45's emotions. Hooldoon?"

"We'll have to pump up the confidence, get rid of some of his frailty, make him less depressed. We'll have to lower the introspection, but obviously it's a damaged soul."

"Drugs can't be ignored," sent Reemo. "That's what messed things up."

"It's linked to his despair," sent Cantoon.

"It's linked to his imagination," oozed Beeel.

"Look," implored Hooldoon, "I think he did damn well. I love DM's imagination. He just got some bad luck!"

"What about getting in touch with God?" posed Beeel.

"Loose cannon," returned Thodol. "Anyway, he's too busy creating his wacky little planets. No, it's part of many things and you can blame anything. It's somewhere inside the inveterate memory."

"JUDD101?" sent from Peelah absorbed everyone with a split-second history.

"Yes," from Cantoon. "I didn't expect it to be so immoral."

"They're having fun that's all," sent Reemo.

Thodol's frequency had agitated impatience: "It's their philosophy. They're as idealistic as ourselves, but when it comes to Earth they've absorbed too much cynicism. They aren't our concern, it's sensory viewing they're interested in. If you look, they've altered JUDD101 very little on his return."

"But he still doesn't care about Earth," came from Reemo like a bleep.

"If he doesn't get into any tricky situations with JUDD101 I think the DM will be fine," offered Cantoon.

"They were good together. We can't take that away," came inconsequentially from Hooldoon.

Thodol summed up a coil of subliminal moods with "Maybe," about to release more when Hooldoon intercepted the vibe:

"No, definitely. The Foulahs aren't as bad as we think. I don't think harming the DM was in their plans. Sure, they want to see the end of Earth, but they know it'll happen without JUDD101; it's not enough to do anything on its own.

JUDD was just partying. He'll be harmless if DM can keep his head. JUDD101 did nothing directly to accelerate the end of Earth. He only dropped DM in it because DM let himself get into a bad situation."

"Pause," from Thodol nullified everything. "There's not much we can do and there's not much time. We should have all learned something from our mistakes. None of us can escape from that, but at the same time, as Hooldoon made felt, we did come very close. We can be proud of what we started and we can have hope that there is a second chance. No more bickering, no more theories, no more debate. We have to concentrate, tap into the memories of our parts in DM45's creation, prepare for some minor adjustments. Cantoon, some repair work from you is needed. Reemo, some loose historical data which DM45 can connect for himself. Also, DM needs more information on The Men. Leenen, I know it'll be hard, but DM requires a new compartment which can run through the consequences of his actions much more quickly and thoroughly. Beeel, some more language. We'll be in a different time, so you can use your imagination, but try to piece it to the way language has developed. Lahro, work with Leenen, get the new compartment up to speed. Hooldoon, your part is very important. We haven't time to alter too much, but you know what to do. Peelah, we are going to have to work quickly once Leenen has opened the inveterate memory, use all our strength to influence DM's soul."

Leenen counterbalanced with: "Opening up DM's inveterate memory will work as a kind of reminder to his soul. It will add a whole new dimension to his fate. There's a possibility of flashbacks, a possibility that he will connect with the truth."

"Then we must be aware of that," commanded Thodol. "But our primary aim is to equip DM45 with the capacity to ignite a successful revolution. May the force be with you."

THE BROUVAHS

"I say we make sure we get JUDD101, that's all. Fuck the Foulahs."

"Stay calm. Enough of the Earth vibes. We should learn from what happened. KRIST2000 had faults too"

"The drugs."

"The whole philosophy. I'm backing the Marchous. We've got to do something more. It seemed sex would help DM45 but we didn't think it through, and we didn't account for KRIST2000's soul."

"Well I've had enough. Fuck Earth, humans have no respect for anything."

"Enough! KRIST 2000 is going back, if not for us then to show fellow Inuthuans that we won't let The Vicrips or The Foulahs dictate what kind of society we will become."

"But why did he kill her?"

"Only what is deep inside JUDD101's soul can tell us that."

"We make KRIST stronger. We can help the Marchous."

"Why are you so concerned with the Marchous all of a sudden?"

"I think they offer hope for the future. They can help guide Inuthua. The Immortal is too busy, we have to work it out for ourselves."

"Don't release that mood!"

"The modifications need to be made. Let's go to work."

The Fanaters

"Hey happy heads, how y'doing?"

The four heads were in a semi-circle on the ground, their eyes straining from side to side to see each other, bemused by the collection of Inuthuans metamorphosing before them.

"We're tripping," Dan thought, his eyes circling.

"You aren't boys. Check this out, you're on a planet millions of light years away from Earth."

"Yeh, welcome to Inuthua, home of the weed."

The young Inuthuans transferred an approximation of laughter to the four heads.

"A short summary for you lads," began Flim. "We made you four. We got your souls from those drifting about the universe. We got John Lennon for you, Dan, Jimi Hendrix for you, Dean, Andy Kaufman for you, Jon, and Stuart Sutcliffe for you, Richard. You are, respectively, DAN1, DE1, JO1, RIC1. We made you and sent you to Earth. How cool was that?"

The four heads had become aware of the ESP and were sending haphazard signals all at once.

"One at a time, boys," sent Shile. "Dean."

"How can you prove that we are not just tripping?"

"Whatever we tell you would be too incredible for most humans to believe. If you think it's a trip, then enjoy it. You just have to believe in your imagination," answered Gotby.

"Yeh, look, it's like this," summoned up Gouevhuo: "Here on Planet Inuthua there's been a lot of interest in Earth over the years. There's been these groups on our planet who've made humans to send to Earth, usually for something boring like saving Earth or destroying it. We love Earth. We've watched it for years on sensory screens, looked back at its history. We love the old music they used to have, so we got together to create a band of humans. We thought it'd be a wheeze. Life on Inuthua is pretty serious and boring most of the time, so we made you lot."

"You are so fucking good. A lot of the younger Inuthuans were watching the visuals you sent back. Your music was good," praised Shile.

"This is mad," thought Richard to the rest.

"You can't communicate with each other," sent Molk, who then proceeded to connect all the heads, taking the Proul to beam a visual screen. "Now, if you want to think something, the words will appear on the screen."

"What's it all about?" experimented Dan.

"We're just having some fun. We're going to send you back too. We want to hear more music. Some older Inuthuans have criticised us for being frivolous, but we don't care what they say. Everybody else is sending their humans back, so we are. But, we have to make a few adjustments, try to get you in with DM45." Gotby jigged the beats, bounced them around to affect all.

"Yeh, he nearly made it," ascended Gouevhuo.

"What's DM45?" questioned Dan.

"Daniel Manion to you, the revolutionary back on Earth," answered Shile.

"Yeh, we know him, he was in the papers," sent Dean. "Didn't he murder some people?"

"All a frame up," returned Flim. "So, look, we haven't got much time, what do you think of it all?"

"A pretty cool trip," Dean sent to the visual screen.

"Far out and chilled in," layered Jon.

"The thing is, once you've been sent back you probably won't remember this. Just, y'know, enjoy yourself, keep playing those tunes," summed up Shile.

"Any requests?" sent ripples through the sensitive nooks and crannies of the Fanaters' subconsciousness.

"Anarchistic Dream," boomed Gotby.

"Do some Lennon songs," beamed Flim. "We'll have to programme that into you."

"Time is of the essence, get busy."

Bleep.

THE VICRIPS

Disgruntled slabs of ominous vibrations had ideologies clashing before finding the same deafening beat. The idea of the Marchous drifted between the cacophony until its vision was shattered by determination and insidious belief.

Each of the Vicrips sent out images, plot developments and conclusions: they tangled but found the same thread.

TUM3, they decided, needed only a few minor alterations before it would be seen as the superior model. Shifting mechanisms abbreviated their communication until one of their number threw a spanner in the works:

"The worst thing TUM3 did was meet DM45."

"That couldn't be helped, he was a patient, but as you reveal, DM45 was a problem. Again, only a slight alteration will have TUM3 meeting whom he was meant to meet."

"But the Foulahs, can we trust them?"

"Inconsequential: an inferior, ratings-winning model. They have only sent down for so-called fun; we can ride over their probe's idiosyncrasies quite easily. I am more concerned about GOD3, and from what I can see it'll be on the scene unchanged."

"GOD3 was an irritation, but I don't think her function had any real effect on our plans."

A vacuum of sound was created, motion still for some seconds of colossal contemplation. Then the black, deep booms, arrogantly reverberating outside their group into the surrounding space.

"Marchous fools, believing in Earth," demonic bursts. "I'm sure The Immortal disapproves, and if The Immortal doesn't it is not our concern. We are the future of Inuthua now. Things will change. It's time we started to think about ourselves."

"That is heresy and it goes against everything in The Koubah. How can you release that?"

"Times change, we must change with them."

HAVE BRED, HAVE MADE SEEDS, NOW WATCH DISPLAYS OF OTHER LIVES

"Quiet you two, control yourselves!"

"We're bored. Why isn't there anything on the display?"

"I've told you, they've recalled most of the probes!"

"But what about ConchJUDD101?"

"It's just fires, I've told you. Behave yourself, it'll be back soon."

"Why don't you get a Proul re-call?"

"Yeh! Yeh! The one wiv the action!"

"We've only got two Prouls after this."

"Can easy get some more."

"Orright. You want the end of the world?"

"Yeh, yeh, yeh! Put that on! Put that on."

"Right, but any more complaints and I'm not gerrin any more Prouls, and you can just 'ave the ConchMARX edits."

Misour connected the Proul to the display unit – the Proul's death sentence – appeasing the two demanding offspring. Misour located the memory where JUDD101's consciousness was stored and the Proul began relaying highlights of the end of the world.

Misour's partner, Finhou, was drawn to the visuals, couldn't resist settling for another look.

They fast-forwarded through the helter-skelter of diminishing natural resources, expanding population and unabated pollution; to the searing heatwaves culled from news bulletins, followed by fires, shortages of drinking water. Death. Destruction. They paused and absorbed again civil unrest, uprisings quelled by brutal force and pointless wars.

Speeded up stock exchanges in panic, slowed down mobs hanging and butchering investors and speculators.

They absorbed ravenously: anarchy, and streets savaged by various natural disasters. Cities were underwater or all burned out. It became dog eat dog, voyeuristically irresistible to watch human beings raping, pillaging and looting whilst The Men drew up futile plans.

Then the scenes the whole family had been waiting for; the decapitations. Heads were hacked from probes in a rich variety of ways, the transmissions going dead, switching to another probe until finally all probes were decapitated, bar one which kept a flickering image of the catastrophe as flames lapped all before them.

"Again, again!" demanded the offspring.

Misour didn't need much persuading, having enjoyed it too, rewinding gleefully to a point just before the decapitations started.

"It makes you glad to be an Inuthuan," Misour proclaimed proudly.

"I wonder what the return will be like," pondered Finhou.

"Bank on The Vicrips I say; more of the same. I dunno what the Marchous are up to, but if you ask me they haven't got a clue."

The offspring duly noticed a legacy being left and sent contagious gratification out in waves.

Misour rammed his hands into Inuthua's soil for a feed to give extra taste and enjoyment to the images.

Marnou

Marnou patiently crafted, positioned on the little piece of ground Marnou claimed territorially, working with delicacy on the butterfly's head. With fingers extended to a fine minuscule point Marnou could work on the intricate wiring required.

Marnou had begun work on the creature before Earth's last dimensional turn; a labour of love and hate. When a section was completed Marnou would test it through a self-constructed display unit. Finding certain small points wrong Marnou would set to work again, altering them until they met specifications.

Marnou had been working like this through endless loops of time without break. Marnou was something of a loner on Inuthua, an enigma wrapped in a riddle who had such intellect that brain transmissions from Marnou could be hidden from other Inuthuans. Thoughts stayed firmly inside Marnou, gestating into big ideas.

When the butterfly's head had been completed Marnou began crafting a body, an equally precarious job but one which Marnou could approach with greater enthusiasm and fewer definites having finished the difficult part.

This would be perfect and beautiful, Marnou thought indulgently, infusing the wings with symmetrical colours, so fine and delicate as to not be noticeable to a human. Marnou liked that; the apparent insignificance of the art balanced against what Marnou knew to be its importance.

The body accounted for some time loops before completion, the wings' attachment achingly slow. Marnou tested the butterfly on the display. All was perfect.

Marnou sent a thought to shatter the display screen. Transmissions would be hard to pick up through thought and Marnou knew instinctively that Inuthuans would not bother; and if they, by accident, encountered visuals on their display units they would quickly switch consciousness transmissions to something less apparently innocuous.

But Marnou would see the beauty of nature, using original mind power to travel to places never discovered by Inuthuans. With this sensation Marnou felt contentment, feeding from self-cultivated ground, its weeds offering an alternative perception to that engaged by most Inuthuans. Marnou turned briefly to The Immortal as millions of tiny flecks loaded The Immortal with more information, absorbing contemptuously before returning to the butterfly that had been created.

THE EXISTENTIALIST ALIENS

DM45's inveterate memory unspooling slowly before them, the Marchous absorbed with empathy.

"Such poetry in a child's view of the world."

Images of riding on a float with other children, each in various fancy dress guises; crowds waving and cheering from the pavements, willing participants in the conspiracy of innocence. The sequence ended with a photographed reminder of Daniel Manion in scarecrow garb, a wooden poll across his shoulders and through his coat keeping his arms in permanent crucifixion pose.

A child with parents, picnicking in the countryside, then running wild and free; a lost era like every generation's lost era, much lamented after progress has eaten up memories and left only an idealistic and pure semblance.

In snatches of news, Dunblane: a massacre of infants, never fully explained or comprehended: a tragic meeting of fates, strengthening the faith of some and shattering that of others.

Parties celebrate the beginning of the last year of the millennium. Daniel Manion is passed around the comforting arms of recognisable faces, excitedly caught up in the world he seemed to rule.

School uniform and the colours change, more realistic but substantially duller, like footage from an old CCTV camera. Images flash in quickening bleeps before pausing at the contorted face of Mr Marx, his face gorily disfigured.

Bleep. Slowly the image wound on, pale visuals of newspaper cuttings on a noticeboard: *I WANT MAM AND DAD*", "Bad Luck Boy".

Bleep. An arm in view, blood trickling steadily to a pile of papers, soaking through the print, forming a rising pool. Chaotic images came back from the inveterate memory before a long "Bleeeeeee—"

"You can see the point of realignment and re-connection there," sent Leenen.

"You did a very good job," sent Peelah. "What can be done?"

"Significant events can't be changed, but we can re-direct some of the messages created by these events, find parts of DM45's subconsciousness where they can be buried. As I warned, this will push other things closer to the surface," returned Leenen.

Hooldoon floated away from the main group, disconsolate vibes picked up by Thodol who followed.

Softened questioning grew around Holdoon: "I'm not sure we should have tampered," Hooldoon sent.

"I understand, but when DM's spirit finds enlightenment he will agree with what we've done. He will see his sacrifice saved Earth."

"Do you think The Immortal pays attention to what we are doing?"

"I'm sure. The Immortal has much knowledge coming in each second, from all over infinity, but I'm certain this little storyline interests The Immortal. If you look at the way MARX1 connected with DM you can see The Immortal must be on our side."

"But the others, the killers, the lunatics—"

"The Immortal had to balance things," Thodol enraptured with positive touch waves. "Have faith. We can change a whole planet's way of life, and indeed save a whole planet's life. The history we know tells us about all the opportunities missed by all the planets now glowing as stars. If we can make a connection of consciousness it may give us the key to our own existence. Look at the attention to detail, the human frailties that exist in MARX1 and you see that deep inside The Immortal has acknowledged the importance of humans, the need to be a part of that. We need to connect with Earth, its mystical qualities, its once finely balanced eco-system, learn its intricate subtleties, then we can produce a blueprint for the rest of infinity. With our capabilities combined we could create planets as stepping stones into the darkest chasms and black holes of space. We are better and more unique creatures than this and all eternity is our playground. But we need Earth to survive, and we can do that, Hooldoon."

Hooldoon enjoyed, absorbed and acknowledged but was not fully ameliorated: "Do you think we, and The Immortal, are just workers for some ultimate omnipotent being?"

"Over the passing of expandable time the idea that some other force created us has become dated and discounted. Whether you believe in The Koubah or not, you cannot deny The Immortal's knowledge and the facts we can pluck from our own history. We have a visible god and we are what we know we are. I understand what Peelah feels and I have faith in that. Here and now we are what we are and we have to live with that, and we are honestly convinced we are nourishing the experience of consciousness. At the same time I cannot dismiss the idea of a higher force, otherwise there would be no point to our lives."

"But you can't express that idea around Inuthua."

"You didn't just imagine that, did you? We are free; not to kill, not in competition, not to seek power. We have a higher awareness than humans so we use our freedom for galactic philanthropy. The Immortal doesn't order us to be good, we just know from our evolution and history that that is the only way for progress to continue. And I tell you this as a truth: The Immortal's greatest ponderance, The Immortal's reason for collecting so much information, is to find out who created The Immortal. The Immortal's quest is: 'To find the source of all life, from microcosm to microcosm, from omnipotent creator to omnipotent creator and absorb that for the furthering of existence,' The Koubah."

"It's just a chemical reaction."

"We know too much to believe that."

"Maybe there isn't any answer, maybe we should just live for today."

"A noble idea, Hooldoon, and that is one of the reasons why we needed you for DM45. Your soul is strong and it will have an important part to play in the next life."

Leenen arrived with signals: "Completed."

Thodol reciprocated good vibrations as Leenen made to lead the way. But Hooldoon held back.

Hooldoon confessed in a motion his worries. "Most Inuthuans think Earth is a terrible place, but I like lots of things about it, and if it goes we might lose so much."

Thodol transmitted comfort and adopted a human "voice": "We are part of an adventure called life. History may or may not record us, but the most remarkable things aren't always recorded in history. We've got to take our experience from this, that's all. It enriches the soul, which is all we have at the end of it."

Hair Of The God

"You look like shit," said Joe.

"Nothing so pure."

"Fighting talk. Let's be full on the meter impure. Virtue doesn't exist anyway. Let's blast 'em."

"You are fuckin' indestructible."

"Come on man, this is the time, the time is now. We need a karma fix. I'm dry and if I know you, you, DM, the DM, must be too. It's time to trip the light fantastic at Club Independent."

"We monkey men?"

"Monkey."

Heavy boots hit the ground, dropping the experience between meltdown-thoughts to register a feeling; the toe curling, sole feeling resolute concrete, kicked off at the heel. Repeated and forgotten; the experience missed its opening, missed its beat.

Side by side, Walker Avenue rolling by amid soundwaves and sirens concerned with elsewhere; houses shaking, excitement waking, insomniacs celebrating or grating against sleep.

Inside Club Independent a fake, untuned guitar looped over a synthesised scream; floor vibrating as the doors kept swinging. The ins and outs, the dilated pupils of the poor and needy, all winking hints at the drug chauffeur.

Drinks in, eyes aware of every little move from the bloodshots. A voluminous, exemplar, bearded man is telling a line along the bar about how he made 400 dollars on a job by just driving a van.

The eyes were looking for someone – a loser – to play pool. Money slapped down invited a challenge.

"I'll play 'ya son."

The voice came from the face of a drunk's sculpture, all hashed and hacked chiselling of a face nobody and everybody recognised.

236

"Take him, DM," whispered Joe. "I'll get us filled up."

"On."

He took up phlegm like it were a preservative, keeping it in his mouth and bouncing it off each cheek as he stabbed the white ball into the pack. He recoiled, spat into an empty glass and lapped up the aftertaste as the balls scattered with none potted.

"Fuck."

One minute and twenty seconds later five balls had choked down jaws without reply from the sculpture.

"Here," Joe presented a drink. "Yor toying with him, DM."

"Break for a drink." A miss. "Needed more time."

Three balls crashed into pockets, each followed by the sculpture's, "Fuck," as he found himself out of position, a "Fuckin' fucker", concluding his stay at the table.

Number 7 and 13 were swallowed before the black bounced off cushions and into the middle pocket.

"You lucky fuckin' cunt," summarised the game for the loser.

"You make your own luck. You do the do or you do the dodo."

"Agen. Am jus fuckin' gerrin' warmed up. Purra century on it."

A nod confirmed as he carelessly began to set up the balls.

"You cool, DM?" asked Joe.

A roundabout nod was received.

"You apocalypse?" asked Joe. Another nod prompted, "Then beat this shit and let's monkey and get the fuck outta Dodge."

"Hey, the fuckin' gods are with me."

Smack, crack, Lady Luck kickin' two balls into corner pockets. Two evens. No hesitating, cue sliding between finger and thumb, cruising for a bruising. Bam – in the teeth of a pocket licking its lips. Slow and sleazy – right corner. A mad woman dancing, out of the endless rhythm's beat. Boom boom, bleep bleep, slam bam, hanging over the edge before motion took it down. A break for a gulp of legal narcotic.

"Smoke 'em," Joe trailered, shuffling in the background. "The monkey man is a-calling."

Parading around the table like a neanderthal, grunting to take the piss way above his violent intellect. In a whirlwind the balls were secure before a flamboyant black ricocheted off number 7 and went in.

"Fuckin' jammy cunt," he said, rolling up his sleeves determinedly, a tattoo of S*T*E*P*H*E*N* revealing his identity. "One more 'ya fucker. Double or nowt."

"Don't," whispered Joe impatiently.

"Make the monkey wait," cut him off.

Stephen bit again, rattling the balls with no success.

"Fuckin' cunt!" He dropped his cue to the floor. Bending to retrieve it, "Fuck" came as he watched the kitchen knife fall from his pocket. "Double fuck," came as it clattered on the floor.

The knife found a place back inside Stephen's jacket, like it was nothing, a mere inconvenience that it had happened yet again. The knife's point cut deeper into the pocket's hole, filtered through dried blood of those injured and deceased whom now strengthened the padding inside his jacket.

A miss and Stephen thought he was in. But he shot too violently, skipping the cue ball off the table.

The bloodshots freaked, heads down like a bomb had been rolled towards them. A shriek went up. "Fuckeeen' 'ell!" A drink spilled, an arm tried to steady, cigarette ash hit a leg and pandemonium ensured for ten seconds. Then they were all laughing. Stephen didn't like that. And he didn't like the man who told him he wanted a new drink. One grotesque scowl, wonky teeth showing, sorted that out. He snatched the cue ball from his accuser, slammed it on the table and backed off belligerently.

Too easy to pot three balls in quick succession. Too easy to tempt Stephen back by missing a black.

"Right 'ya fucker," growled Stephen.

But there was no substance other than violence and he missed an inviting pocket.

"Fuck!" of course.

Black ball down, end of game.

"Fuckin' lucky bastard. Y'lucky y'cunt. Eer, a 'aven't goh no money." Stephen placed a bag on the table. "Take it, no fuckin' arguments."

The small polythene bag contained a kind of dust, a greyish matter not seen before. Stephen slunk towards the bar as Joe demanded, "Monkey."

Joe and DM laughed, at nothing in particular, just some absurd notion that they were living and in control of their lives. Outside, the disenfranchised were laughing too, hooked on something that got them through. Police sirens wailed, spotlights searching, cameras whirring, planes hovering overhead, helicopters pursuing.

But Joe and DM were safe because they weren't under suspicion: they had the front of employment, and the respectable type too.

Music cam from every wall, beating back and forth a disc with sounds originating from 1969 and excerpts from Joe's compilation disc of Robert De Niro movies on the televisual unit. The claustrophobic sensation threw out agoraphobic cards ready to play for their lives.

"This match," began Joe, holding a burned-out match between two fingers, thrusting back and forth, to and away from his eyes with a greater emphasis than was necessary, "This is this. Y'see, this is this. This match is the person I want dead. This match is Noel D'Steadmonds."

"This match then," began Daniel Manion," is Rupert C Donald, capitalist cocksucker."

"I'm killing Jim Tarbski, bam bam, blood everywhere," added Joe.

"I'm killing Norman Terrick, genocidal poisoner."

"This one's for Randolph Hiller, headmaster and all round ball-breaker."

The dead matches were resurrected from the ashtray, laid down when cards were defeated, but in the early rounds neither Joe nor DM cared as long as someone died.

"Heter Pitchens."

"Susie Baster."

"Robert Parsons."

"Dim Davidson."

"Mitchell Portman."

"Rob Monksmith. Kill, kill, the sad sick entertainers."

When they'd snorted enough dust in their world the planet had been ethnically cleansed of the dumb fucks of a dumb fuck culture.

DM left the dead bodies behind, satisfied that he had done something for mankind. The idea whirled about his mind as he touched the paving stones like piano keys, careful not to wake the surveying camera lenses marking every street corner.

"Just walk normally. Keep your head down, ignore everything. Ten minutes to home...Ignore the siren, the sound of breaking to enter. Keep walking, four minutes to home...Nearly there. Going fine. Not arrested. Just act like normal people act."

DM cut through a back alley, disturbing a bag of burned-out technological devices. He coughed, as he always did when out after midnight, when the factories released all their poisons. A smattering of rain, heavy with particles of pollutant dust, caused him to cover his mouth, quickening his steps indoors.

The number he tried at his flat building did not release the door and he searched his memory for what might be the correct numbers.

Again it didn't work and he felt himself grow more desperate as the rain thrashed down noxiously, trying to remember numbers he had lived with for nearly five years.

It might have been luck, but eventually the digits fitted and bleeped the door open, DM ascending the steps, passed the fake plastic plants and the chemotherapy of the white plastic staircase and walls.

At the entrance to his flat the numbers didn't work, each frustrated bleep not letting him enter. He tried numbers that meant something to him but that didn't open the door. He then rested in the automatic lottery of four-digit guesses, knowing the odds were poor but unable to indulge. Paranoia pulled one way, the absurdity of it pulling another, until an amalgam of the two got him cackling sinisterly.

Two times lucky in one night, he finally entered, believing he would remember the numbers when the drugs wore off in the morning.

MONKEYS CAN TALK

On the televisual unit they talked of death. The Manchester Slicer had struck again, a body just outside of Leeds bearing all the hallmarks: flesh ripped from genitals to neck. A net poll was being conducted on the age, size and background of the killer. After an hour they had a five foot nine inch computer operator who lived alone in a flat in Manchester city centre.

Then the ads came through the visuals; everything from Coki Coli to plastic surgery, "Vote NRP" to genetic improvements. Daniel knew he had to get out.

A measure of the dust he and Joe had split the night before got him to "Bleep" purchase a newsdisk in no time. He sat on a plastic bench in a small, suffocated park, noting the graffiti into three categories; Abuse – "Tiana's gorra whore's cunt": Dissent – "Fuck the NRP"; and love – "Kath luvs Rob".

He placed the newsdisk into his handcom, chain-smoked through world events – noting some for memory – then took up to a bus queue of busy bodies:

"A know mate," said the young man with stylised hair and ragged, unmatching clothes. "Tha fucker down our street, Daz Steel, ee's fuckin' pushin' ih. It's shit stuff n'all. Billy James is gonna fuckin' tupe 'im. Av ad nowt to do wivim. Ee's fuckin' mad for it."

His companion with expensive Reeback trainers incongruous at the foot of his cheap imitation clothes, steamed in with his bit: "Who int pushin' it? Ma fuckin' mates can't even gerra crust these days. And tha don't fuckin' care who's afta um. Our 'ole street's fucked."

"Aye, that fuckin' tart, Mary Dicko's gorra slag in the bag uzwell. Mind, ad fuck a."

"Fuckin' yeh."

"Come on, fuckin' bus, a gorra fuckin' sure shot on tha fuckin' robes today. Gorra gerratha fuckin' bookies."

"The fuckin' robes is fixed man."

"A fuckin' knows tha. Y' jus gorra back tha fuckin' one that's fixed to win. Cobs sez it's that fuckin Devil 2.3."

"Ee's a fuckin' smacker cracker."

"Ee fuckin' still knows tha robes though. C'mon, fuckin' buses."

"Uh, a nah."

"Uh."

Their life stories were revealed in snapshots: not working, but drinking and gambling and taking the odd hit when they could get some good stuff from a guy who "isn't a cunt, ee's oright": spending their time under the illusion that they might have some function.

DM abandoned the queue, made several detours to vidboxes on his way home, using memorised codes to connect to updates from Grassy, Aisha and Jake.

"Lights," returned Daniel to the brightness of a place where he had started the day.

"Coffee!" he shouted loud enough for the machine to begin boiling in his kitchen.

"Screen." The televisual unit loaded up.

"Crack a tune," got DM's walls rumbling.

He pondered playfully. "Lights off. Lights. Lights off. Lights. Hey, fuck you."

"Bleep bleep bleep"

He moved into the kitchen, poured out the hot coffee and stirred into it a milk tablet.

"Shower," began water running in the bathroom.

"Now get me a whore."

"Bleep bleep bleep."

"OK, OK, a little love then."

"Bleep bleep bleep."

"Hicksoff."

A "Bleep bleep" switched off the voice activator.

After the coffee-shower-cigarette-quick meal routine had been completed Daniel disconnected the power panel at the foot of his televisual unit, lit three candles and rolled a joint.

As the marijuana's aroma floated through the darkness and swirled around the candles' glow, he felt his sense of reality and plausibility submerge. He touched the covers of his old copy of J D Salinger's *The Catcher In The Rye* and it brought back a reminder of the atmosphere inside a library. He turned to the first page, pausing on the imagining of visiting a library, determining he would do it by re-creating the scene.

Buzzers were humming all around the block, distracting Daniel, causing him to re-read parts of the novel. When his buzzer went he ignored it, but soon the other disparate noises on Pourische Road were entering his awareness; windows smashing, people shouting, kids yelling, alarms sounding, sirens approaching, tyres screeching.

Daniel put the book away, turned on the power panel and re-booted his televisual unit.

Joe was next up, one buzz, one bleep before being face to face with DM.

"Here's the plan," he began. "We do a few rounds at the Indie, pick up some more of that dust 'cos it was damn good shit, and then we hit the town and find us some monkey women."

Daniel felt the weight of expectation, but Joe was in too quick to let it linger: "There's no no to this, it's just a question of how many degrees you are up for it."

"Tell me it'll run smoothly and I'll go ninety."

"It's on, be blissed."

Kids and adults in Halloween masks awakened both Joe's and DM's paranoia, but when they got to Club Independent they renewed themselves with a sense of excitement; everything going to plan.

"Ow, a wanna fuckin' re-match with you cunt," shattered their illusion; language pulled from S*T*E*P*H*E*N*'s bowels.

Joe shrugged.

"Sorry," said DM, "we're in a hurry, but let's do lunch sometime."

"Cocky fucka, y'gorra fuckin' play me."

"Next time, eh?" said DM, his tone clinging more to condescension than appeasement.

"Fuck no!" barked Stephen, yanking a kitchen knife from inside his jacket.

Two of the drug chauffeur's heavies were on him immediately. Trouble attracted the police, and it wasn't going to happen on their patch.

"Not here," said the man with the shaved head parted by a deep scar. He must have been reminded of its infliction as he cracked Stephen's wrist with his fist, forcing the knife to drop.

"I'll fuckin' av ya," shouted Stephen, eyes fixed on DM, held back by four arms crushing his body.

Joe had been in and out of the toilets between the beginning and end of the incident, flicking his head to signal the exit.

"Mad bastard," said DM as the two swiftly negotiated an exit through side streets for fear of being chased.

"What did I tell you, cracking night. Hey, stop, let's have a quick snort."

They found an alleyway where no cameras whirred. Joe took out the small polythene bag.

"This is cheap shit," he said, placing some in DM's palm. "The pot's gone way up."

They took a snort in one.

A light spooked them simultaneously.

"Penny for Halloween, mister," said the short figure from behind the mask of a deformed one-eyed, blood spattered character; one fictional and one real-life serial killer at either side of him.

Joe and DM laughed with anticipation.

Joe shovelled in his back pocket for an archaic 1p coin, placing it in the boy's outstretched hand, both accomplices peering over his shoulder to see.

The taker threw it on the floor, "Fuckin' bastad" came over the chimes leading to the coin's resting place. "Y'can't use tha."

The three moved off with curses directed at the two adults. Joe quickly found and picked up the penny.

"Heads," claimed DM.

Inside the warmth of O'Malley's , gulping on drinks, both Joe and DM were static, wordless for minutes, contemplation wrapping up dreams as they surveyed the scene

"She's beautiful," said Joe, gesturing with his glass to a woman turning away from the bar.

"Just your type," said DM ironically. "Beautiful, quiet looking, smartly dressed. She's certain to be unnaturally drawn to a hedonistic bum like you."

Joe took the joke. "There's yours over there," he said pointing to a statue moulded onto the staircase. "You can probably handle that. You wouldn't be able to bore her to death with your politics."

"I like them passive."

Their well-practised routine of ball-busting continued until Joe spotted two women leaning against a wall at the back of the bar.

"Look, those two. No, don't make it obvious."

DM composed himself, sweeping his head to leisurely survey the bar, a semi-circular movement in which his eyes did not move when they'd fixed on the female targets.

"Nice. A bit above our league though."

"Hey, come on: we're bright, witty, charming—"

"Drugged up fuckers."

"DM."

"OK, OK. You do the talking."

"I'll start if off," announced Joe as they wove between bodies. "How 'ya doing, what're y'doing, etcetera. Then you come in."

"One liner, get them laughing. One liner, get them hysterical. Bam, where you going later?"

"Bam bam."

"All tied up."

Just as their motion was coming to a halt, just as they were reaching their prey, just as Joe was about to speak, one of the women burst out,

"No thanks," before dismissively returning to conversation with her friend.

"No thanks?" said Joe, displaying bewilderment but already resigned to disappointment and now playing it for laughs. "But you haven't even heard our pitch yet."

"We're just not interested," said the first woman, more sophisticated now she was engaged.

"Just a conversation that's all," said Joe with his best innocence.

She snapped back, "OK, how about the state of a supposed democracy engulfed in capitalist ideology?" she laughed abruptly as a kind of signing off.

"It's a paradox that's ultimately unworkable," chipped in DM, standing to the fore. "Capitalism is inherently undemocratic because only the rich and strong will survive."

Shocked, she shaped her body to face the two men.

"Y'see," said Joe smoothly, "We've got any conversation you want. How about a drink on us?"

The woman who had not yet spoke registered her protest: "Just what I was thinking, ironically enough."

"No, no," pleaded Joe, "just a friendly drink. It's so rare to meet such startlingly intelligent women as yourselves in this city."

"Most of us are stupid then?" asked the first woman.

They moved away together, into another part of the bar where they conspicuously turned their backs on Joe and Daniel.

"You blew it," said DM in Joe's ear. "That intelligent women crack went down the wrong way."

"Fuck 'em, they would've been no fun. Let's get back to our league."

"Yeh, yeh, but it's three strikes and yor out tonight; I'm not being humiliated all night."

"Not us, we're the kids, we're on the ball. We got fun in the blood, good times in our genes. Neck these and we'll be doing some pubs before a club. They'll be loads of freak girls pissed on Halloween. Even we can't fail."

Fat waves of noise bounced from the entrance of Gigi's nightclub, security men outside like top-heavy weebles, making you wait until they confirmed passage inside with a nod.

You buy a ticket and wait some more, the whirlpool of beats drawing you in. You show your ticket to the check-in guy, his moment being the ripping off of a portion of the ticket, handing you back a stub, then taking your card and bleeping you into the computer to check you are the right type. Bleep and you're almost in.

You have the freedom to walk for a bit, down stairs before meeting a burly figure who takes sight of your stub before letting you move along the corridor, security cameras scanning back and forth at corners.

The beat is beginning to seep into your consciousness, pulling you until you reach the main hall, a final nod from a tough nut letting you in.

Scattered, various coloured flashing lights give some presence to the bodies yearning to move faster, whilst a bar drags in the addicts. Glasses in hand focused attention like centres of gravity, guided to a point where they could sip between lengthy lulls in conversation, dictated by the beats which only subsided to anticipate an explosion. The glow of cigarettes offers an outlet, a pause to fill a pause and a potential burn-mark for all to avoid.

You just get flashes of faces, eyes meeting instantly, your brain trying furiously to log them; but no memories remain as smiles and frowns fade away, replaced by the comfort of strangers.

At the bar, a thickness of people striving not to be impatient, waving their credit cards, minds turning over as time expands and the wait aches.

Joe departs for the toilet as DM waits functionlessly, smothered by the beat, fixed on faces and bodies until they grow discernible: there's the middle-aged cool god, deep lines in a weather-beaten face, an earring through his nose and a decade old haircut, blending fashion sensibilities to appeal to all ages; there's the suffering white corpse of a girl laced with black, bending her face to look at others, looking to look active, to find someone compelled by her deep-rooted sensitivity.

Daniel likes her, but he's racked with doubt. He knows females can be choosy: there's enough unemployed monkeys who've saved up their benefits and dodgy deals to go around. But DM thinks he's got the talent, running through his files of achievements, his little web-library of philosophies and enactments.

He can't make a move because right now he's in another world, and he knows he's in another world, and for that time he's one version of himself which is shy and detached and can't bear to enter the fray.

He is hypnotised, intoxicated by the thunder in his brain. All seems to stop still, then move on when he isn't concentrating. They become statues for a brief spell, placed around him to add to the effect of living. DM sorts out his perception, gets them to move slowly, in slow motion jolts, grunting and grappling. And he is still waiting.

It seems to be a vendetta, that everyone in the club has made it their duty to knock him as they pass.

"Guinness times two," he shouts when he is served.

Boom, Joe's back when the money's been spent.

"How's your equilibrium, DM?"

"I always come to these places and hate these places. When will I learn? Everybody's too perfect. We missed the cloning bus Joe. We haven't got those perfect pop star noses and movie smiles."

"Hey, that's what makes us unique. That's why we can pull, ugly is the new beautiful."

"Three strikes, that's all."

"Be cool DM. Be your cool self. Be the man."

"Lemme snort, then I'll be the man."

DM exited to a toilet cubicle in a land far, far away, snorting to numb the sound that bleeped and burned. He listened to the men who came and went and pissed so extravagantly to mark their existence:

"Uh, f'in, gu. Cu, wan, uh," was followed by laughter.

"Uh, oow. Uh, fa'in, gr'. G'n" followed by laughter.

These monkeys could talk if they wanted, but then they'd be eligible for employment and that would discomfort their carefully constructed lives of waking late, dabbling in crime and drinking some. Splice in some televisuals and they are retreating, retreating, retreating to what they can understand.

DM entered the eye of the bloopy loopy beats, noticed Joe talking to two young females, their features impermanent beneath the revolving lights and interfering beats.

"This is Dan. Dan, this is Shana, this is Chantelle."

"Hi babes, and you do look like babes," DM slurred, followed by the loudest and weirdest laughter.

"I hear you are a teacher," said the female with flashing lights dancing across her body decked in black catsuit.

"Yeh, we educate the masses," said DM gloriously. "Whatta you do?"

"I'm assistant telesales director for Siezens and Shana's an advertising executive sales manager for Friedland and Co."

Shana giggled. "I suppose I educate the masses, tell them what they should buy in order to help their lives." She thought that connection was hilarious.

"Boom yeh," replied DM as Shana moved forward and Chantelle fixed on Joe. "So what have you sold us then?"

"We worked with The Institute Of Science y'know," Shana said enthusiastically. "We helped with their regeneration range."

"Didn't they use rabbits, pigs and dogs when they were trialing?"

"Oh, I don't know," replied Shana, taken aback. "I don't deal with that sort of thing."

"Then make a fuckin' stand. They torture and kill rabbits and dogs and probably the homeless." DM laughed hysterically in an attempt to impersonate Shana. "If yor in advertising or marketing, kill yourself."

And with that the date was over.

"Dan, what's the problem? Two nice young femmes, and we were in there."

"Sorry man, just landing. Delete it, that makes us even."

"Never mind. I saw those women from O'Malley's. They smiled at me. I think they're just playing hard to get."

"Go for it. I've seen someone already. Let's split and go Dutch."

"Who is it? She nice? She got a friend?"

"I don't think so. Even if she has, she wouldn't be your type."

"Let me guess; pale, sullen-looking?"

"Yeah yeah yeah. Well you stick to the androids and I'll stick to the revolutionaries."

"OK kid. Go out and get 'em, and if they move, kill 'em. I'll see you later or I'll see you tomorrow."

A handshake followed like a deal, Joe moving into the maelstrom of bodies, Daniel searching around for the pale girl.

When she reappeared she was with a trendy male in his brightest clothes, wearing his widest smile. His hand on her arse, she laughed exuberantly before snogging him; and she didn't look so pale, introspective or interesting anymore. Daniel made an early exit.

Returning to his flat he wrote down the digits which again eluded him on entering his flat. He remembered the ad girl from Gigi's and was spurred to contact some subversives, make some plans for a future that didn't need selling. He set about working at his computer, adding ideas to file *AL*, for the 'novel' he felt could never be finished until life ceased to exist.

THE MEN

The Advertising Manager creature at Dizzy instilled in his employees: "It doesn't matter whether the product is good or evil, just that it is consumed. Remember that.

"We need to know what the under tens feel, how they think, what motivates them. If they want a hero, we'll give them a hero. If they want a laugh, we'll hit the lowest base and get them all laughing. If they feel insecure, feel threatened, we'll give them safety. If they want us to impress them by killing someone, then we'll goddam kill someone."

Jace Meadows slept at night. Sometimes he engaged his wife with the pills which could send babies to sleep in seconds: "'Peacetime', for your peace and theirs." Sometimes he lost himself and fantasised about a product which could replace the cigarette, which would get people hooked but appear harmless until long after he'd sold the company and achieved immortality through the latest cloning advances.

His conscience-free dreams had him going to America to pitch his idea to Shelby Thurston Junior, getting the big break and the big money.

"Family entertainment," had long been a money tree shaker for the Thurston empire. Through Dizzy films and their merchandising to Dizzyland's sprawling virtual parks in Florida, South Africa and West Germany, the company had made enough profits in a month to support a third world country for three years. Kids were raised and conditioned under Dizzy's watchful eyes. Under the façade of "Family values" puritanical fanaticism festered. It paid them well to preach innocence as a virtue, gave them a mandate to exert pressures on less powerful bodies to censor and deny.

Shelby Thurston Jnr met with Matt Levinson and Jim Proctor, or their representatives from Coki Coli and MacDolland's respectively, once a month. They discussed strategies to absorb the whole youth market, stretching from eight years to nineteen years old.

"It's obvious now gentlemen, and all our surveys prove it, the consumers we embrace span eleven years. We are taking sixty-eight per cent of them through their formative years and managing to keep hold of them for some time after. But there's thirty-two per cent whom we don't control, and that's our target."

"Fear and greed are what motivates people. If we can get them when they're thirteen or fourteen we can instil that in them; the subliminals would be easy to insert."

"And that gets us our place at The Paradise Table. Donald isn't going to deny our potential role in his plans."

Jim Proctor's flight to England enabled him to formulate the idea for MacDolland's latest advertising campaign: Images of war in the Middle East, the Balkans, East Germany and the former Soviet Union; in each clip people are seen living inside the chaos and destruction, struggling to survive. There's a young couple, a family, a group of friends and a solitary boy. Each one is on the move, moving towards their local MacDolland's store. Inside; ragged, lost souls gather, huddled around tables, nibbling on burgers and supping Coki Coli. The plotted figures are embraced, encouraged by the warmth of those around them. The words on the screen read: "There's always a chance of peace at MacDolland's. Branches all over the world now."

Proctor had to work on the slogan, but he was pleased the way everything else had come together. He chose then to summarise his life, something he invariably and frequently did during peaks or troughs in his life. They helped remind him how great he was, how much success he'd had, all the obstacles he thought he'd overcome. He would have convinced himself he was a messiah by the end of it and that fate was always going to deal him a good hand because he controlled it.

The closer he got to the present with his recollections, the more detail he found, and he anticipated building to a climax.

No one talked anymore about MacDolland's burgers being genetically modified, about MacDolland's plundering the planet's natural resources. He, Jim Proctor, had sorted that all out with the help of Rupert C Dolland's *Shine* empire. And now he, Jim Proctor, would take a seat at The Paradise Table.

The meeting with Rupert C Donald's right-hand man, Tony Prior, went well. So much so that it seemed something of an anti-climax for Proctor: ten minutes to agree the deal, then a handshake goodbye. He expected more; some champagne, some stimples, some wild party in honour of his achievement.

But Tony Prior was a busy man, well aware that he needed to make himself indispensable to Rupert C Donald. After Jim Proctor he bleeped info into his handcom and made his way across London for a meeting with Norman Terrick.

Terrick didn't like having to meet Tony Prior. Terrick had a fuck-everybody attitude because he thought everyone was less important than himself. Only Rupert C Donald was of equal stature and he resented having to meet a second-in-command.

"I need to see Rupert. Tell him that. Tell him to call a meeting of The Paradise Table because we are ready."

"Panamera?"

"Panamera."

"And its final properties?"

"All done to RCM specifications."

Terrick was cagey. He wanted to see the whites of Donald's eyes, wanted to know for sure he would have a place at the table. Prior seized on this weak spot and got all the details he needed to relay to his boss. Terrick didn't know what had hit him when Prior left, but his ignorance kept him feeling superior.

Prior worked on his handcom on the flight to Newcastle, re-assessing information, opening up new files and re-coding sensitive plans.

On arrival he directed ten minutes of his time to visit the city's zeitgeist junkie. It only took that time for him to expel imaginative urges, allowing the zeitgeist junkie to relay his memories.

Shuffling and jiving as always outside the city's tech-centre, he rapped out the benefits of what he was selling.

"Hey sir, long time no see?"

"What's the news zeitgeist man?" asked Prior coldly.

"I've got all these Virtches," he said, sweeping an arm to present his table of assorted technology. "It's all saving souls now. They's wanting to keep life going, do everything they can do for as long as they can do. I've got a DIY cryogenic unit coming next week, only, huh, it's not really DIY if you think about it."

Zeitgeist man was off, and Prior would allow him four minutes of this.

"...Oh, I remember those days, back after Spencer's going. It was easy then; something simple, something sentimental, all that believing in giving. Phew, the dolls I shifted. Five good years outta that; easy sales, easy money..."

Prior only glanced at his watch to confirm it was time for him to switch roles: "I know for a fact that it's gonna be about satisfaction, peace on Earth, contentment and gratitude. Put that out, get in the market."

Prior arrived for his scheduled meeting with Dr Lewis Tumblety at The Institute of Science four minutes early, though he *had* timed it that way.

Tumblety was mutedly deferential. He didn't like having to run through details he thought were perfectly in progress. He placed his finger on the thumb-pad then bleeped digits into his computer.

Prior looked at the screen: "All those on the programme are fully functional?"

"They're living. Shellac has taken 303 with only a thirteen per cent recall rate. MacDolland's has taken 758—"

"Yes I know the statistics. Call up one for me."

Tumblety bleeped to show information on the screen.

"Tell me about this one," urged Prior.

"Leonardo M Smith, one of our Unpeople. They have been easy to alter and we can easily programme them to carry out basic tasks."

"What's this one done?"

"Stole documents from the home of a subversive, set fire to an eco-camp, picked some pockets, all very simple, but effective."

"Show me an exterminator."

Tumblety grudgingly obliged, bleeping up another subject, leading Prior through the points:

"Stephen Davidson, not one of our better examples. His methods are crude, but again, effective. He's being used to push the Reeto Dust right now. We took him off exterminations after his second non-programmed killing, but before that he'd finished off three tasks. He may well suit the pushing. The latest Alters are much more controllable."

"And the Automatics?"

"An eighty per cent success rate. They're buying the products, watching the visuals and easily absorbing the subliminals. There must be at least one in every street in England."

"Good, and the Reeto Dust is being consumed?"

"Ravenously."

"Are you any closer to tracking down Marx?"

"We made some progress with Edward Blissett's brain and as we suspected he is within a fifty mile radius. When we get R Sampson we should be able to reduce that."

"It's important we do. There isn't going to be much space at The Paradise Table, but Mr Donald will be very pleased if you can find Marx."

Alone in the basement of the asylum, Dr Tumblety replayed Prior's last words, resentful that he was a mere cog in a bigger wheel. He could not concentrate as he scanned through parts of Edward Blissett's brain, desperately trying to find something which would pinpoint the whereabouts of Marx.

Tumblety thought The Men owed him a lot, thought he should automatically get a place at The Paradise Table. He had seen that insanity was a booming market and he had developed the use of drugs, psychology, soundwaves and education to rehabilitate patients. And now he was effectively an employee of RCM Enterprises. Maybe his one-time partner, Henry Ragalana, was right when he told Tumblety no capitalist could be trusted.

RCM Enterprises had taken control of Dr Tumblety's experiments when they'd taken control of The Institute Of Science. With that came Friedland electronics, Siezens and Menworth Hill.

Menworth Hill was the jewel in Rupert C Donald's crown. Under the guise of MoD operations it worked as a spying system for hire. Big business could pay for information on anyone; Menworth Hill could track any individual or any organisation and with information gathered from the census, the electoral roll, police files, security services, health services, social security, Inland Revenue, local government, banks, loyalty cards, subscription agreements and consumer monitoring, they could produce a comprehensive dossier.

Rupert C Donald knew what his rivals were doing, what governments around the world were planning, and had bugging devices in most of the population's homes: Friedland Electronics, makers of most things from house alarms to chemical weapons, invariably played a part in most people's lives. Donald could assess and decide who sat at The Paradise Table.

Through his televisual channels and multimedia control he could dictate taste, manipulate thought and shape culture. The NRP and New Labour were in his pocket because they knew he could fix any election.

With these tools Donald could put into action his master plan. Sitting around him at The Paradise Table were the most powerful and influential men on Earth and he delivered to them a glimpse of the future: his media would dumb down culture, making people easier to control. With RCM Enterprises perfecting cloning Donald could decide who lived forever, who lived to rule over a population dead from the neck up, distilled by drugs and pre-programmed to run on automatic.

The Paradise Club would eventually have whole countries to themselves and would be able to build a new civilisation. Early meetings of those involved determined that their new world order would need to keep them amused: nubile females for sex, the finest foods and drugs, and regular technological innovations to allow them the finest virtual opera, virtual film and theatre, and virtual art. These would not be shared with the masses, and as the process of dumbing down and exterminating continued all threat of insurrection would fade.

"England does not need well-educated people but good subjects."

"At the touch of a button anybody and anything is yours. The possibilities are endless. We can explore space and colonise all eternity. Gentlemen, we are one small step away from becoming the new gods."

THE MISTS DESCEND

"Who am I?" he asked to the mirror. "The man who goes through life getting wasted, or the man from years ago, the one with ideas and purpose?"

Seated in a fog-enveloped park he pondered the question, numb to the horror show he viewed on his newsdisk.

An old man with thick white gelled-back hair sat beside Daniel, nodding an acknowledgement. He then tapped his wrist to know the time.

"Ten passed twelve," said Daniel.

"Hank-u," he replied unclearly.

He was deaf, but began to strike up a conversation with his hands and fingers, asking Daniel what was in the news.

DM put his handcom down and told him about the Manchester Slicer, the tidal waves in the Mediterranean and the election build-up.

The man's name was John, twisting and tapping his hand to convey displeasure at the news. He began a tale about the old days when he was young, when they used be a left of centre ideology in British politics. He used to stand on picket lines when that was legal. He talked about how people used to stick together for the common good. He liberally sprinkled swearing into his description of Margaret Thatcher, identifying her system as a turning point, concluding that Fascism had found a respectable front in Capitalism.

Daniel questioned whom he would be voting for.

At a push, Adam Benn and the Labour Party, but he didn't think voting would count for much.

DM posed that maybe the people could come together again, if enough people really wanted it.

John agreed but communicated that the working class and some of the underclass would need to be involved, and that most people, even liberals amongst the middle-classes, ignored them.

DM returned that it was that fucker Rupert C Donald with his televisual channels and Shine media outlets who had emasculated the working classes.

John laughed, joked about the probability of DM's first use of sign language being to swear. DM confirmed, then asked what John did now.

"Survive," John uttered slowly but considerably clearer, much practised in frequent use.

He returned to sign language to reply that he painted pictures by the seaside, that he could see the beauty, smell the fresh waves when the factories weren't over-polluting, and that he could still imagine the sounds he'd experienced in childhood. You've got to enjoy nature, he added, before communicating that he had to leave, thanking DM for the conversation.

The mists were descending, pouring from skies that had been a patchwork of whites for nearly a month.

Taking heed of John's message, Daniel made for the hills, to feel some kind of cleansing, away from the drugs.

Ascending the hills, visibility diminished to about one meter before the fog thinned as the ground levelled out. He could look down on the city, layers of white resting over the whole town. The higher peaks – some office blocks, churches – peered through the space between sky and fog. To the north, cooling towers and chimneys formed an ever-changing dark construction, hinting at an existence vaguely through the poisons they chugged out; disturbing grey strands into the whiteness.

DM pondered a population readily accepting this, fumes and poisons routinely pumped into the air they breathe. It's there in front of their eyes on clear days, and if they only read the reports about CIC Newcastle they could see facts about leaks, carcinogenics released into the atmosphere, and the higher than national average statistics on cancer and leukaemia in the region. If they could all get together and say enough is enough, then something might change. They could block access, invade the site, do something they can't ignore.

It was so wrong. CIC's owners didn't care, didn't tell the truth about what was being pumped out. It was business, strictly.

Daniel moved on, through pockets of clouds over undulating wet land, absorbed by his thoughts until something flashed in the peripherals of his vision.

The figure emerged from a cloud, like some kind of magician's entrance. His skin was a dark ebony, his hair like wool, his face the colour of brass. He had a slim figure, sported facial hair of the unkempt kind, wore white T-shirt and white jeans, muscles taut beneath and from them.

His outstretched hands beckoned Daniel to hold them. Daniel felt inclined to back off but some power source drew him to engage hands. He felt a scar initial itself on his palm as the stranger massaged a welcome.

"Daniel. I have been looking forward to seeing you." He released Daniel's hands. "We have to do something, you know that. The world is running out of ideas. I look down and all I can see is despair, anger, tragedy, intolerance. I had to come back, and I know you are going to help."

"Ted?" asked DM disbelievingly.

"No, but he will be back soon."

"Who are you with?"

"All of you good good people."

"How do you know me? Where have you come back from?"

"Be calm, brother. Trust me. There are others out there, we just need faith."

As soon as Daniel replayed the incident it seemed to have changed. It grew briefer on each subsequent recall from memory, the stranger's face growing vaguer and less realistic. It eventually dissolved to become one of a number of Daniel's weird trips.

In the streets characters flitted between clouds, cigarettes dancing as they criss-crossed. In neon-lit alleys, mutterings and some angelic voice yearning "Nobody loves me" like a fragile town crier. No reply came, just the swell of lights emitting blobs from the back entrance of pubs.

Voices seemed suspicious, all actions full of intent. Each one had some scam, tripping up to make some money from you with an undercoat-sale. Sirens bumbled in spirals, stacking up and building up to a constant.

"Wanna live forever mate?"

Daniel turned and nobody was there.

SHARKING

In Sector 8 three of The Sharks lived a modest existence in a terraced house. Taff, as Dr Edwards, was once one of The Medikals in Sector 3 before the killings started. Jez worked as producer on a small televisual channel devoted to the arts and occasionally documentaries. Phil, a freelance media analyst, had done some work for the government but all the sharks knew the work he had done for them was innocuous and what he had learnt and passed on to subversives was invaluable.

The Thursday ritual of cards frequently got interrupted but always continued, usually taking place in Sector 8 for convenience, and because they had a nice rectangular card table there.

If they ever write *The Truth About Marijuana* it will probably include comprehensive chapters on its history (first cultivated in China around 4000 BC), its environmentally friendly properties (one acre of hemp will produce as much paper as four acres of trees; hemp is a source of fibre for cloth and cordage for rope) and its medical benefits (it alleviates symptoms of glaucoma, multiple sclerosis, AIDS, migraines and many other debilitating ailments). But they should find room for a section on the vibes it gives the user, the openings it creates in the thought process.

Conversations circled in pockets as joints were rolled and participants settled.

"What do you reckon for the election, DM?" asked Phil.

"We've gotta hope, but I can't see anything getting the NRP out. You?"

"No chance. I've heard all that stuff about it being close is just a bluff. They expect a landslide."

"They're all fucked anyway," piped in Joe. "Don't trust any politicians, don't trust anybody in power. They're all lying cocksuckers."

"What about Adam Benn?" questioned Taff, taking DM into conversation, letting Phil argue the case light-heartedly with Joe.

"Yeh, good bloke, but he'll never get enough votes."

"It's all fixed, DM, that's the truth," let in Jez, ending abruptly as he licked the Rizla papers.

"Too true. Benn'll never get in as long as Donald owns the media. He'll pick our governments for as long as he's alive."

"Come on Jez," urged Joe, busting Jez's balls over his slow perfectionist technique.

"Just think of all the power Donald has," Taff said incredulously. "Just think what he could do. He could make England a more culturally enlightened society, he could promote the arts."

Phil spilled into conversation with Taff and they were talking about art's subjectivity, about great artists, about Picasso, Van Gogh, Monet...

"I like Dali," said DM seizing on a pause. "But I find him obvious. He's accessibly weird and his paintings guide you in an obvious direction. His imagination consumes all his work and allows only a small, well defined space for your own."

Jez began a conversation about the idea of a god and found all the sharks attentive, pulling them all in to offer quick theories on God. But they weren't ready to explore the concept and their ill-thought out conjecture confirmed to Jez they were impatient for him to light the joint.

Cards were dealt, concentrating the scene with anticipation; and for one millisecond they were all static, like an old photo in a old book.

The only comments exchanged during a game were bites at fear and relief, culminating in Joe losing to Taff.

"If there is a god," began Jez, "He must've made dogs, and he must have been aware that dog was god spelt backwards. Dogs must have some amazing powers that we don't know about."

"The big god," began DM," "is stuck in a white cupboard, from where it controls all of creation."

The subject of gods tailed back to Rupert C Donald. Joe, preoccupied with rolling a convincing joint, had no room to comment.

"That's just it, DM," said Jez. "The whole of the media are now helping the government. You can't get the truth anymore. Look at this Manchester Slicer thing, it's just entertainment, and anything that affects our lives is distorted and twisted. You have to look hard to find the truth."

After numerous card games and with night-time now old, they slowly parted: first Phil, then Taff, then Jez, then DM, leaving Joe and shuffling home alone.

In the air, sirens formed a distant bleeping. With statistics showing two alarms from a variety of appliances go off on average twice an hour along most streets, Pourische Road would get its turn.

DM prepared for sirens, but none came, and in the unnatural silence he became aware of footsteps following him. When he quickened the steps mimicked. He could see his flat building and made to burst into a run when a hand grabbed and spun him around.

Ted K

Ted moved quickly on seeing DM's associate leave him. He moved closer but kept at a safe distance, pausing behind an object to weigh up the next stopping post: car, wall, bush or gate; he pinpointed the spot and scurried to it to begin the assessment over again.

He had time to weigh up the situation and project a successful conclusion. He even had time for contemplation; he worried that DM might have changed, might have grown bitter after the failure of the last revolution, might have settled into an automatic life.

Ted became aware of his footsteps in the silence he'd plyored. He realised DM had speeded so he did, with a little some extra, then sprinted in anticipation of DM's burst away.

He caught DM's shoulder, the motion of pulling away exaggerating his turn to an unbalanced spin.

"DM, it's Ted, ssh."

"Fuck! Ted! Wha? How? They let you out?"

"Served my sentence, though I didn't except them to let me out this early. I haven't got long, I just wanted to know you were still with the plan?"

"Yeh, of course."

"Have you been keeping in touch with the groups?"

"Most of them. I've been busy y'know," DM replied apologetically.

But that didn't bother Ted, more worried as sirens approached.

"Just get organised good DM, I'll be back in touch."

Ted left as flashing lights turned into Pourische Road, diverting DM to scurry for his flat.

Ted was always one stop ahead of any law. Every movement he made was part of a carefully constructed plan which had taken shape during his time in prison.

An important part of that plan was DM, the conduit for most organisations he needed to involve. Ted would spend the next three weeks igniting the fuses of his ideas, travelling around the country setting things up, sending tasks for DM to carry out.

He saw the NRP's election victory as inevitable, didn't allow it to knock his plans off course. This time around the revolution would succeed.

After the election victory had been officially announced at 12.45 a.m., Joe and DM went sharking, playing some cards to get Jez and Taff to go to Club Independent and score some dust.

They returned with a newsflash about the extortionate price of pot against the cheapness of the dust.

The games were muted and lacked any sense of adventure.

Ted caught up with DM on his route home, again following first before turning DM. Again, DM's shock needed quelling.

"OK, DM, it's me."

"Hey, fuckin' NRP again!"

"It was always going to happen," replied Ted before focusing DM's mind on the jobs he needed doing and the people he needed contacting.

Inside his flat DM was tempted to dip into the dust, but flashes of pain in his stomach pushed him to do the work for Ted first.

Automatic People

Seven a.m. the alarm bleeped, pure automatic and without remorse. Daniel twisted to pause its noise but found himself wide awake after an electric shock made a connection from finger to brain. His heart pounding, he noticed loose wiring at the back of the alarm. Calming, he took another hit of the shock to lift himself out of bed.

On the televisual unit politicians from the NRP were talking about "A great day for England" with no trace of irony. They were talking about the reintroduction of capital punishment, "for the terrorists, the rapists, the paedophiles who torment our innocent little children".

"TV off."

The side of a cereal box took his interest with "The Chance Of A Lifetime" emblazoned on its side, a trip to Dizzyland to live like a cartoon, sponsored by someone else, all in the pocket of The Man.

The food didn't appeal, soaked as it was in diluted milk. He scraped it into a bin and poured some more hard caffeinated coffee.

On the coffee jar a competition to guess the number of granules in a jar. Just guess, phone a number and listen for what prizes you could have won. Calls cost thirty dollars per minute. Calls should last no more than four minutes. "You must win something."

It's all about competitions. We are all unsatisfied, all want to get lucky with guesses and draws, Xs exercised like targets.

8.05 a.m. waiting for a bus. Just waiting, shuffling on the spot, trying to load up on nicotine, eyes darting like mad fish.

Shaken on the bus, walking to the train station from memory, passing through the throngs of those Automatic Living.

Daniel Manion has no dreams, switched on like the rest to look for numbers, gaze upon screens and bleep digits into machines.

Walking around him are numerous Inuthuan human probes, mostly older models who burned out years ago and switched to automatic, a function which would keep their systems working for between fifteen and thirty-five years after. They no longer transmitted to Inuthua or served any particular function other than getting through a routine.

A number of these probes would be intercepted by newer models and downloaded, after which they could not be reactivated and were usually destroyed.

Mixing with these probes, various clones and genetically modified people. These were soulless creations identified by their outer beauty and likeness to famous people; plenty of grown up and grown old Emily Spencers, some movie stars like Michael Grant (the older and now rather embarrassing version done before he was arrested masturbating in a men's public toilet), and the frequent oddity.

This new species of supposed immortals were prone to aberrations; genetic breakdown, mental illness, flashbacks and even violence. RCM Enterprises contrived to play these down in the media, baffling the public with the latest extraordinary developments in cloning.

Shift-working petty criminals had perfected looking ordinary, able to blend in with the automatic masses, their targets, whom they would track diligently before moving in to make some money.

These automatic people were a mixed bag; average humans who'd succumbed to the cultural genocide around them. They had no aspirations and they felt fairly content, although if pressed they couldn't say what with. Covering all classes, they went through days guided by a routine they thought they'd decided for themselves.

The underclass were surviving, the working classes were trying to keep their heads above water, much like most of the working middle-class, and the rest were counting their money and not mixing with the street people.

Infrequently emerging from their homes, bleary-eyed and ill-equipped to deal with the outside, were computer workers and addicts. They communicated with plastic cards and numbers then rushed back home to evolve into a new species.

Intelligent life was out there, but it had no heart; emotionless intellects bleeping off the tasks on their lists of challenges. Amongst them, televisual unit repair men and women; super-intelligent techno-wizards, absolute mathematical geniuses. In their brains they held a mass of information concerned with technical details and specifications and problem-solving strategies. They could assess, solve, fix, rationalise anything. But they were misfits, severely lacking in social skills. From a lifetime in front of a screen their skin had an anaemic hue, their soulless bodies a withered look. Though they were wealthy, they too were automatic living.

Added to this melting pot were the psychologically challenged, roaming the streets under the liberal supervision of "Community Care".

Blank-eyed, drugged-up on suppressant and mind-altering drugs, most had little purpose other than to tire themselves out so they could sleep. There was no common thread as to why they would suddenly snap and become violent: a wrong look, a misplaced word or action, anything could pull the trigger.

Even those from the asylum in Sector 3 who had been instilled with a mission could snap. Ronan Jacobs had begun treatment at the age of eighteen. He'd been released several times on trial runs to see if his bitterness and resentment had successfully been re-diverted. He walked the streets most days to buy a meal at MacDolland's, drink Coki Coli and stalk people.

On this day Ronan Jacobs would follow freelance artist and co-founder of "Newcastle Ef", Anthony Tennyson. He would wait two minutes after Tennyson had entered his home, then knock on the door. Jacobs thumped Tennyson onto his heels, pushed him down, closed the door, cut his throat then left. He purchased a meal at MacDolland's then went to his flat in Sector 3 to watch The Universal TV channel.

There were no witnesses to the murder, no clues other than "missing" CCTV footage. Life continued on automatic, the population mapping out their objectives, no diversion from routines carefully aided by the creation of zones: Education Action Zone, Health Zone, Consumer Zone, Crime Zone, Drug Zone. Zones were good, they told us simple people where to go to get what we wanted.

5.30 p.m. Daniel re-entered the scene and noted it had barely changed since he'd been at work.

"It's just been bugging me lately," he said. "Is my life first person or third person?"

"First, I replied."

"No, I am detached, barely third, more like second."

"It'll pass, I said."

"Why are you talking like that?" asked DM.

"That's it, be the kid again, urged Joe, the strikingly handsome young man."

"The man had a sense of himself which would get him through many scrapes, but which would ultimately be his downfall."

"Joe realised this, and that's what he liked about it. It was time to monkey."

"What about Stevie?"

"He can't be there all the time," reasoned Joe. "In fact he can't be there for most of the time. We'll take a chance, we are as much likely to get killed standing here as the Indie. Let the fates decide for us."

They clocked in at Club Independent and clocked out with no hassle.

"I told you, blissed," said Joe buoyantly.

By 21.40 p.m. the Reeto Dust had them in its grip. In their time capsule they set off, the world outside DM's window whizzing by until they were jolted to a halt.

They surveyed the scene in shock, the land burning for as far as the eye could see.

FRICTION

"DM, DM, be sweet! All we need are our big hearty hearts. OK, so we didn't make the make. Y'know, two big time intellectuals like us aren't gonna find a fizz on New Year's Eve. Everybody's just too happy right now."

Joe was on his high-style-trip, a million miles from Daniel. This moment was a repetition of other loveless moments: going out high on life, returning dejected.

"Hey, you at least got a number."

"Oh yeh, some stupid Yorkshire bitch who was fuckin' somebody else's pocket by the end of the night. Big deal."

"It's love I need," said Daniel forlornly. "Maybe I should just be me in future. No cocksure guises."

"Taking a risk there, DM."

Down the steps from Gigi's nightclub, they waited at a taxi rank, a cold chill gradually detoxicating them.

Simultaneously they became aware of a woman descending the steps, grasping the railings for support.

"What's this?" pondered Joe as she slumped against a wall.

"She looks well off the meter."

"Pretty crushing though," said Joe, ironically mimicking a teen-phrase like he were some unsophisticated adolescent. He moved to her, Daniel following reluctantly.

"Hello. Are you looking for a taxi?"

She nodded.

"Where are you going?"

She mumbled a reply, then flung her arms around Joe, who did the same to her but with greater precision.

"Sector 5," she slurred with the cut of a foreign tongue.

"That's near us," Joe said. "You can share our taxi."

She smiled, began kissing Joe lasciviously on his lips. Over her shoulder Joe's eyes were wide and knowing, indicating to Daniel that he had found some kind of panacea.

She let herself fall away from him in mid-snog, leaving Joe diminished and puzzled as she addressed the sky in her own language. In one sweeping movement she had her arms around Daniel, her lips planted on his. He too was willing to indulge, all sensitivity abandoned.

When done she slouched back against the wall, verbally graffiti-ing it with babbling.

"No taxis here," said Daniel. "Let's walk."

The long route through town saw the woman alternating her affections between Joe and Daniel, ignoring the wasted generation, incoherent and abominable.

"Giz some money!" pleaded a withered young man from his humped ball beneath a street lamp.

The woman stopped first, drawing in her two charmers.

"What's up?" asked Joe impatiently.

She fingered in her pocket, Joe sharp enough to see an opportunity for his hand to go in, ostensibly to help her, feeling inside the fabric for her flesh. But she pushed him away, taking out a purse which she couldn't prevent from dropping.

The man in the heap snatched at it but was too wasted to fend off DM sneaking it back. When their eyes met, recognition flickered beneath the pale light.

"What ya fuckin' lookin' at?" growled the heap. "Goh any stimples? Come on, fuckin' come on."

"Who are you?" asked DM.

"W' the fuck's it t'you?"

"Tell me, I'll give you some money."

"Who the fuck're you?"

The woman was taking several round trips to withdraw some money from her purse; dropping insubstantial coins in the heap's lap.

"Come on DM, let's go," urged Joe.

DM persisted, pulling notes from his pocket as bait. "Come on, tell me."

He snatched the money and buried it in his groin before answering: "Nick Tallant. Who the fuck're you?

"Daniel Manion. You were in my fuckin' class at school."

"Fuck school."

"You were in Mr Marx's class weren't you?"

"Fuckin' yeh, fuckin' mad. Fuckin' good ideas though. Fuckin' lunatic. 'Ole new fuckin' way of finking. Lateral revolution. Fuckin'."

"Come on Dan, yor not a goddam social worker."

DM resisted, intent that the heap should continue and earn money.

"Fucked me up like. Fuckin' crazyhouse for me. Tha fuckin' scared of him there. Crazy fuckin' brains." The heap started laughing, clogging his throat with phlegm, soon suppressing his emotions to ease the pain of coughing.

"Scared of Marx?"

"Fuckin' gorra go, y'not gerrin y'money back." He shuffled on his ass to retreat.

"Come on, Dan," sounded Joe, taking the woman's body to lead her away.

In each direction both connections were pulling away from Daniel. He couldn't feel frivolous anymore as he watched the heap scurry away.

Joe's was still in the mood, but the cool fresh air had had a sobering effect on the woman and she was now only using Joe for support.

He tried some sweet talk with, "Where are you from?"

"Denmark," came out exhausted.

In bursts she revealed her name, Kristen Ingersson, that she was in Newcastle to study English literature for a year, that she had drunk too much and taken too many dodgy pills.

"I live over there," said DM. "Do you want a coffee?"

She yawned the same language as them. "No, no, I need to sleep."

"I'm just around the block," said Joe, making to kiss her.

He had no chance to develop the moment as she extravagantly attracted the attention of a taxi she'd spotted.

"Thanks for helping me," she offered as she stumbled into the vehicle. "I'll see you."

"Not if we see you first," said Joe as the taxi drove her away. "Fuckin' hell, DM, we're cursed."

"Too existential for love. It wouldn't have been right anyway. Come on, my brain's buzzing, I need dusting."

They booked seats on the flight to the moon. DM downloaded File *AL* from his computer to bury there before they came back to Earth.

5:35 a.m. they were outdoors with DM determined to find a spot on Earth to bury another disk of *AL*.

"We've just been to the moon, DM, we need some rest."

"Fuckin' hell, it was so fuckin' real. I've got to do this, it's my destiny."

"Too much Reeto man. I'm going for some zeds. Later."

Stood alone outside his flat, the greyness of the night emissions giving way to the white skies of daytime, DM felt the holitude of modern living.

He returned indoors, upstairs and inside his flat to find a metal box to put the disk in. Then, downstairs, stood outside, checking off items on a list. Inside again, upstairs again, making sure his televisual unit was turned off. Outside again, alone again.

Convinced he was being foolish he went back indoors, re-connected his televisual unit and slumped in the armchair.

The news devoted ten minutes to people around the world celebrating new year. Three minutes of the Middle East war followed with footage supplied by the military. All the talk was of weapons; weapons which could hit a pin from forty miles; weapons that could turn corners to find a target. There was no mention of people. Two minutes were found to skip through the conflict in the USA where some southern states had declared independence, their numerous militias involved in a process of ethnic cleansing. In ten-second bursts the war in East Germany, the conflict in Nigeria, the rise in oil prices. Three minutes for the boy whose parents had been murdered, then five minutes on minor ceremonies to commemorate the thirty-fourth anniversary of Emily Spencer's death. It served to advertise a night of programmes on the channel which used the generation gimmick for an angle.

Local news was merely headlines: a woman's body found in Sector 5, humans losing jobs, replaced by robots, New Year celebrations.

He toyed with the large control, grew bored with the supposedly endless possibilities the televisual unit offered.

The televisual unit, from basic model to super model, was a feature in most homes. First advertised as "The world at your fingertip", it had become a substitute for living. The system incorporated television, computer and phone. You could watch transmissions from all over the globe, and even outer space. Any CCTV camera around the world could be dialled, its recordings viewed live. You could work from home on it, order products on it, gamble, play games, record information and visuals, even edit. It served as communication through e-mail, voice and visuals. Updating the power-box could add all sorts of novelties like voice control of your residence's electronics. An upper-class toy, middle-class necessity, it even inhabited the homes of the majority of the working-class, though its capabilities were meagrely enhanced: visuals and phone.

It often disgusted DM, to the point that he would frequently disconnect the whole system. What it did give him was contact to the groups whom he and Ted K had gathered together for the last revolution. In his present state of despondency he reminded himself of the fact and logged on to an old hidden site.

Cryptic notes there alerted him to check his own hidden e-mail box. Its memory was bursting with coded instructions from Ted, of individuals to contact and plans to formulate.

The realisation he had things to do immediately called up a backlog of sleep, leaving DM in two minds. He felt a sharp pain in his stomach, his blood boiling, his time and space contracting:

If he neglected the work he had to do, chose instead the dust, he would put Ted K's plans in jeopardy. If he convinced himself they could wait, he would have more work to do at a later date.

He would make seven contacts today, fifteen tomorrow and ten the next day, then he'd be up to date when he returned to work.

Impulse inspired him to take the tin with the *AL* disk in as he once again found himself stood outside his flat, though this time the holitude had a backing track of sirens and angry mechanics.

"Bleep" as he deleted "1PHONE" from the list on his handcom, having contacted the group "Phone Bug" via a vidphone booth at the end of his street. DM gave a coded message to an unanswered phone, an alert to the group to begin plans on the interception of phone lines around the country.

"Bleep" as "2IND" was deleted, the Industrial Anarchists given plans to disrupt operations at The Institute of Science.

"Bleep" after one drink in O'Malley's had initiated contact with Hemp World: free hash cakes for the masses.

"Bleep" to "3WILL".

"Bleep" Freedom Coalition.

Bleep to The Redskins.

He wandered in a daze before deleting the final target, "Newcastle Ef", still in shock after hearing about Tense Tony's murder.

He was still in Sector 27 but he didn't know the streets surrounding him. He wasn't lost – he could use the pollution filtering into the sky as a guide home – but all the same it felt eerie. Under the pale sky, coming down from the Reeto, without sleep in thirty-one hours and with thoughts of Tense Tony's murder running through his head, DM grew monstrously paranoid. Aware that he was conspicuously motionless, he put his handcom away and began moving, directionless until he realised he was directionless, then he perfected the role of standing in front of a shop window and apparently looking in.

He saw it was a second-hand shop, in its window an old video cassette recorder priced at "Only E1000". He imagined buying it to play his old cassettes but the antique was well out of his price range, and he would need to find a connector for the televisual unit anyway.

His paranoia worked hard to slap him awake, but DM's attention was taken with a book, *Cracking Codes For Kids*, displayed in the window for fifty dollars.

Bleep: strange place, standing still. Bleep: home. His confusion needed a cigarette to calm down, take stock.

On the red cover, beneath the title and author, the rough white tear where Daniel Manion's name label had been pulled off. It was his. He instinctively knew. He recognised the features and they connected with a memory and unlocked a sensation; a powerful re-experience in a flashback.

He had read it seemingly every day in his childhood. He had looked at and absorbed the cover so many times during his formative years that he couldn't be wrong about its origin.

The truth was confirmed when he noticed a spider's web doodled in the right-hand corner, black ink following lines of white where the book had creased at the edge. It was going to be a river, but at eight he'd reasoned that would need to cover the whole page to be effective. The spider in the corner looked much more secretive, and he'd been told once that spiders used their webs to send messages like Morse code.

He cursed that the shop was shut, cursed again on seeing it wouldn't be open again for four more days. He so much wanted to buy, to flick through the pages and relive the excitement of his innocence once again. There would be his own codes on the pages at the back of the book; the little workings of his embryonic mind.

Moving slowly away, Daniel tried to piece together some picture of his childhood, but each vague recollection was misread and the memory unfound.

He then tried to order his past chronologically, hoping this would eventually lead to a fuller picture of his early years. But as he retreated he realised that even the most recent past had long periods in which nothing significant could be recalled. Back into his teenage years he recalled the gunshot of Mr Marx's attempted suicide.

He turned around, walked back down the street to look at the book in the window again. Below the eye-catching and bold 3D lettering of *Cracking Codes for Kids*, in small italic lettering "*A D Marx Production*".

"Mr Marx?"

"I'm talking to myself on the street. Too many weird things are happening. I need to get a grip," DM thought. "Note that I must give up Reeto Dust and get my head straight. This is just a mad flashback. Walk away, stay sane."

In analysis he realised that he could only remember the most significant events from his childhood: his parents disappearing, Mr Marx, and Emily Spencer (though being reminded of her death every year was also a factor). He'd never been one to think about his boyhood, but only because it had little relevance to his present and therefore was infrequently called upon. Now, the determined effort to explore deeper into his past seemed to be reaching an end at the point where he was writing "My Last View Of Life" as Mr Marx held a gun. He got a sense of himself, alone, closing out the world and closing out the past.

Analysis complete, he switched awareness to his surroundings.

Gripping *Cracking Codes For Kids* behind that wall, passing messages onto his friend in the next garden along, preparing to crawl to the next mission post; "the lamp post we sealed with glue on Mischief Night, the one we used to get people out playing hide 'n' seek with the other kids in the street:" the same lamp post Daniel now stood at.

"Where are all of my friends now? Where are you and what were your names? Where are you, my parents? Why did I give up hope of finding you? When did I stop grieving over you?"

There was the stretch of road they used to play kerby; the best spot because the kerbs weren't disintegrating and there was a speed controller over the road so you could get double points for a ricochet. Every gate and wall triggered a memory, swirling loose around his brain.

He had reached his house, igniting a sensation of the return to it as a child; the warmth, the safety, the imaginative tools in his bedroom, the endless hours creating and plotting, pushing heroic inch-high soldiers to their doom, flicking goals in the Subbuteo World Cup Final, making characters out of pens and scissors; his parents, comforting and perfect.

Knocking on the door in an unknown neighbourhood has an above average chance of being dangerous. Society's make-up was a concoction of murderers, people who knew murderers, people who had murderers in the family, people who'd witnessed murders and the relatives of murder victims. Add to this those who had either ordered, planned or merely hypothesised a murder: of a boss, a husband, a wife, a brother, a sister, a son, a daughter, a neighbour, a politician, an entertainer. Whoever answers the door is going to have to be religiously devout not to want to hit Daniel. And then there's the chance of it being a religious fanatic and they'll kill you just because you're not like them.

He was trying to make lots of connections all at once, felt himself going dizzy, his stomach sending shock waves of pain around his chest. As the door opened he re-experienced the physical presence of it from his childhood. Blood was swamping his memories, flowing over the screen he was watching, rewinding back into a deeper past filled with flashes of words and images bleeping towards a conclusion. Blood was pouring from his nose as he began a sentence, its flow exacerbated when the burly and briefly glimpsed occupier punched Daniel in the face.

"Fuck off, religious cunt."

As the pain throbbed, as he walked with his natural homing device bleeping instructions, he repeated to himself, "*Give up the dust. Give up the dust.*" "Give up the dust," caught him talking to himself, noticed by strangers. He continued on, one "*Give up the dust*" every five bleeps.

When Joe called around with suggestions and statements equalling answers, Daniel was rooting through his storage cupboard.

Joe was out of dust and he took up Daniel's offer swiftly. But he checked himself and took another, more dignified route to his evening's dénouement: "It won't be the same if yor not sharing the trip, DM."

"I'm giving up for a bit, so it doesn't feel so bad when we go back to work."

"It's going to feel bad anyway. We've only got three days to get through. If we take it to the limit, we can cold turkey those three days, and you know we can do it, 'cos we've done it before. We'll have a chilled weekend, ease out the Reeto and we'll be back to full fitness for the Monday. You pull out now you'll be in a deep one by Thursday."

"It doesn't add up, Joe, but I like the idea."

"Then fuck 'it doesn't add up', life was never meant to be an exact science."

"Yor good, yor very good, but you've been watching too many De Niro movies." DM had a wacky ball-busting punch-line to finish off, but he came out with, "And you can't be yourself anymore, you don't know who you are."

"OK, Mr Manion, I can see you've got some serious issues you'd like to discuss with yourself, and I've always been one for human self-nourishment. See ya later, OK?"

His tone had been carefully crafted throughout the brief speech so that it touched acceptance, sarcasm, resignation and finally warmth and concern. He'd chosen that instead of "Fuck you".

Daniel's storage cupboard revealed little of his last fifteen years let alone his first fifteen. He did find the newspaper cuttings dealing with Mr Marx, but there were no mementoes of the previous years. He reminded himself of the information in the clippings: Declan Marx, thirty-two years old, Geography teacher, attempted suicide in front of classroom of pupils, still alive but in a coma.

What he had not connected with before was that the incident occurred in Newcastle. His childhood, east of the river, had been such a distant part of him that he'd always connected it with another place he'd moved away from; a place that until today he couldn't even imagine.

There were no cuttings following what became of Mr Marx: Daniel stopped keeping a scrapbook a few weeks later when he and his parents were on the front of pages. Daniel had always assumed Mr Marx never came out of his coma, or had died.

His mind was racing again, speeding along inconclusive superhighways, typing "Declan Marx" into his TV, reading information about the record for the person who'd been in a coma the longest, from 2017-2022. Mr Marx's biographical details were very bland, and pages recounting his suicide attempt were simply regurgitating what Daniel already knew. Mysterious benefactors had paid for, then taken

Mr Marx into their own care after three years at the local asylum. Believed to be relatives, they had maintained Marx under the supervision of local health authorities for two years, maintaining their secrecy even after Mr Marx's death.

Daniel's opening up of the whole site revealed its origins copyrighted to James Cross, dated 2024. Nothing in the site's memory explained the lack of additional information over those twelve years since.

He couldn't control his mind, couldn't defuse the ideas colliding and splitting in two, exploding into numerous questions and possibilities. He just kept repeating the mantra "Stay off the Reeto" as his head went into paranoid overload and cut out, something bleeping as it crashed with him to the floor.

LAURA GODFREY

Thundering rain instilled a greyness in the blemished sky. The smoker's room felt like Daniel's own little world and he got a sense of security from the isolation.

The woman who knocked briefly before entering was not a teacher; didn't look anything like one. Her long thick blonde hair, icy red lips, and deep blue eyes cast her more like a movie star. Her swagger swung hips from side to side, then stopping and calculating a smile before speaking: "Mr Rogan?"

"No, Mr Manion. Have you tried the staff-room?"

"Yes, they said he would be in here."

"He might be in his room in the maths block, second floor, room seventeen."

"OK, thank you. Are you the Mr Manion who teaches English and who has Reeback form?"

"Yes."

She held out her hand: "Mrs Godfrey, Kelly's mother."

"Oh, really? How is Kelly?"

"She's fine. She'll be back in school next week to see through her exams. I've just come in to make arrangements. One of the things is that I would like you to take her for English. She has talked about you in the past."

"You'll have to see the headmaster."

"I already have and he said it would be no problem."

"Good. Well, she was a very bright pupil."

"Yes. Anyway, nice to meet you. Room 17?"

"Yes."

She sauntered out, her perfume settling under the cigarette smoke.

She caught Joe smoking in his cupboard, causing him some embarrassment before he realised there was no point in trying to hide the cigarette.

"Mr Rogan?"

Joe nodded.

She held out her hand for Joe to take: "Mrs Godfrey, Kelly's mother. Don't worry about the cigarette. I believe you taught Kelly in second year?"

"Oh, yes, I remember her. She's been off a while, since. Oh, I'm sorry."

"Don't be, we've both had a lot of time to put Kelly's father's death behind us. Kelly will be back next week to see through her exams, and knowing how important maths is I was wondering if you could be hired as her private tutor?"

"Well, er, I don't know—"

"I appreciate the demands it will place on your time and that's why I have another offer which will go hand in hand with the tutoring." She took out a cigarette case, taking a stick and dangling it between her fingers to initiate a light from Joe. "I am connected with the asylum in Sector 3. Its work is concerned with educating and rehabilitating patients, making them—" She paused, just enough to add irony to, "good citizens," then neutral with, "My associate at the asylum has been looking for a top class educator, and after looking through public records we saw that you could fill that role. Your wages will be much better and there will be less hours involved than at your present occupation."

"This is a bit out of the blue. I'll have to have a look at a contract—"

"Of course, of course. I just want to know if I can confirm your interest and move on from there."

"Well, yes, it certainly is inviting."

"And I'm sure you will enjoy working with Kelly. She has matured into an elegant young woman and is eager to learn."

"I'll think about that as well. The bell will be going soon, but if you can arrange some kind of meeting so we can go through the details that would be appreciated."

"Certainly. I'll arrange something and call you." She dropped her cigarette to the floor, definitively stamping it out, twisting the toes of her shoe into the butt, concentrating on it before facing Joe as if to appraise him: "You certainly don't look like a teacher, Mr Rogan. Can I call you Joseph?"

"Joe."

"Joe. Laura."

She offered her hand again, like a blessing, departing with an air of reluctance.

Daniel waited with the rest in a bleak, underfed bus queue, waiting for spluttering buses to emerge from the smog, craning his neck along the line.

A display at the stand flashed up red figures illuminating the time at twenty-second intervals. In between, bus information and messages such as "Ever thought of a holiday? A free trip to the Amazon theme park. See Coki Coli cans for details. 16:49. Eat at MacDolland's. Three burgers for the price of two. A great family day out. 16.50. The Bremar Bus Company thanks you for your support."

No one spoke in the queue, merely checking watches, growing more impatient when several bleeped unsimultaneously at 17.00.

Language had become redundant. Too emotional. Apart from confirmations, instructions and brand names, words came as commodities with a price. Words could get you killed. So everything has been worked out for society, from bus numbers to credit cards, pass numbers to prices; communication is no longer necessary.

When the bus finally arrived, those boarding ahead of Daniel merely presented credit cards and uttered a number and a cost to indicate their destination.

"Roseberry Hill, Pourische Road," said Daniel insouciantly, which seemed to alert everyone on the bus to blink in his direction before nervously turning sight back to the grubby windows.

As the bus jolted forward no one spoke, all avoiding the sticky business of eye contact, glued instead to the vidscreen convulsively spewing out adverts and "Infotainment". It was an escape from living, one they held onto desperately, fully concentrated on glamour adverts for *The Shine* and short news bulletins about the NRP's bright shiny plans for the future: A new cancer-preventing water scheme, a further investment in Workscheme, statistics on booming consumer-spending paying for healthcare schemes, health trusts lowering prices and improving productivity due to a competitive market place. This was a new and gleaming Capitalism with a social conscience and you had to be proud of it.

In white neon at the foot of the screen, bleeps preceded the appearance of a number, indicating whose ticket was up and had to "Please alight the bus".

Joe turned up at Daniel's flat late evening, had the stuff to take them into the cold labyrinth of the Stoned Zone, where everything lasts a lifetime, where the everyday objects of an automatic life become infinitesimally interesting. You can penetrate the surface, give life to the inanimate.

Joe shuffled the pack of dog-eared cards, selected one and placed it face down on the table." Nine of spades," he said, turning the card face up to confirm its identity. "Your turn."

DM selected a card, laid it face down, touching the corners: "Queen of spades," and he was right.

Another card for Joe, "Ace of hearts," correctly guessed.

"King of diamonds," countered DM. "Piece of cake."

A fresh pack of cards was presented, Joe holding aloft the old pack above a bin: "God, or whoever's out there, bless this pack which has served us so well." He dropped it and crossed himself.

DM dealt as Joe fiddled with a joint.

"Enjoy this, DM, because it was goddam expensive and I'm not buying anymore while the price is so high." He lit, inhaled deeply. "What do you reckon to this Laura?"

"Nice body."

"She was flirting with me."

"You gonna take the job?"

"Probably. Do you know much about Kelly?"

"Great pupil. I don't know what she'll be like after nearly two years away." He dealt the last card at Joe. "Your luck's out Joe."

"She's a cruel beast. I wonder if we added up all the games we've played over the years who'd come out on top."

"Evens, sure shot. Tens of thousands each."

"We've played a lot of cards."

"We're the gods 'n' the cards we play determine the fates of distant planets as yet undetected by science."

"You certainly have an imagination, DM."

"Life is vivid if you use your imagination. And the imagination excuses everything. You can get away with anything just by saying it was your imagination. But you can never fake it. There has to be some link with the real world, albeit tenuous, to draw people in. You've got to use that bit of reality as a springboard to leaving it behind."

"Did you ever get round to burying that disk of your book?"

"Yeh."

"Where?"

"Shit, I can't remember. It was on New Year's Day, down that street. Yeh, fuckin' hell, that street I grew up along. Joe, I found where I used to live. I, I, I'd never remembered it until that day—"

"OK, OK, get blissed and don't get heavy. Tens of thousands each and this is a decider. If you win I'll listen to your crackpot childhood, if I win you'll join me in the Reeto."

"What was your childhood like, Joe?"

"Come on, take the bet and I'll tell you the fantastic and amazing adventures of Joseph R as a child, and even listen to yours."

"On. I've got a three."

"Go…"

Joe won the game and DM only remembered what his forfeit was for losing.

"You can make anything interesting because everything is interesting. This Earth is fascinating and I can find everything in it interesting. Look, pick a subject, a word."

"Huh. Er, aviation."

"Bummer. Well, what makes a great pilot?"

"Getting off the ground, flying somewhere, landing."

"Yeh, but imagine being one, being in the cockpit. Imagine the control, imagine what goes through their heads. He's checking dials, high in the clouds, and he can't think about bread and butter stuff. It's got to be fifty-cups-of-coffee-awareness, pinpoint accuracy in everything he does. A minuscule fault in a plane's structure once brought it crashing to the ground. He's got to know everything, know the consequences of everything. He hits turbulence, something is wrong, and he has to get the plane through it. But suddenly he's thinking about his wife, his marriage falling apart. It would be so easy for him to crash it. He remembers the training he went through, learning what circuits do, what metal fatigue is, all the details of how an aeroplane works. But it's all empty. It doesn't mean anything. He's going to take this baby down. He's going to see if there's a heaven. He puts the plane into nose-dive. He wants passengers to feel the fear, to touch their god. Plunging at hundreds of kilometres a minute he can hear the screams but he's oblivious to all but his destiny—"

"DM! Fuckin' stop! I'm there! Fuckin' stop!"

"Me too! What a trip!"

"Fuck. Here's one for ya: carrier bags. Go on, make them interesting."

"Think about those crinkled supermarket bags you always see stuck in trees. Think about where they've been, whose hands they were held in. From production line to supermarket, intercepted by some lonely male with no family or friends, packing his weekly shopping of meals and sanitation for one. Give him a history, give him a storyline, and he'll be bleeping at your door to murder you."

"Yor exhausting me, DM."

The televisual unit kept them hooked; a clock stuck at 23.58; the world outside burning.

A plane crash had killed 250 and the news had amateur footage to revel in.

PM Mitchell Portman was shaking hands on his "peace mission" in the Middle East. He made time with diplomats from Saudi Arabia, finalising plans preventing Iraq from lowering the price of oil.

From there, Portman met up with US businessmen in Indonesia… "Making efforts to provide aid for Indonesia whilst also being aware of the needs of East Timor. We are trying to use diplomacy to bring peace."

At a weapons fare in Jakarta, Portman urged businessmen from third-world countries to buy Anglo-American "machine tools" which could be easily converted into deadly weapons following a few simple instructions. The news only reported "A big agricultural tools order." Missile launching tractors no doubt.

After the success of his space flights to The Moon, millionaire Rupert C Donald was planning to build a theme park on Mars and start a colony, offering executive packages taking in The Moon and Mars.

A second female murder victim had turned up in East Tyneside, this time in Sector 27. Her body had similar mutilations to the first victim. Police discounted a theory of the Manchester Slicer moving north, though the killings did hint at a copycat. A spokesman for the police talked up their record in catching criminals, seeking to convince that, "The murderer will be caught."

A man had been arrested at a Techno-market for selling home-cloning kits and the DNA of famous dead people. The news presented the story with a humorous slant, skipping over the facts to present visuals of whom among the famous dead might be cloned. Expensive graphics and laconic vocals took viewers through possibilities from Noel Edmonds to Hitler, ending with, "Just think, your next door neighbours might even have Madonna as a lodger."

A final item told the story of a young man who had taken drugs and thought he could fly. He jumped from his bedroom window, broke both his legs, damaged his spinal chord and fractured his skull. He was in a garden, in his wheelchair, kicking a football then wheeling himself forward to kick it again.

"William regrets what he did, every time he watches his mates running around on a football pitch."

There are images of William on the sidelines, watching his friends athletically chasing a ball, shouting and laughing.

"But he has used the tragedy to re-shape his life. He's grateful that he didn't die and he wants to pass that message on to schoolchildren."

William's in a classroom, edited to say, "I thought it was a good buzz, I thought I could do anything, I thought they'd lied to me about drugs. Oh yes, feeling cosy, feeling blissed, I thought it was the best thing in the world. But it messed with my head and now I can't walk, can't play football, can't do most of the things I used to take for granted…"

"What a dick!" exclaimed DM. "If he thought he could fly why didn't he try taking off from the ground first. Check it out. You don't see ducks lining up at elevators to fly south. What a fuckin' dick. He's a moron, he deserves it. Use your fuckin' brain, work it out. Shit!"

In disbelief DM had to continue, to use and expel something within him. "For once I wanna see a positive drug story on the news: 'Today a young man on pot realised that all matter is merely energy condensed to a slow vibration, and there is no such thing as death because life is just an illusion and we are the imagination of ourselves. Here's Tom with the weather.' "

"Sounds familiar," said Joe.

"Only to the sacred few."

The weather skipped over rain, low clouds and temperatures to get to the country's air pollution warnings, red triangular symbols indicating the worst affected areas and how long people could spend outdoors.

"Are you here, Joe?"

"Is there acid rain coming down?"

"Yeh."

"Is everything burning?"

"Yeh."

"I'm here."

Daniel went through the register at a leisurely pace, hangover still working its way out of his system. He only really noticed his surroundings when a voice perked up, "Sir, my name wasn't read out."

He looked up to where the hand was raised.

"Kelly, oh, sorry. It's nice to have you back."

She had grown elegant indeed, her face somewhat pale and distant, flourished by a hint of natural rouge in her cheeks; her smile the perfect antidote to the century; her long blonde hair thickened by the darker strands of womanhood.

The face and the moment stayed with him in the smoker's room during a free period. It had been so long she seemed like a different person, a stranger with no past to know about other than the death of a father in a car crash.

He found his mind walking the street where he had grown up. His half-formed self-questioning produced no answers, never finding the source of his problems, merely running around in ever-decreasing circles.

During the day's lessons thoughts of Kelly Godfrey and attempted thoughts about his childhood disrupted his teaching. But he got through it on automatic, retrieving errors masterfully and playing down mistakes with a joke.

Fifteen minutes after the bell sounded to end the school day, science teacher Kate Flowers intercepted Daniel's exit.

"Hi Dan. Thank god that's over."

"We keep ticking off the days."

"A few of us are going for drinks if you want to come?"

"Who's going?"

"Peter, Mike, Liz, Cameron, John, a few others."

It wasn't Daniel's scene; fishing for conversations, forcing anecdotes, trying to appear witty and clued-up. These occasions always turned into a ritual back-stabbing of those not present. But he liked Kate enough to be persuaded by her smile.

"Good," she said, genuinely happy amid her surprise. "I'm driving if you want to come with me."

"Thanks."

Daniel had shared a night of inter-spatial exploration with Kate five months ago when she'd first begun working at the school. They'd never been as close since, though they often engaged in conversations about the universe to escape the confines of work.

During the drive Kate talked about her latest investigations. She had a soundwave monitor and had been taking readings from various points in the area, learning that those from the hills, the asylum and The Institute Of Science matched those coming towards the Earth. In her big imagination she envisaged an alien race trying to make contact.

This led to Kate and Daniel discussing the strange lights that had been seen recently over the hills, dismissed by the news as an electrical storm.

In the pub all the usual suspects were sat around several tables pushed together. Daniel wanted it to end as soon as he sat down.

John Cogburn had interrupted his flow to flick out greetings before continuing: "What have innocent people got to fear from the reintroduction of the death penalty? They are gonna have rigorous checks to make sure people are guilty. This country's going down the sewer with all these terrorists, murderers and paedophiles. It's about time we had the bottle as a society to do something about it."

"Little" Frank Horation clocked in (and the "little" referred to his intellect): "Well, it's bloody lunatic liberals. I mean, I'm a teacher so I'm pretty liberal, but some of the ideas that some people put across are ab—so—lutely crazy. I was hearing today that the boyscouts were being forced to allow homosexuals to become team leaders. Imagine that– your child on a camping weekend with a homosexual! I sometimes think the NRP allows these things to show how stupid the left have become in this country."

Heather had some voice of reason but, "Maybe we should have the bottle to be a more liberal society," was always going to be drowned out.

"What will fate throw up?" pondered Daniel. "How can I get away from this? What moment is going to mark my presence in this scene? Something embarrassing? I spill my drink, make pathetic apologies. God, I could be at home by now. What am I doing here? I have a list of six things to do for Ted K and I need to find some time for a drug-bliss so all this shit can slip out of me."

Daniel noticed Cameron urgently massaging his pen and wondered if the pen-top was going to be caught, flicked into somebody's drink for all-round hilarity. Boom, it was.

Liz repeatedly lifted her wine glass to her lips to sip, not bending her eyes away from the speaking faces, ready to add her bit: "Well, I didn't vote for the NRP but at least they are trying to change things."

Daniel had disengaged the conversation, wondering instead at Kate and wanting to fall in love with her. He wanted to be alone with her, to have fate bring them together so he wouldn't have to make the effort or risk the ignominy of rejection.

He grew angrier the more his beautiful thoughts were battered by raised voices spewing bullshit.

DM could feel himself warming up, waiting to speak, waiting for a pause. It was going to be so powerful, so impressive. He felt himself reach a point ready to explode.

It was a moment when all the principal speakers seemed to be happy, having reached agreement on what kind of society they wanted; a consensus formed by disinterested nods.

DM clicked in: "You can't call these people lunatics, they're radicals, and at least Radicalism has an agenda. Give me Left versus Right so we can at least see their colours. Then all us lefties can take clubs and bats to these moronic, bigoted liars on the right. 'Cos that's all they are, dressing up their policies with appeals to morality, saying single mothers are a burden so they cut benefits to keep families together, locking up petty criminals and activists in order to maintain a so-called stable environment. Just watch the news, everything's all right. No, the new immigration laws don't hound minorities out of their home, out of the country, back to countries where they will be persecuted; they decrease the burden on white middle-class families. Praise be! They help cut taxes so everyone can absolve themselves through their unanimous shared greed. Wake up you people, they're lying to you. This government still sells arms to dictators, still make deals with The Man. Fuck 'em. It's simple what should be done: hound all capitalists from their homes, chase them through the streets with cattle prods, then chuck them on a bonfire. Guy Fawkes was a genius!"

A stunned silence: a deep, burning silence more embarrassing than throwing up all over the table.

"Sorry, I thought I was at the meeting at the docks. That must be tonight," added DM with some panache, just to get them laughing and forgetting.

He remained quiet during the subsequent small talk before making his excuses to leave.

Daniel found some sympathy from Kate on the way home, instilling him with the courage to ask her into his flat for coffee. She had something planned already. And maybe she did, but for Daniel it was heartbreaking and he would never try it again. "Because that's what adults are like," he thought to himself as he found consolation in the dust.

On returning to her flat in Sector 5, Kate immediately bleeped on all the machines inside her attic before opening a window in the roof and positioning her telescope. At her computer she looked through the ultrasound waves that had been recorded in her absence. Again she was able to decode them into the English language. Though they were garbled they had a semblance of meaning:

WARSDB FNHASE KAF TO CLEARKL OF ASYLUIME.

Kate noted the 131st use of the word "TO", the 98th of "OF", the 8th of "KAF" and the 15th of a word like "Asylum".

Having tapped into the asylum's computer previously she had found little information other than patient records of varying detail. She had selected records at random, like Adrian Mearson whose file merely showed date of admittance and list of numbers. Some, like Emma Brannigan had considerably more detail; admitted 2018, released 2021, a list of medicines and "Altered", a file which gave evidence of the woman's new life in Manchester as a computer operator. Whatever the records did reveal, Kate could make no connection with the ultrasound waves from outer space. The fact that those readings also matched those coming from the asylum only made her more convinced there was a connection.

Her brain meandered through a maze of ideas, finding dead ends then rewinding to take another route. It would not come to her though the conspiracy theories kept her amused.

Taking a break she made contact with Moz from The Astros, her astronomy group. They had been following up her leads, concentrating attention on what was happening on the hills.

Moz had taken the Cocktail Suicide 8 up to the hills to investigate with him. He relayed to Kate that they had found a frost-like substance covering patches of grass and that they found it worked as nourishment for vegetation. In addition, Institute Of Science vehicles had been making regular journeys to the hills. Moz had also linked events to the asylum but could only suggest that it had something to do with the rehabilitation of inmates, and that perhaps the brainwashing had an even more sinister purpose than they supposed.

Unable to make any further progress Kate took to working on her reply to the ultrasound waves.

"We are waiting for you, DM. You know what to do..." boomed a voice from his wake-up system.

Then the character began singing, very slowly, the words backwards.

"Fuck!" Daniel choked in aggressively hushed tones, planting his fist in the pillow, reaching up to connect with the electric shock from the loose wires at the back of his alarm. It got him upright and ready to move.

He felt ill, a pain in his stomach demanding that he slow down, that he didn't enjoy the cigarette so much as he waited for a late bus.

Six minutes and one second late, he though as he checked his watch. Six minutes and three seconds. Six minutes and ten seconds. It would come within the next minute. He would count it down.

In daylight the CCTV cameras seemed peculiarly more sinister, moving slowly in semi-circles, the whirr always audible if you concentrated. Maybe it was just the sense of vulnerability from being viewed in daylight, but Daniel kept his head down and continued counting.

Eight minutes and twenty-three seconds late and two buses arrived.

Numbers, directions, signs. Automated Living, here is your path and your destination.

"Bleep", he paid for his newsdisk. "Bleep", he took his ticket for the train, behind all the bleeps complaining about it being four minutes late.

Joe met him on the train, but they didn't talk much – their unwritten rule for working mornings, giving them time to get their heads in gear.

Through rubbish-strewn waste-ground the train eked out a slow progression, taking in all the sights: factories bellowing, buildings crumbling, shiny new shopping complexes, vandalised walls, violent streets.

Daniel was struck by the slow insidious deterioration, deteriorating into an ugly, mechanical world. All the beauty had gone, replaced by machines desperately eating the air to squeeze out one more dollar. There was no more beauty to see, no more innocence in the little foolish things that once sparkled.

Life to Daniel no longer felt like some great ride filled with little unexpected pleasures. It had become a pulseless, hard, inexorable slog. Even finding compassion was difficult.

He remembered something in his memory banks, a picture of a man, high above the ground, balancing on a branch, his arms in a locked hug around a tree. And many of those who had gotten access to the picture probably thought he was a harmless fool. And they would never realise why he loved that tree. They would keep thinking that the job they had, the lifestyle they lived and the possessions they surrounded themselves with were important, that these things gave their lives meaning. Sure, it would all work out.

By The People, For The People

Crawling through the tunnel, they kept communications open with handcoms, timing it so they all emerged from the ground at the same time. When they did "Birmingham Ef" had already secured the vehicles and machines. They charged on Siezens Electronics' main building whilst its security was diverted by the Effers. Rampaging through the building, each of those from The Techno Anarchists used individual skills to delete files, sever communications and overload memories.

This carefully crafted and swiftly executed plan was helped by police being detained dealing with The Guthries blocking streets, playing their music and entertaining the crowds with their carnival.

Two weeks previously The Guthries had approached the police with their plans for a carnival, collecting money in aid of "Arts For Children". The police couldn't refuse. That the carnival got out of hand and blocked their route to Seizens was an unfortunate accident, thought up by DM during a free period.

'Phone Bug' finalised their plans by making a recording of the statement DM had given them. An estimated eighty per cent of communication lines would be intercepted to broadcast the message.

"Nature Against Technology" were working closely with "Phone Bug", setting up explosions at power-points throughout the country to disable communication lines for a few hours whilst activists began the revolution. They needed to be very precise so that widespread confusion would allow the activists to take some sort of control before "Phone Bug" re-opened lines to broadcast the message.

Ted K moved houses every day whilst in London, directing "Phone Bug", "Nature Against Technology" and "Corporate Watch" in their operations. He used The Freedom Network to pass on instructions to DM or request information.

DM circulated information to those revolutionaries working in the media, preparing dossiers on RCM Enterprises, Coki Coli, the NRP, CIC, MacDolland's, Shellac and Su-Hi Incorporated, principally. This would be made known to the masses at some point midway through the revolution in order to gain support.

Some printed pamphlets were already distributed to lay the seeds of the truth, placed into some of the nation's consciousness to incite or merely inform.

DM drew together environmental groups to begin demonstrations at sites where buildings now replaced landscape. Places where protests were already operating to prevent construction beginning would be reinforced by people in nearby villages and towns.

"Reclaim The Streets" were placing organisers all over the country, carefully selected to appeal to the general disposition of whatever village or town was targeted, able to encourage them to join in a "Peaceful protest". In addition, "Reclaim The Streets" were receiving plans from DM on which motorways to block and where to join "The Guthries" in street carnivals.

Those groups against cloning and genetic engineering would be protesting outside various outlets of RCM Enterprises. The more militant were planning arson attacks.

DM passed on locations to Ted K of left-wing groups dotted around the capital. From there Ted K drew together minority groups and unemployed musicians who would surround the Houses of Parliament.

It was important that the revolution was as peaceful and good-natured as possible so artists, theatre groups and street entertainers were contacted to add to the carnival. Even Adam, down and out busker with an acoustic guitar who plied his trade around Newcastle city centre, got involved.

They were a multi-racial, multi-faceted collection of groups and individuals, but DM found a common thread which linked them and gave them one ideology.

THE BIG COMEDOWN

The Red section of *Stoned News* had quite a bombshell:

A recent report, disowned by the government, suggested that in the past thirty-five years mental illness amongst twenty-fifty year olds has increased by 400 per cent. The report blamed the proliferation of designer drugs, particularly amphetamines, charting the boom in their consumption back to the turn of the millennium.

Angela, thirty-eight, was one such case: "Me and my friends used to pop pills every weekend. It was a good buzz. We always managed to get it out of our system though and get on with life." Angela had stopped taking the drugs regularly when she got married nine years ago. She gave them up completely four years ago, mainly because she had a home, two children "and not enough energy to go clubbing anymore". But over the last two years she has been suffering from insomnia and hallucinations. "They're like flashbacks. I'm too scared to sleep. The doctor gives me pills to help but now I'm dependent on them and I don't even know what they might be doing to me." Angela, though, was lucky. One of her friends committed suicide after years of suffering from paranoid schizophrenia. Another was agoraphobic and on medication.

The report criticised the police for being ineffective against those who made the drugs. Reference was made to five cases where scientists employed by RCM Enterprises were cleared of concocting drugs which subsequently found their way onto the streets. None were convicted because they won their argument that they were not directly responsible for the drug being manufactured outside science labs.

The report estimated that over half the population of Europe took drugs on a regular basis; a statistic which mirrored England's. One of the co-authors of the report, Professor Henry Ragalana, believed that in a generation's time there would be five times as many people in psychiatric care as there are in prisons. Indeed, psychiatric treatment was now the biggest growth area in England over the last fifteen years. "Curing mental illness," said Professor Ragalana, "is now an industry in itself. Government subsidies for treatment and reintegration mean it is a highly profitable business. Major companies are involved because they can employ cheap and disposal people from the treatment programme, doing menial jobs under the government's 'Workscheme' initiative." In conclusion Ragalana warned, "The success rate is still moving slowly and there is the danger of supply being unable to meet demand. Sometimes people are released too early. The number of mentally unstable people on our streets is probably five times conservative estimates."

The article switched attention to its own opinions:

"It remains the great irony of these times that in Holland where cannabis and other soft drugs are legal, and where hard drugs are strictly controlled, there are the least problems…"

"Cannabis is still classified as a dangerous and illegal drug in England," said Davon Hemp of Hemp World. "But when people try it and find out they've been lied to about cannabis they assume they've been lied to about all the other drugs. So, they'll try whatever's out there.

"However, the NRP refuses to budge on cannabis, merely condemning all drugs with spurious soundbites about ridding the world of evil influences. It is obvious too that the police aren't putting enough effort into catching street-pushers, but then they are worth only eight points. It certainly is the big comedown with a society waking up, dazed and insecure."

Dr Tumblety's Plans

The process could take a matter of months or sometimes many years depending on the complexity of the problems a patient suffered. Drugs were used to subdue and then delete parts of the patient's brain. The altering process required stronger drugs to make patients susceptible to new ideas through multimedia manipulation. After re-wiring parts of the brain, wordless music consisting of beats, bleeps and loops helped mesh the system together, ready for psychiatric treatment and education.

Dr Lewis Tumblety and his partner, Professor Henry Ragalana, had been pioneers in psychiatric research at the end of the last millennium. They used soundwaves to tap into people's thoughts, analysing the brain's ultrasound waves. Understanding that soundwaves are reflected back by red blood cells in the brain's arteries, and that blood flow increases when people are thinking, they were able to detect sites in the brain where schizophrenics hear hallucinations.

Tumblety was the first to see the commercial value of this and began seeking investment from businesses. Not until after Emily Spencer's death did business pick up and attract finances.

Henry Ragalana did not like the direction Tumblety was taking and he deeply resented the idea of using people to make a profit. He left Tumblety and began his own research, most notably into what goes on in the brain when a patient is in a persistent vegetative state.

Though bitter, Lewis Tumblety carried on his treatment programme, business growing every year. He took more specific alters, treated to order and had a belief that he was making important progress in securing his place in history. But as The Men began to call the shots he gradually realised he was just a cog in their wheel. His misanthropy found something to hold on to with the government license he had been given permitting him to kill a human for experimentation and research. Though he had all the guinea pigs he needed at the asylum, he used this license to exorcise his demons. Although the license was specific in stating "Homeless vagrants, criminals and old people, or unpeople with low-level intelligence" being the only ones he was allowed to kill, he found it easy to attach labels to any victims traced back to him.

From his third floor window he noticed an unmarked van arriving with police escort. He took a stimple and made his way down to sign for them. It was the first time Dr Tumblety had left his room in two days.

The police had two men bound and gagged: two more of the subversives and artists he had begun taking in in increasing numbers. The NRP paid poorly but the work didn't take long, sometimes even only involving a few injections and electroshock therapy.

After subduing them and allotting them a cell, Tumblety went through the orders' file on his handcom. One from MacDolland's wanting "Unthreatening facial features, basic grasp of English, basic level of intelligence and easily controlled". The order was for eighty-three and Tumblety could plunder from his own mind to get sixty-nine ready to go. Fourteen others, near to completion, could easily be found.

The biggest money-spinner was from Menworth Hill with an assassination order. Tumblety pushed that to the top of his list and returned to his room to look at "AL File 2" on his handcom. From the list of candidates he chose the most provenly effective, for he had always had a good record with Menworth Hill.

One incongruous name on the list reminded him of his next appointment; Laura Godfrey. There was nothing particularly disturbing about her treatment, but she had asked him to delete it from the files. Instead Tumblety kept it with his own secretive file just in case he should ever need it to use against Mrs Godfrey.

Joe felt smooth, having dressed in his most expensive clothes, bought some classy after-shave and cleaned himself to the bone: all for Laura Godfrey.

"It's a pretty rough sector," said Joe as they cruised through the debris of burned-out cars and abandoned houses.

"Yes, but I never travel alone here." She opened the glove compartment. No gloves, but a gun.

"Neat. Every modern woman should have one."

"Have you got one?"

"No, I like to use my hands if my deadly charm doesn't work."

She smiled, slowing at the asylum's gates, flashing a card to be bleeped in.

More checks followed, Mrs Godfrey bleeping them aside with flippant ease.

The cries were about; the mad pangs of pain.

"Party time," joked Joe.

"When we're done here I would like you to come to dinner. Kelly can come along as well so you can get acquainted."

"Yeh, good," he replied, somewhat perplexed and disheartened by Mrs Godfrey's need to bring her daughter. He guessed they were close.

Two knocks and she was opening the door to Tumblety's office, his secretary stuttering behind.

"Dr Tumblety. This is Mr Rogan."

Tumblety arose from his desk and shook hands with Joe, his palms cold and clammy, his eyes assessing Joe subjectively.

"Take a seat Mr Rogan," he said neutrally, though he meant it to be encouragingly.

Mrs Godfrey lit a cigarette and seated herself beside Joe, opposite Dr Tumblety.

"As Mrs Godfrey has told you, we are trying to add weight to our programme of educating and rehabilitating patients. Your record is good, Mr Rogan, and maths is a key area. You are interested, I understand?"

"Yes."

"Well, we have a syllabus you will need to look at. Not only will you be teaching maths, but also helping with inputting an ideology and philosophy. Will this be a problem?"

"Not at all. What kind of ideology?"

"Well, we take the maths, its structures and calculations, and we try to apply that to everyday life, to give it some foundation, some meaning. Our society is held together if you like, by mathematical formulae. The thought process can be made to function normally if the patient's mind is made to realise that solutions can be found for anything if a broad scientific formula is applied. On a very simplistic level, if a patient once released had to make a choice between things, he or she would be able to work out the answer and not succumb to wild impulse, paranoia or the imagination. A mathematical strategy would be able to control the mind, enabling the patient to live a successful life. You see that, Mr Rogan?"

"Sort of. I get the gist."

"It's all about creating good citizens. Drugs work as part of the programme, but we need a structured education in place as well. And we cannot get too idealistic about this. These patients have been violent to themselves and to others and what they need is to focus on obeying the rules of society so they can live effective lives."

"I'm sure Mr Rogan knows exactly what to do," said Mrs Godfrey laconically and dismissively as Joe thumbed through the file Dr Tumblety had given him.

Tumblety tried to ignore her words, concentrating on Joe: "I think it would be a good idea if you had a look at some of the work we have done."

"Well, can we make it quick, Mr Tumblety?" interrupted Mrs Godfrey. "We have plans for later."

Tumblety twisted his lips to suppress an anger about to surface as condescension. "It will be," came tersely from his mouth.

Despite a "No smoking" sign Mrs Godfrey continued to take licks off her cigarette as she followed Joe and Dr Tumblety along the yellowish corridors.

Joe enjoyed the horror of it, the sense of excitement and superiority, hearing the mad screams and glancing through small windows to view broken bodies going through the gamut of idiocy.

When Mrs Godfrey had finished her cigarette she halted the other two by announcing she had to make a phone call and would return to collect Joe in ten minutes.

The patient Joe viewed was a girlish looking woman with straggling long mousy hair. Her pale skin quivered with a fevered look.

"Melissa Stanton," began Tumblety. "She's under sedation at the moment due to her aggressive behaviour. She fears everything that is living, even down to tiny insects. Her way of reacting is to hit out and kill. Still a virgin at thirty-three, she has extreme agoraphobic reactions. This affects her whole personality, but we have made some progress reducing her violent tendencies. Melissa, look at me. Look at me, Melissa. Now, tell me what your dreams are, Melissa."

Melissa quivered, made several motions with her mouth before the words came out: "A nice house. I want a nice house with a nice televisual unit. I want a nice car and a nice family and to be normal again. I want to take my kids to MacDolland's for their birthdays—"

"OK, thank you." Tumblety turned away, led Joe out of the cell. "You see, Mr Rogan, we have been able to take her recovery so far, but we need that extra push to be able to get inside and re-wire her brain. Come."

Joe stood a while, voyeuristically peeking at the agoraphobic virgin through a small window in the door.

Inside the next cell a man was seated at the edge of a bed watching an old television. He looked up, flashed a fake smile then returned his eyes level with the screen. He had big ears at either side of his bald skull, standing out like inverted commas.

"Hello Frank."

"'Ello doctor," he replied morosely.

"Are you looking forward to leaving us?"

"I am, Dr Tumblety," he replied, a deadness in his tone. "I am a hundred per cent looking forward to being happy."

Mrs Godfrey breezed in to stifle Tumblety's communication with Frank. "You need to look through our curriculum, Mr Rogan," he said. "Perhaps you can come in next week?" Then he glanced at Mrs Godfrey. "I can arrange transport. There's no reason to inconvenience Mrs Godfrey."

Joe was alive to the subplot being played between the two, hazarding a guess that a relationship may have been cooled.

"Mr Rogan will be busy, Dr Tumblety. I think we should give him time to consider the offer. Besides," and she languidly smiled at Joe, "I have first grabs on Mr Rogan teaching Kelly." She squeezed Joe's arm and reaffirmed the smile.

Mrs Godfrey had arranged the meal in a restaurant in the Sheadle Sector; a gloriously expensive area occupied by rich American refugees parading their swanky dollars and patronising English culture.

Mrs Godfrey knew everybody at the restaurant, using her credit card like an aphrodisiac to add extras to the meal. She controlled the conversations with her exploits and ideas and how wonderful her daughter was. To this Kelly made little response. When they'd finished eating she spotted someone she knew and left Joe and Kelly at the table.

"You've been quiet, Kelly," offered Joe.

"I hate her," Kelly bit back. "She doesn't care about me."

"Woah. I think you are being a bit harsh there Kelly," said Joe, although he had come to the same conclusion throughout the meal as Mrs Godfrey exaggeratedly praised her daughter in between embarrassing her with innuendoes.

"She only cares about money. She's a fascist."

"Hey Kelly, check your history books, she's up against some pretty stiff competition."

"I do know my history books. I know very well what's inside a fascist and how their minds work. She voted for the NRP you know."

"So did a lot of people."

"Did you, Rogan?"

"No. Shouldn't somebody your age be listening to music and chasing boys?"

"I'm not a stereotype."

"Good."

"Sorry, I didn't mean to sound horrible, it's just her."

"So, how's school?"

"OK. I like English with Mr Manion."

"What about maths?" asked Joe, trying to bring in a jocular mod. "You know I'm going to be teaching you if I leave school for this job your mother's offering."

"Yes. I suppose I do need to improve my maths, but not for her."

There was no getting Kelly away from the subject and Joe grew increasingly impatient. Mrs Godfrey was either not interested or playing very hard to get. Joe didn't like the odds, deciding he would play hard to get himself when she returned.

"Sorry about that Joe. I hope Kelly's been keeping you entertained."

"Sure."

"I insist you come back to the house and let me fix you a nightcap. We have a spare room and I can take you to work in the morning."

"It's a nice offer and one that only a fool could refuse, but tonight I am that fool. I have a lot of work to do for school tomorrow. Maybe next time."

He caught sight of Kelly smiling as her mother was lost for words before quickly riding the disappointment and composing herself finger-click quick: "Oh well. Still, at least I know I've got a professional."

Mrs Godfrey returned Kelly home before driving Joe back to Sector 9.

"Thanks for the meal," he said.

"My pleasure." She leaned over to kiss him on the cheek, resting her left hand on his thigh, letting the kiss linger before pulling back. "I look forward to working with you." Her hand remained in place a while longer.

Joe had a flashback of the state of his flat with its empty beer cans and porno mags possibly left conspicuous. He couldn't invite her in and therefore he couldn't make a move. But he contented himself that although she was playing hard to get it wasn't hard enough for Joe not to crack.

In Action

Back on the beat. "I hate this. I hate this," Daniel muttered to himself as he shuffled from flat to bus-stop feeling the well-oiled conspiracy crunching between metal cogs. He was part of it; getting up at a prearranged time, catching the 38 bus, bleeping the fare, timing it to catch a bleeping train to a bleeping job. Dog-tired, he tried to remember the last time he was sane and acted like that.

The bus moved a few centimetres every minute, stuck in traffic behind other buses from other companies and cars whose drivers drove because buses were too slow.

The machine breathed as gears wrenched themselves to change, wheels spluttering to get moving before slowing in a queue of cars spluttering and coughing, feeding out to pedestrians spluttering and coughing.

It wasn't worth it. DM got out and began to walk. It gave him pleasure to move passed stationary cars, the engines growling out their poisons, the drivers blaming the rest of the world for holding them up.

DM waved at them for kicks, got some V-signs back for bigger kicks.

He reached the train station late and had to catch the next train, which was OK because it gave him time for a cigarette. A really good cigarette. A really good drug that he knew could give him cancer or heart disease. A legal drug making pots of money for the government. He remembered a fact about ABT (American British Tobacco) having developed a safe cigarette and a memo showing that Sir Patrick Sheay had suppressed it because its production might imply that ordinary cigarettes were dangerous. DM felt guilty but there was no other choice: he was addicted like millions of smokers throughout the world.

The train came its usual eight minutes late. On it, no human being showed happiness. They were slouched, their hands hung on leather rungs, desperate to make it to their employment on time, crossing off hours to the weekend.

Daniel arrived late to his lesson, receiving a message from the teacher minding his class that the headmaster wanted to see him.

His mood didn't improve, though he was past the point of caring. When he noticed an advertisement had been pinned up in his classroom extolling the virtues of MacDolland's, he tore it down in front of his Year 11 class. Against his will he had been compelled to allow advertisements in his classroom for things like milk, computer games, magazines. He didn't like it but he could convince himself he could rationalise the products' value. MacDolland's was too much and he used the poster in his lesson to explain the evils of Capitalism.

At break-time he went to see Randolph Hillier, the head teacher. He was warned about his lateness, told he was very close to falling into the bottom three of the league table because of the paucity of his parent-contracts. With this the head worked himself into a frenzy, climaxing in notification that representatives of the examining board were coming in to look through his lesson plans. The essays Daniel's class had produced in the interim exam had revealed diversions from the curriculum.

Daniel reasoned that he wasn't preparing them for model answers, but to think for themselves.

Hillier wouldn't budge, issuing further warnings but not revealing when the examiners would be coming into school.

It only fired DM up for the day's remaining lessons. He took his first-year class on a wondrous flight in their imaginations, landing at a place where people enjoyed themselves, playing games under pollutionless skies.

His second year class was a little more difficult to motivate. By age eleven or twelve children have all the basic education they need and those at East Tyneside Comprehensive had few aspirations because they knew they could never afford them. DM did well to introduce a passage from *A Kestrel for a Knave* to get the second-years to discuss how those in power abuse it.

The Year 11 class he had begun the day with returned for last period. David Weaver, who had recently returned to school after a year away, had lost his Ritalin tablets and was in an antagonistic mood. Daniel only had the energy for sarcasm to combat his belligerence, eventually sending him out when he lost control.

At the end of the day as he packed his belongings away, Kelly Godfrey lingered back into the classroom.

"Hello Kelly. Is everything OK?"

"Yes. Those were good lessons today, especially the first lesson. I really enjoyed it."

"Thank you. It's nice to be appreciated."

To Daniel she looked beautiful, poised as she was, slightly nervous as she prepared to speak, playing with and repeatedly pushing back her hair.

"I was wondering if you had any disks about Marxism I could borrow?"

"Marxism! Gosh Kelly, I didn't know you were interested in that sort of thing."

"Dad used to be a socialist. When I was off I looked at lots of political disks, and I've joined lots of environmental websites. I'm in the Eco Warriors y'know. I kind of thought you were probably a socialist."

"Well, don't tell anyone," he joked, placing a finger on his lips. "They'll lock me up."

A refreshing laugh invigorated her whole body, relaxed her tension.

Daniel felt clumsy in the pause, like the lovesick teenager he had never had the chance to be. He couldn't help but stare longingly into her eyes until it vaguely unsettled her.

"Yes, I can copy some of my disks if you like. I can bring them in on Monday."

"Thank you, sir."

He had the idea to say, "Call me Daniel," but his in-built corn-monitor would never allow it.

"I hear Mr Rogan is going to be taking you for maths tuition?"

"Yeh. I suppose I need to get better in maths."

"It can't hurt. Your English skills certainly don't need any extra tuition."

"Pity. I love English."

Daniel could feel himself becoming entangled in something, feeling an incredible urge to offer his teaching skills.

She left abruptly to be picked up by her mother, but the experience had heartened Daniel enough to join Joe for a drink in O'Thwacke's pub.

"How are things with Kelly's mother?" he asked Joe. "You in?"

"Oh yeah, she's keen. She's playing hard to get though. She's classy but I don't know if she's worth the effort. I think she's working on commission too."

"Why?"

"She's got something going with this guy at the asylum, Dr Tumblety—"

"Tumblety? Big bloke, grey beard, glasses?"

"Boom."

"He's my doctor."

"No shit. Well, I'm gonna be teaching his crazies. There's some friction between him and Godfrey and I don't know what it's about.

Mind, the money's good and there are fewer hours than this teaching bullshit."

"I don't trust Tumblety. I haven't been to see him in years 'cos he's so weird. He's certainly working on commission."

"Yeh, it must be working with all those crazies. But y'know, if this Godfrey's as keen as she seems then I might retire and live off her in her swanky mansion."

"You've got it sorted than. How's Kelly?"

"Well, she's a little weird but she's got her head screwed on. She hates her mother though, thinks she's a fascist."

"She's got some tough competition."

"That's what I said."

"Hello boys," announced a foreign female voice.

It was the woman from New Year's Eve, outside Gigi's. Joe wanted to speak but was preoccupied with trying to remember her name.

"Kristen, isn't it?" asked Daniel.

"Yeh. I saw the both of you come in and I tried to think. Then I remembered you two helping me one night."

Kristen had a dynamism in her eyes that hadn't been there on that drunken night, a lucidity in her pale complexion like some kind of re-awakening. She wore a black jumper, casual, faded blue trousers. Her long brown hair, smartly combed and straight, added to a restrained sex appeal which both Joe and Daniel were drawn to.

"I'm sorry, but I don't remember your names," she said apologetically.

"Joe."

"Daniel." He was halfway to being in love with her, but then he was halfway to being in love with a lot of females. "You are from Denmark right?"

"Yes."

The lilting accent in her English gave off a sensuous vulnerability as she talked about why she was in England, what she liked and disliked about England and how she was concerned about the rise of nationalism throughout Europe.

When Zeke, Aisha and Barney arrived to collect her, DM couldn't let the coincidence pass.

They spoke with hints and innuendo, enough for DM to realise Kristen was joining in with preparations for the revolution and that they were targeting The Institute Of Science that night.

"Was that the army of the people's revolutionary front?" asked Joe sardonically as Daniel returned.

"Yeah yeah yeah. Come on, amon nino."

Two empty beer glasses were left with froth slipping back into the base.

The city centre was warming, carefully regulated excitement festering with neon beats as police cars patrolled to pick up some points before the end of the season.

S*T*E*P*H*E*N* had snapped. In one hand he held a cue, in the other he swished the air with a kitchen knife as the crowd closed in on him. On the floor a young man lay, bleeding from the stomach, screaming for help, his bloodied hand trying to plug the hole.

"Back off you fuckers! 'Ee was fuckin' screwing me."

Seeing his chances diminishing as the group moved closer, he charged for the exit and into the darkness.

Shavenhead leaned down to the blood-soaked youth:

"Listen. Shut the fuck up and listen." The youth calmed his sobbing. "This bloke 'ere is gonna take ya down the hospital right. You don't make any noises and don't give 'im any fuckin' bother right?" The youth nodded as a fat bloke dragged him up and out through the back door. From there he would be taken to the river, finished off and dumped.

Joe and DM entered cautiously, always giving some percentage to the chance that they might meet Stephen.

"Shit," said Joe on seeing the blood being mopped from the floor.

DM had sussed the place: "It's clear. Let's monkey."

Joe made for the toilets.

"A century of dust," he requested. As the drug chauffeur fingered in his soap box Joe asked, "What's gone down in there?"

"Some fuckin' mad cunt stabbed a kid. Nowt special."

"Any chance that it was an ugly-looking guy, plays pool, has the name Stephen tattooed on his arm?"

"Y'know him?" he asked, withholding the drugs briefly.

"Nah, just ran into him once."

"If the fucker comes in 'ere again 'e's dead."

Joe nodded sagely, took the drugs, overstepped the mopping and joined a worried DM outside.

"The pot's gone up again, DM, so it's the good old dust. But hey, good news: that little piece of art on the floor was our friend Stevie's work. Our man said if he goes back in there he's dead. Looks like we got lucky."

"Aaaah, it's good to be back."

"We have been blessed," added DM.

"God spun the roulette wheel, placed his bet on Joe and DM and got damn lucky. Ha-ha."

Meanwhile, God, enjoying a spell in his male side, had his feet up, balanced on a star, lifting them off at intervals when his feet got too hot. In one hand he held an enormous spliff, in the other he perfected his art of the yo-yo.

His latest planet had zero gravity, inhabited by flying creatures and insects whose lives were brief due to the considerable energy spent hovering. God had given the insects all the brains just for fun, though for the moment the massive flying creatures were the brainless rulers. God had plans to create a highly developed insect which would enter his new planet to preach his world, but for the time being he merely contented himself with enjoying the spectacle of watching the insects trying to survive.

A tap on his shoulder disturbed God. It was Archangel William.

"What is it?"

"Sorry to interrupt you, God, but it's Earth."

"Oh, what now?" God sighed.

"The humans are going to destroy the planet."

"Tell me something I don't know."

"Well, er, Jesus has gone back to sort it out."

God took his feet from the star and straightened.

"Why?"

"He said he wanted to get back to his roots, to try again."

"Well good luck to him, I've washed my hands of Earth. But keep me informed."

"There's something else, God. The Inuthuans have sent some of their creations down; some to help save, some to help destroy."

"The information-gatherers? What are they playing at?"

"They think they have some sort of spiritual connection with Earth. They think it can give them clues to their own existence. I have heard they want to take it over."

"Really? I will have to seek out The Immortal then. Have the Inuthuans no sense? Earth is meant to take care of itself, that's the whole point of free will!"

"You don't have to tell me, God."

Two figures, bulbous bodies and balloons for heads, burst into Joe's flat.

"Wake up! Wake up! Reality Police, get your senses together!" shouted the blue figure.

Joe and DM sprung to their feet gracelessly.

The red balloon, his head steaming, pointed an accusing finger:

"Daniel Manion and Joseph Rogan, you are hereby charged with violating reality under Section 23, Paragraph 19.2 of The Reality Act."

The blue balloon slapped DM, the red balloon slapped Joe.

"This is a warning!" growled the blue balloon. "Any more offences and your imaginations will be revoked. Is that clear?"

"Is that clear?" repeated the red balloon after neither Joe nor DM replied.

They both nodded.

"Now," continued Blue, "Repeat after me: This is 2035."

"This is 2035," they replied simultaneously.

"The NRP is the right government for the country."

"The NRP is the right government for the country," said Joe.

"Speak!" directed Red at DM. One slap to the left, one slap to the right. "Imaginative capacity will be withdrawn if you do not speak."

"The NRP is the right government for this country," said DM, suppressing laughter.

"I'm warning you! We have the power," boomed Blue. "Repeat after me: we live in a good and free country."

They were both sniggering as they followed the command.

"You are warned!" said the increasingly steaming Red. "One more violation and it's reality for you both!"

"Look out of the window," ordered Blue. "See, it's all burning. This is reality. One more indiscretion and that's all you'll be seeing. Now, keep acting the part or you'll be burning."

A sharp pull of air drew the two figures from the room, a stench of burning in their wake.

"Fuck me," said DM. "What a goddam trip!"

"The fuckin' kitchen's on fire!"

So they panicked, put out the fire, laughed a lot and wondered how the fire had started.

"OK, best of three," said Joe, "Then I'm done. This dust has taken me some place and I don't want to go much further."

DM didn't pull himself away from the window:

"It's still burning out there, Joe."

"Come on, DM, it'll have cooled enough when you leave. The cards..."

DM took several attempts before being persuaded that it was safe to step outdoors. He moved in quick bursts on clunking streets, pausing at points to assess the dangers, his paranoia played out under the constant buzzing of overhead police planes.

A hand on his shoulder caused him to scream, turned him round to be muted by Ted K's hand.

"OK, DM," he said, letting Daniel breathe out. "Tell me how things have been going."

"Good. Where've you been?"

"London mostly, but I'll be back up here a while. We've got news that Trioxide've been letting out poisonous chemicals. I need to get something sorted for up here so I'll be back a few days. While I'm here I need you to get in touch with the CS8. I've heard they're up to something and I don't want it to mess with our plans."

"No problem. Can you give me a date yet?"

"Not quite, but things are looking good. You are very important to our plans, DM, and don't forget that. DM, are you listening?"

"Uh, yeh, nothing, it's OK."

"Have you been on the herbs again?" Ted joked.

"Uh, yeh."

"Just make sure that's all it is. Listen, get in touch with CS8, get Will to send Cassie to me and organise Newcastle Ef to help you take the city hall."

"Did you hear about Tense Tony?"

"Yeh, big shame, he was a good man. You better keep your eyes open, I suspect the NRP was behind it."

Ted K had instilled DM with enough confidence for him to search his files for disks to copy for Kelly. Daniel had decided that he loved her, that she would be this week's object of his unrequited affections.

Daniel awoke after a sleepless night with a gnawing pain in his stomach. He half-heartedly went through the net to make some contacts before downloading some news, and then he felt even worse.

The body of Louise Woodling, missing since New Year's Eve, had been found, badly mutilated. Police refused to link the murder with two other recent killings, all of them baring the hallmarks of the Manchester Slicer, or a copycat. The article reported that police wanted to contact everyone in Gigi's nightclub on New Year's Eve.

Joe's reply to the news was, "Yeh, and—?"

"We need to go to the police."

"So? We're innocent."

"It depends how you define the word, but it's only the flip-side to guilty. If we go to the pigs they'll have us."

"So we don't go."

"And then they come to us and we look guilty."

"How about flip a coin for it?"

"Heads we go to the cops. Heads would make sense."

Joe took an old penny coin from his drawer, gave it an indifferent flick and declared, "Tails."

"So the gods have decided, OK."

DARKNESS FALLS

"OK, OK, I've got to concentrate, I'm not that wrecked," thought DM, trying to sort out his brain. "I'm killing fascists tonight."

DM waited with Chuckie E, Zeke, Barney, Aisha and Kristen.

"Time," said Chuckie E.

DM straightened his Cross of St George T-shirt and made for the pub across the road, All the others except Chuckie E then dispersed into the darkness.

"Time to kill fascists. Time to kill fascists," repeated DM in his head. "OK, work it out: I'm wrecked. Just play it drunk if it shows. Think, tonight, Daniel, I'm going to be a fascist. I'm a fascist, here to share my ideology with fellow intellectuals. The man on the door is fat, his head shaved to just over one centimetre. He's very ugly. I nod to him, flash him an ID card. I imagine sticking a knife in his gut as he bleeps me through the door. I'm trying to get the smell for murder.

"People I've seen before at meetings are nodding to me. The music is an intolerable thrash, but it's a live band. Shit, a live band. They have guitars too, and a drummer. I am almost drawn in until I hear a chant about lynching Asians. I want to tell them I'm going to kill them. I've got the pleasure and feel for murder."

Deep in Sector 3 Joe has just left Dr Tumblety. He's kept himself off the dust for a bit because he wanted to look the consummate professional. But as he walks, relieved at what he'd thought was a successful day, he feels bored, tense. He finds himself accidentally on the heels of a middle-aged man. He can see the back of his head, thick black hair greased back, a clipboard in his hand.

"He's on his way home, proudly clutching the results of some survey," thought Joe. "He's not going to be missed. It would be easy, so easy, and such a thrill. I can't get caught, I'm too lucky. Life's got to be savoured, hasn't it? Every experience is something.

"This man's telling me about the niggers who are taking over England and Europe. He's telling me and I'm nodding at the right moments. He's got a little anecdote about how he and a few of his friends drove some Asians from their own home. I should have seen them crying. I should have heard all the whites in the street who came up to him and thanked him. I need to agree, to join in, then make my excuses.

"All the men at the urinals are looking at each other's cocks, nodding their heads to the dumb fuck ranting coming through the walls. I take a cubicle. I'm pulling the explosive from my arse, groaning appropriately but really feeling the relief. All's going according to plan. Kristen is so beautiful. Having her with us is such a warm coincidence, but Kelly's more beautiful. She has such innocence about her she could let me be whoever I wanted to be. Put the bomb behind the back of the toilet. These bastards are going to be blown to smithereens. So much fun to be had killing a fascist.

Joe's waiting outside a massage parlour, ruthlessly enjoying his sixth cigarette, noting the name and location of the place for future reference. He watches the clipboard man leave. Curiously he has became more human through visiting the knocking-shop; but the idea is already in Joe's head and he's already imagining how it will feel.

"Just turn into a quiet back street. It's a short cut and you need to be home. Yes, that's right, you'll be OK, nothing can happen to you. Good man, your face is going to show fear."

The flames are behind DM, sirens and alarms exulting the satisfaction within him. But one of the fascists has staggered out, quickly making his way from the scene of the crime. DM is in furtive pursuit, tapping digits into his handcom to alert Chuckie E and the others.

"Little scaredey fascist, running away, thinking he's lucky, thinking he can continue his hateful crimes. This is going to be some pleasure."

The escapee stops at a pub.

"Nice. So I'll get myself a double, neck it, and imagine how I'm going to kill you."

DM follows him out. He's feeling the thrill of the chase, the foreplay of murder.

"Are you following me?"

Joe's smile is malevolent, a pleasure fed somewhere deep inside of him.

DM's smile is malevolent and he enjoys showing it.

"I see his glossy face with the fear; the fear of the unexpected. And here I am with my complimentary asylum pen, smashing it into his eyes. He screams but I'm on top of him, holding the pen in my fist, smashing down on his throat. He's slipping away and giving up the fight. His life is at its twilight: how must it feel?"

"I kill fascist fucks!" barks DM, his words simultaneous with his boot going into the escapee's head and groin.

Chuckie E, Barney and Aisha arrive, but they stand back in shock as DM lays into the man.

"You have found the unexpected," DM thinks. "Red blood. Red blood coming from an eye socket. Mr Marx, this is for you. Bleed, you fucker."

"What's your name?" asks Joe, holding off the pen as his victim gargles through blood. "Tell me and I'll stop."

But he can't speak and he can't scream, too preoccupied with choking for life. Joe lunges the pen into his chest, his vocals produce some spat grunt, and Joe seizes on this to stab out some kind of code from his mouth.

DM's boot kicks more desperately, long after the grunts have turned to mere squelches.

"DM, he's done!" shouted Barney.

DM stepped back, breathing heavily, looking on his work.

"Fuckin' 'ell DM, and yor not even black," said Chuckie E.

"It's the ignorance, the fuckin' ignorance. The fuckin' givin' my species a bad fuckin' name. It's that what's fuckin' ruining it for all of us. I hate him 'cos he's a fuckin' racist, but more than that I hate the fucker 'cos he's ignorant and he probably reads *The Shine*. Fucker."

Joe backed off, the exhilaration coming again as he viewed his subject. He fingered inside the victim's inside pocket for an ID card: "Joseph McCreal, Jehovah's Witness."

"Now that you've found God, say hi from me."

SCHOOL'S OUT

Daniel would have stayed off work but for his desire to see Kelly and give her the disks she had requested. From the train station to school he became aware of the usual sirens, only this time they were all making for the same direction.

Fire engines, police cars and ambulances filled the school's entrance, a plume of smoke hanging over the science block. Chaotic bodies darted back and forth as short sentences ordered and exclaimed.

Randolph Hillier stood in front of a television camera:

"We have stepped up security since the last bombing, but when someone is set on planting a bomb at as necessarily open a place as a school there is little we can do."

"Do you think it was a pupil, Mr Hillier?"

"I very much doubt that."

Daniel joined Joe behind the police line.

"Anyone hurt?" he asked.

"They've taken Kate Flowers out, but I saw her, she was OK. The caretaker and the two others I don't know. The police have carted off David Weaver."

"They think he did it?"

"'Course he did. He's mental like his mother." Joe paused briefly. "Still, an early end to the day and a few days off isn't bad."

"Hillier'll want a staff meeting first, a crisis emergency debate in which he can tell us what we already know. I'll take bets it'll beat the thirty-five minutes it took us debating pupils wearing coats in corridors."

Sure enough, once the pupils had been dispersed and their joyous yells given way to the operating of vehicles, the head called a meeting. Fortunately for Daniel his stomach pains had drained his face of colour and given him a fevered brow. As he slouched past the secretary she asked what was wrong and he convinced her that she needed to tell him to go to the doctor's promptly.

"Third floor, room 4b," said a male secretary at the asylum.

Daniel guessed his way up the stairs, came to the third floor and recalled Mr Marx putting a gun to his head. Through his headache vague screams filtered; noises from fractured voices. Daniel had an unalterable sense that he had been here before.

A man in a long white coat, carrying a box under his right arm, approached Daniel. The centrepiece of his rosy face was a long white moustache that curled at the ends. When he spoke there was some degree of aristocratic eccentricity in his voice: "Can I help you?"

"I'm looking for Dr Tumblety's office."

"Ah, well, Dr Tumblety is very busy today. I am taking all his regular patients. Dr Schrödinger." He held out his hand, shook the shake with full enthusiasm. "I work very closely with Dr Tumblety. Please, come into my office."

The doctor walked cautiously along the corridor, opening an office door, looking in, then entering.

He placed the box on a desk, seemed excited as he gestured for Daniel to sit down.

"Now, you are—?"

"Daniel Manion, six seven two six nine."

"Ah, yes. And what seems to be the problem?"

He made phoney gestures as he spoke, emphasising when he added, "Don't be afraid to tell. I am a professional," like he suspected something indiscreet ailed Daniel.

"Well, I keep getting these stomach pains."

"I see. Please roll up your jumper."

The doctor's cold hands felt around Daniel's kidneys, then chest and rib cage.

"Mr Manion, from my examination it seems to me you have a problem with your kidneys. Do you drink a lot?"

"Twenty-five, thirty units a week. Is it serious?"

"Very," he said, moving around the desk, placing his hands on the box. "But we have made such strides in medical science over the last few years that your condition is not beyond our help."

He pulled open the cardboard box and took out a sheepish looking cat. He fumbled in his pocket for a pill which he forced into the cat's mouth, keeping its lethargic jaw shut as it gagged to swallow. The cat looked decidedly stoned.

"Please allow me to demonstrate, Mr Manion," he began. "This is where all the badness comes out." He lifted up the cat's tail and pointed. "Just like your kidneys the cat has a system which needs to rid itself of all bad things. And when all the bad things have gone you can have a normal life with your car, your TV, your home, your Coki Coli." He had lost but quickly recovered himself. "What we have to do is make an insertion here." The cat's eyes sparkled to life as it whined. "Therefore we can alleviate any problems with discharges."

He smiled excitedly, liked he'd stumbled on his own genius.

"When we place the organ in here the cat will either fight it and ultimately die, or will take the medication and live. I'll show you."

His rosy cheeks bulged as he steadied the cat with his left arm and began unzipping his flies with the right. As he fumbled he said, "Believe me, Mr Manion, this is an amazing advance for humankind."

Daniel knew it was wrong but he'd suddenly caught that English disease of reservedness and couldn't move from the spot.

The door being swung open coincided with Schrödinger's trousers dropping to the floor. He protested as they dragged him from the room, the cat having collapsed with relief.

Dr Tumblety appeared from behind the two bouncers:

"Give him fifty milligrams of Psecho, and then come back for that stupid cat!" He addressed Daniel with, "Mr Manion? Please accept my apologies. If you could follow me."

Room 4b: thick with the claustrophobic pungency of being lived in.

"Sit down. Number?"

"Six seven two six nine."

He called up Daniel's details on the computer, curiously involved in reading them for some time. Once he'd examined Daniel with a cold stethobeam he reached much the same conclusion as the fake doctor: "Cut down on the alcohol and try to eat better. Try to relax. Stress kills more people these days than cancer. It might be worth buying some Balance tablets."

"It's nothing to worry about then?"

"No."

"And you are always here these days?"

"Yes. If that's a problem then I can give you the name of another doctor."

"No, it's fine," replied Daniel, aware of all the paperwork that would involve for himself.

If it was only stress then Daniel could comfort himself with learning that school would be closed for a week. On the net news it was revealed that Billy Smiles, the school caretaker, had died in the explosion, not from the blast but from a heart attack. David Weaver and his mother, Melanie, had been charged with the bombing. Three injured members of staff had been released, but Kate Flowers was being kept "under observation" a while longer.

GOD STRIKES BACK

God announced his arrival with a blast of white light followed by a nonchalantly conceived rainbow. He swaggered from the heavens to float face to face with The Immortal.

"God, nice to have your presence," thought The Immortal. "Found out why we are here yet?"

"I'm sure you can work that out," thought God. "You've taken a keen interest in my planet."

"Is that a problem? I'd been led to believe you'd given up on Earth."

"I left them with free will, that's all they need. Your planet's involvement is not part of the grand scheme of things."

"Inuthuans have free will too. Surely you can accept that?"

"Yes, quite big fella, but I don't want other gods going down there."

"Rest in peace, God. The creations we have sent down are just ordinary people. They have no really special powers."

"Jesus has gone back. I hope your machines aren't going to fuck with him."

"No, no. I am surprised Jesus was interested."

"He's got a bee in his bonnet, wants to save Earth."

"Good. Many of our beings want that too. It's nothing personal. My beings are not trying to usurp your authority. Please, feel free to have an input into our world. I would dearly like to download some of your knowledge."

"I bet you would. Why don't you just read my mind?" teased God.

"Well why don't you let me?"

"Ha. Not quite all-powerful yet? You've put on some size though."

"It's knowledge, something I can see by your figure you seem to lack," thought The Immortal bitingly.

"I just take in experiences, big man. You can have all the knowledge you want but it won't give you the answer to existence. That's what infinity's all about. You are chasing your tail with this knowledge trip."

"Oh, but you don't know what I know, you've gotten complacent. Have you been to Dstbll galaxy?"

"Passed through."

"Then you won't know that all the planets in that galaxy and all the space it occupies are just a small science project in the arms of a young offspring of one of the Sun Gods."

"Really? And who created the Sun Gods?" **questioned God cheekily.** "And if you find out who created them, then who created the creators? What you won't have experienced is dancing on planets with the most beautiful gods in all infinity; creating strange and wonderful planets, each detail beautifully balanced, each colour carefully added down to the most minute detail. Like Earth. Maybe I even created you lot."

"Oh, let's not get into creationism, and let's not argue. We are both good and believe in goodness."

"Goodness doesn't mean you have to be serious about everything. Have an argument for the fun of it."

"It's not that we Inuthuans don't appreciate your sense of humour God; scattering marijuana all over Earth was good trick—"

"Yeh, get that, and they banned it!"

"We are a serious species because we have work to do. I hope you are cool with that."

"We cool. You can send your little jobs down to Earth, but if they start acting like gods or show signs of any god-like powers, then I might have to do something."

"That's fine, but it seems you are a bit behind technological and biological developments on Earth. They can create their own gods. Your little experiment has grown up."

"As long as they know I can still destroy them in a second."

"There aren't that many who've read the Bible, let alone believe it."

"That may be, but apocalypse is still just a finger-click away."

Censorship By Omission

The NRP had the support of most news websites and televisual channels as well as all the tabloids still in circulation and two out of the three broad-sheets. Rupert C Donald owned them and owned the NRP. Radio stations not closed down for "Being offensive" or "Inciting anarchy" were deemed irrelevant, reaching too few listeners.

It wasn't difficult for everything the government did to get a neat, palatable spin. Underground pamphlets and disks flourished, but of those in the mainstream only the *Guardian* site, its infrequent newsdisk and paper, and *Stoned News*, gave anything like the truth.

For the re-introduction of capital punishment the NRP had the support of the loudest voices. Parents of murdered children were dug up from getting on with their lives to proclaim "Now little Julie Can Rest In Peace, And So Can I" when it was revealed a retro system of executions would take place. Tickets were already on sale for the first lethal injection and first electrocution, set up by Rupert C Donald's "Justice Channel" who would string a whole evening of programmes around the executions.

Not many people got to hear about a clause in the new act concerning the appeals of those condemned. These would be chaired by government appointed officials who could bury files after execution and legally keep the information suppressed for a period of sixty years.

Also in the government's programme to deal with crime were powers given to the police to use drugs on suspects in order to induce flashbacks, "in order to reveal the truth behind their monstrous crimes". No mention that the side-effects were likely to mean flashbacks for the rest of their lives, guilty or innocent.

No mention either that the Indonesian government had secured weapons through the NRP whilst simultaneously continuing its ethnic cleansing of East Timor. Indonesia was: "A prime example of the New

Asian democracies" and the weapons were: "to help stabilise the country against the threat from neighbouring countries who hadn't yet achieved a total state of democracy". The fact that the only reason those neighbours were a threat was because the west had sold arms to them found no place in the news

"Infomercials" were used to gloss up whatever the NRP was doing: "Panamera is the miracle we have all been waiting for," as scientists with goggles boggled with statistics. "Panamera is the miracle we have all been waiting for" was repeated in lulled, warm tones whenever a pause allowed.

You had to look hard for the truth, had to look at what wasn't reported, but with TV guiding perception in easily digestible form, very few people had the capacity or initiative to think for themselves.

WHAT ADY MEARSON DOESN'T KNOW

"You have surpassed my expectations, Mr Rogan," said Dr Tumblety. "I think Mr Mearson is going to do very well."

"It should be interesting. How are we going to know what he's up to?"

"We have a tracking device in his stomach and a camera behind his left eye."

"Fuckin' ingenious."

"Quite. I think we should now move on to other patients and start some paired sessions. Our benefactors have a lot invested in this programme."

"Laura Godfrey?"

"Well, yes, though her concerns aren't important to our programme."

"So what's her story?"

"Well, I'm sure you know all about how conniving women are. Suffice to say she got her claws into one of our shareholders; a married, respectable man. She told him she had a disk novel of their romance written. That's how she got her shares. Do not trust her, Mr Rogan."

"I don't know what her interests in me are or what the thing is with her daughter."

"As I said, do not trust her. Enough of Mrs Godfrey, it's time we viewed Mr Mearson.

Ady Mearson walked hesitantly from the asylum. With each step away he grew to realise he had freedom, with all its possibilities. For a moment he imagines white dust. The cocaine does not give him pleasure. 'I will be the loser. I pay and I have nothing. I could spend that money on a TV.'

He heads to the safe house in Sector 3, shows his papers to an unspeaking landlady who gives him a key, puts out her fag and goes to bed.

He's alone in his room and he starts to create a picture in his head; a landscape of luscious green, a bright sky patterned with large white clouds; remembering school and learning how they were formed, remembering lessons and the excitement of knowing. But with that feeling came a switch-off and sleep.

For a week his life amounted to little more than this until he got his first rehabilitation cheque, with which he bought an old televisual set. Though the picture quality was poor, now at least he had something else to do. Whenever he thought of suicide he would either sleep or go out walking.

Once, whilst walking, he enlivened his day by phoning the police with details of where he had seen a scruffy looking woman giving out leaflets.

Norman Terrick arrived at the asylum just before daybreak, ushered quietly through the building to meet Dr Tumblety.

"You've got something for me?" Terrick asked coldly.

"Last night's transmission from Adrian Mearson."

When Tumblety received no gratification he pressed "bleep" to display the recorded events.

Ady Mearson was on one of his walkabouts, though this time invigorated by a purpose, following in Barney Cradley's footsteps.

The night-time vision made Terrick ask, "Who's he following?"

"Barney Cradley, known activist."

Terrick nodded as the action continued to unfurl. In three abrupt movements the visuals were at Cradley's back, a kitchen knife appearing as he turned, lashing down into his skull. Blood blurred the screen before a hand appeared to wipe it moderately clean.

It was over quickly, a brief view of the lifeless body before images rushing unsteadily over paving stones, at which point "bleep" turned it off.

"What happened next?" asked Terrick.

"He went back to the safe house, watched televisuals and went to sleep."

"Excellent. And what becomes of him now?"

"He'll continue going about a routine. We may give him menial tasks. He may make it as an Exterminator, but we'll test him out on other things first."

"Good. What about Marx?"

"I'll know more tomorrow. We may even have him by the end of the week."

Terrick puckered his lips, satisfied with his evil:

"Keep up the work Tumblety. I'll report your success." By way of a side comment he added, "Does Mearson drink Coki Coli?"

"All the time, and eats nothing but MacDolland's. He only watches the RCM channels and he's been a good informer too."

"Good. And remember, we can't have too many psychopaths out there. We need a few model patients who can shake hands with Portman."

"Oh, yes," agreed Dr Tumblety like he'd just remembered.

"I've got thirty tonnes of Reeto for you to disperse. Get back to me as soon as anything happens with Marx."

When Terrick left it was Tumblety's turn to indulge a diabolic smile, rewinding the tape to play again.

A Cultural Chernobyl

From out of the turning world emerged the words *Your News,* growing to fill the screen and kick off a pounding techno-soundtrack. Amid recordings of wars, disasters and images of sensational headlines, came the faces of news-presenters, looking tough and determined, their names and labels in bold letters.

"The slaying continues. Another victim of the Manchester Slicer is found."

A thud-thud pause.

"Police under pressure. One hundred officers add to investigations." Thud-thud.

"Iraq bombed again. MoD reports best attack yet."

The soundtrack changed subtly, not exactly mellow but moving in that direction, the thud-thud pierced by a simultaneous bleep-bleep.

"Pop sensations Superkids call it a day."

"Bleep-bleep."

"And Newcastle beat Brixton in Championship Decider Weekend."

Bleep-thud-thud, *Your News* from the centre of the Earth.

"Good evening. Police today identified the Manchester Slicer's latest victim as Rachael Sampson…"

"There was a Rachel Sampson in my class at school," announced DM, then abruptly left the idea. "Is it gonna be on time, Jez?"

"Sure, this is an easy one," he said, his eyes and fingers concentrated on a handcom.

In the small cramped room DM and Kristen looked on as Jez fiddled with wires at the control panel and adjusted the camera at intervals. A televisual unit kept them disgusted.

Although Renaissance painters might disagree, the full-bodied women on *Homecam Live* were not attractive. They displayed themselves in a range of costumes, from ill-fitting bikinis to lingerie, for votes from viewers on who should strip after ten o'clock. It was a tawdry show dubbed "Postcard humour" by the makers.

Viewers of the following quiz show, *Naked Lies,* were in for a shock.

Jez found a solution, connected wires and flicked a switch before finger counting DM in, a balaclava masking his appearance.

"Good evening fellow citizens. We are interrupting this programme to wake you up. You will want to listen to what we have to say, and tape it if you can. Rupert C Donald owns this channel and he puts on the cheapest, most insulting rubbish he can. It's stuff that won't make you think because he doesn't want you to think. He wants to keep you under his thumb. These programmes assume you are stupid and that all you are fit for are stupid programmes.

"He also owns *The Shine* websites, newsdisk and newspapers. All of these tell lies which keep people stupid and help keep the NRP in power. The NRP doesn't care about us, the people. All they care about is making money. We are better than this, and if we all get together and make a stand we can make a difference. We can be better as a race. We can care if we take a chance. Rupert C Donald doesn't want us to care, because then we wouldn't buy his products.

"Everyone is affected by Rupert C Donald. Some older people might remember the time when we could watch football for free. Now, if you want to see your favourite team you'll have to pay Donald—"

"Just got cut off," said Jez. "We'd better move."

Daniel and Kristen were enjoying some pot, watching lights dancing above the hills.

"What do you think it is?" she asked.

"Aliens. I don't know."

"Maybe they've come to save us."

"I hope so." DM took a sachet of Reeto Dust from his pocket. "You want some of this?"

"Reeto?"

"Yeh."

"No thanks, it's too strong for me."

DM put it back inside his pocket, wanting to create a good impression. He had a desire to kiss Kristen, have sex with her, fall in love. But she was too self-assured, nothing like the person he'd met on New Year's Eve. Life would be complicated with her: he'd have to know how to play the part of a lover in what they call a relationship, and he'd have to know the rules.

"It is OK, DM," she said, seeing a sadness permeate his features. "I just heard some bad things about Reeto."

She leaned forward and kissed Daniel on the lips, withdrawing to assess his reaction. He longingly drew her in for another kiss.

"I don't want love, Daniel," she said. "Nothing complicated."

He nodded with an acceptance somewhere between relief and disenchantment.

After the clinical sex Kristen was back on to talking about the revolution. Soon she was gone like none of it had happened.

Daniel tried to sleep, but the barracking and violence on Pourische Road was too much, and it would continue through to the early hours then start all over again.

ON POURISCHE ROAD

Their hideous traits had been handed down from generation to generation, each one less evolved: like clones from clones they lose their validity.

John was born the third of five kids. His older brother ran away from home for a life of crime leading to a life in prison. John stayed until aged sixteen, taking the beatings and learning the moves.

His parents liked the idea of kids, particularly the idea of them being babies. His father thought it showed off his potency, his mother liked playing at dolls. But as John grew older, as with the others, they lost interest. It was too much hassle and John became "A little bastad". They grew frustrated at having to tell him things even they didn't understand. So they didn't talk to him, didn't take the time. But at least they had their legacy.

John didn't do very well in school. He struggled, and unable to catch up, he gave up. Shoplifting, vandalism and mugging brought him success and respect.

He got in with a gang, got drunk a lot, didn't get a job but got a girlfriend and got her pregnant. Then he left her, got another girlfriend and got her pregnant. This time he hung around, got into a routine and bred some more.

They're all at it on Pourische Road; drinking, gambling and screwing because there's fuck all else to do. And they like Rupert C Donald's channels, his papers, his flashy quiz shows.

Things stay static for these people and they get cut off from society. They become the underclass that nobody knows or cares about, and they're growing because they're breeding, because there's fuck all else to do. Morality and culture are expensive tastes and when your taste-buds are being bludgeoned every day, every generation, by mindless TV and puerile news coverage, you lose sight of the things outside your sphere of existence.

Choice is something they only have the illusion of enjoying. No access to opera, theatre, Art, great literature, anything that will improve them. It's just fags and booze and weekends of both, maybe some sport if they can afford to watch it. It's cheap fast food and irrelevant showbizz news, seeking to keep them down, low and dirty, valueless, underclass pigs snuffling around for a scrap of something thrown down to keep the rich amused. They are conditioned not to question it.

The middle-class pays lip service to it but they don't want to change anything until they themselves are threatened. And that won't happen because they are never given a picture of what is going on amongst the underclass, the unpeople who are swept under the carpet. The middle-class would be shocked and horrified to learn that heroin addiction is common amongst eleven to nineteen year olds: kids in school talk about it, talk about their lives beaten up by the police and kept enclosed in their locally infamous ghettos. But this is never noted for history, for these lives die out and progress will dissipate them.

John doesn't care about politics. He didn't even vote because "it does fuck all". And he and his friend Mackie don't want to talk about it when they're out.

The Dragon's Tail isn't a pub you go in unless you look like those inside. If you look different you'll be out, with a punch in the eye to remind you not to come back.

DM's with Kristen because having a female there usually tempers local anger. She just had to be careful not to look at the men attached to their women. So she had to lock arms with DM and kiss him regularly. Daniel knew it was an act, and though he admired Kristen's proficiency and sacrifice for the cause he also grew cold towards her.

DM was playing pool with a man in his fifties, a big man with tattoos and short-cropped grey hair. DM played to lose but had to keep the game going long enough and put his opponent under enough pressure to make it exciting. He intended that the man should savour his victory and be magnanimous.

"Go on!" said the man when he'd finally potted the black. "Al av a pint of best."

DM played the part, presenting a drink to the man and sitting with Kristen near his table.

"Ya played well, but missed some sitters, son."

"Must be the fuckin' cue," joked DM

"Oh yeh, and the table was wonky too," added one of the winner's friends jovially.

DM laughed on cue and began reading a copy of *The Shine*. After a cursory look he put it aside knowing full well that one of the group next to him would ask, "Can I av a look at that, son?"

"Yeh," he said, handing the paper over. "It's full of shite though. Did you see that fuckin' thing during *Naked Lies* last night? Did you 'ear what they said about *The Shine*?"

"Aye, fuckin' mad, wonnit."

"Better than fuckin' *Naked Lies*," added a stubbled man from the group.

"Fuckin' yeh," replied DM.

"Fuckin' wankers talkin'," said John. "Ey, don't you live down our street?"

"Pourische?" asked DM.

"Yeh."

"Yeh." DM wasn't going to get into where he lived and what job he did. "A wuz watching that shite *Naked Lies*, and then this fuckin' thing came on, and a thought, he's fuckin' right about *The Shine*."

"Like what?" asked the grey-haired man.

"*The Shine's* full of shite. Who gives a fuck if some puff film star is shagging someone? Why does *The Shine* think ar fuckin' care?"

One of the group, his face worn-out and battered, was in partial agreement: "I don't even like it. I only gerrit for the robes."

"Yeh, but you can go down the bookies for tha," replied DM. "Y' get much better tips."

"Ee's right," said the grey-haired man. "*The Shine* doesn't give a fuck about ordinary people."

DM saw and seized the window of opportunity: "worra fuckin' hate about *The Shine* is that it tells so many lies and thinks we're so fuckin' stupid we'll believe 'em. Y'remember when there was that disaster at the match up here, and *The Shine* was saying that fans were to blame, fuckin' ordinary people like us? They don't give a fuck about us."

"Yer fuckin' right," said the grey-haired man. "My old man was a miner last century and he stopped buying *The Shine* when they wrote lies about the miners."

"Aye, that fuckin' Donald supports the NRP and worra they doin' for ordinary people? Fuck all," said DM.

"I'd love to fuckin' do over one of those toffee-nosed bastards," said the stubbled man.

All over England the same scene was being enacted every night. Casualties were surprisingly few, usually activists who couldn't act the part. Generally, the proletariat who had been kept down for so long they'd become proles, were turning around again.

Confidence gained, suggestions were made and ideas for direct action were discussed. Permeating the logjam of dissatisfaction on Pourische Road came focused anger

Bad Luck's What You Make It

Jake dropped DM off in the town centre during dawn's early light. He felt good after the success of a job. A weapon's manufacturer had lost ninety million dollars due to six middle-aged women destroying an aircraft, using hammers and screwdrivers.

Daniel felt invigorated and the need for impulse took him to visit Kate Flowers in hospital.

Kate was sat up in bed scribbling something on a notepad.

"Dan! How nice of you to come."

"Hiya."

She put the notepad aside, revealing mathematical equations and chemical symbols.

"How are you feeling?"

"I'm OK, a few bruises. It could have been worse but I was leaving the science block to come and see you. I have found out some things about the asylum of particular interest to yourself." Kate sat up further, excitedly drawing Daniel in. "I couldn't really get hold of what was going on at the asylum so I made sure I went through every avenue of exploration systematically. I went through patient history, workers' history and all the little offshoots of them. This Dr Tumblety who runs the asylum used to work with a man called Henry Ragalana. I've met him a few times, he's an expert on ultrasound waves. I found one of his old essays about certain people in society sending out ultrasound waves which could subconsciously influence those around them. The essay had case examples and one of them was Declan Marx."

"My old geography teacher!"

"I know. I'm going to get in touch with Ragalana because readings I have been getting seem to be sending a message. I've made up a

326

dictionary and Marx keeps getting mentioned. It's the same with the asylum. If you decode the soundwaves into English the asylum gets mentioned very frequently. There's also a file there that I can't hack into: AL File 2 it's called. Do you think Joe can get any information?"

"He wouldn't be interested. Mr Marx died, didn't he?"

"Supposedly, but all records of him stop at 2022. Some of Ragalana's recordings match very closely with what I have got from space and from the hills. If he's still alive he's in the area—"

"A man I met recently, an old classmate, told me that the people at the asylum feared Marx. Surely he can't still be alive."

"I don't know. I looked at old school records and some of those he used to teach have been in the asylum. Some of them are recorded as having basic treatment and leaving, but others have scant details and are coded with AL File 2. I need to find out what's on that file."

"I'd certainly like to see what you've got on my old class. I can hardly remember anyone from it."

All at once Daniel was overloaded with ideas he couldn't spit out. He felt the pain in his stomach again as he tried to articulate his forgotten childhood.

"Dan, are you OK?"

"Got these stomach pains."

"Dan, see a doctor here, you look really ill."

"I can't remember who I was when I was young…"

Daniel awoke groggily, the white room slowly defining itself as his eyelids flickered.

"How are you feeling?" asked a wobbly doctor.

"Ooh," he felt his stomach, a small scar rippling under his fingers.

"It'll be sore for about an hour. This little thing was the problem." The doctor presented Daniel with a small clear bag containing a barely visible metal object. "Any idea how it got there?"

"No."

To the same question he gave the same answer to Kate.

"Want me to have a look at it?"

He gave over the object, felt again the scar under his shirt.

"I'd better go, Kate. I've got some things to do," he delivered plainly. "Like?"

"Y'know, think about the universe and our place in it," he replied, more awakened by Kate.

"When you find an answer tell me why the world's such an unhappy place."

"Because we live in a society where individuals carry a heavy burden, and they carry them as individuals. They are manipulated by the system to think their neighbours are happier than they are and that if they do certain things or buy certain things they can be happier than their neighbours. But these things are impossible, and disappointing if ever accomplished or bought. There's no sense of equality because this society only shines on winners."

"It sounds like you rehearsed it."

"Pre-programmed through hours of finding out the truth."

She liked that and Daniel was in love with the laughter he left her with.

Daniel felt little inclination to sort through the coded messages in his e-box, but the work needed to be done and they were things he needed to do before he could do the things he wanted to do: make contacts, "Then begin my autobiography," he thought.

In his e-box he found what appeared to be meaningless gobbledegook:

DM45. INUTHAU WATCHES ANHG SUEPOTTS. BEAH THE OEN DJOIE RTOAGAN.

He laughed at first, the final words so similar to Joe Rogan. Then some paranoid thought process set him worrying; a worry that excited and tempted him. It must be dust time.

The buzz buzzed on cue. "Old Joe must've received my brainwaves," said Daniel to himself.

"Yeh?" he said through the wire mesh.

"Daniel Manion?"

"Yes."

"Inspector Howard. May I came in for a word?"

Daniel checked on the televisual unit's security channel. A police ID card covered the whole screen, withdrawn to reveal two figures. One of them said to the screen, "This is my partner, Inspector Collins," his voice coming through the intercom. Daniel bleeped to let them enter.

Their steps could be heard, overlapping, pausing at levels, continuing to grow more thunderous.

"Inspector Howard," greeted the first man, ostensibly charming. "Inspector Collins" introduced his sullen, business-like partner.

'Which of my crimes am I under suspicion for?' wondered Daniel as he let the inspectors in.

"This is just routine, Mr Manion," said Howard, one metre from and opposite Daniel as Collins, the short, bald partner, surveyed the room, noting details on his handcom. "You may be aware of the murder of a young woman called Louise Woodling."

Daniel knew how to contort his face to portray surprise: "Yeh, the one from Leeds?"

"Yes. We have been checking up on everyone who was at Gigi's nightclub the night she was last seen. Did you see our requests for information in the media?"

"I didn't pay much attention. I suppose I should have come forward, but I didn't think I had anything to say."

"Of course." His tone changed as Collins' bleeping on the handcom continued apace. He had a hardness in his voice, like the preliminaries were over, when he said, "Many were like you, as if they hadn't heard the emphasis we placed on EVERYONE coming forward. It has made our task a lot more difficult. We had to sift through hours of videotape from the nightclub and then contact all those we could identify. It has taken much time. Perhaps in that time we might have caught the killer. Still, you will know for the next time."

A pause was left there, to fester.

"I'm sorry. What can I tell you? I was in Gigi's but I left quite early."

"We know. And we know you left alone. Our footage was from the exit and the bar area. As I said, this is routine and you really shouldn't worry." Howard produced a photograph, showed it to Daniel. "Look again, try to think about maybe seeing her, talking to her."

Daniel affected looking closely, but the image did not register.

"Sorry, I don't recognise her."

"Yes, we thought that would be the answer," Howard said. Collins looked up, cynicism peering through his thinning eyes. "You were with Mr Joseph Rogan that night."

"Yes."

"You didn't stay with him."

"No, I wasn't feeling too good."

"Do you know what Mr Rogan did after you left?"

"Talked to a few people, nothing much. Ask him."

"We have, and as I have said, this is just routine. There is absolutely no need for you to feel defensive."

"I don't" never made it to Daniel's mouth as he reasoned it would sound panicky. *"And Joe's no fool, he's not going to give them anything."*

"Where did you go after you left Gigi's?" asked Howard.

"Straight home."

"You live by yourself?"

"Yes."

"So no one can verify that."

Boom!—"Check Nero's Pizza. I ordered one that night."

"Fine."

DM had played his way to innocence. He was on a roll to roll them out: "I can have another think about it tonight, see if I can remember anything from that night, but as I said I didn't stay long at Gigi's."

"Of course," said Howard, his patronising tone elongated, like hammer blows in a coffin which he imagined sealing his victim. "We will be in touch again. And do remember that when a police request is made it is the duty of all citizens to comply. If you are not part of the solution, you are part of the problem."

Daniel nodded. Howard moved away whilst Collins loitered to bleep some more notes, looking Daniel up and down before scurrying behind his partner.

Daniel waited, searched his drawers for some dust but found them empty. He needed to see "Joe Two times"—"Two times".

The skies were a thick dark grey, large full clouds suffocating the white. Speckles of light danced to the west, though tonight they were vaguer than usual above the hills.

His steps were cloaked in caution; a sense that his legs were detached from his body, the CCTVs whirring a backbeat narrow and hard to master.

Daniel buzzed twice at Joe's flat entrance to no reply. Only a departing third buzz found a voice – "Yes?" – deep and eloquent and not Joe's.

"Is Joe there?"

"No."

"Do you know when he'll be back?"

"No."

"Tell him DM called."

"Thank you," discommunicated the voice.

A violent flash of light filled the skies, veins of lightning surging across their canvas. A long, low growl followed; a beast awakening.

The beginnings of rainfall stung him as he dashed back to this flat, so that he had to change and shower to clear his body of pollutants.

The rain came in big lumps, thudding on windows, pounding on the roof as slap clap light threw shadows on the walls.

An explosion cut out all the lights, sent a groan through dying electrical equipment. Daniel tried to open the door to the stairway but the electronic lock had jammed it shut. There was no way out. The inches of air in his flat were sucked out with each crash-boom-bang, fading away and simultaneously gearing up for another psycho-yawl. The boom slammed down, sent a tremor through the building.

What was that shuffling in the room? Just the rain? A shadow flickered across the wall, leading his eyes in circles then disappearing before they could catch up. *"Is someone here?"*

Another flash, anticipation growling before the omnipotent reverberation. A spark flashed from a plug, sent the televisual printer spewing out letters joined as words.

Daniel picked up a pair of scissors to attack the threatening intruder, stalking intermittently darkened corridors for his prey.

Rain whipped windowpanes, caught his attention. Then a flash swung him to make something from the shadows. Then the chattering printer birthing paper.

Daniel stepped steadily in and out of the spotlight before returning to the main room, waiting for lightning to illuminate his safety. The flash though, in his mind's eye recognition, didn't leave every corner accounted for, provoking his imagination to unwind a mystery. He clenched the scissors, leading with shadow stabs as he investigated the corners, ready to rip out a throat.

He retreated to his bedroom where the handcom printer babbled. He locked the door behind him, hesitantly watched the print-out reeling off, then took an electric shock to his bed as he tried to take hold of the paper.

THROUGH INNOCENT EYES

Kelly shrugged off her mother's routine farewell at the school gates. She felt trapped, reluctant to enter, to go through the meaningless slog with only English to excite her. She composed herself with thoughts of leaving in a few months.

In her mind she rehearsed what she had learned from Mr Manion's disks and the net news. Mr Manion wouldn't be interested in the capture of the Manchester Slicer, even though her gender gave the story some issues for women. He might be slightly interested in the suicide pact by a religious cult. He might be interested in the US invading South America to "stabilise the economy". She knew it was about saving their own economy by imposing the dollar on them as part of a "Recovery package", and about diverting attention from their domestic problem of white supremacists taking over the southern states. With the war in the Middle East boring the American public a new enemy was needed. And Mr Manion would certainly be interested in NRP legislation.

She sat through tutor-period listening to Phoebe and Tiana talk about boys, film stars and "Ooh isn't he crushing", then about their brothers on drugs and their neighbours being arrested. She told them they should read books and they told her to "fuck off" before asking her if she wanted "to go on the piss tonight". She told them she was "Fuckin Tom Creaney tonight" and they said, "You fuckin' wish."

She was glad Mr Rogan was absent again. She had shown little interest in his maths tuition the previous night and her mother had embarrassed her, arriving home drunk and barking about her bankers.

Mr Manion seemed to be looking at her throughout form period, breaking off to make notes. She imagined them to be subversive plans.

The day dragged and acquaintances stayed with her briefly, only until she showed her sore-thumb point of view. It wasn't making sense to them and she grew frustrated.

All through lessons she was conscious of her dog-tired eyes, inclined to let the day drift by until English.

Mr Manion talked about language changing throughout the years, taking Shakespeare as a reference point. When he said, "Language gives people power," and continued about television and popular culture denigrating language to dumb people, she felt inclined to speak:

"It's because the less the masses have to say, the less they can articulate their feelings, the less power they have, and the less they will question. That's why the NRP made education, especially higher education, expensive and elitist. They want to keep ordinary people in their place."

An "Excellent Kelly" pleased her.

She felt some credit too when Jenny Simpson added, "Sir, it's like those mags that're supposed to be for our age group and they're like for little kids."

She added to the debate that erupted, felt herself riding on the crest of a wave. Each time Mr Manion praised her, paused on her, it made her special.

Some fifteen minutes before the end of the lesson two suited visitors – one male, one female – entered Mr Manion's classroom. He seemed to freeze immediately, praising the class before handing out worksheets.

As a bell sounded them out Mr Manion followed the two suits from the classroom. Noticing he hadn't collected his bag she remained behind, waiting for his return…

"Oh, Kelly, what are you still doing here?"

"I just wanted to tell you that I've read all those disks you gave me and they were excellent. Marxism is really interesting. It's a shame people are too cynical these days to go for it."

"I agree," he replied, somewhat wearily, though bemused enough to take an interest. "It's amazing that someone of your age has such an enlightened philosophy."

"I don't want to be like the other girls, all the stupid ones who only talk about who they fancy."

"I think I can copy you some more disks if you want."

"Yes! Have you got anything by Naom Chomsky?"

"Yeh. I'll get them sorted."

They walked together to the school gates, Mr Manion's enthusiasm lifelessly efficient.

"Are you OK, sir?" Kelly asked.

"Well, yes, it's nothing."

"Is it something to do with those people in our classroom?"

"Yes. Nothing for you to worry about."

At the school gates Kelly's mother had her head poked impatiently from a taxi.

Kelly put her lips to Mr Manion's ear: "She's in a taxi, she'll be drunk."

"Mr Manion! Just the man I wanted to see," she slurred. "Oh, hello Kelly. Good day?"

She didn't reply, watching, with rage seething, as her mother artlessly beckoned Mr Manion to join her in the taxi.

"I insist on taking us all for lunch. The driver can take you home, Mr Manion. I have a little proposition for you."

She communicated over the backseat, wilfully ignoring Kelly as she flattered Mr Manion: "I've heard such wonderful things about you, Mr Manion…" She began. Kelly didn't say anything despite knowing she hadn't said a word to her mother for three days. "…This offer will give you more free time to enjoy yourself, which, after all, is what life's all about."

"Certainly," replied Mr Manion uncomfortably.

Kelly sensed his unease, sought to help him out with "You must spend a lot of time planning lessons."

But her mother, lighting a cigarette, butted in: "I've been thinking about your teaching skills Mr Manion and I'm ready to put it to my associates at the asylum that you should be offered a job there, in much the same capacity as Mr Rogan."

Her giddy words, filled with incongruous peaks, came to a full stop, her cigarette tossed from the window, her butting-in reassuming control.

"Really. Well, that is indeed fortunate as I will be leaving school at the end of the year."

Kelly's shock subsided instantly on realising she would have left by then.

"So yor interested?"

"I'll take a look at it."

"And of course, you can earn some extra pocket money if you can begin private tuition with Kelly. She doesn't seem keen on maths so we're going to concentrate on English."

Kelly had a feeling her mother was up to something. She remained mute as she sized up her options on the appropriate time to alert Mr Manion.

At the bar restaurant in Sector 20, Kelly's mother drank some more, freely anonymous amongst those she never usually rubbed shoulders with.

"She's up to something, Mr Manion, don't trust her," burst out Kelly during her mother's absence from the table.

"Why, what's she up to?"

"I don't know, just don't trust her. She only cares about herself. I hate her."

"That's a bit harsh, Kelly."

"I can't help it, it's the way I feel."

"You shouldn't feel such hatred, it's bad for you. I tell you what I want you to do," Mr Manion began playfully, "Imagine with me. We're going to take a nuclear bomb and drop it on that hatred. Then we're going to take the dusty remains and put them in an envelope, put the envelope in a file, in a cabinet, and put the cabinet in a big metal container. We're going to take the container to the deepest chasm in the Atlantic Ocean and drop it in. Then we're going to seal it up with concrete. We're gonna put booby traps all around so that your hatred can never get out again. Bury it away Kelly, you're better than that."

She smiled despite herself, let down a barrier.

"Whenever you feel hatred just remember where it's buried."

Her mother's return brought an end to the evening. She enticed Mr Manion back to their house, but immediately on arrival Kelly went to her bedroom, not wanting to be further embarrassed by her mother.

She turned off her lights then automatically locked the door.

In her headset she once again inserted the 'Virtual Sex' Virtch, once again saw movie star Tom Creaney at the foot of her bed; all curvy muscular torso and sharp angular face. What could she do with him tonight?

He took off his clothes and stood blankly awaiting instructions. But she wasn't turned on. She took hold of his head and placed it between her legs, holding it there as they went through their familiar shtick.

Soon bored, she had some fun making him wank himself off. Then, when that bored her, she made him strike ridiculous poses.

She pulled out the cartridge and tossed it aside. She needed something new, her mind unable to prevent Mr Manion entering.

She flicked on to a short-wave radio station from Liverpool where the JP Wing Ding was broadcasting. Her task, which she set about like some TV unit repair woman, was to find footage of Mr Manion from the CCTV camera at the front of her house. From there she switched to the computer on her portable televisual unit and wired it up to the Virtch headset.

Occasionally she broke off to make notes of the messages being broadcast on the Wing Ding from a code she had cracked long ago.

She used her expertise to give a clearer definition to Mr Manion's face, then superimposed one of the spare bodies she had in her computer.

The hours passed before she had the right image loaded into her VR programme. When she put on the headset and saw Mr Manion entering her room she initially felt guilty, not because she didn't think it right to use him, but because seeing him made Kelly think of all the constructive things she could be doing: fighting the capitalists, nourishing her mind, uncovering truths. She would save Mr Manion for later.

On unlocking and opening her door she gasped at the sight of Mr Manion.

"Oh, sorry Kelly, did I wake you?"

"Uh, no. How come you're still here?"

"That lift home never materialised."

"Typical of her."

"Now remember, that hatred is buried. Where?"

"In the deepest chasm of the Atlantic Ocean."

He left her smiling, and after taking a glass of water she kept him intact, in her memory, retrieved when she had virtual sex with him.

KILLERS

Dr Tumblety and Joe watched the screen avidly, its visuals following loitering eyes: a backyard identified. The body appeared to be loosely shuffling, waiting, humming words before they grew audible: "Who am a? What am a? No, fine. Good. Freedom."

The display turned to a window, an elbow gently cracking it, fingers taking out pieces of glass before feeling inside for a lock to pick. A larger window opened and a hand took a hammer from a supermarket bag.

Moving inside, all was vague shadows in darkness, three steps taken before an alarm sounded.

"Who am a? Nobody knows mi."

A female appeared, a light turned on. She couldn't expel the words, muted with fear. It seemed to last for a prolonged time, as if the assailant didn't want to break the moment, the alarm whirring. He weighed the dangers against the fact that all streets have alarms regularly going off twice an hour. For him it equalled a chance to understand the moment.

Dr Tumblety studied methodically, his fingers massaging his chin. Joe took vicarious pleasure, feeling her fear amid the sense of anticipation.

The assailant found a negative in his contemplation as the woman began to cough out sounds, trying to find a word to hold onto.

A hammer went into the women's face, cracking her stuck vocals to a scream. Another blow and his voice could be heard: "Bang." Smashing her face again as she fell backwards: "Bang." She collapsed under his chant, heard the words coming as echoes in her unconsciousness.

Each step from the house was accompanied by his "Bang" mantra, fading as he moved further away. Dr Tumblety noted his brainwaves switching to automatic as he took a route away from the scene of the crime. He tossed the supermarket bag into a field, threw the hammer in the backyard of a crackhouse, and made his way back to the Carehouse.

"Hello Frank."

"Make a nice reply because if she likes you she'll think you're OK, and then you'll keep being free."

"Hello Mrs Robinson."

Dr Tumblety turned off the display unit.

"Fuckin' amazing viewing!"

"Quite. It shows our treatment is working, Mr Rogan. How do you feel about what we are doing now that you've seen it?"

"Hey, it's fate as far as I can see, and we've got to keep the numbers down."

"Yes," Tumblety added, a low growl running through his words. "Murders every day, sick, sick murders, limbs ripped off, orifices bunged up with all manner of objects, unbelievable torture and mutilation."

"Are your bosses happy?"

"Yes."

"Are you going to tell me who they are?"

"Not yet."

The words dripped into his movements, making some subliminal association as he pulled open a drawer and retrieved a disk which he inserted into his computer.

He turned the screen to Joe to see Daniel's face and details.

"What's this?"

"Your friend, Daniel Manion, he has been involved with activists in the past. We have concerns that he still is."

"No," replied Joe disbelievingly, confidently. "Yeh, I know he has some weird friends, but he'd rather get wasted than start the revolution. I don't think you have anything to fear." Joe laughed to dismiss the point. "Certainly hasn't been involved in any of that stuff since I've known him."

"You can be sure?"

"He's OK. He likes the good times like me. He gets wasted, enjoys the crack. He's just like me. I don't know if he'd approve of what we're doing but I'm not gonna bring it up over cocktails."

"You need to be sure. Keep an eye on him."

"OK, no problem."

In the asylum's underground laboratory Dr Tumblety began work on dissecting Rachel Sampson's brain, inserting monitors at strategic points inside what remained of the skull.

338

For hours he went through readings from the brain's memory. During breaks he added to his own urine and semen collection, beginning a new shelf in the deep freeze. The readings confirmed his suspicion that Declan Marx was situated somewhere near the hills in East Tyneside. Conflicting readings pointed to Sector 5. With logic he reasoned that Marx, even if out of the coma, would not be able to exist on the hills, especially with The Institute Of Science so visible up there. It had to be Sector 5.

He switched to his air frequency monitor to match up the ultrasound waves, then switched to his ultrasound monitor to pinpoint a location.

Tumblety felt satisfied with himself. He felt every genius idea he had could reach fruition and there were no limits to what could be done. He had the means to develop anything his imagination came up with. He had known that a fresh head would yield him clues as to Marx's whereabouts and he had altered the person who'd killed and helped him prove his theory. And he, Dr Tumblety, had programmed the Manchester Slicer, Emma Heardman, to commit suicide within twenty-four hours of being caught. No clues would lead back to him. He could control anybody. "Fuck the Paradise Table. I own the future," he thought to himself.

He pulled one of the Unpeople models, Leonardo Smith, from his file, made some alterations and sent him out to find Marx.

◻ ◻ ◻

"Hey, DM—"

"Where the fuck have you been?"

"Hey, I don't need school anymore, and I'm due a few sickies."

"The pigs came asking about Louise Woodling—"

"Don't worry, DM, they've seen me too—"

"What did ya say?"

"Nothing, just routine. Don't sweat on the small stuff."

"What about them fitting us up for the crime?" demanded Daniel.

"They'll be fitting up somebody else: somebody too stupid to question it. They ain't gonna fit up two respectable teachers. We're double good citizens."

He delivered it with a mellow dose of irony, enough to lighten Daniel's worries.

"You should be getting fifty cups of coffee with your alibis. She was the one you chatted up wasn't she? The one who gave you the flick?"

"There was no camera where we were. Say what you like about paranoia, it certainly helps you cover all the bases. Anyway, she was playing me out. Fuck her, she must've played it with the wrong guy. Serves her right for not choosing Joe. Come on, let's monkey."

"Nah."

"DM man, come on. We are the lucky sharks around a sinking ship. Let's get snapping. We're the hot-to-trot lucky penny motherfuckers."

"I can't, I got things to do. Y'know about Mrs Godfrey offering me the same job as you at the asylum?"

"No. When was this?"

"Couple of days ago. I'm gonna be teaching Kelly too."

"I've heard nothing about you coming to the asylum. I know Laura's dropped the maths lessons. Thank god. Kelly was starting to bore me."

"You must've been boring her."

"Too sure. So when do you start?"

"Nothing's final yet. Lucky break really 'cos they gave me my notice at school."

"Why?"

"Not teaching the curriculum. So fuck 'em."

"Yeh, fuck 'em. Looks like the two desperados'll be riding in the nuthouse then."

"May—be. I gotta go and get born right now, but I might be round to get dusted later."

Joe would wait a long while, growing increasingly isolated as he consumed other worlds in snorts. It played to his ego, got him supremely confident of his omniscience before he went prowling the streets, homing in on Sector 6.

Daniel's intentions to take in some news, make some contacts, then call on Joe, were diverted by what he learnt:

News of an NRP bill to "rid the net of evil paedophiles and terrorists" focused his attention. Reports exposed the net as a nurturing ground for molesters, rapists and "hateful terrorists". What the presenter called "hours of hard research" linked infamous criminals with time spent surfing.

The NRP's "new tough measures" were going to close down sites and reduce access so that "innocence can no longer be corrupted".

Friedland Electronics were sponsoring the bill, "using technology to create a better world" according to their spokesman.

It pricked Daniel into action; making contacts, setting up secret sites and alerting organisations to the threat. He was so involved that the idea of visiting Joe only returned to him in the early hours when his body had stopped functioning.

RAGALANA

Professor Henry Ragalana sifted through his notes as the train rattled into Newcastle, ordering them chronologically so that in his memories he experienced again the excited drafting of his first report on Declan Marx.

At first he and Dr Tumblety had treated Marx as an ordinary coma patient, but as their research into ultrasound waves developed they began using him more as an experiment.

Many months of noting Marx's brainwaves led to the realisation that there was some communication there. They gradually broke the code, deciphering descriptions, imaginings and messages. Many of these proved prophetic, events translated from Marx's brain precipitating events around the world.

Whilst Tumblety concentrated on altering patients, Ragalana developed communication with Marx. He discovered that Marx responded to music, and that it could affect his mood, which in turn affected world events.

Once Ragalana had seen the direction Tumblety wanted to take, he knew he had to end the association. The mysterious benefactors who had paid for Marx's upkeep agreed that the patient should be in Ragalana's care.

Ragalana made further progress with Marx. He wired up the patient to an ultrasound monitor and printer. Through headphones, Ragalana sent ultrasound messages, repeated questions like "What colour is white paint?" which could only produce one answer. He found that after five to eight attempts Marx would send back the correct answer.

The question repetitions were reduced from two to four and grew a little more demanding, like, "Is dying bad for you?" Eventually Marx began to send messages directly and independently.

Marx had a description he wanted to relay. Called "AL: How The Earth Destroyed Itself", he would add to it during every session with

Ragalana, alerting the professor to begin taking dictation by causing a sharp bleep on the heart monitor.

Through his notes Ragalana recalled the event in his life he had never told anyone else about. His rare nightmares – the sleepless visions he hadn't mastered control of – threw up headlines and exposés of "Mad Professor Says He's Talked to Aliens", images of him committed to an asylum where a grotesque replica of Tumblety performed alterations on him.

He shuddered with the halting train to think of it: the animated human-plant creature taking him to outer space and telling him he needed to hand Marx over to the benefactors because he was in danger.

Although he had never met the benefactors, they had known how to get in touch with him and at first made regular contact for advice on maintenance. Even after they'd put out that Marx had died they maintained communication. Over the years this had become less frequent and Ragalana had conditioned himself to concentrate less on it, placing it at the peripherals of his life. It became more of a hobby to take readings from Mr Marx, emanating from Tyneside, and thread them to the plot development of "AL", which he had copied before posting the originals to one Edward Edwards. A private detective he'd hired followed Dr Edwards through a string of conduits leading to dead ends, helping Ragalana to consign the whole business to an amusing pastime. Until now.

Kate Flowers met Professor Ragalana at the train station and they engaged in the small talk of apparent old friends as a Pup Taxi took them to Kate's house.

"Are all the taxi-drivers like that?" he asked as they approached her front door.

"I try not to take taxis but my car got in a crash the other day so I'm meeting some interesting characters until the end of the week."

Her humour, seemingly timed to perfection, crashed against an imposing dimension and never found direction, withering instantly as Kate gasped.

Of all the stories she had to tell, the first would be to reason why her whole house had been smashed up.

The day was stunned with a large sheet of white pasted precisely around the materials which served as an immediate background for the automatically living.

On each street corner characters loitered, their mere presence changing Daniel's direction, until it was no longer a sense of escape but a means to trap. He had to think hard, stay looking normal. He couldn't find the second-hand shop that had his copy of *Cracking Codes For Kids,* and he couldn't find the street where he'd grown up, because neither existed. It was the dust that had gotten to him to him that day. He was clean now: clean-ish, less frequent, hardly at all, but sometimes, but now and then, but too much.

He stopped, assessed, changed direction like a robot. "Don't go that way. Change left. Walk. Observe. Danger ahead, turn left."

But why couldn't he piece together his childhood? Why couldn't he make distinct recollections? Where were his parents? *"Where did my parents go? There must be somewhere. Something's going on. Oh, it all looks perfect: every detail done to perfection. Of course, I'd expect to see a lamp post there, a CCTV there. CCTV, my life-story in black and white."*

A safe place to go would be the hills, to seek Ted. *"That's what I'm here for. See Ted."*

"Newcastle Ef, CS8, Tech-one…"

Thick mist hung over the hills, Daniel seeing dancing lights amidst the whiteness.

"My eternal friend, Daniel Manion," whispered firmly from the mists.

He turned, Ted K not visible until the veil parted for his entrance.

"Don't get paranoid, Daniel, it's me. Have you been busy?"

"Fuckin' hell Ted, something's going on! My head's spinning."

"Be calm, brother. Your eyes suggest you've taken something. How long have you been outdoors?"

"I dunno, it seems like ages."

"Didn't you see it was a low air quality warning day today?"

"No, it's not that. I can't remember my childhood—"

"Daniel, we've been through that. You know you closed it all off when you were fifteen. Come on, be calm, remember who I am, where you are, what we are doing, and what your hopes are. OK?"

"OK Ted."

"Did you see the CS8?"

"Yeh, they're OK. What they're doing will help us. They're pushing this drug they've made. They call it Wantok. It's OK, it'll help us."

"You've taken it."

"Yeh, it's based on that village system, Wantok, where everyone in the village, uh, helps out with things in the village. They, like, use their skills, exchange them, and, uh, help each other. It's a nice trip. It'll open people's imaginations."

"The Effers?"

"They've made all their connections. You hear about Kathy?"

"Yes, terrible. Very sad. It's definitely the NRP, hiring killers to take out activists."

Ted guided Daniel to walk with him.

"I've seen the Techno Anarchists too. They can have everything done within ten hours."

"Try to get them down to eight."

"Is it soon?"

"Very soon. You feeling better?"

"A little"

"It's really peaceful up here, Daniel. There's a strange presence, especially at night. You can think clearly, come up with the most brilliant ideas. I feel some mystical force is on our side, guiding us. There are many groups up here, in little caves, underground, amongst the trees, all protected by this divine mist. It's not like that pollution hanging over the town, this is fresh, invigorating."

"What about all those Institute Of Science people up here?"

"They're closed off in a small area of ground and not ventured out from there. It looks like they're taking air readings but we can't be sure. We've got a few people watching them."

From the skies a pattering sound, slowing. Ted looked up and raised his arm, drawing in the pigeon which landed there.

"Cassie, old girl." Ted stroked the bird. "Still going strong."

"Do you think she recognises me?" joked Daniel, a little flippantly for Ted's liking.

"I'm sure she does, Daniel. She's very clever." Ted took the paper attached to Cassie's left leg. "Good, good," he said whilst reading. He stroked Cassie when finished and turned to Daniel. "DM, you need to see Will. Tell him to feed the XYs with Feemo on Wednesday and Thursday, and to send them out on Friday." Daniel nodded.

Ted took two notes from his pocket, swallowing one and fastening the other to Cassie's leg; a poignancy on his face as he sent her off.

"It must be soon then?"

"As I've said, DM, it is. Be patient." He placed his hands on Daniel's shoulders. "I heard about your sacking. Don't worry, you'll be OK after the revolution. Teachers will be valued and paid a good wage and pupils will be able to achieve their dreams. Stay off whatever you're on for a while, and be strong."

They hugged before departing. Daniel's sense of clarity was immediately tainted by a feeling of solitariness. He stumbled through the undergrowth, feeling lost, thoughts of Kelly Godfrey encompassing him until he gradually became aware of a humming underneath slow, low bleeps.

His body vibrated. He looked to his feet, lights gleaming around them on Mother Earth, giving the grass an animation he had rarely seen or felt since childhood. It was an intense moment that felt like some strong and real escape from automatic living.

"I am not of this earth," he thought to himself. "I am not of this planet that regurgitates useless ideals with media tart-up. This society has no place for a free thinking, sensitive, beautiful, artistic, passionate man. I am a new being in a visionary universe. The aliens are speaking to me. My brain speeds up the low hums to make bleeps. The message is to trust instinct. There is only this moment."

After a few hours with Will Correca, Daniel made his way home to find the sleep he needed to be awake for the job that made him need to sleep in the first place.

THE PAST COMES CALLING

The display screened Daniel as he left the pub. It followed at a distance, catching the flight of cigarette smoke, mimicking the rhythm of his heels. As the jolting visuals progressed, curious figures flitted by: a woman offered sex, a man offered sex, a man offered drugs, a woman offered drugs. The display ignored them all, the "Fuck you weirdo!" as they backed off.

Daniel Manion moved into Sector 9, his head down. Turning into Pourische Road he halted to strike a match and suck on a new cigarette. The display closed in rapidly, Daniel turning as it reached three metres away.

"Uh, wha—" Daniel's match fell. "Whatta ya want?"

The display halted, heavy breathing coming though the speakers. No movement, just a staring into Daniel's eyes.

"Pete?" questioned Daniel. "Peter Wheaton?"

No reply came.

"Peter Wheaton, it's you isn't it? Danny Manion, remember me? We were in the same class at school."

"Danny Manion. I, I don't know."

"What's up? Are you OK?"

"I've been ill. They let me out. I've been following you."

"Why?"

"Because you don't add up. You aren't the right decision. I don't know. You were there when he did it, weren't you?"

"Yeh. It was bad, wasn't it?"

"Ya fuckin' cunt!" was heard before a figure appeared from the darkness.

Vision immediately focused on the stranger, a knife gleaming in his hand, lunging at Daniel.

Another knife crossed the scene, thrust out to the third character, caught him in the arm.

The visuals were accompanied by a soundtrack of heavy breathing and grunts as blows rained in and blood obscured the scene.

It spun around, caught sight of the night sky, then settled quivering on Daniel Manion's face from above.

"Hang in there, Pete, I'll phone for an ambulance."

Sky occupied the screen, sounds on the peripherals cluttering the moment's serenity. Stars blinked behind waves of pollution, visuals flickering, then shutting down. Bleep.

Daniel felt himself shaking, each misplaced bleep on his door lock tightening a noose around his neck.

"Steady yourself, Mr Manion," said Inspector Howard.

Inspector Collins began moving around the flat as soon as they entered.

"What's he doing?"

"We have a warrant," said Howard, producing a plastic card. "All just routine."

"But I haven't done anything!" Daniel made to follow but Howard held him back.

"Leave it. We don't want to have to take you in. Tell me what happened tonight."

"I've told you, the guy who killed Pete was called Stephen. I beat him at pool and he's had it in for me ever since. They were stabbing each other, then Pete collapsed. Then this Stephen just blacked out."

Daniel heard a noise from his bedroom and darted to see Collins turning out drawers.

"Stop!" demanded Howard, placing a painful grip on Daniel's shoulder.

"What's he doing? Why are you searching my flat?"

"We've got to follow everything up."

"Just arrest that Stephen!"

"We will speak to him when he comes round. Now, where did you play pool with this Stephen?"

"Club Independent, why?"

"Club Independent? An interesting place for a teacher to go."

"He's just throwing my things about!"

Howard intercepted Daniel's movements again, taking his arm and twisting it behind Daniel's back:

"Now I can make this hurt more," he breathed into Daniel's ear, pulling tighter, making it hurt more, "And I can take you in and arrest you. So, last warning, be fuckin' still."

Collins promptly announced that he was "Done. Got hair and skin samples and some letters."

"What do you want them for?" asked Daniel.

"Just so we know exactly who you are," replied Collins eagerly before Howard could answer, his previous reticence making his words all the more bloodcurdling.

"We will be in touch," rang hollowly from Howard, imitated in the echoing clank of their four-footed departure.

He couldn't help feeling he was being set up for a frame-up. An internal dialogue questioned and answered his paranoia, his contemplations fully aware of the fine line between truth and insanity. He found substance in the notion that voices were talking to him, struggling to keep his thoughts objective.

DOPE BEATS ON THE STREETS

Sector 11 had all the beats, populated with mixmasters like Morse. Most others had abandoned the area because of the high number of cancer and leukaemia cases, widely believed to be due to the encroachment of factories and chemical plants.

Morse liked the desolation. He liked that some nights all you could hear along shadowy alleyways and run-down streets were the beats and bleeps of those experimenting with sound; cutting and mixing and looping.

With his face mask on he hurried home, ideas running through his head: how to create "A track which would inspire people to revolt", as he recalled Daniel Manion saying. He had thought of the idea himself many years before, but somehow, on time's divergent paths, he had neglected to nourish it. Now the loops were running around circuits in his brain, the beats and bleeps full of hope and belief.

Once he'd climbed over the cemetery wall and was amongst the gravestones his motion slowed. He took in the inscriptions on gravestones, lamented for the people he'd grown to treat as friends. Over the years he'd gotten to know them, imagining their appearance, their character and the lives they'd led.

He paused at the headstone whose dates were Dec 1971-Jan 1972.

"Why do people die?" he thought to himself.

Morse cleared a supermarket carrier bag from the grave and knelt down. He imagined David's life, imagined him growing up, playing with friends like Morse had played with friends when he was a child. He sketched out a life in his thoughts somewhere close to his own, but with different faces.

"Why do people die?" he asked the ghosts of gods all around him.

Inside the church Morse flicked on the machines: a mixing deck for discs, a radio transmitter and receiver, a sampling deck, a televisual unit, a computer, and various sound imitators, tape decks and editing facilities.

He began to experiment; a siren he could elongate, a speech he could manipulate, a corrosive guitar he could distort, a big and booming baseline he could lay over the sounds.

Some three hours after speaking to Daniel Manion he had the beginnings of a track. It was going "dum-de-dum" as Daniel pissed to his own humming:

"Dum-de-dum," and he'd cleared Morse from his memory, more interested in where the alcohol high was going to step to next.

"Hey, DM, let's town it," said Joe as Daniel returned to the table.

"What about the sharks?"

"They'll be up all night."

"Cops?"

"Fuck cops. We'll just have to try and not be near any murder scenes. Come on, monkey man."

"Monkey man."

Through red lights the chasers spun crowds on their heels, as equally unconcerned as their tormentors with not killing anybody. Somewhere along there'd be a crash, and it'd stand out from windows smashed by the disgruntled, too drunk to move, taking beatings for their pride. There's a tall man, all on his own, looking for love in the wrong places. Money's hot in his steaming pocket, ready to buy experience.

Those who went about it like they'd always gone about it, went with a swagger adopted since their youth; now rather worn, but they clung to it because better times were always in the future and that was the manifesto they'd always bought into.

Little Slick Johnny had his decks on a street corner, mixing the sounds, speaking with his hands, begging for loose change to pay for his habit. In breaks you could hear guitar man Adam strumming, loose change rattling along with his finger licks.

Queues were more patient than remembered, but it was only temporary and, when the wait got too much, curses and fists splattered in the air.

Joe and DM were ghosting in and out of pubs to find their panacea. They were the beat kings with snatches of dialogue in a style they'd mastered: "Move the crowd, she's the one."

"Her friends got class, nice call son."

"Hey baby, you move like yor money-makin'."

"Yor words seem like you are faking."

"No baby pop, we only chat with the best."

"I'm DM."

350

"I'm Joe. Let's start the test."

You like this tune? Wanna waltz the room? Hey, they're laughing, time to zoom.

What you do? I'm in the bizz. Fizz? Not tonight, we just want laughs. You, me and us got some pretty laughs.

"Would you like a drink?"

"I don't think."

"Come on ladies, this is it."

Yeh, one moment, one time and Joe's unrehearsed kiss.

But they're laughing: something's amiss.

"Lost it Joe, too cocky, too cool."

"Ain't worth it, D, makes us a fool."

Onto another bpm slot where the roof is bouncing and the neon is hot. Bodies rub, looks get musty; figures shaking, dusty lusty.

They get their doubles and a bottle to parade, down them in minutes and wait for the raid. Cops gatecrash and take some snaps: people hauled off just for points, just for laughs. But the cops can't find the buttons to turn off the beats, and bodies are dancing around villains they seek.

A quick exit for the two, into another hive, swinging for a stinging and talking the jive: "One two one two, get the lines ready."

DM's loaded, took a snort at intermission: he ain't too steady.

"Hey, how are you doing?" begins the chase.

"Fine."

"I'm Joe, this is Dan."

"Tessa."

"Peps."

"Nice names, nice viewing."

"Rhyme?" DM's hush in Joe's ear.

"Let's shine."

"Like you wanna fuck the man."

"Tessa?"

"Peps? We've been perusing."

They smile at Joe and fake it with anxious DM.

"We've been in a story for too long. We're stuck in a story and we need you to help us get out."

"Run it, DM."

"It's about these bad ass blokes and their block rockin' beats, and they like to run around and chase the tail of time. We likes the thrills and spills."

"The chills without ills," added Joe.

"We need some actresses in our story."

"Your beauty and intelligence in all its glory."

"I've got a boyfriend," says Tessa.

"Peps?"

"No."

"It's yours man, this is my end," says DM, lucked out as he ducks out. "I'm sharking."

Pup Taxis' driver has a weirdo hairdo: a black grease back, shocked out and on end at each side.

"Sector 8."

"Right, forty kilometres an hour, four kilometres to go. Lights and stops, add one kilometre. Arrive in 7½ minutes."

"Fine."

He put his foot down, bleeped on the clock, fixed his eyes on the mirror to log the face in the back.

"Out on the town?"

"Yeh."

"I don't like it down there. It's got dodgy people. I don't need that. They're wasting their money."

"Yeh, that's why I left," humoured DM.

"Good. Don't I know you?"

"I don't think so. What's your name?"

"I've seen you somewhere."

"Well, we've all had our fifteen minutes."

"Fifteen minutes out of, say, eighty years, is not much if fame is what you believe in. Like, ten million, five hundred, and twelve thousand minutes, and you pin your life on fifteen. Might as well save up those minutes and buy yourself a whole life."

"Yeh, right. You been doing this long?"

"Couple of weeks."

"What did you do before?"

"Watched the walls closing in."

"Yeh, I know what you mean."

When DM paid him he said, "Nearly got that vidphone," before speeding off as he looked at his watch. The car screeched to a halt at the end of the street, slowly turning right.

The dice were rolling as Taff led DM into the front room. There, Phil played disconsolately with dice, rolling to produce the numbers he imagined would come up.

"Daniel, well done. We didn't think anyone was turning up tonight."

"Joe's fishing for a fizz. Where's Jez?"

"On a job."

"Oh, yeh yeh."

"Some cards, Mr Manion?" asked Taff gleefully, a joint in one hand and a pack in the other.

"Deal 'em."

The cards were mythical. They madeth the man. They befitted a ceremony: a soundtrack of flea bitten guitars, storms raging, stray cat blues and hot rock licks was ignited; cans burst in anticipation; the air filled with smoke.

A fresh pack lost its innocence, mixed up, shook up and dealt out: once round, licking lips as slaps sounded on the table.

No reaction escaped as the players looked at their cards. Taff laid first: ten of spades, hunting out its queen, The Black Mariah, wanting to damage somebody. With no takers he gave it a second flush with a seven of spades.

DM laid the ace of spades. Once Phil had laid a nine of spades, DM became prime suspect as holder of The Black Mariah. DM knew Taff had it, unless Phil was foolishly making early moves towards shooting the moon. It was unlikely, so Taff had it and was playing some elaborate game to weed out all the spades. He thought Phil would suspect him, but Phil knew exactly who had it.

Phil knew exactly what Taff had and Taff knew exactly what Phil had. Both knew exactly what DM had and when he won comprehensively they both affected shock and praise.

They carefully controlled DM's karma: four straight wins, one defeat, two straight wins, until he could take no more and burst out: "I'm sorry good people, but this is too easy. It's like I know what you are going to play."

The irony wasn't lost on them, but it was tempered with concern, for DM needed to play and win two more of three more games.

"You can't give up now, Mr Manion," urged Taff. "You've got to give us the chance to retain some dignity."

Daniel relented, somewhat relieved that he lost the next game.

Taff and Phil played to lose the next game, but in the one following they used all their skill to give the game a competitive edge, taking it to the wire before DM won.

"Listen good people," announced Daniel, exhausted by the cards. "I don't know what's happening to me or if I'm going crazy. I keep hearing voices, I keep imagining things before they happen. I can't remember what my childhood was like. I can't stop thinking about my parents but I keep forgetting to remember that they went missing and that I never tried to find them. I'm fuckin' crackin' up."

"Be calm, Mr Manion," Taff soothed. "Have you been taking that Reeto Dust?"

"Yeh."

"It's fuckin' you up. You need to get hold of some Wantok to get your equilibrium back."

"Oh god, I want to get out this. I want to feel real again, back in the real time and place."

"You can get back, Daniel," said Phil. "Stay off the dust."

"I'm fuckin' desperate. I've read about it, I'm showing all the signs of a paranoid schizophrenic. It creeps up on me and takes over me and I exhaust myself trying to keep it at bay."

"Don't do anything silly, Daniel. You're not going to join the stupid club are you?" asked Taff, apprehensive with concern.

Daniel shrugged it off: "No, that'd be too like Marx."

Taff and Phil worked to eke DM out of his insanity, bringing him back to a card game with no consequences.

They were the keepers of what to them was an innocuous secret. Their purpose on planet Earth was simple: to save their own planet, Finhouha.

Finhouha; a small, delicately balanced planet, orbiting the planet Zshrr and on the outskirts of Inuthua's galaxy, had been an insignificant speck in the universe until Inuthua began sending their androids to Earth. A leisurely planet of intellectual pursuits had at once taken note of the effect DM's card playing was having on its way of life. After analysis they had learned DM's successes and failures at cards were influencing the vibes on Finhouha.

Taff and Phil were dispatched by the highest authorities on Finhouha to make sure the outcomes of DM's card games were conducive to life on their planet. But Taff and Phil were sharks at heart and they were in it for the thrill of using their games skills to manipulate the outcome of the cards. They had their own little game going, racking up points around whatever result was necessary for DM. If DM was first out of the five sharks they would compete for second. If DM was due to come last they would play for the four higher places.

The secret they kept to them was of minor inconvenience; a means to satiate their philanthropy in between card games. They were in regular contact with Daniel's parents, using them to help determine what DM would do next and when he was available for cards; keeping them content with information about their son. It also kept The Immortal off their backs with them aiding Declan Marx's continuation.

Phil and Taff were now both hooked on irony. They could emotionally exist in irony, loading themselves up on the possibilities of every action and thought DM had. That Daniel thought things were weird now hit their mainlines full on. If only he knew how weird things really were.

THE TWIST

"Kelly, you stay in Dr Tumblety's office dear."

Tumblety grumbled. Mrs Godfrey returned a satisfied smile. DM winked at Kelly. Kelly, all attention focused on her, remained disciplined.

Daniel followed Tumblety, Mrs Godfrey nonchalantly interfering at their backs.

Through one window Daniel saw a patient imitating walking, but not moving from the spot. On his face, some determination and vision, staring blankly ahead, seeing something only his imagination could explain. Beads of sweat poured from his brow, his breathing heavy, the movement of his lips mouthing, "Water, water…"

The cell had little furniture, a string-less guitar in the corner focusing the voyeur's vision.

"That's King Creole," said Mrs Godfrey condescendingly. "He walks in the desert for hours then he picks up his guitar. He hasn't quite grasped the rudiments of playing it yet," she added, self-satisfied with her wit.

Daniel remembered a pupil from his geography class. Mr Marx had given him the nickname "King Creole" on learning he played guitar, got him to write a song naming all the planets, got him to play it in front of the class. Daniel couldn't remember the kid's name, it was just King Creole, but *he* certainly could play guitar.

"I suppose it makes a change from teaching," suggested Mrs Godfrey.

Daniel nodded, his eyes fixed as the new King Creole picked up the guitar. Mrs Godfrey, against Tumblety's murmurs, bleeped on the intercom: "Dum dum, da da da dum dum," came from his lips, scratchily mangled through the wire mesh. "…There's a man in New Orleans who plays a rock 'n' roll, he's a guitar man with a great big soul. He lays down the beat—"

Tumblety bleeped and peripheral movements were abruptly finalised as feet began to sound.

"...Y'know he's gone gone gone, jumpin' like catfish on a pole..."

Feet like rainfall pounding harder. Daniel's father had his vinyl records out. It must be a Sunday, it must be his father's old vinyl retrospective.

"...He sings some blues 'bout New Orleans..."

The pounding thundering to a conclusion, muscular white spooks bleep into the cell. At a socket in the wall one places a disc, the other pinning the patient onto his bed.

Tumblety's mutterings and impatient saliva slappings urged them on, but Mrs Godfrey was feeling playful:

"What are they putting on, Lewis?"

He hurrumphed and seethed before bleeping into his handcom for an answer:

"Er, Phil Collins, 'Another Day in Paradise.' "

"Piece of shit," spat Mrs Godfrey gleefully, moving into Daniel's space to view the patient.

DM traced the song back to November 1989, its indeed piece of shit sounds evoking an era at the end of the excessive 1980s when concern and sympathy allowed Zeitgeist Man to sell many recordings. It probably stayed in the chart for eleven tortuous weeks: VS 1234.

The patient began to wail, began to scream lyrics, causing feedback over the intercom. DM could decipher it all:

"...There's a hot spot in space, y'know it's called the sun, it's a great big ball with a fiery core..."

An injection sucked the patient into a black hole of his own subconscious.

Daniel took in the patients which followed, absorbed each one of their idiosyncrasies. He showed little interest in answering Tumblety's questions, but played it well enough to keep the doctor probing. Mrs Godfrey loitered, used the spare time to practice one-liners on the audience in her mind, perfecting them for precisely timed deliveries. Tumblety grew more impatient, more exasperated, continually replaying the genius of his life and finding a scene where he stabbed Mrs Godfrey to death.

By the end of it Tumblety had realised he didn't want Mr Manion employed at the asylum. Daniel himself had merely played a part, merely bought time for Kelly. He wouldn't need to take the job because the revolution was coming and ulterior motives thrilled him, fuelled his performance. Mrs Godfrey didn't much care which way it went: the asylum job was a carrot, and now that Mr Manion had bitten on tutoring Kelly she didn't need it. She just enjoyed her wit and planned her next move.

"I'm sorry the job fell through, Mr Manion, but remember, I've got you tomorrow. At least you've got that," she said whilst practising belligerent driving skills with the car's wheel. "Where is it you want to be Kelly?"

"Here," came succinctly from Kelly's lips, the prospect of her mother's attentions forcing her to leave the car early.

"Who is it you're meeting?" Mrs Godfrey asked belatedly.

"Phoebe. I'm staying with her—"

"OK darling, I'll see you tomorrow," cut off Mrs Godfrey, pulling the car door shut.

Daniel's lift home endured Mrs Godfrey's regret (no work at the asylum), hope (Daniel helps Kelly achieve good exam grades) and frivolity (Kelly likes Daniel, looks up to him, is inspired by him).

Fifty minutes later the CCTV cameras for Daniel's flat block were out of action and Kelly was at his door, holding a comdriver like a trophy.

"It's a very old system here, Mr Manion," she said, handing him the tool and taking out her handcom.

"Have you looked at it?" he asked Kelly.

"No," she replied, bleeping in a code, presenting the handcom to Daniel.

"AL File Two," he read from the screen. "Automatics, Unpeople, Exterminators." He bleeped for "Automatics". "God, there's hundreds, thousands of names here." He bleeped on one – Keith Hammond – and read through the details: "Ten day alteration, 2020. A list of drugs, names of immediate family, wife Cindy, job with MacDolland's, claiming benefit. Equipped to play lottery, drink Coki Coli, eat at MacDolland's and watch RCM channels. Fuckin' hell, what is this?"

DM bleeped back to the index, bleeped on "Unpeople": "Hundreds, thousands again." He halted the unscrolling list of names with a bleep, landing on "Leonardo M Smith" from whose details he again read: "Admitted June 2032, released 2034. List of drugs again, no immediate family. Equipped for purchasing, petty theft, surveillance, burglary and stalking. Possible exterminator."

DM quickly returned to the index, bleeped on "Exterminators" and impressed the details on Kelly: "Hundreds, hundreds. Not as many as the other two categories—"

"Look! Go back. There. Forward. There, Emma Heardman. She was The Manchester Slicer."

DM bleeped on the name. Kelly continued as details flickered on the handcom:

"She killed herself. She had bits of bodies in her flat in Manchester."

"A big list of drugs again," noted DM. "Working as a computer operator for Suh-Hi Incorporated, Manchester. Equipped for automatic life, has capacity to kill at random with no evidence. Fuckin' hell, they're creating assassins! Does your mother know about this?"

"Probably."

"You know?"

"No."

"Fuck! This is. Fuck! Sorry Kelly. I need to check out all these names, track some of them down."

A yawn preceded Kelly's, "I'll help you," and led Daniel on another path, touched as it was with innocence.

Here before him was the potential of love, more perfect than any Daniel had come close to touching previously. But here was a dangerous love he couldn't see through, couldn't pin a label to.

Her infectious tiredness resolved all problems until the morning. She wanted to take the couch despite DM's thoughtful insistence, and she settled into a coil there to urge him towards sleep.

He was walking in a desert in no time, and all the friends he'd had were passing him by, bleeped and deleted. Thirsting, they passed by and were bleeped off; his childhood running from him, the feelings and possibilities of an era slipping through his grasp. In the skies a vague hand tried to squeeze the clouds, but they were dry, coughing out dust. Sirens were coming in.

There was an apparent mirage, an oasis where naked women danced; "To music like a tommy-gun…" came through a hailer.

His eyelids flickered, the sirens drawing closer. He felt something. He was being masturbated. It felt beautiful, his subconscious touching reality, the waves of pleasure mimicking the approaching sirens.

He groaned, licked his lips, whispered, "Water water…" as King Creole started strumming.

He could stay here forever. When reality threatened to wake him from the dream he could ignore it, submit to sleep and throw himself back into the fantasy with a back-flip.

The sirens drew closer, grinding to a halt as his eyelids flickered; gradual awakening connecting him back to real time, real place, real action. Kelly sat at the side of his bed, her hand slowly, eagerly, pushing and pulling on his cock.

Sudden shock reared him upright, worked out a Karma check in operation.

"Are you enjoying it, sir?" she slurred hazily, her doey eyes opening and shutting in a slow-time.

"My god, Kelly!" Daniel pulled the sheets over him. "What—"

"Reading your mind sir. The desert, the burning, the whole world burning. Just you and me and all the water gone. We're fucking, urh, we could save this fuckin' planet. Take me with you in your time capsule.

It's my mind that you need." She lolled onto Daniel, slipping her hand under the covers.

Daniel felt her hand at his groin, his battle between morality and pleasure indulged before he took her hand away.

"Stop it Kelly. It's wrong."

The sirens died, a voice coming over in faint echoes with, "He's pulled out. No Reeto arrest here."

"D'ye wanna stay, see what happens?"

"Reality's breaking through, we'd better get outta here."

A suspicion took Daniel – using the bedsheet as a robe – to his coat, to its pocket, to the place where the Reeto Dust should have been. Into his living room he saw it scattered on the couch and accompanying table.

When he returned to Kelly she was in deep sleep, her legs hanging off the bed. Daniel positioned her body for comfort and covered her in a fresh bedsheet. On the couch he contemplated sleeplessness before cut and paste dreams subtly played out the prophecy.

Kelly looked weary in the morning, slumping into the living room, rubbing her eyes in a pause to focus on direction.

Daniel had half the feeling and half the hope that she'd forgotten the previous night, until she spoke: "I made a fool of myself last night Mr Manion, and I'm sorry."

She sat beside Daniel on the couch, burying her head into his shoulder, succumbing to the tiredness left unpurged by her frantic dreams.

"It shouldn't have happened, but we'll forget about it," he said, his hands soothing the back of her head. "It could cause a lot of trouble."

"Only if I tell, and I won't," Kelly replied, pulling herself out to face Daniel. "I'm not stupid. What I did was because I was high, but deep down I wanted to do it. I don't feel like a fifteen year old, some stupid schoolgirl. I think I love you.

"Don't say that, Kelly. It's, it's, it's—"

"OK, if you don't love me, then I was stupid and I can forget about it. Don't worry."

He consoled Kelly, touching her face with the backs of his fingers:

"Yor a wonderful person. I've grown very close to you recently. Let's not complicate matters. You've got exams to get through and I've got plans to make—"

"I want to help you with the pupils."

"You can," appeased Kelly, pulling her gently to him.

He was crumbling and he knew it. A past life came back to him in emotions and he had the idea that Kelly could be a part of the perfect future he was planning. He seized the day:

"Maybe I love you too, but right now we should just stick to words and feelings."

"And when can it be more than that?"

"When the world's a better place."

A Joint, A Mind, Some Good Tunes, And Your Imagination

No problems, we got this all under control. I am me, you are you, and we, we are the one-consciousness. Let's get back inside this thing.

So, do we jump or do we step? Could we make it in one jump?

I say we step, we amble, we take our time, we hang here. But not for too long: we don't wanna look like crazy bums.

I got this under control, no problems. Left foot, right foot; it's easy. It's not far, we can get back into it. Right. No, left.

Look, I told you, we still cool. We got this under control. Boom! I'm in space looking down. *Resurrection Vitaque Sum*: that's one of crazy Beeel's.

Right, left. Left, left. Jesus! Nearly flattened by a car! Even so; life, death; all down to fate. Keep moving.

Things are getting really strange. I wish I hadn't got so out of it. There's sirens in the distance. I need to get out of this. Think.

Bleep. Checked up on The Pointless Fanatics.

Bleep. Final details with The Redskins.

Bleep. Dusted.

Bleep. Pointless Fanatics.

Bleep bleep bleep.

Walk. There's a woman following. Walk. Keep walking, DM.

She's out there, screaming about disasters she had foretold, screaming that she can see me meeting a horrible end as she yanks up a knife. Yeh, she's good at seeing into the future when she controls it.

Bleep: I've been sacked. Bleep: I'm having a relationship with a minor. Bleep. Bleep. Deaf John's got the old miners, railwaymen and dockers together. Bleep: I keep hearing voices in my head. Bleep: I need to get off the dust. Bleep. Bleep: I am superhuman. Bleep: my mother was called Helen, my father was called John. We lived in a house in Sector 26. I was the bad luck boy.

It's just a dream half a world away. I've got to stay on the tracks of an automatic life. Keep walking.

You are safe now. That's the house. I'm OK, I can cope with this.

Kate introduced Professor Ragalana then took DM through the tidied debris of her house up to the attic.

She took a disk copy of "AL File 2" from DM and bleeped it into her battered, aerosoled computer wall-panel.

"Automatics seem to be just concerned with buying products. The Unpeople seem to be used for petty crime. And The Exterminators, well—" said DM, putting commentary to the display Kate had bleeped up.

"Then I'll bet our man's one of the Unpeople." Her head tilted slightly to address DM, though her eyes remained on the screen. "We took prints from the front room. The police haven't got back to us yet, but it didn't take long for us to identify the intruder. There."

She bleeped up Leonardo M Smith's details.

"Wow, Kate, that was the name I chanced upon when I got the file. What a coincidence."

"Coincidences happen all the time, it's just that nobody notices," interrupted Professor Ragalana, a joint smouldering between his fingers. "Coincidences can be linked to every moment in history, and what people don't seem to realise is that careful planning can throw up all sorts of useful coincidences. It seems to me that's what Tumblety's up to. He's planning lives, choreographing emotions, making the right people for the right time and place..."

Ragalana was feeling loose, enjoying the thrill of knowledge. He had spent enough of a lifetime distancing himself from the fantastic reality of Declan Marx and the aliens. The business of experimenting, recording and assimilating had been like an addiction to keep him sane; logic ticking over to suppress illogical theories. He'd regulated himself to the point of insanity; so tight with functioning perfectly that even the slightest hint of his past experiences tore him up. As hard as he tried, Ragalana could not rid himself of the memories.

But now the prof was cool. He was going to cut loose, use his knowledge to ignite his imagination. All those crazy ideas about aliens were going to be allowed to flourish. He was going to enjoy himself, and by the end of it he was going to be purged. He had met people with parts of his jigsaw and they would be witnesses. They would meet the aliens on their fantastic adventure and he would know he was sane. And if not, then at least he would pin his insanity down, use his mental powers to cope and live with it, even to indulge.

Yes, Ragalana was embarking on an amazing adventure. His imagination was going to run riot in the fields of his consciousness, going to explore and play, touch and feel the extraordinary ideas drifting about infinity. He would be able to fantasise, using rationality only as a last resort to shoot down concepts getting out of hand.

He was free at last to live by impulse, to even feel a sense of innocence, to be truly open-minded about the possibilities of the universe. Little did he know that he would be dead within five minutes, although ask him now he's dead and he appreciates the irony: killed by one of his own little coincidences. That one step into another dimension put him in the town Wrong Place, Wrong Time.

"Sorry, have I been hogging this?" he asked with a roach-biting butt as presented evidence.

"No, Prof," said DM, "I just gave it to you."

"…This is unbelievable. Once we expose this it'll bring down the whole establishment."

"It's got to be the right time," said DM cautiously. "You've got to plan it right, not get it out half-cock—"

"I once treated a man with half a cock," Ragalana said, eye-catchingly deadpan. "The least of his worries, really."

DM continued: "You can't chance the authorities getting a sniff or they'll have it suppressed long enough for a cover up. You need to have all the right media outlets at your disposal."

"I think I know what you are talking about," said Kate. "A Sun, Right wingless aircraft, Quarter, A Sun, Twenty-four hours," came straight from *Cracking Codes For Kids*.

DM acknowledged before a flood of memories kick-started his paranoia. He was about to seek resolution by opening discussion with Professor Ragalana, when a stunned Ragalana exclaimed: "What the fuck was that about?"

In the time it took Daniel to prepare the dialogue for a second delivery, Professor Ragalana had worked out that he'd let himself go too far and that he needed to take a break from the chimera and get back to business: "Sorry, I haven't had the 'Erb since the turn of the century. I fully agree with the need for mass media coverage, but there would be little danger of a successful cover-up. If you look at what all the various types of Automatics have been treated with you will see that their present existence is enough evidence to prove Tumblety's plans. These drugs, these functions, do not allow for much retention of memory. You would need only one of them from amongst, well, possibly millions, to prove what is apparently happening. Ask them questions about their childhood and they will only have vague moments, possibly the most traumatic, to recall. Also, certain functions which require nurturing to understand would be beyond them, violence their probable method of dealing with it.

"Those in power would have to commit genocide on an unprecedented scale to cover this one up. Although history charts mass murder and ethnic cleansing throughout each century, it is usually only the big one people remember. This would have to be this century's big one for a cover up to be successful. Unless the future is a catalogue of appalling holocausts and this possible genocide is just a minor precursor, then I doubt it can be covered up."

Daniel made to approach Professor Ragalana a third time when Kate's words came to distract: "It's going. Check the tracking switch is on Dan, it's at the side there."

Daniel felt around and, not wanting to show his incompetence, touched the nearest switch. He felt an electric current keeping his finger on the button.

"No," said Kate. "It must be Leonardo's handiwork. What's up Dan?"

"I'm getting an electric shock. It's OK."

Ragalana pulled Daniel away from the controls, made to examine the tracking switch. "You got the wrong one," he said before touching Daniel's incorrectly chosen option. The electric shock flung him backwards. His body shook briefly, blood pouring from the back of his head. Then, Professor Ragalana and all he knew, left the Earth for the next life.

"I don't know how to react."

"React how you feel," said Kate.

"I feel like I'm going insane. I feel like I've done everything before, but this time it's all collapsing."

"Is it the stress from all your big plans do you think?"

"Maybe."

"It'll be OK, don't worry," said Kate sensitively.

Daniel loved her, but his mind was with Kelly Godfrey.

"My mind was racing when the cops were here. I thought I was going to crack."

"You got through it. You should really lay off this Reeto though. I can get you some Wantok if you want."

"Maybe. Look, we'll do the hills tomorrow night if that's OK. I've got some things I need to do."

"No problem. Are you going to be OK?"

"Yeh. You?"

"Yes. If we keep our handcoms with us we can get in touch if there are any problems."

"Good idea. Be careful good Kate."

They were into each other's minds, accepting and touching ideologies, moulding them together; their imaginations ignited with infinity their playground.

"And then everyone would be free to think and feel the way they wanted," added Kelly. "We could spend our lives exploring our inner selves, projecting that to our outer selves."

"The mind would become so powerful. There would be peace on Earth with everyone just exploring the possibilities of their thoughts, just going to the ends of their imaginations," said DM as he took Kelly's intricately rolled joint.

"But there would be no end. There would always be new directions to explore. And we would grow so strong with the love of our fellow humans that we could share. World hunger could be ended rather than people just trying to get richer and richer."

"The world has enough natural resources to feed everyone. The NRP spent seventy billion dollars on their defence budget last year. Imagine spending that on food for the hungry, or even helping the underclass in this country."

"It can happen," said Kelly enthusiastically. "And then we can explore space together."

"Only when we end capitalism, when we put an end to the idea of life being about making a profit. The true function of our lives is to find fulfilment, in our inner and outer selves."

Inner and outer, slipping in kisses, exploring each other's particular innocence. DM felt inspired, reminded himself of the power of "The 'Erb" as Professor Ragalana called it. He'd been on the dust for too long and now he felt like he was escaping, releasing at last a part of his emotional development that had been closed off with his childhood.

Kelly began unbuttoning her blouse. Daniel couldn't say a word, though he had many speeches queuing. He wanted to see her pure, smooth flesh. There had been too many brief, unimaginative, experienced lovers in his life. The sex had been arbitrary, cold, clinical. Anger had successfully distanced him from these moments, so that he had never known the depths and thrills of First Love.

She reached the last button and slipped off her blouse; her skin, sculptured, timeless, ageless.

She reached down to unzip her skirt, wriggling from its confines to stand before Daniel like perfection: her soft, pale face flushed, veins pointing like arrows at her carefully crafted facial features; demure pale blue eyes flickering above the carved artistry of her innocuous nose and naturally pink, pursed lips. Plain, white underwear served a prosaic function for Kelly but smoothed into Daniel's desire an eroticism he had never experienced before.

A kiss between them forced retreat into shells, their nerves shuddering from a primeval power. They were hardly daring to taste anymore, but the risk and its red-blooded fancy tempted them to break through. They kissed again for a longer connection, retreating deliberately to touch the aftershock impatiently. They felt it inside, let it linger, felt it like nothing else as important had touched their lives before or would touch their lives again.

Each motion hesitated before acceptance then paused for reciprocation, nervous that the love might not be real. But each movement strengthened their souls until they were turning as one, feeling as one, holding the world as a grain of sand.

Across the thick night air bleeps floated, seeming natural with the hushed rustle of bushes and trees as wildlife settled.

"Hey DM, all ready for the big day?" asked Red.

"Just about. You?"

"Wantok-a-gogo."

Cocktail Suicide 8 had known DM since 2021. They'd known Kate for seven years through her astronomy group, The Astros, which had three of the eight as members: Moz, X and Roget. They'd kept the contacts separate for the sake of their belief in fate and yen for frivolity.

Kate only worked out the coincidence twenty-four hours earlier when she'd asked them to help with an exploration of the hills. DM, last to know, got the full glory of commenting on it.

"There are some beautiful vibes up here," said Tina, passing on the carrot-shaped joint, introducing it with, "This is the cock-eight carrot, let your imagination fuck."

"We've felt something when we've been up here," said Roget. "There's all sorts of weird shit going on, but it's all positive. I don't know what the Science 'Tute are doing here, but we don't get their vibes man."

"Your friend Ted's up here," said Maggie playfully.

"Have you spoken to him?" asked DM.

"Ah, well, y'know Ted. I don't think he approves of us too much. He told us not to do anything rash." Maggie laughed and the other seven followed. "He shouldn't worry about us though. We won't blow his big day. It's soon, isn't it?"

"We've heard it's Sunday," interrupted X as DM lost a witty reply.

"You know more than me," was all he could offer.

Maggie edged closer, her face a few inches from DM's: "We know all you know. When you see Ted he's gonna tell you it's Sunday."

"Yor very good," said DM. "What about the winning lottery numbers for the draw after Sunday?"

"Oh, too easy. Thirteen, thirty-seven, thirty-nine, forty-six, forty-seven, and, er, big number one. But that's only 'cos we've fixed it so everyone's a winner."

"Tuned in."

Maggie kissed Daniel's cheek: "We believe in you, DM. Sunday's gonna be the beginning of paradise on Earth."

The badinage running wild, Kate interrupted to give directions. In pairs the group set off to look for the source of Kate's recorded brainwaves.

Daniel followed Kate, using the yellow brick road which wound up the hills as a focal point to maintain a position. Kate used her handcom to guide them, taking and noting readings as DM kept a watchful eye out for people from The Institute Of Science.

The yellow paving flitted in and out of thick, coiling fog, inspiring vague memories of paths DM had crossed in his infancy. More permanent were the strange lights, flickering in no apparent rhythm with a low level humming: a heavy bass oozing and fading over intermittent bleeps.

"The strongest reading is around here," said Kate, circling before halting. "The ultrasound waves match with recordings of Marx's. It seems to be under the ground though. Are there caves around here?"

"Many. We used to go in them when I was a kid."

"Are they big? DM? DM? Daniel."

"Sorry, no, not that big."

"Can you take me to the closest one?"

"I can't remember where they are exactly. This fog won't help, but I'll have a go."

Daniel found that as he walked there were natural icons which triggered experiences from his past. He remembered the way stones were piled, the positions of trees and the shape of grooves undulating beneath his feet. He sensed their presence from childhood adventures, guiding him to a cave he felt his family had once picnicked in.

Kate was leading again, using her handcom to follow the ultrasound wave readings. Daniel laboured, took in the scenes and absorbed the memories.

"This is it," echoed back to DM and took him towards Kate. "It ends here, but the readings are coming from that direction," she said, pointing with the handcom at a cave wall. "Are there any other entrances?"

"Yeh, but none of them go very far," replied DM. In the pause he picked up something in his hearing.

"Shush, listen. Someone's coming."

He took hold of Kate's hand, led her some metres before she picked up the approaching mutterings spinning around the cave's walls.

They knelt behind a triangular rock and watched as two figures wearing Institute Of Science uniforms reached the dead end.

As one took readings from the cave wall the other muttered, "This is bullshit. There's no way in."

"One kilometre of dense earth and rock. No apparent way in or out. I reckon it's just an alien decoy transmitter, but what do I know?"

"We know more than those fuckers."

"Come on, this isn't the closest, let's do the others."

When their footsteps had faded Kate moved back to the rock face: "There's something in there, they know it. But it can't be Marx."

"The aliens. He said, the aliens."

Kate tapped the rock: "Maybe they have landed, maybe that's why the Institute is up here."

Just over one kilometre behind the rock was a hollowed-out space ten metres wide, twelve long. There, Taff and Phil were reporting back to Helen and John Manion, the space's centre occupied by a table, on which Declan Marx lay.

Marx was hooked to a drip, wires from his head connecting with a wall panel and monitoring screen. Crowding around the table were luscious green plants, some of which appeared to be linked to Marx's body. Slow, subdued bleeps marked out time uniformly.

Helen and John, their appearances unchanged from when they were thirty-three and thirty-two, expressed concern for Daniel's well-being. Both Taff and Phil had some sympathy and support, but dealt mainly in cold, hard information.

For Helen and John the carefully constructed cave had been their habitat for over seventeen years. Only rarely did the time pass slowly, for the Inuthuans had kept them amused with wondrous, fantastical spiritual flights and experiences. Only when they pondered Daniel's whereabouts and life did the minutes move laboriously. Even then they never considered leaving and abandoning their mission.

From the moment they had been taken to Inuthua and shown Earth's possible fate they'd known what they had to do. They were shown worlds beyond their comprehension, shown the possibility of the mind and the longevity of the soul, and they were converted to The Koubah. With the promise of their own immortality and eternity with their son, they agreed to follow instructions: "Their destiny", as it was put to them.

Taff's factual account of Daniel's mental health worried them briefly, their mood tempered swiftly with images of meeting him again.

"It is soon, we are getting close," said John Manion. "Marx is nearly done and the Earth is nearly saved. Keep an eye on Daniel and don't go back to Finhouha without telling us."

"I don't know if we're ever going back," replied Phil.

"Just tell us if you do," concluded Helen.

After Taff and Phil had departed, Helen and John took up animated discussion, went to Inuthua and back, and then assumed their positions in front of the monitor to view life through Molly Simms and John Barrett's eyes. Both probes allowed them muted and infrequent visuals of their son; mere highlights of a life that inspired them to believe in their mission.

In the wee small hours Kate and Daniel regrouped with Cocktail Suicide 8 back at their mansion in the luxurious Sheadle Sector.

Lal and Red had been spying on the Institute Of Science's operations. They had seen a diaphanous box, in which was caged, "Some kind of green creature. Little aliens," said Lal excitedly.

Moz had someone with him; the tall black man with hair of wool whom Daniel had thought he'd encountered on the hills before.

"He says he knows you and he's in with the plan," said Roget. "He says he's—"

"DM, I have news from Ted," interrupted the man, his velvety and authoritative vocals commanding everyone's attention.

"Ted who?" faked DM.

"Trust me, Daniel. Ted Kandinsky is fifty-one. He used to be a union leader on the trains. He is part of the revolution both you and I believe in. He has a pigeon called Cassie. He has first-class honours degrees in Chemistry and Psychology. He was married to a woman called Lena who disappeared one day twenty-five years ago. If you need any more proof, remember the man who built walls."

The code was enough to convince. "Do you know the day?" asked DM.

"No rest," replied the man.

"Told you," said Maggie before DM could digest the information.

When the man left, Moz told everyone that he had called himself Jesus: "I asked him if he was THE Jesus Christ and he said, 'What do you think?' "

"You think he's mad?" asked DM.

"What do you think?" returned Moz.

X marked the spot where she had prepared a joint and where she wanted the group to sit and pool together their findings.

All had witnessed something "Amazing, people", in the recounting of their adventures. There had been many encounters with activists upon the hills, all preparing for the day. Each had information to pass onto the CS8 pairings about the Institute Of Science's activities.

As each couple described and explained, a one-consciousness sensation linked them all in piecing together the fragments.

DEPENDENCE

The stupid and foolish thought they could get away with anything in the run-up to the European Championship semi-final. But the cops were watching them, taking bleeping notes in preparation for the first leg – at home – of the semi-final. The stupid and foolish thought the cops weren't bothering with them, the small points fry. But the cops were just waiting, logging potential easy-points-scorers for the home leg, hoping to accrue enough points before going to Amsterdam for the away leg.

DM meanwhile, with a little sophistication, pinpointed blind spots and went about subverting. He was the luckiest man alive.

At Primal Scream The Pointless Fanatics were playing to a full house, the venue ceiling-dripping crammed. Guitars crunched; vocals elevating above the sound, pleading for defiance.

Bodies bounced off the floor in union, their appreciation reverberating when a song ended.

"No rest!" shouted DM in Dan's ear.

The applause subsided as Dan announced to the crowd: "This is nothing. If you like this then be at the most important gig ever on Sunday. It's free and it's gonna blow your minds. Be at Freeman Park at three o'clock on Sunday. We're gonna play music like it was meant to be played; from the fuckin' heart!" A rapturous cheer as the instruments tuned up. "Tell all your friends and tell them to tell all their friends and our one-consciousness will be joined."

A big cheer followed, merging into the next raucous song. DM made his exit, to Casino Bob's to meet Joe.

Once inside, Joe must have sensed his presence, breaking off from a conversation with a waitress.

"DM, I thought you weren't coming! Here's the plan; we take a snort now, play some cards, make some money, then make the make. We go through tomorrow on Auto, getting stocked up with dust before the home leg, then get whackoed to infinity."

"Bleep me onto point one."

When they emerged from the toilets the regular busyness of Casino Bob's had changed.

"That waitress is eyeing me again," said Joe. "I'll see you at the Mariah table in fifteen."

The patient was seated in a corner, his head in his hands, buried in and burying in, his body statically intense. He was seeing it all there, in the free picture show in his mind.

At the roulette table the devil cracked his knuckles, his fiery eyes following the ball's jumping around the wheel as steam wafted from his bald red scalp. He got lucky, licked his lips and collected winnings all round.

The patient lifted his head up and everything stopped: all movement, all emotion. He smiled knowingly, put his head back into sweating palms. The people jolted back to life like nothing had happened.

DM had already won a few rounds before Joe seated himself at the playing table, a contented look upon his face.

"There she is," said Joe, nodding to direct DM. "I'm meeting her later on."

As his words rang hollowly, the waitress they viewed trod on a discarded beer bottle. She lost her balance, dropping the tray of drinks from her hand, teetering as they smashed, flapping to keep upright. Gravity pulled her body down, her head hitting a virtual game machine and taking the weight of her lifeless sprawl to the floor.

Uniformed figures were quickly at her side. Those playing games mostly ignored the incident; only a few losers distracted.

She was picked up, blood dripping from her head, her limp body suggesting something serious.

A man whose hushed tones were shocked with volume, said, "She's dead."

He was quickly admonished by an employee before her body disappeared into a back room.

"It's OK, just a little accident," said a uniform, seeking to convince observers.

"Shit," said Joe. "How fuckin' unlucky."

The patient in the corner looked up at DM, took away his reply to Joe, whose eyes were firmly fixed with disbelief on the death scene.

The patient mopped his brow, wrung out his palms and made a sharp exit from Casino Bob's.

No taxi came so DM began the long walk home. On his way he saw a man pissing against an antique book shop, another breaking into a car. He saw a woman chasing a man, wielding a hammer and spitting invective. He saw a man kicking into someone's body. Alarms sounded from houses and cars, tyres skidding, bottles smashing, fires crackling.

But DM was the luckiest man in the world and he walked through it like he were superimposed.

Footsteps followed, DM turning as they were upon him. It was the man from Casino Bob's who'd been sat in a corner.

"Whatta ya want?" demanded DM, standing his ground confrontationally so as to halt his pursuer a metre away.

"I knew you were going to say that, Daniel Manion. I know because I make it happen. That book yor writing, it's all my ideas."

"Wha—"

The man made a stop forward, rotating his head on its neck-axis, apparently trying to shake something off.

"Stop right there! Reality Police!" shouted the air-filled, thick-veined, smooth-skinned ball of a face.

"You have broken Section 23 of The Reality Act, paragraph 5.3," added the other similarly featured balloon. "Imagination bridging with reality is an offence. You have had your warning—"

"Chief," interrupted his colleague. "This is Ronan Jacobs. He's a special category imaginer. We can't touch him."

"Can't touch him? This fucker's broken—"

"He's protected. We must have got the wrong one."

"What about The DM? Check Jacob's memory."

The balloon did a quick scan and replied, "Yeh, DM was here, but he's gone now. We won't be able to get back in, his unreality is fading."

"Fuck! But he'll be back. Then we'll have the fucker. OK, Jacobs, but be warned; I don't give a fuck who protects you. If you think you can let your imagination go anywhere you are in for one fuckin' shock."

Jacobs woke and DM was gone, so Jacobs found somebody else to kill.

Joyous music – ethereal bleeps and harmonising waves – led the news into, "Panamera is saving lives…" Fifteen minutes were devoted to the success of the NRP's "Water scheme". Mitchell Portmann, sincerely humbled, spoke slowly and lowly:

"You know, many people criticised our plans, but if you want to be radical and want to change people's lives you sometimes have to ignore the dissenters. You have to have strength and faith and you have to be tough. We have earned people's trust and they can see that what we are doing is for them. Yes we take risks, yes we can come across as stubborn, but you know, in the end, it is the people who benefit..."

Opinion polls showed "The people" significantly impressed. Opinions, dependent on selection, had been noted and the NRP was "overwhelmingly supported by the majority."

"Anarchists" had been arrested, "their murderous reign of terror ended". They had been opposing the government "with violence and murder". They were challenging "democracy" by "threatening democracy".

From homes in "modernised streets" people were in contact with the world through their televisual units. It gave them a semblance of awareness and put their lives in some perspective to know that "allies" in the Middle East were "close to destroying the sadistic dictator..." It gave them vicarious fulfilment to learn that their country had sentenced another three paedophiles to death. They could share in the grief of Mr and Mrs Elton as they watched their daughter Sophie's coffin being lowered. Another victim of The Manchester Slicer-copycat-Newcastle-Slicer, they were provoked into determination as East Tyneside's Chief Inspector spoke of "leaving no stone unturned, no avenue unexplored in our relentless pursuit of the killer". Their determination found substance as clips re-ran news items showing how East Tyneside had reached the European Championship semi-final: muggers, burglars, murderers, rapists, paedophiles and "terrorists" added to their fifteen minutes of infamy with replays of their hands in locks, their faces in shock, sentences from performing judges echoing on the sound effects. Self-esteem was nourished with a sensational videography of Michael Grant following his arrest for drunk-driving with a minor in his company. They dutifully sniggered at the mock-solemnity of a report on the Michael Grant clone who'd killed himself after hearing the news.

Ultimately they were left with hope, their bitterness satiated with statistics about "the NRP's Workscheme programme reducing the unemployment figures". An edited re-tread of a "Once homeless and hopeless man's life" got them involved, got them to feel "The pain, the madness", before a prick of guilt numbed them with, "No one helped him, no one cared for him, no one bothered with him. But the NRP knew who he was. They cared about him..." Carried along, they clung to images of a different life, in a new home, with money and opportunity. Subliminally, "It could be you," bleeped out from the screen.

They were left with a laugh or four: life on Mars, an award winning star, a cheeky son and the man whose bottom "holds the record for the most appearances on televisuals". He was The Moon King and his next challenge was "to show my arse in outer space".

374

"The weather" recommended that people in Tyneside should "enjoy the indoors for only eight hours tomorrow. That leaves sixteen to spare, and I know those people up there like to party!"

They had no knowledge of peaceful protesters being arrested without charge, of the *Guardian* newspaper and website being closed down, or of the genocide in East Timor. Into their oblivion went news that a Home Office-funded report (The National Audit of Offender Employment Policies and Practice) had been published but had excluded details linking unemployment to crime. Baroness Blitchard had spoken at a seminar, Improving the Employment Prospects of Offenders, and had quoted the Prison Service as considering "work to be one of the principle means of reducing re-offending post release". The report also said that the unemployed or "partially unemployed like those on Workscheme" were more likely to commit crime. This passed them by, as did a relevant "off the record" quote from Sir Patrick Sheay, head of American British Tobacco: "We've killed millions of people, particularly the working class. They can't get off it, it's their only pleasure."

None of this mattered to those hooked to omniscient televisual units. Their emotions had been fixed and now they could switch on/switch off to pursue their purpose.

THROW YOUR HOMEWORK
ONTO THE FIRE

———————

"…So all you need is your heart and soul. Your minds are the most powerful things you possess. You don't need junk TV and you don't need to just sit back and take it. I'm sorry I have to leave you, you've been a wonderful class, even when I've had to shout at some of you. I wish you good luck in the exams, and I hope that you achieve your potential. Don't let anybody tell you what to believe. They're usually wrong. Fuck 'em."

The class fell silent, hushed in shock briefly before some giggles, then applause and tears.

Pupils crowded round to talk to him during lunch break, gradually peeling off as their feelings got squeezed.

"It's so sad, sir," concluded Kelly, now alone with Daniel. "But at least I'll see you again."

"Of course," said Daniel abruptly. "It's on for Sunday, Kelly. Can you get things organised for then?"

"Yes," she replied, quickly locked into the seriousness. "It's all ready. Tell me what's going to happen."

"I can't now, Kelly."

"Can I come round tonight?"

"Tomorrow." She accepted. "Do the CCTVs before you hit the street. Everyone's after me."

"Like who?"

"Everybody. Just keep your eyes open and be suspicious. It's the only way we'll get through this."

His Year 9 class, first after lunchtime, he treated to newspaper headlines relating to the NRP, explaining in detail the truth behind each one. Integrated into a story to mollify the information, he biased it with excitement, making it palatable to their young and adventurous minds.

"This government," he concluded, "lies to the people, making them believe everything is fine. But in this country we have thirty per cent unemployment, double that if you add those exploited on Workscheme. The crime rate is at an all time high just as the points tallies have set new records for forces around the country. Something doesn't add up, but they baffle us into submission with statistics and gory visuals. There's an estimated million and a half people homeless. They can't vote; it's the law. There's an estimated six million people living in poverty; the so-called underclass who can't make their mark on most statistics.

"They get away with it. People don't speak out. We, here in East Tyneside, breathe in all sorts of poisonous shit every day, but we don't question it. It's all good jobs for the area, keeps the local economy afloat. The fact that cases of cancer and leukaemia are above the national average doesn't even deserve a mention.

"CIC are killing us and we don't even question it. You need the intelligence to be able to question. You need education so you can think for yourselves and challenge those in power. Don't think you are being non-conformist by hating school: that's what those in power want you to be. They want you to be stupid so they can fuck with you! Get an education and do what you want with your life. You can decide what you want to do. If you don't like what those in power are doing you will have the mind to do something about it.

"Imagine, you get together in a group, persuade other people to join your group so it gets bigger and stronger. You can wake in your dreams, just imagine.

"I'm leaving you, against my wishes, earlier than expected. It's been interesting and enjoyable and you can feel proud that each and every one of you have something to offer. Good luck in the future."

Having devoted ten minutes to "Final speech" in his lesson plans, Mr Manion finished two minutes early and left them laughing with thought provoking one-liners. He gently eased away the emotions to let in his Year 7 class.

"I've had a look at your My Perfect World projects and I've been very impressed."

For each project he had praise, carefully nurturing his class by coaxing their imaginations into believing in what they had written. Mr Manion had a detailed description to tie together the possibilities of their recorded thoughts.

"Believe in this, children, and believe in yourselves. If you want a perfect world, make it happen. Sometimes you've got to take the chance, go with what your heart tells you. If no one out there understands start your own revolution and cut out the middle man. Have confidence in yourselves. You've made an excellent start to the year and I'm sorry I won't be seeing you again. Thank you."

Daniel felt empty, saddened at leaving. He consoled himself with hope for the future, that one day he would teach again in a better and more flexible world.

He made arrangements with Kate before leaving without ceremony. Joe left him at the train station, urgent in his need to be on time for Dr Tumblety.

Each step through the blank faces in town took him further into depression. He felt the past rearing up, felt its joy and pain, the loss of innocence, the endgame of adulthood. He felt tempted to slip into the dust, fatalistic that with the revolution so close his unrivalled expectation might lead to the bitterest disappointment.

Sirens were already in a frenzy of whirring as he locked himself indoors. He would be staying indoors for the first leg of the European Championship semi-final, one of the guilty and innocent cowering not to end up on East Tyneside's points tally.

He used the net to make contacts and prepare groups for Sunday: birthday greetings were sent to members of The Guthries all over England whilst favourite recipes found their way to diverse groups in the Green movement. He sent an e-mail to Will Correca to send over Cassie, using her to get a hand-written message to Deaf John Barrett. Deaf John would then make final arrangements with the old miners, dockers and railwaymen. A rhythmic bleep with a bass hook went to Morse, initiating his deployment of "Revbeat" – his subversive anthem – to disk jockeys, MCs and net mixers throughout the country. For Jez and members of "Media Truth" Daniel sent out times and durations.

He had the spirit of Father Christmas within him; a fanciful notion of a mythical philanthropist coming to town to brighten lives. A naïve anticipation filled him against his will as he white-knuckled through the fluctuations of his emotions.

They were hardly any sirens in the Egdon Sector of town, just faint echoes infiltrating from the town centre. Kelly worked at her computer, chatting over the net to her schoolmates; inciting in between gossip. Her mother also worked at a computer, putting the finishing touches to her novel, *Laura*.

Laura dealt with her "extraordinary life" (she had the blurb, the reviews and the reaction already typed and saved). From Laura Williams and her "horrific childhood" through to her "perfect marriage" and the subsequent "tragedy of love". She had her fight against depression and her "encounters with the stars" (exaggerated profusely from her experiences on cable TV). Laura Godfrey's "business success" found considerable space in the computer's memory, whilst her "struggle" to raise a daughter "with care and attention" merely came through in carefully integrated soundbites during lulls in the plot.

The novel's climax concerned Laura's experiences with a man whom "I thought could help me learn to love again". But she was "betrayed", "cheated" and "used and abused" by him. The man had seduced and "manipulated" her "heartbroken", "vulnerable...and innocent" daughter. She fought off her "anger and depression" because "I realised my daughter meant more to me than anything. I was determined that I would have the strength to fight back my feelings and do what was right."

The media "torture...drained me...and put unbearable strains on Kelly." Kelly "had a breakdown...was pushed to the edge of insanity." Laura "realised that she needed urgent treatment." Laura had to cope with "my own heartbreak...my daughter's descent into insanity...and a media hungry for my life story."

Laura "battled everything that was thrown at me," and agreed to appear on *The Susie Baster Show* to "open my heart. I remembered Princess Spencer and all her battles and I found strength from that. When I went on that show, feeling vulnerable and innocent like my daughter, I felt Princess Spencer's spirit within me..."

Laura poured through her cathartic broadcast; describing in detail the words she would say in her "...outpouring of deep and fragile emotions".

The novel ended with "...a fragile grasp at hope", and her plans for the future, all mapped out in glorious Technicolor.

The publication deal was already signed: her web library bought up by *The Shine* on condition that she could produce evidence that her story was "True Life". All Laura had to do was re-draft the last five chapters.

She added names, descriptions and background to the novel, sipping at the expensive wine she'd bought on credit with some self-satisfaction.

Self-preservation compelled Kate Flowers' actions as she loaded all the most important information she needed onto a handcom. She dodged the flames to exit but paused when her morality checked. She pulled the still stunned intruder's body from her home and laid it on the pavement.

She had to think and plan as she drove away. All lines to Daniel were dead and she was tensely hunched around the wheel believing "They" had gotten to him. "He isn't safe. Cocktail Suicide 8 it."

Daniel had cut off all lines of communication, all his tasks bleeped off a list "that could burn" He was trying to find equilibrium in his mood, running through withdrawals and hitting extravagant highs and lows.

"Trying to plan time, to make some time, just to plan some more time to make time for a future you can never have. There is only now. Keep that in thoughts, DM, work this out. See the present tense, live in the present tense. If you see the present tense, boy, do you see it, and boy, can you celebrate it."

GODDAM BIBLE!

A splintered crash released Daniel's grip on Kelly. She murmured from the deepest sleep as he sat upright, alert in an instant, forgetting his de-conditioning programme had started.

A light exposed them, ghosts of inspectors Howard and Collins forming through the bedroom door. Four uniformed females circled as a red light from a laser gun homed in on Daniel's forehead.

"Daniel Manion, you are under arrest," sonically came from Collins' vocal chords. "For the murder of Louise Woodling, sex with a minor, supply of pornographic images, drug-dealing and the murder of Peter Wheaton. You have the right to remain silent and this may be used as evidence…"

Kelly started screaming as two policewomen pulled her from the bed and tried to clothe her nakedness.

"Calm down Miss Godfrey," said one of her assailants. "You won't have to see this man again. He is a paedophile and he's brainwashed you. You will receive proper counselling."

She kicked against the vaginas as six hands dragged her away. Kelly raged to break free of their reassuring words, screaming back at Daniel for help.

Howard and Collins remained in the bedroom with one female officer, her laser still pinpointing Daniel's possible catalyst for the next life.

"Got you," came asthmatic from Collins.

"What's this? Fuckin' murders? Pornographic images? What the fuck—?"

"We've got everything we require for the murders, Mr Manion," replied Howard. "And if we could allow you to see the disks Kelly's mother uncovered you'd see quite a performance. We have your evil as our evidence, Manion." Howard bit the sentence, more desperate the closer it came to a climax. He flicked his head impatiently to dismiss the female officer.

"Get clothed, bitch!" screeched Collins.

They watched as Daniel dressed, their contentment recorded with Collins' punch into their prisoner's stomach.

"Don't fuck with us, Manion," warned Howard, suppressing his clockwork need for violence. It was what gained him respect in the force, allowing him to paint himself as a wise old-timer and idealistic pragmatist. Colleagues never knew he purged this impulse by beating his wife. Because, deep down, he hated her because she was the woman he didn't dare to be. Hard words helped sell his image: "We've fuckin' got all we need on you. You couldn't remember talking to Louise Woodling, but we've got a witness says you did just that. And Peter Wheaton, killed by some man you met at your drug den. Why is it that this man has been diagnosed as a harmless loon? Why, you evil fuck?" Howard let it out in an untraceable blow to Daniel's stomach. Collins smiled. "We've got six officers to witness you in bed with a fifteen year old, we've got a disk of you raping her: How fuckin' pornographic is that? Enough? You evil fuck. You are fucked, and we haven't even started yet."

Howard flicked his head again, jerked-off to Collins who immediately began rampaging through Daniel's flat, displacing its identity.

Collins' enthusiasm was at a precipice, gleefully abandoned as he realigned Daniel's belongings and imagined Howard accompanying him to a transvestite's ball.

Collins raised his arm twice, each time to produce a drug. First the pot, then the Reeto. Howard lapped it up, uncoiling his superiority.

"So there's the drugs' charge all wrapped up, Manion. Do you know yor fucked now?"

Collins pulled Daniel's hands behind his back, bleeped a lock on them.

"Fucked," reaffirmed Howard. "Yor only hope is to give us information on Ted Kandinsky."

"Fuck you!"

Howard faked a laugh. "Record that, Collins." Collins bleeped. "We'll get what we want from you, Manion."

The police car dodged and deflected debris thrown at it from the gutters of Sector 3, the criminals out and about to breathe and release a pent-up violence contained over the previous night.

"What the fuck are we here for?" Daniel asked, perplexed and fearful.

"Psychopaths need special treatment, to help them get well," slithered Collins.

He screamed his rights like all those who had passed into the asylum before, found the same deaf ears and the same brutal clamping.

Strapped to a chair by two muscular white spooks, he felt an injection coldly and precisely take him away from the moment.

Daniel felt a warm sensation on his cheek, a tingling spreading, cutting sharper and growing discernible as pain. The slap of flesh hitting flesh registered as his eyes rehearsed opening, slowly and laboriously lifting until another blow shook him.

Dr Tumblety stood before him; Collins insidious with glee at his right, Howard stoical at his left.

"Mr Manion," began Tumblety, his melting face glowering with contempt. "You are mentally ill. I am here to help you. You don't know what you've done; that's part of your condition." Tumblety took theatrically contemplative steps, his head reading the floor for a prompt: "You have Binswanger's Disease, a progressive deterioration of the brain. Intellectually you know the difference between right and wrong, but the part of your brain which can relate to the emotions of others has been wiped out. You will recognise the symptoms of loss of memory and cognition, mood changes and depression." Tumblety's pacing expostulation halted, his sights trained on Daniel, resuming a position in between but slightly ahead of Howard and Collins. "I will help you. Don't try to question it, you will find no answers. You have murdered, taken drugs, raped a girl and who knows what else. It's not you, it's the other person inside of you. We will get rid of that person so don't fight it."

Howard moved forward into Tumblety's space: "Tell us about Ted Kandinsky and what he plans to do."

Collins slapped again, hitting Daniel's bloodline, igniting a fuse back to the primal scream.

"Faaark yow!"

Tumblety retreated, Collins and Howard moving shoulder to shoulder.

"You have very few options," said Howard. "We have all the evidence we need."

"Just in time for the death penalty," added Collins, his tone squat and husky.

"Fuck you. What have you done with Kelly?"

"Undergoing treatment to get you out of her system."

"Fuck no!" Daniel wailed. "Fuck no. You bastards, you fuckin' bastards!"

"Stop, Mr Manion," intervened Tumblety, re-emerging from the peripherals. "Try talking sense. Try to avoid what you imagine is what you should say. Say what is the right thing to say. Say something realistic."

"Yor fuckin' crazy! Yor fuckin' mad men! I'm fuckin' sane!"

Disgusted and impatient, Tumblety retreated again, obliterated from Daniel's view by the two inspectors' bodies.

Collins whined eerily before words functioned: "Well, huh, when we apply some of Dr Tumblety's medicines maybe you won't be so convinced. Really, you never realise how complex the human brain is until you hear all the ways it can be completely re-wired and fucked up."

"You fuckin' storm-troopers!" shouted DM at their backs, all three leaving abruptly, animated discussion in their murmurings.

A few minutes later a thin man entered the cell backed by two guards. The thin man took a needle from his case, sucked a blue liquid from a capsule, injected it into Daniel's arm.

Got to stay alert. Got to stay with this, overcome it. Nothing seems to be happening yet.

I feel suddenly awake, like I've broken through something. My life is flashing past me and the sudden realisation that it was all just a dream, that I hadn't been tapped into a pure vein for most of it, that my mind had become like a sieve, all experiences flowing through, the dirty particles clogging it up over the years so that no innocent light could pass through. All just a dream, my perception altered from that early "Bang!"

A youthful breathing in, taking in the magic and loss, seeing and feeling a pure, sharp definition; breathing out: the older, cancerous soul.

I had nothing I could cling on to, I didn't know who I was. All I knew was the descent into the blackest depression, a forced descent like some devil's soldier were prodding me down the helter-skelter, down which I would slide, falling into the pitch-black emptiness I had circled, observed, but never fully immersed myself in before. The scary blackness, whose mists I had let cloak me and drag me down, moved in.

I grew more intense as minutes passed, my thoughts clouded, growing tighter, cracking to crumble in on themselves. Stop. Control it.

Sucking at the air, gasping, coughing. The lenses in my eyes were tainted with blue. I felt hungry. There was a machine that delivered food with nicotine relish, quickly, efficiently. I ate and wanted more. Everything blue and suffocating.

BOOM!

An explosion came to me as if smothered by a pillow. I felt its vibrations and the beginnings of sirens, but nothing stayed permanent in my register, vision coloured by a haze of blue. Shards of alarms interrupted sleep to awaken briefly my consciousness. Heckling, screaming, shouting and psychotic laughter impaled transient faces in my mind. A shot was fired.

I was back there, in the classroom, staring at Mr Marx's surreal face; blood dripping as my classmates screamed.

A boom-boom hammering at my door preceded its smashing open. Little red corpuscles with eyes flooded in, coagulating around me. I screamed and writhed, fighting off the hallucinations which screamed to the back of my eyeballs, pounding them bloodshot with fear.

A needle went into me, shots echoing all around, clanking against the sirens and smashes: a chaotic symphony over the mad language of jumbled emotions.

Another injection, bones bruising my struggling inflexions until the needle was withdrawn. Hands released me to an endless field of experiences.

"Isedanel. Dowey."

I felt myself being carried, floating above the smoke and mayhem. *So this is death and its magnificent transition.* I moved swiftly in jolts through the corridors of blood; *the soul leaving the flesh.*

Gunfire solidified the movement, the journey paused at vague grunts rewinding me back to primitive man, back past the dinosaurs, back to the beginnings of life: asteroids from Mars bringing to Earth bacteria, water particles and algae. Highly sophisticated amoebae from Mars had concocted the evolutionary stew, sent to the barren planet to ignite life. "And God took all the goddam credit!" fumed amoebakind as God's human additions fucked up their plans.

Back through blue-hued time to a world burning. Humans screamed, technology crumbled, history was reversed again. Mankind's brief and destructive existence terminated; sucked images flashing through Cainozoic, Mesozoic and Palaeozoic. A thud announced Precambrian; 4,600 million years back.

The thud-shot got me moving again.

Elements heating, their inviolability wilting: The End Of The World. All burning, all melting; Mother Nature's wrath soul-splitting. Blue came to the internal visuals, then red, then blue fighting back. Clarity grasped at a semblance of language. A darker red and a world burning; diamonds cracking, lava flowing and some idea that a greedy man was pushing buttons, smiling sweatily. Or maybe there's an evil god. Or maybe there's a schizophrenic god. Nature had taken enough, biting back, melting all the metals, all the man made, creating a new jewel for another future; another chance at Martian creation, another god, another attempt at civilisation. But it's all just the same old story – blood, red, blue, red – over and over again. Just ask The Moon. We've all been to The Moon at least once on Coki Coli flights, to that marketing paradise in outer space where Earthman dances on his own grave and leaves litter.

The machines are screeching; oil-less. The morning birds have gone and it's just that sonhorrific demand to get up.

"Comeuh deeeem, weeeney."

I have no skin to feel, no decisions to make. I have only questions to ask. Which way? Left or right?

"DM!"

My name; the skin that represents me. My mind, my heart, how I think and feel, what I think and feel. My memories, my ideas, my goals. My imagination, sparkling primal energy. The worlds I have created. These mean nothing; their sums don't add up. Life is focused on doing a job, having possessions, believing you belong, convincing yourself you are happy and you have a function. It's haves and have-nots and the have-nothings. They steal and curse and they don't get educated. They don't think for themselves and they have been around for centuries (one classic model, late twentieth century, bought *The Sun* newspaper, laughed with Noel Edmonds, thought Arnold Schwarzenegger was an actor and had no real understanding of the situations in "the former Yugoslavia", the Middle East, East Timor and Rwanada). They are dictated, unaware that they are being kept down, low, cursing and fighting. The Man wants them all to slip into this life, these televisuals: a TV dinner, lager and fuck life. The Man wants to keep us like this. Pragmatism not idealism: a gaudy, tacky, cheap pragmatism. And don't stick your head out if you're not perfect.

"DM!" My name repeated, infiltrating the lines of connection.

I felt flesh, stinging, saw the end of the world again; my head being cut off, my veins being severed. I am—

"DM! Come on DM! Wake up!"

I am teacher, drugs, sex, drugs, revolution, Ted, arrest, drugs, innocent, asylum.

"DM! DM, it's me, Kate. Do you understand?"

So they speak English in the next life. So I was born gifted and I am of some importance. Jimi Hendrix will probably be here too; "see you in the next world baby" he said to me.

"DM, it's Kate. Just nod if you can hear me."

I nodded.

"Yor OK now. We are getting out of here, OK? Yor gonna be all right."

I nodded, mouthed and thought, but didn't deliver "Yes".

I was moving, the surroundings of a van becoming clearer.

"Ted? Where's Ted?"

Gunshot words…"Dead…It's Saturday morning…You know Ted's plans…We need you."

"Kelly? Where's Kelly?"

"We've got to get started. Rest a while, DM."

Start Your Own Revolution

It's really easy to do, and there's just a general starting-point of getting into the nation's consciousness:

Distribute leaflets and pamphlets explaining to people how big companies screw people to make their money: CIC, MacDolland's, Shellac, Coki Coli, Dizzy and all Rupert C Donald's businesses. Their wealth combined, they could alleviate most of the suffering on planet Earth.

Use underground publications to further the message and expose the truth about what these companies are up to: raping the planet and exploiting people.

Bring together all the various left-wing and environmental groups, all the thousands of them active throughout the country. These groups will involve themselves with non-violent direct action to disrupt the machine of big business. If their profits are threatened, then they will have to listen.

Direct action involves green activists disrupting motorway and building construction. In their tunnels, chained to trees, using walkie-talkies and handcoms, they form a formidable force.

Disruption is essential: technoheads hacking into computers, sending viruses into machines—typically through a disk or an electronic message—and co-opting a host's resources, making copies of itself and ordering up deviant behaviour like posting out messages and wiping out hard drives.

Then you need people in work to strike. Though they need their job security you can persuade them to have a cold on Monday, and because so many of them will do it their bosses can't fire them all.

Essential components of the strike are the transport workers, for so long squeezed by their bosses' need for more profits. Thatcherism didn't crush the unions, it just crushed their will. But they still have the power and with a collective ideology they can rise again and stand up for themselves.

You need carnivals, street parties and parades to block roads and give the revolution a sense of fun. You can't rely on the musicians who are making money selling their songs to advertisers, but you can get plenty of unsigned artists as well as actors, magicians, performers, writers and painters. Carnivals and festivals can draw people in, make people appreciate that life can be about fulfilling and unique experiences. People work too hard and they make just enough money to get by. Each and every individual has the potential for creativity but can never find the time to indulge it. The biggest party England has ever known can usher in the revolution on a mood of euphoria.

Giving the disenfranchised a voice is essential: "Imagine us, like we are in the soaps, like we're always seen as in the media; all fucked up, incapable of making a decision, of keeping a secret. We're too fuckin' stupid to matter and there's nobody to vote for with our interests at heart."

Encourage these people, give them hope, make it known to them that it is easy for a government to solve their problems. Deposit your manifesto in as many of their homes as you can. Explain to them that after the revolution your promises will be fulfilled:

A progressive tax system which takes more money off the rich and uses that money to train people in what they want to do. Everyone will have a skill, newly acquired or already gained, and these skills will be used in creating a new England. The defence budget would be scrapped to save more money. There is no need for new weapons: for one, we are no threat to any country, and, for another, no country is any threat to us. Besides, the weapons we have just need maintenance as they are capable of wholesale slaughter already. This money could be used for better hospitals, education and transport. And once you make a convenient and reliable transport system, it will thrive.

Your manifesto might also want to throw in the legalisation of marijuana, another money-spinner with its medical, environmental and recreational benefits.

Initially you'll generate enough money to phase out the idea of an economy, which is fake anyway. England has sufficient natural resources to trade with other countries for the ones it requires. People won't need money because they'll use their skills, give them for free, receive services they need for free. You may have to give a little something to receive, but what you have to give will always be needed.

With your manifesto you can gain support from the disenfranchised, adding to your number of supporters.

With all these bodies you can begin the final stage of preparations for the revolution.

You need to reach an audience, explain your plans, wake people up, tap into the zeitgeist and infiltrate hearts and minds. You need media exposure, and, armed with the truth, you can rouse people from their routines.

So you've got groups of activists broadcasting from their own radio stations, Citizens Banned channels, websites and chat lines. And you've got Jez interfering with transmissions, getting your wanted face on televisuals during *The EC Donald Easy Show*. Just at the point where Evan-Christopher is laughing at his own joke about his guest's low sperm count, your face appears on screens throughout the land. Molly Simms has used her old skills as a set designer in the theatre to give you a style; you look rugged, flushed with passion, honest, innocent and determined. You speak to the public as Jez feverishly monitors the broadcaster's attempts to locate the transmission:

"I'm sorry to interrupt your entertainment but you must know that Donald's show is shit and just an ego trip to promote himself. He's just like his father, Rupert C Donald. Neither care about you and both are only interested in exploiting your basest impulses.

"I am here to talk about important things, to talk about the future. Our society is in a mess and you know it, and all these programmes on this channel are just candy to help us forget it. But we can change things. We can do it if we have belief. Many of you will have received The Democratic Marxist party manifesto. We intend to do what we have promised in that and change this country for the better. Collectively we have the power. Don't trust Rupert C Donald, don't buy his newsdisks or his papers and don't watch his TV channels. Don't trust people in advertising and don't believe anything this government tells you. All you need to know about this government is that it still sells weapons around the world. Weapons are made to kill people. Ask yourself, can there be any justification in the arms trade? No, it's not good enough this government telling us that countries need weapons because of the threat 'from aggressors'. We armed the aggressors! Just think about that fact and don't ever trust this government. Soon the people will rise up to create a better future for everybody, not just those with money. In our next broadcast at ten o'clock on Saturday night, we will produce evidence that this government, in cahoots with Rupert C Donald, is conspiring to brainwash the entire population of England. You won't believe it now, but we have the proof."

Jez wound in gestures with his hand.

"We will be on a European channel, but I cannot reveal which one yet. Take a few seconds to flick and you will find us and learn something which will shock the world.

"And finally if Kelly Godfrey's watching, or if you can tell her about this, I want her to know that I love her truly. I know she loves me and it's honest and pure, and—"

"DM. We gotta move."

Their eyes – wide, glaring, determined – reveal something of their souls; accentuated from the elaborate patterns of green and brown on their faces, shifting from side to side, alert for danger and throwing directions with glances to their comrades.

They numbered about forty-five, shifting in shadows as they moved on the city hall. Molotov cocktails in their hands, catapults in their back pockets and kitchen knives in their jackets, they manoeuvred into position.

Mayhem filled the late evening as sirens pursued their tail-less asses, changing direction as another more important incident came through in bleeps.

As pitiful Frank Riykard was presented to the nation on televisuals, revolution was beginning on the dance floors, Morse's "Revbeat" inspiring the young, free and bored. Riykard looked big and gormless, his bald head and exaggerated ears giving him a Shelleyian innocence. He spoke slowly as the beats revved up around towns and cities. He answered questions in the presence of "experts" and played the part of "The brainwashed" with realistic realism, his performance based in reality. In the unreality of the living world "Revbeat" raged into the early hours and beyond, seeping and inciting through the wakings of morning.

From the north one huge cooling tower pumped out a heavy smog; the non-carcinogenic fumes of pure, smouldering, marijuana. Already people were starting the party, jit-jiving to guitar licks and street beats.

Sirens wailed all around, descending on fires, going to save alarms, dispersing gathering crowds who spun off to form new groups; pockets of resistance growing stronger.

Confused Dutch policemen were swept up in the euphoric release, rolling up joints to join in the mood, disinterested in the bitterness and panic of local police not chosen for the squad policing Amsterdam East.

Scattered torches and burning beacons descended from the hills, pouring down to "Revbeat" from various portable music systems. Synchronised to almost perfection the beats and bleeps had a maddening repetition, growing louder as they sucked in the city centre.

As grainy daylight squeezed through the night, the streets were filled with dancing and singing, chanting and laughing.

London bristled with sirens blaring through streets, trying not to knock over those few who went to work amid the carnival.

A wind licked up papers blowing from the east. A bronzed figure in tainted white rags, a gleaming determination on his unflinching face, moved into the City. He seemed impervious to all around him: a single vision with a purpose.

He paused at a human bundle meekly crouched in a ball for warmth, pulled a fist of money from his pocket.

"I could give you all this but it wouldn't get rid of the disease affecting society." He tossed the notes to the wind.

The homeless bundle looked at them skip away, an urge to chase suppressed by the bronzed man's air of authority; his enigma vaguely threatening.

"Are you the coming one?" croaked the crouched man.

A restrained nod confirmed, restrained the bundle from rising with a hint of secrecy and need for patience.

"A great prophet has risen from us," thought the cowering man as the bronzed figure moved away.

To the stock exchange he went, breezing through tall glass doors. Two police officers fell back as he outstretched his arms and flung forcefields at them.

The messianic one moved on aggressively, his wrath boiling on hearing numbers being called out. He kicked open a door leading to the main room; to a scene of panic and fevered scurrying, calling out and trying to sell worthless pieces of paper as world stock markets crashed. On screens numbers were bleeping on their descent into the negative. Some people were burying their heads to escape, slumped on the floor, all burnt out.

As the messiah strode to the centre of activity, those around gradually focused on his presence, stepped back from sweating as he kicked over tables and sent paper deals fluttering into the air. He kicked out at those who fell into his path to grab at the papers, halted to address the room's occupants: "I have come back!" boomed to draw attention, silence coming like dominoes drawing to a conclusion. "You have filled my house with sin and evil! You will listen to what I have to say!"

"Who the fuck are you?" one voice called.

"I am the one."

"He's one of those fuckin' anarchists. Look at him! Get him out of here!" came a bellowing cackle from an obese man on the balcony. "Get this scruffy bastard out of here. I've had enough of them this morning! Dirty, smelly. Fuckin' guards!"

A look stood the guards in their tracks.

"You talk of appearances," he directed at the obese man. "This is of no concern. People are what matters, and they are being pushed off their land, being made destitute, unable to eat enough bread for a day. And you sit here piling up your money. Your conspicuous consumption of wealth is offensive. But now the time has come. I am back to save the Earth and money and shares don't matter anymore."

"You think yor Jesus?" mocked the man on the balcony. "You look a bit poor for the son of God!" and he laughed, a long, gristling laugh which infected others and encouraged the guards to edge forward.

"And what did you expect?" demanded The One. "Nice shirt? Expensive suit? False trappings of modern society." He sent an angry stare at the guards, making their bodies shake and crumble, then returned sight to his accuser: "William Franklin, forty-five, married with two children. Benefactor of the NRP. You, Mr Franklin, have pushed through developments in green belt areas, destroying wildlife and putting another squeeze on the Earth's precious oxygen supply! You have torn down housing!" He jabbed at Franklin with his finger. "You have made people homeless so you could build business parks and factories!" Franklin, unimpressed, made to speak, but was silenced as accusations raged and shook the building's foundations. "You exploit people and use your wealth and power to circumvent morality. You WILL see the error of your ways!"

He turned to speak to those standing stunned around him: "All I see around me is chaos and deprivation; in people, in countries, across the whole world. Still this emphasis on money, still the belief in consumerism. How can you be so ignorant and morally corrupt not to see that millions of your fellow humans starve to death each year? Is this not wrong? This planet was once a paradise with a carefully created and balanced eco-system, and enough natural resources to meet everyone's needs. Now Mother Nature is choking. Beautiful and precious species have become extinct, rivers have dried up, the air thin and clogged with pollution. And no one does anything!"

The building shuddered, dust clouding at corners, plaster falling from the ceiling.

"You are beyond sin. You believe all this is important. Capitalism is your faith and money is your god. Get out." Turning, he spat at all angles "Get out! Get out of here!"

There was an uneasy shuffling, some eyes returning to screens, hypnotised by numbers.

"Jesus! The fuckin' walls're cracking!" shouted a young suit.

The bronzed man's face grew taut, weighted with anger: "Get out!" He pointed to a screen, blew out its glass, then sent a chain reaction along the walls to shatter visuals in screaming succession.

The suits began rushing for the exit, pushing and scrapping to get out as the building crumbled. Spilling onto the street they were mixed up and submerged by the Revbeat. People snaked on roads, surrounding traffic amid futile attempts by police on horseback to control them.

As the bronzed figure emerged onto the Stock Exchange's steps some of the crowd recognised him and cheered. He opened his arms to suggest an embrace with all those before him, feeling a sense of equilibrium and hope. He began to communicate his joy: "This—"

Two shots cracked the celebration; one to his head jolting him back and to the left. His arms flapped, a second shot into his heart curiously balancing his body. Time stood still as he tottered on the steps, falling face down on concrete edges.

From the crowd a rock swung over the slow motion, smashing into a policeman's face, knocking him from his horse. "Revbeat" got cranked up as anger found expression, turning on those expelled from the Stock Exchange.

Newcastle had fallen by mid-afternoon, thousands dancing along streets, twisting all the way to Freeman Park where The Pointless Fanatics were celebrating rebellion with real instruments, singing from their hearts. Covers of John Lennon and Rolling Stones' songs roused the crowd, mixed with their own songs and speeches about freedom, liberty and "Tyranny is dead! People of one-consciousness, come together!"

Late evening, hundreds of thousands were amassed around the Houses of Parliament where those who could make it convened an emergency session. The chanting and dancing crowds, colourful banners flapping their feelings, were kept at bay by four lines of troops, rifles held nervously at their chests.

Prime Minister Mitchell Portman appeared indecisively on televisuals crackling with interference: "My country," he began gravely, "My people. Today has been one of the blackest days in our nation's proud history. Many of you sit in your homes tonight in fear. Those anarchists who have disrupted our lives are being hunted down, and I assure you that these traitors will be caught and dealt with severely. Because of the NRP's re-introduction of capital punishment you can be confident that what has happened today will never happen again. The army, as I speak, is rooting out the ringleaders. You the people can help, for these violent troublemakers are not invisible. Do you know who they are? Do you know where they are hiding? If so, it is—"

DM appeared on the televisuals, wearing a sombrero, silly sunglasses and clown nose:

"We are not anarchists, we are freedom fighters. We want a democratic society where everyone has a say. We have taken over the country because we want to change what is wrong and unjust. You have nothing to fear from us, but you have hope. The information we have distributed about the NRP is all true and provable. Don't let Mitchell Portman try to persuade you with talk about democracy. There is no such thing in this country anymore. Twenty per cent of the population is ineligible to vote. A further twenty per cent didn't vote in the recent election, disillusioned with politics. Of the sixty per cent who did vote only a quarter voted for the NRP. From the independent monitors willing to speak out we know there were an estimated sixty thousand ballot papers unaccounted for. George Orwell once described how censorship in an apparently free society was more thorough than in an apparent dictatorship because unpopular ideas and laws can be kept secret without any need for an official ban. With Rupert C Donald's help the NRP have used the media to hide truths, like its genocidal brainwashing programme. They—"

The prime minister's face returned to the televisual screen:

"Don't listen to the anarchist. These people have murdered hundreds already. You have probably seen their violence first hand. Don't trust them. Help us to get rid of them. Think about your families, your homes—"

"Back again. We are going to build a country and a world where no one goes hungry, where everyone enjoys life and can make a contribution to its richness. The air will be cleaner, the pace of life will be slower and people will have more leisure time for amazing experiences. There can be world peace and we can make it happen—"

"This is a mad man, look what he's wearing. We know all about his evil ways. His name—"

"This channel has now been taken over by The Democratic Marxists. Stay tuned for public service information and full explanations of what has really been going on in England under the NRP."

The End Is Nigh

The hills had become my sanctuary, living off the hallucinogenic and therapeutic vegetation. Travellers and groups passing through kept me in contact with the outside world, as did my handcom.

A week after the revolution things were beginning to settle, though there were still pockets of resistance from the right-wing, who were using gangsters and criminals to aid them.

Mitchell Portman had been ousted in a snap election, organised by New Labour's Anthony Breff. His party, holding the centre-right ground, won convincingly. Adam Benn's Labour Party, with fifty seats, was the second largest party in parliament. The NRP managed to hold on to twenty-five seats, the old Conservatives increasing theirs to forty-four through capturing many very angry former NRP voters. The Democratic Marxists managed just eight seats though they took as many votes as the NRP.

Breff talked of "A new England" and "The slow and difficult path to recovery". It would be "a painful journey, but together, as a united nation, we can succeed." He acclaimed "those activists" who had provided the damning evidence of what the NRP were up to, but in the same breath denounced those who "merely went along to indulge their need for violence. These people will be rooted out and dealt with severely."

The *Guardian* was back on line with lengthy essays on the rights and wrongs of revolution, rather hedging their bets; saying it was necessary but that some of those who had committed violent crime should be arrested.

My handcom also revealed news of an unidentifiable man being shot dead in London. Though his claims to being Jesus were dismissed there were three witnesses who said they'd seen him walking away from the morgue three days later. His body had certainly gone missing.

Reports also dealt with attempted uprisings throughout The West and their effect on its politics.

For the most part there was a sense of tempered optimism amid extended metaphors, and though this comforted me I could not rest easy. I needed the safety of the hills and the camouflage of thick fog, which had remained permanent since the Monday after the revolution.

Mrs Godfrey had sold her story to *The Shine*, which was doing its best to ignore the revolution, save for outrage at the NRP and demands for New Labour to "string up the anarchists like they strung up Mussolini." *The Shine* "had been too trusting in the NRP, and Rupert C Donald deeply regrets being tricked. But he is determined to use his power to shape a brighter future for England." Mrs Godfrey's story was an elixir for them: a sensational exposé to distract attention from the bones of domestic affairs whilst also revealing "an evil anarchist" to be "a monstrous abuser of the innocent".

"DM – Dirty Molester" accompanied a picture of my head in a noose. "My Tragic Love" stood under a picture of Mrs Godfrey, dressed in black, breaking down in tears (from a re-enactment of her husband's funeral, photographed the day after she'd completed the serialisation deal). "For The Love Of My Daughter" rested above a photo of Mrs Godfrey and Kelly, taken seven years previously, digitally enhanced to age them and bring them closer together. A subheading in the article, "I want mam and dad" quoted Kelly, who was now "undergoing treatment". In two paragraphs it covered her father's death, "her need for her mother" and "the devastating effects of The Dirty Molester's seduction".

The piece summed up with sympathy for Mrs Godfrey, whose "emotional outpouring on *The Susie Baster Show* certainly brought tears to this reporter's eyes. Her book, *Laura*, is published next month."

The revolution had not yet rooted out the corrupt figures involved in public and private law enforcement agencies. I would have to lay low until such a time when the optimism and idealism the uprising would bring could allow me a fair hearing.

"But society will only ever see you as a paedophile. They'll want to lynch you. You can't get away from that."

My schizophrenic dialogue answered, "Once we get rid of Donald we can have a free media and people will be able to see my truth."

"Maybe it's time you came back to us," entered my head.

Humming, slow-chilled-out bleeping came to me from the mist covered undulations imagined all around.

I had analysed my childhood into beautiful experiences and *Cracking Codes For Kids* followed by the trauma of Mr Marx's shotgun and my parents going missing. My blocking off the past had preceded a present life: modern youth culture; so banal, trashy, cheap that drugs were the only answer to anaesthetise me from Automatic Living; then the activists, the revolution that failed, the slipping into a job. Then Kelly and the successful revolution, all detailed and thoroughly described in my memory. I'd easily rationalised the vagueness of my memory as being due to a conscious shutting-off in 2018, the progress of time, and, possibly, my vast intake of drugs.

I had to forget about searching for my parents. It was up to them and I couldn't dwell on why they'd left and where they'd gone.

I hauled on my sandwich board with its chalked proclamation of "The End Is Nigh", behind which I hid my handcom. Into the city I descended, my bum-looks a sufficient disguise: a beard, unwashed hair, Kate Flower's old reading glasses over black-rimmed eyes, and dirty, torn clothing. I was the harmless lunatic, my pathetic attention-seeking innocuous with all the real psychopaths, gangsters and factions moving around shrouded streets.

It took ten minutes of buzzing before Joe answered, sleepily, "Yeh?"

"Joe, DM, let me in."

"Fuck." He said as he bleeped me in, and "Fuck" again as he greeted me outside his flat. "I thought you were dead, man!"

The couch was comfortable to the point of pain, so I crouched on the floor.

"Y'know they're after you?"

"Yeh," I said. "I'm really in the shit."

"Fuck yeh. Kelly Godfrey? I kind of admire it though."

"D'ye know where she is?"

"No—"

"You haven't seen her at the asylum?" Joe shook his head. "What about Mrs Godfrey?"

"I haven't seen Laura since she got this book deal."

"What have you said to the police? What—"

"Daniel, stay calm. All the other things about those dead bitches yor supposed to have murdered haven't been mentioned. You'll be OK once everything gets nice and blissed again. Nobody knows what's going on at the moment so yor OK. Nobody goes out with all this fog. And then there's all those crazies running loose after the asylum got attacked. You go out there it's like you're the king of all the world and you can do whatever you like as long as you've got a weapon handy. Of course, your lot are still roaming around trying to maintain order, but I think even Amsterdam East did a better job than they're doing. You were in with the revolution weren't you?"

"Don't believe everything you read in the papers," was all I said. "So are people going to work? Is life functioning?"

"Just about, but there's not much going on with all this fog. It's sort of adding to an uncertain atmosphere. I haven't even been down The Indie. You fancy it?"

"Yor joking? I'm fuckin' on the run! You know Tumblety had me at the asylum?"

"No."

"Have you been in touch with him?"

"No, nothing's happening. I've told you, Dan, yor OK for now. Come on, let's monkey, man."

"Fuck Joe!" I exploded at the same Joe Rogan. "They're gonna get me eventually!"

"Look, once your revolutionaries have gotten rid of the filth you'll be OK. They won't fix you up, you'll be a hero."

He placed his hands on my shoulders and squeezed to reassure: "Don't worry. Come, let's be The Boys, the monkey men. Let's do it one more time. Fuck this world. If Tumblety was into all that shit then they're gonna come looking for me before too long. Let's go out fighting. Let's monkey."

His charisma was in overdrive, his facial features sorrowfully crushed inward with humility. A wry smile crept onto his lips as I paused before reply.

MONKEY MEN

We had to keep our wits about us in the swirling fog, walking almost back to back as we sidled down the long road we could negotiate from memory. Figures flitted in the whiteness, and some pain could be heard in the corners, but we reached Club Independent intact.

Little had changed inside, except that it was so unrealistically quiet. All the figures were slumped on their chairs, around tables tight with uncollected glasses and over-spilling ashtrays. There was no music and people only communicated in a hushed murmur.

The drug chauffeur and his three cronies were seated near the toilets, each one with a spliff, leaning back on the couch. The place had a welcoming serenity and familiarity.

"Get the beers, my friend," I said to Joe before nodding to the drug chauffeur, following to make contact.

He barely existed in my sphere, so stoned he didn't recognise me, going through the motions from memory.

The price of pot was too much, but to my surprise the Reeto Dust had become cheaper. I took fifty dollars of it, led him wearily back out.

Joe had racked up the balls on the pool table, ready to be break. "Monkey?" he asked, looking up from his crouched position.

"Monkey," I nodded in reply.

Smash. The balls scattered clanking but didn't disturb the bloodshots from their statuesque positions.

"Wanna bet?" Joe asked.

"I've got nothing."

"How about," he began, "this penny if you win, and I'll throw in the fate of the world? Lose and they're both mine."

"On."

He slapped the penny on the rim of the table.

I felt the cue, felt the past, crouched down to take aim. As I concentrated I grew more uneasy at the silence in Club Independent. No one looked up or at anyone else. It was like Joe and I were the only living things in some piece of contemporary art, like we were imposed on a paused picture.

I raised myself to look around. Still no sign of reaction to life, just movements of drinks to lips, cigarettes to lips, spliffs to lips.

I moved back down, took a shot and hit a ball in.

"Wham bam, the king of the table is back."

"Disputed," added Joe with a smile.

I missed the next. He cracked a ball to be eaten by a pocket, then he missed.

I pocketed, missed. He did the same. And it went on without interruption, a pot and a miss for each of us, until I potted the last of my balls and was on the black, which if things were going to go as previously I would miss. I did.

Joe potted his last ball and he was on the black.

"This is very interesting isn't it? A very nice pattern has developed and it's up to me to break it. It's a nice symmetry, one that appeals to my brain, but—" He bent his body and eyed the cue ball in line with the black. "Future of the world," he whispered to himself before striking the ball with venom, too much venom for it to make the right contact. The black rattled in the jaws then threw itself out, a kiss on the white re-directing it slowly towards the middle pocket. It hung over precariously before succumbing to the drop.

"Lucky bastard!" I said.

"The world is mine," Joe said, picking up the penny.

"Ah, DM, it's good to be back," said Joe reclining on his sofa. "So, how do you think your revolution went?"

"Not my revolution, Joe. But, it seemed to go all right. It changed some things, got rid of the NRP."

"Oh DM, DM. How many times do I have to tell you? All governments are lying cocksuckers. Nothing's changed, they've just put a new spin on it. Rupert C Donald still has everything in his pocket, even Breff. Especially Breff. He can easy get rid of Breff, and when he does he'll be running England. This revolution will be used to strengthen his position. Watch this space."

"Such a cynic, Joe. The people have changed things and they'll do it again if needs be."

"And you'll be their leader again, right?"

"There were no leaders in the revolution, just good organisation and people working together."

"But you were behind it?"

"Hey Joe, stop talking fuckin' politics and deal 'em."

"Yeh man. GET THE LINES READY."

I shovelled the dust into lines as Joe dealt the fresh cards.

A thankless three, a faulty four, a fuckin' five! The insignificant cards mounted up between snorts, upping the ante, teetering on the brink of implosion. A truculent ten wiped them out. A frivolous four started again. A significant seven edged us past the point of no return, into a jumpin' jack flash. I picked up.

A nightmare nine. I returned the jack, got hit with a kicking king. Got to pick up again.

The pack in my hand got fuller until I had all the avenues of counter-attack.

Thrifty three, forgotten five, sassy six, eager eight. Slapped down with no time to rest. Jumpin' jacks, quarrelsome queens. A king for a day, a shmuck for a lifetime? An antagonistic ace to tease Joe. He slammed the saviour of a two and we went round again, our options becoming more limited.

He licked up the fresh cards from the dwindling pack. I thought I was working up to execute him, but he slammed a set of nibbling nines to take out the expelled cards. We began again.

The deck piled up with high cards was tempting, but the fresh deck was finished and we each wanted to get onto our face-up cards. He laid an ace. I laid a two. He had a queen. I had a king. He picked up.

A transient ten said hello and goodbye, the prelude to two queens. He took them out with his two queens, chanced my faced down cards with a nine.

I bent the face down card, peeped a look at a jack, laid it with relief.

The snorts were brief, desperate, between the figures mounting up, the cards dwindling. He hit me back with an ace, laid down his face-up kings, got the ace back, waited for the slow drain of my cards, taking a chance on the two face-downs I had left.

I tried to feel some divine force guiding me to chose between the two face-downs I had. The one on the left.

A ten. Taken out, game over, a perfunctory seven to unfold a famous finish.

"Five-three Joe. Can I have the world back?"

"Sorry, DM. But take a penny."

I rose to look out of the window, half knowing what I would see. All was burning again.

"Your world's going up, Joe," I said to beckon him over.

"Good," he replied, peering out of the window. "It's about time we

402

got the fuck out of her. I'm getting bored with this life. Anyway, who needs the outside world? We've got all we need here." He looked around his room.

DM looked too, newly aware of what had drawn him into Joe's company in the first place; the deep interest in literature, original copies of classic books from Salinger to Dostoyevsky; the compact disc collection of everything from The Rolling Stones to The Smiths. The film collection of everything from Goodfellas to Clockwork Orange.

"Our little time capsule," said DM, remembering something of another trip they had taken a million years ago.

DM noticed the clock, its red figures hovering at 20.49.

"2049 Joe. We're in Extreme Future World."

"I'm there. Tell me about it, DM, in that good old fashioned stylee."

Extreme Future World

The alarm bleeped just once. There was no staying asleep beyond that bleep.

In an instant Daniel stood erect from his bed covers, addressing the unseen all-seeing eye secretly deposited somewhere in his habitat: "Daniel Manion," he began, pushing back his fringe to reveal numbers tattooed indelibly on his forehead. "One eight seven zero three four seven, Sector 9 Area 51, Location 45, Country 69. Ready."

He takes E472e, E471, E322, E202, E270, E160a for breakfast, consumed around three cigarettes.

Bus number 13A, train 7 on platform 9. Arrives on time.

Each class gets a disk to work from; their task to fill in blanks in the curriculum. Daniel can't leave because they can't leave until they've got the right answers.

On his way home he purchases a "Nutrition burger" from MacDolland's and a can of Coki Coli, recording his activities as evidence of the fulfilment of his duties, to be bleeped off a list for the day. Then he can either slip into anonymity by getting drunk and stupid or by watching televisuals.

America is bombing the Middle East in response to the latest terrorist attack on a western business.

The American government has sent troops into its own streets to counter the threat from extreme right wing sects who have used chemical weapons on government buildings

The recent flare-up in The Balkans is "under control. The international community ['those western governments where capitalism is in swing'] has sent thirty thousand extra peace-keepers…"

Work had begun on replacing the millions of species wiped out throughout history. Government bodies had decided which species to clone first, their decisions based on "environmental contribution and aesthetics".

"Though Dizzy had helped pick some cute animals to be used in ad campaigns," thought Daniel. With furtively acquired facts and his deliberately far-fetched imagination, "At least I still have my fuckin' mind."

And he knew too that Shellac had influenced "The Evolution Project" to include extinct birds which they could use at places wherever there had been a dangerous oil slick or chemical leak; to show they cared enough to repair the damage.

Baby elephants were seen strolling in deserts, using CGI and twentieth century footage.

Go on, choose a desert, any desert, there's plenty of them around the world now.

Daniel's body barely moved as he slouched on the sofa, a can of Alkoka in his hand. He was playing the part, looking like he was switching off and looking to be switched off.

He made a face like he didn't understand the financial news, yawning at, "Trioxide announces record earnings..."

Not that exciting when you realise that a decently managed company should have that statement in its reports every year. Even an individual with twenty dollars in a savings account should expect record earnings every year if the capital remains untouched.

Daniel checks his watch, flicks onto The Lifestyle Channel and waits to be officially switched off.

He times it, then estimates three hours of free time before the all-seeing eye returns to check up on him.

He heads to a club in town where a clone of comedian Bill Hicks is loose: "...Your children are not special...I know YOU think they're special, but I'm just trying to tell you, they're not...Every time a man comes he comes two hundred million sperm...And you mean to tell me you think yor child is special? Just because one out of two hundred million sperm – that load. We're talking one load! – connected...Gee, what are the fuckin' odds?"

The words released Daniel, made him The DM, explorer in the imagination. He concurred with Bill's words:

"Our seeds are our souls and through them we will live on. And I haven't got time to mould a child: the attention, love, energy, time, compassion and money it takes I do not possess. The rutters on Pourische Road can't even give attention, but then I wouldn't be having a child for novelty value."

Bill is speaking from his heart, driven by the truth, disbelief in his mocking laughter as he exposes a mad, mad, double double bad world. It was inevitable the police would break in, arrest the comedian.

Daniel makes his way home with thirty minutes to spare before "Supervisional Social Safety" returns.

He finds some pornography on the televisual net, finds a woman who will talk to him and perform for him. He places his credit card into the computer and watches as it clocks off a number from his soul. Then the sex and the guilty bleeping off, waiting for the supervisionals to soundlessly bleep back on.

"Daniel Manion, number one eight seven zero three four seven, Sector 9, Area 51, location 45, Country 69, signing off for sleep. Condition: drunk."

The mantra is repeated, through his sleep until its back to the wake-up bleep. He's crunching numbers again, pushing himself to places where the dice determine.

Clones predominate streets, faces and bodies based on corpses' secrets. The same faces from the last generation – their parents' favourite pop stars and movie stars – stumble about in their worthless, though perfectly engineered, bodies.

Daniel is ugly, which makes him different, which makes him attractive. All the women want him, but they all look the same, all act the same. He wants to meet an eccentric ugly woman but they are so few and far between, and all the rich men have got them anyway.

It's a cloned world; history repeating itself; nothing original despite the expectations and advancements of science. A charitable organisation even cloned the opera singer Emily Spencer and the one-time princess, Diana; both to help promote the charity. But Emily killed herself again and Diana is just dandying with playboys, merely paying lip service to the cause when her popularity ratings drop.

The Adolf Hitler clone got locked up for trying to create weapons of mass destruction (without a license), but the Jimi Hendrix clone is doing his stuff, rocking till the broad daylight. It's only a matter of time before the authorities arrest him too.

Hey, and everyone thinks it's great, because it means anybody with enough money can live forever.

A burst of electricity blew out the lights, flashed open eyelids to focus on a sharp neon glow. Two large male figures took shape; one red, one blue, each like a helium-enhanced mannequin.

"Stop right there, you fuckers!" screamed the blue figure. "Got you, Daniel Manion. You have broken reality law, section 23, paragraph 2. No fuckin' appeal."

"Joseph Rogan, you are charged with conspiracy," added the red balloon.

"Fuck him," said Blue. "Manion, you are ours. Your imaginative capacity will be reduced, and one more further transgression and we'll have the basic shit as well. Fuck you, welcome to reality."

"Mr Rogan," said Red, "your special circumstances means we will only invoke the minimum, but you have been warned."

I felt my head shaking, a force pulling from the inside to suck out. Joe's the same, though briefer so that he could watch through me the process he had just endured.

Once over, my head whiplashed.

"Fuck me, DM, what was that?" asked Joe, shaking with disbelief.

"Fuckin' trippin'"

"Time to rest. Take the couch."

"Time. Yes, time. Eight thirty-five."

"The clock's fucked. Powercut, karma check. Later."

Before Joe left his flat he fixed the clock for 08:35.

Within ten steps Joe was sweating, unpicking his collar button and loosening his tie. Smog bellowed around his person and he tried hard to imagine being the last person on Earth, but solitariness was frequently punctured by head-aching alarms.

Joe checked the temperature on his handcom, saw it was pushing seventy and bleeped urgently on the air quality forecast. Seeing that the recommended time outdoors was only two hours he fixed on his air-filter mask.

The heat gave imaginary presence to buildings and life existing somewhere inside the smog. The air's claustrophobic squeeze on Joe dragged him back in time, so that direction and time checks on the handcom revealed laborious progress.

He had too much time to think; starting emotional fires and coming smack up against the hubris waiting in cloudy cul-de-sacs. Rushing through his miles of memory files he found nothing of substance. Pushing through the prosaic mosaic of his experiences he located only fading possibilities. His search grew more frantic, desperate to place himself in some real place where he could leave a lasting impression. Inevitably, through the law of averages he based his life upon, he stumbled on his conscience; there at the asylum gates.

Armed guards took checks before bleeping him through.

"Rupert C Donald is a bastard. He's not evil though: very few people are. Most of the schizos and psychos have a disease. There's only a few of us who enjoy evil and who can perfect the art," thought Joe.

Three more guards made checks before bleeping Joe into what remained of the asylum. It seemed a continuation of the outside world's sense of isolation; smoke-coloured white walls, strewn debris and people-less corridors. Only a few vague mad wails reminded Joe where he was, what he had come for.

"But Donald has no verve or passion. He's all dull yet expensive spices. Money buys crass. Crass makes a racket, crass gets a deal, and crass gets to copy crass. Dull, dull in any yawned language. Kill the man, he don't give a fuck. Nice idea, good buzz."

As Joe reached the basement level, armed guards took more bleeps from his soul before letting him enter Tumblety's bunker.

In the dimly lit underground hanger, freezing with air conditioning, two more armed guards checked before reviving Joe with a bleep.

A room, ten metres by twelve, had various white suits around computer screens. They checked Joe's file before allowing passage into Tumblety's bunker, its dimensions similar to the antechamber.

At the room's centre a table had wires resting on its surface, connected to wall panels and televisual units. Space at the table's centre awaited a body.

"Mr Rogan. Is this business or pleasure?" asked Tumblety, surprised yet expectant.

"Y'know I can't separate the two," replied Joe.

"Well, some good news. Our escapees are performing an admirable job. OK, they've taken out some – ahem – innocents, but they have been highly proficient at rounding up the so-called revolutionaries."

"I know where Daniel Manion is," announced Joe without provocation.

Tumblety immediately clicked on: "You do? Where is he?"

"I want to meet The Paradise Club. I think I have proven myself by now."

"Indeed you have, Mr Rogan. Is this a definite sighting?"

"Definite. I can take you to him now."

"Well, our benefactors certainly want to get a hold of him, but—"

"I want to meet them."

Tumblety contemplated, slapping his tongue around his cheeks like a washer with one item in the sludge. He hadn't the authority to sanction Joe's demand, but he delighted his thoughts with the way he could phrase it; as a request, engineered by himself, which would give him a place at The Paradise Table.

Tumblety's eagerness placed him in the front seat, an armed guard driving. Tumblety practised his speech, his mind finding new possibilities to cram into his memory. Joe's thoughts, backseat and pretty vacant, were only able to imagine a contrived scenario; but that was enough for Joe.

The driver held his weapon loosely, following Joe following Dr Tumblety into a superfluously decorated conference room. Around a long and rigid rectangular table he recognised the faces of Shelby Thurston Jr, Norman Terrick, Robert Parsons, Jim Proctor, Aggro Suharto, and Rupert C Donald at the table's head, Tony Prior lurking, standing over his right shoulder.

"Joseph," announced Donald warmly. "I have been waiting to meet you for so long. Your work has been much appreciated."

"Well, y'know, it's been a fizzing wizz."

"Oh!" Donald administered laughter to the proceedings. "Such a like mind. You will certainly command a great deal of power when all this mess is sorted out. So, you can tell us where Daniel Manion is. Why the need to meet us first?"

"To see who I've been working for. To see the faces of the men who control everything."

"Maybe you want to join us?" asked Shelby Thurston Jr, his fascistic sneer pre-eminent amongst various facial ticks.

"Maybe. I guess the idea of a global genocide with only a few left to control everything appeals to me. But, and the thing is, this is a big but, I don't really like Earth that much. All humans suck, especially those in power. They all suck Satan's cock."

Joe didn't have time to enjoy the shock registering. After negotiating enough bleeps to make him a god he had the element of surprise to lower the odds. *Averages are meant to be exploited.*

He elbow-butted the guard, broke a bone and took his gun.

The first shot flung back Tony Prior, the second cracking into Donald's forehead, splattering blood on the faces of those around The Paradise Table.

Screams were aborted as gunshots rattled out in jerks, each hit provoking a deeper, inexpressible fear in those rising to flee. Bullets tore into flesh, caught limbs easily, caught hearts and heads by chance.

A door kicked open ricocheted to the sound of gunshots aimed at Joe's back.

Make sure. Make your mark in history. Kill a fascist.

As he staggered forward, his motion jerked with bullets piercing his flesh, he unleashed rounds of ammunition on Rupert C Donald's prostrate body. Each impact squirted blood, re-animated the body as Joe fell forward to Donald's knees.

Hazily eye-balling the carpet, Joe reconciled his life. Gunshot flashbacks reminded him that he had lived, once before. And at least Donald was dead, most of the others the same or injured. And to the guards screaming confusion, he was now dead.

LOSING THE PLOT

I now think I am officially mad. I've spent the early morning carrying a sandwich board over my shoulders, proclaiming "The End Is Nigh". And I've really been into the part like it were my only mission.

I can't get back now so I might as well indulge in the fantasy which has taken me over; play with madness a little, leave the real world behind, go out with a bang.

Of course Joe was out there, collecting a reward, turning me in. But I was one step ahead of him, able to infiltrate his future and change it. Most able.

Why I was walking in the people-less mists with "The End Is Nigh" exciting me both ways I didn't know, but it felt like a good game, like meeting Peter Wheaton in the school playground at eleven a.m. every day to exchange cracking codes for kids.

When Kate bleeped into my handcom a message: "I've seen the aliens" it became only a minor part of my carefully constructed and unstable fantasy. It was nothing. I'd met the aliens, I'd seen Jesus riding a unicorn.

Hey, but I'm just altering your perception. Tell me what to do next.

I have to try hard to get a flicker of life from my soul, and it's Kelly Godfrey at the end of the line: "DM. Where have you been?"

"Hiding."

"Please come and get me. They've given me things. It's getting hard to stay one step ahead of them. They're doing something to me. They come every day with new drugs and they keep talking to me, telling me what to think. Please, please—"

"Yor at home?"

"Yeh. They've got two men from Su-Hi Incorporated on guard. I've got to get out of here before they finish me off."

"I love you, Kelly."

"I do as well."

"Can I meet you?"

"Only if you've still got your instinct."

"I think so. But Kelly, something's wrong with me. I think I'm losing my mind—"

"We'll make a fresh start, start over again. We can do it, we just need to feel. I can feel you in me. I can meet you halfway. They have Sunday off. I think I can hold out until then. They think they have me, but I can make it. You must be there. It's in our hearts, in our souls. Please."

For two days I lived life like a confined crazy, my stomach rolling grumblings over the hills as I watched the visuals from the CCTV at Joe's flat block.

He never returned, but twice his home was broken into. The first time, Su-Hi Inc. uniforms were in and out in no time. The second, "Fuck Mob", set off alarms before barging their way out.

I turned into a surveillance camera generating images of Joe's flat over twenty-four hours, rewound the visuals to give me time to go back.

His flat had been ransacked, all the features of his time capsule broken and scattered.

I found the last of his Reeto Dust, took it and felt nothing of consequence but self-absorbed contemplation of "Daniel Manion". I felt suicidal and recalled: "...broken shards slash me to ribbons..."

I couldn't escape the darkness filling me with a thick, murky liquid. Here was that embryonic depression.

The world was the same sordid mess, and each individual in it was the same messed up spoke; in a wheel, in a machine, in a box, powering another machine. Cogs. Just me, cog, unremarkable, unmentioned.

I am only here briefly, but remember me, any old DM you like. I fought the law, incited revolution, tried to change something about this unfair world. I am the person who worked nine to five for too many years.

Before that, some young escapist DM, hiding in streets, seeing off imaginary bad guys. At some point, he was blasted out of existence.

Their names are located in a daily register subtly instilled into me. I can't put faces or personalities to their monikers, I can only reel off a list of birth-marks:

"Shanice Baines."

"Yes sir."

"Paul Bellam."

"Sir."

"Peter Bexley."
"Sir."
"Cassie Blake."
"Yes Sir."
"Melanie Blatt."
"Uh."
"Melanie."
"Sir."
"Edward Blissett. Edward!"
"Sir."
"Emma Brannigan."
"Yeah sir."
"Adam Cogburn."
"S."
"James Cross."
"Suh!"
"Stephen Davidson."
"Yeah."
"Sophie Elton."
"Yes Sir."
"Elisa Farrel."
"Yes sir."
"Emma Heardman."
"Sir"
"Ronan Jacobs."
"Mr Marx."
"Ben Lavelle."
"Sir."
"Dan Manion."
"Here sir."
"Ady Mearson."
"Yes sir."
"Frank Riykard."
"Sir."
"Michael Slater."
"Yeh."
"Michael Smith. Michael! Michael!"
"Sir."
"Geoff Spear."
"Yes, sir."
"Melissa Stanton."
"Yes."
"Nick Tallant."
"Yes, sir."

"Peter Wheaton."

"Sir."

"Laura Williams."

"Sir."

Katie Worrall."

"Sir."

Mr Marx was talking about the planets, raising his voice vainly, then giving in and giving up, beginning to talk nonsense:

"...but there are many more planets, as yet not discovered. Millions of light years away: amazing planets. Like my own planet, Inuthua..."

Even Mr Marx's imaginative madness couldn't quell the flow of ignorance.

I remember the shock as his voice screamed louder than it had screamed before, and the deep intake of air as he wielded a shiny metal gun.

No one knew how to react as he made demands, though images of school massacres around the world circled my brain in headlines. The law of averages suggested it filled the thoughts of those around me.

We were writing, obeying him.

"...Just keep writing. Write anything. Just look like you are writing. Just write down everything...repeating fuck fuck fuck. You'll only be seen if you stand out...Use your imagination he says. Use up all the black ink to save your life. Save him and save us. Take it back, renewing time, changing time, time time, time, time. Let us all pay attention. Let history go a different way. Take him back, keep writing. Anything. Just to save your life. Get a life by imagining a life. He looks scared. I can see him sweating. I need to keep writing to save my life. I can see his eyes rolling around the room. He's looking for someone who isn't writing. Keep writing. Famous people like Emily Spencer, Tony Blair, Adolf Hitler, John Lennon, Clint Eastwood, TM, TM, I can't even write this. A list of planets like Pluto, Mercury, Jupiter, Saturn, Mars, Earth, Uranus, Earth, his gun in his cheek, he can't keep it steady, he can't control. Need full stops full stops and commas, capital letters and he's not going to kill us. He's scared and he just wants us to remember something. I think he's doing it for a reason. He needs a reason to die and we are here for a reason. I'm somewhere in the solar system, I am some life. I have a purpose. He's— All the others are. He's—"

In suspended animation, a series of flashbacks kept us absorbed. Mr Marx's face ripped off, blood all over the walls, voices screaming:

"They are all screaming, pissing themselves, running around and falling over. Panic won't let them get out and get away. No one gets out alive.

"He bleeds cleanly, a drip-drip-drip onto his arm, onto the desk, making a red puddle around exercise books. His left eye flickers, but the rest of his body doesn't move. I must keep writing, keep thinking. It's just me and him. Mr Hillier has some rules about that. He's bleeding. How much blood has he *got inside of him? How much longer can he live? I don't know the answer to everything. I must keep writing, just imagine he's teaching us something."*

I can't remember what I imagined. I can't imagine what I must have imagined.

Joe's durable televisual unit was all that worked amongst the debris of his flat. The news led with the aftermath of a nuclear bomb dropped on Iraq by America. Sombre tones commentated on devastated scenes before interviews were conducted with families of those killed in the chemical bomb explosion in Los Angeles.

Short and snazzy snippets followed: New Labour's "Regeneration Programme", the arrest of "militant activists" and some long-lasting humour: King Moon's spaceflight and censored footage of him baring his ass.

Paranoia dwelled on some labyrinthine conspiracy theory, but imagination hadn't the capacity to explore and I returned to "business" over the net.

James Cross, some body from schooldays, had a website on Declan Marx; the same website I had visited before. But in the revolution's aftermath, in the intermission before a recognised order is restored, various new websites had appeared:

"www.declanmarxmystery.co.uk" corroborated Daniel's belief that Mr Marx was still alive. At the foot of an essay: "Are you interested in the Declan Marx mystery?" and "marxtruth@inuthua.co.uk".

I bleeped in, "Yes."

Bleeping back, "You don't know me, but I know you, Daniel Manion. Have your scars healed?"

"It's getting worse. Who are you?"

"My name is Hooldoon, but that won't mean anything to you. I'm on Earth. They've got me at The Institute of Science. I don't think you can do anything about that, but do not worry. The first thing you need to know is that Earth is not the beginning and end of all existence. You are more important than that. You have many lives, but all you need to concentrate on is the present. It's not crazy just because no one else understands. The most important thing you can do right now is find and kill the doctor called Tumblety."

I turned off the machine. This was a joke, designed by a part of my brain which had escaped the logical pull.

I hung "The End is Nigh" over my shoulders and paraded through smoky streets like a sacrifice.

My dying imagination could not find conclusions, diverting me to buy a MacDolland's burger. It's final throws had nowhere to go and fantastical graspings located only the dying embers of used-up catalysts. My imagination was lifeless. It needed some dust. But no, that would be a bad idea, and anyway, I could only stumble upon The Indie in this blinding fog. The odds weren't good.

Endgame seemed to be approaching. I might as well just die. Just switch off, see what the afterlife has to offer.

Brain malfunctioning.

I want to see Kelly. "Have I got instinct?" she'd asked. That meant something. But where was it, and would it be a good idea to meet her?

It had cons: Kelly was being tracked and I'd be caught in a clandestine meeting. It'd look bad. And she was Laura Williams' daughter, and whatever person she'd been in school, she certainly was a cold-hearted bitch now.

It had pros, enough to get me born: I love her. I need her. I have nothing to lose. There's no future for me. I just need to see, get to feel a last time.

There was no fourth pro. All evens, I felt convulsed, stopped walking to articulate vomit.

What's the next step? Where is my life going? I need some idea of fate. I haven't the imagination to take the next step.

A penny coin was in my back pocket. Heads, see Kelly; tails, get lost.

I tossed into the dense white air, lost sight briefly before the coin's browned non-glint allowed me to catch and slap onto my wrist.

"Heads."

I kissed the coin and prepared to release rejoicing fluids about my system.

A black boot, attached to legs and body clothed in black, led to a mangled face: S*T*E*P*H*E*N*.

A knife tore the skin on my throat, nervously resting there with menace.

"I will kill you. You have to come with me. If you do, you will not be killed by me. If you don't I will kill you. What is your choice?"

"I will go with you," I answered prosaically.

He held onto the back of my collar and jabbed me forward with cuts to my backbone.

A bleep accompanied our motion's pause until we were in the hazardous clarity of the asylum's reception area.

He edged me down a flight of stairs, laughing as I stumbled on lumps of concrete.

The large hangar-like area we entered was insidiously quiet, save for some shuffling and the whirr-bleep of machines.

The bleeps grew clearer as I was stabbed forward, into a room where Dr Tumblety loomed over a table, at the centre of which was positioned the body of Mr Marx, disfigured face and all, wires attached to his head and parts of his body.

Bleep. "How are you feeling, Mr Manion?" he asked.

Bleep. "What's going on?" I demanded.

Bleep. "You are sick. You must realise that by now. You have taken too many drugs and only now are you dealing with the trauma stored up over many years. All—'bleep'—caused by this," he said, his arm outstretching to present Mr Marx's body.

My elbow connected in a spirited whack to Stevie's face, sent him backwards, dropping the knife. Each fist in his face punched him closer to the floor, until he collapsed in a bloody heap.

I had the knife in my grasp before Tumblety's bulk had made progress.

Bleep. A chance to fulfil fate.

"Tell me what the fuck's going on? Why the fuck's he here? What the fuck's happening?" I screamed deliriously. "Tell me! Tell me what you're doing! Where the fuck's Joe"

"Joseph Rogan is dead. Sad for somebody I suppose, but not for me. It's just me left. You can be a part of the new world."

"What the fuck are you talking about?"

"Does swearing make you a better person? Think about it, and try, try hard, to get a balance. You know the English language, you have the words. Work it out."

I had to agree. "Then just bleeping explain it."

"Life as we've grown accustomed to knowing it is ending on Earth. The Panamera is seeing to that. It is left to those most powerful to inherit the planet. Thanks to Mr Rogan's efforts, that is just about me. But you can be part of it as well. Your thoughts are powerful enough to take over the world," said Tumblety, adding as an afterthought, "But you need me."

Bleep. "What are you saying? Why is Mr Marx here?"

"To help with the new world order."

"Bleep."

"You're a fuckin' NRP tool—"

"My path crossed with theirs, it is true, but then yours probably did too. We all have visions of a better world, Mr Manion, of the necessary genocide to root out those not fit to be a part of it. This is a different revolution."

Bleep. "This is madness."

"No. Think about it logically." Bleep. "You destroy life on Earth and you have the technology to keep yourself alive indefinitely. We can create better humans, new myths, a new Jesus; for a world which follows a path you have always dreamed about."

Bleep. "I don't understand, this is fucked."

Bleep. "You can't imagine. The Reality laws have reduced your imaginative capacity. You let them in when you took the Reeto Dust."

Bleep. "I'm going to kill you." Bleep. I moved in on him, led by Stevie's kitchen knife.

Gunfire thudded from the ceiling, stopped me in my tracks.

Tumblety's smile tightened his beady eyes: "Killing me would not be a good idea. You are talking to me. I have offered you communication, and you haven't had that for some time. I am the only chance you have of retrieving your sanity—"

An explosion blew open the door, threw me knife first onto Tumblety. Bleep-bleep-bleep went Marx's life.

Kate's face first; jumbled words trying to find a location.

"You OK, DM?"

X, Moz, Red and Chuckie E were with her, smouldering weapons in their hands. I was raised to my feet as X checked Tumblety's wounded stomach: "He'll live," she said, leaving Tumblety prostrate, his hands bloody around the knife wound.

"I've seen them, DM, the aliens," rushed out Kate. "They sent Marx down here. I communicated with one of them called something like Hooldoon. Marx's ultrasound waves are controlling Earth, that's why Tumblety wanted him, so he can tap into the brainwaves."

Bleep. Kate paused, drew breath, all eyes on Marx's body. Bleep.

"Marx has been in the hills. Tumblety's lot got him back, killed the couple who were guarding him. We've got to turn him off, stop the bad vibes."

"You can't do that," spluttered Tumblety from the floor. "If Marx dies, then you die, Mr Manion. What he imagines is what you do, and all of your former classmates. You can't win."

"Yor dead inside, Tumblety," spat Kate at him. "And you can't live unless you make everything dead around you!"

"Marx dies, you die, Manion," he returned, masturbating his own sense of superiority.

Bleep. I lost control. Bleep. Hooldoon's mission; calculated rage thrusting the knife into Tumblety's body, my hands and face covered in blood before Chuckie E pulled me away.

"I'm losing it, people. I've fuckin' lost it! I can't imagine why I did that."

Kate put her arm around me: "You've done too much, DM, you've been under a lot of stress. You just need rest. When was the last time you rested?"

"I can't remember."

"See, that's all it is."

"Of course, yeh, I'm still the DM. Do you think he was telling the truth about pulling the plug on Marx?"

"It's possible, but I can give you proof that we need to end his life."

The coin! Bleep. "Heads Marx lives, tails Marx dies," I said presenting the one pence coin to all those standing.

Bleep as the coin spun stylishly up. Bleep, Tumblety croaking "You need help Man—" Bleep, his death and Marx's verdict. Tails.

Tails? Joe's coin on tails?

"I don't know what this is all about, Mr Marx, but all I want is my imagination back. That's all I need. The answers don't matter to me anymore."

Bleep. I flicked off the life support. Bleep. I watched, half expecting him to decompose before my eyes. Bleep.

"You can go back to Inuthua now."

Bleep.

"He'll live a while yet," said Kate. "You've done the right thing, DM."

"We'd better get moving," said X as she and other members of CS8 set about snipping wires bleep-bleep.

"We're re-organising, DM," said Chuckie E straight into my distracted face. "It's not just changing things now, we've got to take over. You need to make contacts again."

"What're we gonna do?" I asked lethargically.

"It's war. We've got to take out those in power. Breff is doing just the same as Portman. We've got to be in control if we want to save this country."

"Right, good, it's back on. The revolution again, back to auto living. Make contacts—"

"Bleep."

"The aliens are coming, DM," said Kate. "We need to be ready with the good, good people, to join with those who want to save the Earth."

I had to believe Chuckie E and Kate to fit in with the plot spooling out of control in my mind. Everything would work out if I was DM again.

If God Was Kafka, Jesus Was K, What Would That Make Kafka?

"Jesus, nice to see you back. Again."

"Don't tell me I told you so. We could argue this for centuries and I know you'd eventually agree with what I tried. Let's not do that now. I really don't want to."

"Well," warmed God. "At least you tried, but you must've known what they'd do. Why didn't you consult me?"

"I wanted to do it myself. I've learned from this experience. We are just one-consciousness. It's all just a dream and we are the imagination of ourselves. You and me, we're just somebody's dream, somebody's art. You knew that though didn't you?"

God bowed his head as a way of confession, raised it after the pause, acknowledging Jesus' intuition.

"Of course. But that doesn't mean it's meaningless. That's the point—"

"I know. I realise that."

"Earth doesn't really matter, just as we don't really matter in the open scheme of things. But, we matter in the here and now and what we can feel and perceive from all that's around us. That's all the education anybody needs, or will get. Even me. There is only this moment. But this moment is eternal, as long as we believe."

"Yeh, I get the irony."

"No irony. That's too easy. Sure, I've created lots of planets, lots of different ideologies, but the bottom line is we're all in this together. You, me, Earth, the universe, infinity. It's all just a dream. And maybe there's someone who dreams everything, and when that one wakes up, that one wonders about its place in the scheme of things. Earth is unseeable, you and I are under a microscope. So, we learn something, we move on. We've all been through death and we know it's just a phase. Get dreaming, get living."

Jesus laughed, an equanimity spreading over him. "I'm sure that's a dichotomy, if we analyse it, but I like it. You're a hippie and you always will be."

God laughed. "Hippie? They'd call me a Llaaazdr on Shim. A Vyupgyu on Zshrr. Words, communication, actions. Come on, skin up." He handed Jesus a lump of hashish, some papers and a light from his finger. "Let's have that debate after all."

"OK, but I'm not going to go on for decades. I'm going to create a planet in the next year."

RELIGION IS ANATHEMA

The Immortal, though Inuthuans' visible god, had never had discernible features, mainly due to an omnipotent influence on Proul transmissions. But The Immortal was now concentrating on other matters, shedding tons of superfluous knowledge and apparently shaking. Upon The Immortal's mass an expression seemed to be appearing; a tense contraction of fear.

Vibrations could be felt all across Inuthua, winds brushing through the unprotected terrain.

More Inuthuan groups were heading off for Earth to engage in a war they would never have been allowed to indulge in on their own planet. Cathartic carnage would find an answer to their problems, or at least prove a visual distraction.

They went through space on a mission, most under the guise of a religion: some were Jews, some were Catholics. Some Protestants, some Muslims: all fundamentally racists. The Marchous went as Buddhists, ostensibly to save the beleaguered Hooldoon, but still with an overriding desire to impose their will.

Hooldoon sensed all this from a cell inside The Institute Of Science. "It's OK, it's all all right, I don't have to panic. It's just a ride." Hooldoon's forced optimism was clouded though by the ultrasound wave chaos which was unhinging dimensional shifts and disrupting time.

WILL THE REAL DM PLEASE STAND UP?

Eventually I reached Egdon Sector, thoroughly exhausted by the intense temperature; each degree rising giving the suffocating fog more presence.

I felt weaker than I had ever felt, pausing to catch my breath at the gates to what I believed to be Kelly's house, using subtraction and addition to modify the readings from my crashing handcom.

Weighing up the pros and cons of entering I still got an objective draw. "Have you still got instinct?" I reminded myself she had asked. I fought to find the energy to enter.

Nothing stirred in the gloomy house dimly lit by portable battery-powered lamps, some of which were vaguely bleeping to denote their loss of power.

I had the numbers to bleep out the alarm system in seconds then disable it with Stevie's kitchen knife, only to then notice it was switched off anyway.

I felt confident briefly until a pain at the back of my head cancelled it out and re-focused me on a mission.

It took three bouts of gentle knocking to bring Kelly to unlock her bedroom door.

We fell into each other's arms, her weary body and pale face the foundations of my own washed-out and unmaintained features.

Words of love then words of concern: "Are you OK?" I asked.

"They've been giving me tablets. I've managed to throw up most of them. I daren't eat any food. I have to sneak out when I can for a MacDolland's." She was waking herself, fathoming out the situation as she rubbed her hand into her face and hair. "Tumblety's people were coming round, but they haven't been all weekend. And the police went a few days ago."

"What day is it?"

"Sunday. April the first. My sixteenth birthday!" She laughed weakly. "It's OK now, we can be together."

"Where's your mother?"

"She's been in bed all weekend."

"They told me we are going to do the revolution again. I've got things I have to do. I need you to help me."

"Yes."

"I need to get round to people. We might need money. Is your handcom working?"

"Only the main lines. I know where her bank card is and I can drive the car."

Kelly looked in on her mother before we departed. She took much time before saying she wanted to kill her, but delivered the words with little conviction.

Mrs Godfrey breathed loudly in uniform bursts, her fully-clothed body tangled in the bed sheets.

Kelly bleeped the car into gear with a throaty guzzle. She drove carefully in the fog, using the car's flickering route graphics for hazardous guidance.

"One call into Club Independent Kelly. It's just over the river."

"What?"

I bleeped directions into the car's computer then set about transferring *AL* disk from my handcom to Kelly's.

"This is it, Kelly!" I proclaimed as I began to add to *AL*. "Nobody notices anything until it's gone, and then it's only if the news bothers to mention it. But this disk Kelly, this disk will record the truth…"

I barely noticed the screeches from tyres, only the jolts and bleeps on Kelly's mother's car's computer as it racked up minus points for bad driving.

"…You see, it's all here, all the truth in plain English. No, there's none of your fancy shit here," I continued, possessed. "No italics here. Italics to emphasise? No working-class people know what that means." I went into character, "Don't fuckin' know that. CAPITALS man, that's what we fuckin' know." A "Huh" laughed me back to myself. "You can take a survey on it if you don't believe me."

I skipped in bleeps through sections before finding *AL's* frayed ending.

"I'm gonna add to this and finish this Kelly. I'm—"

I typed, re-read, bleeped to delete. I typed again, stopped, re-read, bleeped to delete. It seemed so dull against that I'd previously manufactured. I was too concerned with realism, and try as I did I couldn't force anything fanciful into the handcom.

Kelly was back in the car before I'd noticed it had stopped. She had a full fist of dollar notes ,placing them on my groin indifferently.

"I don't think anybody's using money at the moment..."

I couldn't respond, my mind working out how to spend the money: how much pot I could get and the pluses and minuses of obtaining a smidgen of dust.

"...statement. She was twenty thousand overdrawn until she got the money from *The Shine*..."

"Of course, she's in with *The Shine*. She's from Marx's bad side. That's it—"

But I couldn't find a way to input it fluently into *AL's* narrative and the idea withered to an abrupt halt.

My teeth crashed, my neck cracked, and we were shuddering outside Club Independent; its neon sign striving to shine through the smog, vandalised by editors to "Clu e e e t".

"Shell suit, dodgy eye. 200 on pot, 20 on Reeto."

Kelly was gone for years and I pondered a character who'd said "Our cities are full of dead forests" and "If there's no televisuals in heaven I don't want to go". I couldn't fathom out the dichotomy of the philosophy, couldn't bring it to a conclusion, so I gave up and counted time.

Three minutes later I was an alter, full of praise and anticipation. Yet I never really hit the heights of DM perception and the fall to depression was an abrupt and painful one.

"Got jobs to do, Kelly. This is my last chance. I have no imagination anymore."

"You must have it somewhere!" she pleaded as if at last released from purgatory. "Just THINK, DM! You still have instinct haven't you? Find it! It'll be tucked away somewhere in your heart! Come on, let's get on with the jobs."

"Sector 5," I said, bleeping directions into the car's keypad before returning to my handcom.

"Give me a meeting place," I e-mailed Kate.

After some delay, possibly exaggerated by Kelly's slow disjointed driving, Kate sent a reply: 'Who is this?'

"DM."

"DM who?"

"Daniel Manion."

"Who is this?" came back again.

"Kate, it's me. Five-ten, short, dark brown hair, worn-out face, East Tyneside Comp," I typed back.

Another delay before: "I am DM, who are you? Hooldoon?"

"Who is this? I am Daniel Manion. I want to speak to Kate Flowers."

"Go and tell The Man his days are numbered, you monkey."

The line was cut.

"What's the matter?"

"I think they've got to Kate. We'd better make contacts quickly."

The man who opened the door at Kristen Ingersson's lodgings had a gun in his hand, "Wha—?" he demanded tersely, pointing the gun at me.

"I need to speak to Kristen"

"She's gone home."

"Can—"

"Now fuck off, I don't want any trouble."

The armed man edged inside, clicked and bleeped several locks on the door.

Kelly helped me back into the car. "Where next?" she asked professionally.

"8."

Neither Phil, Taff or Jez were answering the knocking at their door.

"16."

Will Correca's front door was open, the inside of his house like a womb from the vision-less smog outside. But the heat was more intense outside, generating a deathly smell which led us to the back yard.

Dead pigeons were scattered across the grass, each body bloodless. Though they all looked the same, to me it felt that the only living one, perched on a branch cooing from the white mist, had to be Cassie.

I encouraged her to my arm with one of Ted's much-used lines, "Cassie, old girl."

I quickly made a microdisc of *AL* and attached it to Cassie's leg, bird-noising directions to Morse's for Cass. There was no sense of her flight away, no feeling of uplift as the blanket fog encompassed in a second.

It would give Morse time to read it before we arrived.

Kelly saw my weakness and tried to encourage, but on seeing the energy it took me to acknowledge her she retreated into nervous silence interspaced with squeezes at my flesh.

Kelly held me as I led her through the tunnels under Morse's church. I felt encouraged that the readings we used to guide us, taken from the microdisc, indicated Cassie had reached Morse.

Uncovering the floorboard to enter the flickering clarity of Morse's cell I was shaken with flashbacks, shocked into unconsciousness.

The room was clearer when I awoke, several new candles revealing how Kelly had used up some of my void-time. In addition there was a lumpless globule of vomited saliva on the floor. It matched the stain on Kelly's T-shirt as she lifted me onto a chair.

Opposite, Morse's corpse, blood now slowly oozing from his shattered face. A burning aroma drew my attention to a gun on the floor.

"Are you OK?" asked Kelly; her eyes red, her cheeks sore with drying teardrops.

"Yeh. You?"

She nodded stoically. "He left a note." She held it in front of her and read: "This is what I always imagined. *Ars Moriendi*. It's time to cross over." She flipped over the paper. "He's drawn a map of how to get to where he wants to be buried."

I noticed Morse's televisual unit had "..." going to infinity. On pressing and bleeping "Rew" into action I realised he had been reading *AL*, though the computer's memory had recorded a number of "Skip" bleeps.

"It's THE DM," I e'd to Kate.

Delays punctuated my repetitive actions as Kelly curiously tried to clean up Marx's features.

'Who is this?????' finally came back, imagined demandingly.

I flicked to "Vis.Comm." to show my face.

As Kelly used Morse's coat-arms to tie his legs together I impatiently reached the point of starting my persuasion afresh.

Kate's face appeared on the televisual screen. She was looking down, speaking in spells against the pounding crowd noise muttering all round.

"Start again, Kate, I can't hear," I said, turning down the bass.

She lifted the handcom higher to stare directly into the lens. Parts of skulls, bits of noses, clumps of hair and floating, hacked off limbs surrounded Kate.

"Who are you?" she asked in tinny echoes.

I turned down the treble. "It's me, Daniel. Where are you? What's happened?"

"I've seen you before somewhere!" she seemed to shout, though the tone was neutral. "Who are you?"

"It's me, DM. What's the matter with you? Will's gone, Kristen's gone—"

"You killed them!"

"No. I'm DM. Don't you recognise me?"

"You're Leonardo Smith aren't you?"

"Daniel Manion! Fuckin' hell Kate, they've got to you."

She changed tack: "It's gonna be OK. You are going to be cared for. We are going to be selfless. You don't have to worry. Just stay indoors and wait for the all-clear. Watch your TV and you'll be fine."

She lifted the visuals above her head, turned them round over masses of heads crammed together in some kind of dimly lit chamber. "This is the DM. Just believe in us."

Over the sea of heads, at the screen's left, uncomfortably bobbling at the stage's burning centre, a figure sent over scratchy, distant vocals:

"...We've come through a lot. We're almost there: Utopia. But we've got a lot of problems to sort out before we can get there. I have had a dream; THE most beautiful dream. Imagine a world without money, a world full of sharing, innovation, artistry. We can make that dream real..."

In a quick swing Kate was back on the visuals: "You aren't *the* DM and you don't need to try to be him. Be yourself and have hope."

She cut off the communication. Kelly had Morse's body tightly bound up, eager to leave the scene of the diabolic crime.

She pulled the corpse by its arms as I infrequently aided with lifting its feet.

We stumbled on graves as we edged a route though the fog, but because I hadn't the imaginative capacity to interpret the etchings I did not take them in.

"I think this is it," she said, stopping, so that I almost tripped over the corpse's legs and fell onto a kitchen sink dumped in the hole.

Kelly identified a small box at the grave's head: "It's got a button on it."

"Bomb."

"I don't think so. Check that grave to the right." I stumbled over to push my face against it. "David Marks?"

"Yeh."

"1971 to 1972?"

"Yeh."

"Oh, he was only just over a month," Kelly lamented. "Check the one on the left."

I scrambled, clipped my foot on Kelly's and fell onto the left grave-bed.

"Sorry. Is it—?" Her hushed "shit" vibrated with fear. "Is it 1988 to 2003?"

I saw the numbers, replied, "Yeh," then saw the name; a 'Daniel Manion'.

Kelly did all the work: pulled out the kitchen sink, pushed in the dead body and loosely covered it with earth. She pressed the button on what passed for a gravestone and set off "Abide With Me". A choir sang all the prayers she had planned to say and allowed her an eternity of quiet contemplation.

I awoke to "Abide With Me" fading and then heard it replaying on loop as Kelly helped me back to the car.

I caused us to stumble, though when I say "Us" I almost mean "Them", and when I say "I" I really mean "He". There was no sense of existence; just of being carried along. I wasn't the real DM, he was. And I wasn't even the other DM, because he was dead. I was just a DM, just one of the unpeople with an extraordinary life never to be recorded for history. This DM was now enduring a rather listless and sordid finale. "The End Is Nigh" was now remembered with irony, inscribed on back-breaking placards; replicated photos of which flashed through DM's mind.

Kelly spoke, but I took in little; "Where do we go from here? From despair to where? Can't do one, two, three, or, four...thirteen..."
17.7.12.16.6.11.
1.13.37.39.46.47.
It was my flat, now "Your old flat", now "My old flat". But there were different clothes amongst the material possessions, and the food cabinet and fridge illuminated "A healthy lifestyle".
The collection of books, music discs, computer disks and posters were much the same, save for a few reminiscent of Joe's "Old flat".

Online she found a doctor, shadowing the mouse over Daniel's body to get a diagnosis.
The televisual display returned, 'Patient is slipping into a coma. Consult your local doctor. Coma patients can be a burden. Ninety per cent of them don't emerge from comas. It is best, for you and the patient, to end the pain. Research shows that releasing the patient's soul and having a proper funeral can be more therapeutic than spending the rest of your life waiting for an awakening that might never happen. Consult your local doctor. MacChurch gives a dignified burial at a competitive price. Log on to macchrip.com.uk.
Kelly kissed Daniel, trying to smash through his REM, hugging him as tears dripped from her eyes to his face.
Her inconclusive thoughts eventually came up with: "God left marijuana growing naturally on this planet. It has many different purposes, all of them positive. Maybe pot is The Panacea."
She knocked up a joint quickly, its haggard construction the result of her clammy hands. Its ignition produced a cloud of smoke and falling, burning tobacco.
Kelly kissed the kick-back through Daniel's lips, forcing the smoke into his lungs, holding it there, then pushing his stomach to release air.

She repeated, more passionately, the two of them burning each other up as their lips rolled.

DM flickered, uttered, "Kelly." She kissed him again and he grunted back to her, "It's DM. Can you hear me?"

"We're at your old flat, right?"

"Kelly. Pick a noun, any noun."

"Erm, battery."

"A rechargeable battery stuck into the Earth's core. It gives out vibes and it's running low. I'm back!" I locked heated lips with her; a surge of energy leaving me drained. "Kelly, I think I've died. But it's clear now. I've seen it all—"

"Yor not dead—"

"I've always been dead, and I've seen it all. I saw mankind, in a few years, coming up with unbelievable inventions and technological developments. An economist devised a socialist system which made sure no one went hungry and everyone enjoyed a fruitful life. But it was too late, the world had already started collapsing. At least God's little experiment had produced lessons from which The Almighty could learn. God wouldn't make the same mistakes again."

"You've got your imagination back!"

Kelly hugged me but the atmosphere was too oppressive for me to feel touched.

"Change the clock Kelly. Change it to, say 2339."

Confusion gave way to a heartfelt trust in me. She altered the digital clock in bleeps, her face worn out with overriding concerns of "Love".

"Look out of the window Kelly. What do you see?"

"Fog. All just fog." She paused. "There are some fires burning. I can't see too clearly. It must be far away."

"But we can't see two metres in front of ourselves out there. It must be a big fire or it must be just outside. Whatever, the burning will get closer."

I pulled her close to me but was only able to feel the prickly friction of branding clothes. We stripped inelegantly, pulling feverishly the materials from binding perspiration.

Our porous flesh choked on desire, writhing into position for the final fuck.

"Kelly, look. I do love you. I need you to understand. I need—" She licked my salt lips. "When you die, your soul leaves your body. We still exist. I promise you, I will find you. In the next world. I will still feel this. I'll remember to come looking for your soul. This love will last forever."

Bleep. The televisual's speakers ushered in euphonious music and a soothing, imageless voice announcing: "Coki Coli. When it's the last thing you need, but the thirst thing you want."

It Couldn't Happen To A Nicer Planet

Scorpio to the north, Aquarius south, Leo west and Taurus east; the constellations were locking into their final positions. By chance.

Majestically hovering, flitting and swooping near the Americas' coast, somewhere over the Atlantic Ocean, a butterfly recorded waves crashing on desolate shores.

It landed on a rock peeking through the waters, remembered the small island community wiped out by tidal waves. The creature sensed death near, relaxed for a final thought:

"My simple butterfly life, transformed from caterpillar to this. But all I can remember are beautiful flowers and a life spent surviving when I should have been appreciating."

Wings strained to take off, just before a wave splashed over the rock. "Phew. So close!"

An almighty flap forward whipped up the waves below, the wings forced back to stir up a storm.

With each aggressive push and pull of the wings the butterfly rose higher and incited the waves further. Walls of water reared up, steaming towards the land.

As the strain of its motions peaked, the butterfly gave in, its tiny body falling, then swallowed up by the ocean.

Waves crashed for miles into the land, sweeping over towns and cities to reclaim the past. Hurricane winds over 300 kilometres an hour ripped up anything left standing. For humans there was as much chance of survival as winning the lottery.

All seas around the world were snapping at land in vast bites, each action causing a reaction, triggering some foot soldier of Mother Nature.

Some people had time to pray: for their salvation mainly, as irony knocked down doors. All hate was swept aside. All that Hate which had lasted through centuries, even through The Age Of Enlightenment, even through the sophisticated and literate twentieth century, was obliterated by Mother Nature. They should have been thanking God, not singing "Abide With Me".

Magma rose from the earth, exploded into volcanoes; molten lava eating up all the man-made and re-shaping nature's deposited art. Thermometers burst like fountains as fires scorched ground; purging through natural cleansing.

Isostatic movements searched for equilibrium, earthquakes finding fragile fault lines and opening up gaping chasms. Fault lines caused by persistent nuclear testing had left the Earth weak, unable to resist as tremors ravaged through continents.

Forests burned; gasping for water, gasping for air, ignorantly and unknowingly trying to be mankind's saviours. If only the trees could understand, they could comfort themselves with the knowledge that their capabilities would mean them growing again and being part of another planet.

The poles were melting; icebergs cut loose to speed into tidal waves, drowning another population.

The sun's full glare burned through ozone holes and poisoned the air, seeing off those left in Earth's concentration camp.

The planet Inuthua exploded and The Immortal crashed through, its fragments sent hurtling into deep space. The Immortal's implosion propelled debris to the outer reaches of infinity. In one of The Immortal's fragments the memory *AL* was secreted and encased. It contained all the necessary details for an immortal to realign itself to some kind of cosmic reality and live again.

Planets shattered, sent impacts out to other planets and shattered them, Earth's solar system exploding into countless numbers of variable size and importance. One of Earth's fragments contained DM's disk of *AL* and in some inestimable twist of fate it rebounded off a rock from The Moon which contained a disk of *AL.*

Particles bounced off each other as the Sun jettisoned balls of fire to heat up the developing stew. Somewhere a match would be found and creation would begin again.

Tomorrow Is Always Yesterday

In 1668 Nool Hamwoo became the first Hamo to step onto planet Ourth's Muwn. It was an historic day for Hamokind: the planet had solved most of its problems and could now concentrate on space exploration. They were very few who did not join in the global celebrations; only those Hamos in The East who distrusted science and wanted to live a simple, orthodox life.

The six Hamos who landed on Ourth's Muwn stayed there for two years to develop life-forms and manufacture a climate.

When the six returned to Ourth all the represented countries cheered them through streets. Ingsh, an island country, had two citizens returning, one of them being Nool Hamwoo. But they didn't celebrate Hamwoo's return. Though reports were subject to censorship it did emerge that he had had a breakdown shortly before leaving the Muwn.

Some years later, after the Muwn had begun receiving regular visitors, Hamwoo reappeared in the media. He had joined a tribe in the eastern kingdoms because he believed in its way of life and thought all Ourth should adopt it.

In an interview with *The Ourth*, Hamwoo talked about finding a disk buried below the Muwn's surface. He had deciphered the code to find a story, created by some other species which had existed long before Ourth. It was a story about how a planet destroyed itself. "Dictated by Declan Marx", Hamwoo tried to tell the public when he returned to Ourth but was silenced by governments and big business.

Hamwoo was "a crank," the original "Space loony". His revelations were tucked away in *The Ourth's* glossy *Mad World* supplement, available "for laughs".

Now I'm God

On The Universal Channel, deities waited expectantly to compete with me on *Be A God*.

"God number one," began the host, Immy. "Tell me everything you know about the planet formerly known as Earth."

"Er…Creation, Adam and Eve, the dinosaurs…" God No 1 raced out. "…Er, Jesus Christ…The Holocaust…Man on the moon…"

The same question went to gods numbers 2 and 3, each replicating much of the first god's answers.

"OK gods, your marks have come through," said Immy with a finger on an ear-piece. "You've got sixty per cent omnipotence!"

Muted applause rang throughout the solar system, giving way to pinpricks of shouted encouragement for me.

"DM, your first task is to tell me everything you know about the planet formerly known as Earth."

"Bacteria from Mars, the Renaissance, The Age Of Enlightenment, world wars, the Holocaust, Emily Spencer, nuclear weapons, television, John Lennon, *The Catcher In The Rye*, Bill Hicks, global warming, drugs, George Orwell, rock 'n' roll, fascism, racism, socialism, communism, El Nino, tinned food, bar-codes, bleep, bleep, bleep…Salvador Dali, Martin Scorsese…It's all about money…Monet, Picasso, Adolf Hitler. Hate, hate, hate, gunshots. Selling guns, selling bombs, defence budgets. Underclass, working-class. Class-shot, bleep, bleep. Eco-system, education, education, education, bleep, bleep, bleep. Money, economics, famine, death, destruction…Human beings, dodos, eyesight, feeling, hearing, smell, taste. Blood system, eco-system, balance, coagulation, Armageddon—"

"RIP," proclaimed Immy. "Well, it looks good, DM. After the break, we'll see if you can be a god…"

They were advertisements trying to sell uncultivated Planets, decorative stars and passes to other dimensions.

"Welcome back!" greeted Immy. "OK gods, it's select-a-date time. And remember, you can work together on this. Everyone! Everywhere! Give a big Universal welcome to our resident basshead, Adhou Elvhou."

Elvhou breezed in; a spliff in one hand and a gun in the other. He did his karaoke sketch, miming along to Sid Vicious' version of "My Way", then he sent a bullet into "The Time Planet" and took a rock for a reading.

"Well, we gotta ask it," said Immy laconically.

And all of infinity's tuned-in an connected shouted out, "What's the date, Elvhou?"

"Oh, my little one-consciousness," delivered Elvhou's catchphrase. "The date is April the thirtieth 1999."

The gods collaborated but only managed "one point for Jesus-like," in the whole of their allotted time.

When the date was put to me it triggered: "Bombs in London, because people still hate. Hate. Racism, Fascism, Homophobia. Insecure pre-millennium tension. NATO bombs Serbia, NATO bombs Montenegro, NATO bombs Bulgaria. The West oppresses Iraq, and MacDolland's, Dizzy, Coki Coli and American British Tobacco takes over the world. Conspiracy theories for the rich and famous and prosaic burials for the unmentionable unpeople. El Nino is wreaking havoc across the world, the polar ice caps are melting. The Earth's temperature is rising, the Earth's natural resources are diminishing. The Verve have just split up. You might want to contrast that with The Smiths split in 1987—"

A bassy bleep and Immy's hushed, "Bonus points."

"Children are dying when they don't need to be: in Africa, in Poland, in England, on Pourische Road. Suede are about to release "Head Music" and, and, someone got shot in the head. Fates, coincidences, connections and selections are all locking on for what's been wrongly billed as "The New Millennium". Bill Hicks is dead, Steve Coogan is alive. He was Alan Partridge, a character who celebrated on learning his nemesis had died after falling from the roof whilst trying to adjust his television aerial. And Rod Hull, whose fame had been the result of performances with a puppet, had recently died after falling from the roof, etcetera—"

A bleep announced Immy's, "Bonus Narrative points."

"...Ideology maims Earth as Irony rehearses gags about ethnic cleansing. The Earth is so self-satisfied it thinks it can last forever. Oh, they'll be more bombs, more Hate, more death, more scandal, more bizarre cults and psychopathic individuals, and they'll party on towards 2000. They'll make resolutions before the hangover, then they'll get depressed with the new slog. But they've got through it: the world wasn't "Nigh", and they'll clap and laugh through the final year of the old millennium thinking everything's fine—"

Bleep, "and bleep, that's amazing; ending on a bonus Future point!"

The deafening cheering forced all those in space to join in, even the vacuums and black holes (resting from hoovering up infinity: a little bag of dust for "THE GOD").

"Well, DM, this is it," anticipated Immy. "The final round: Weirdo-Bizarro-Extremo-Fishy!" Immy turned to "Elvhou", and laboured out, "So, what mad jape have you got in store for today?"

"Skimmy Immy, call it a seven into the ocean. I got the basest and the most exalted jape for all of consciousness." He turned to "Gods and DM", took a toke of marijuana before commencing: "In fifteen seconds give m—"

The Gods bleeped prematurely.

"OK gods, you got it. Y'wanna take it or shake it?" asked Immy.

"Take it!" blurted out God Number 2.

Elvhou repeated, "In fifteen seconds," before slowing to emphasise, "give me as many names as you can think of for human masturbation."

"Oh, er, wanking," said God No 1.

"Jerking," added God No 3.

"Tossing off," burst out God 1.

"Ooh, ooh," hesitated God 2. "Oh, it's, er, hand-job."

The Gods grunted indecisively but could not add to their points-tally before being bleeped out.

"Well gods, you got four points," Immy said in all seriousness. "But you could have had tugging, pulling, slapping the snake, the hand shuffle, the hand shandy, the ego thrash and The Feminist Panacea. So that means that DM just needs to match you to win."

So that was that, a "hand-shandy, a wank, a tug," and "a Sunday hose," getting me universal adulation.

I increased the thickness of space to slow down the capsule hurtling towards me, its motion smoothly coming to a halt.

Inside, a small room decorated with books I'd ordered. Also, the music, films and paintings I'd ordered.

At two seats near the capsule's front, two piles of dust. I began to scoop them into a beaker.

"Hey!" came thoughts into my head. "What are you doing here?"

I turned to DM's thought-waves, imagined a figure with short, dark brown hair, average height and features.

"Have you been waiting for this vessel?" came to me.

"Yes," I sent back. "I am Hooldoon, of the planet formerly known as Inuthua."

"Did you watch over me?"

"Only as much as you watched over me. In the end it's all one-consciousness experiencing itself subjectively. This soul life is hard at first, but you'll get used to it, and once you tap into it your mind will go on an infinite trip. Everything is ours now."

"I'm getting the hang of it, but it just doesn't seem fair yet. I thought death would be more than this. It's a bit lonely."

"Well it would be: you've got infinity to explore! There's much to appreciate out there once your soul gets on line. Once you've understood communication you'll be able to begin in this life."

"Can you tell me where Kelly Godfrey is?" I thought to this strange creature.

"Just think about it. Feel it. You'll find her."

"You got in touch with me, didn't you?" I asked the creature in reverberations of thought.

"Many times, DM," I replied. "We can slip inside each other at will. All eternity is our playground."

I liked that. I liked this creature's style. I asked it, "Why did you pick up that dust?"

"Yeh, Reeto. That was The Immortal's work. Very clever really."

"Where's The Immortal now?" I questioned abruptly.

"Somewhere," I replied with a sigh of vibrations. "The Immortal duped us big style. It matters little that we now know it was a capitalist mass engorging on space, given nutrition by feeding off living planets. Oh, we were screwed! Talk about working on commission! But The Immortal goes on, and we go on. We're little cogs but we're matter.

"All we've got is the dust of dead lives, dead planets. It gets us to another place, gets us away from the physical. You heard about The Ourth?"

I returned the negative.

"I just got the signals. They've discovered a new planet. Wanna go?"

"The bones?"

"Y"know, the usual fuck-ups. They've got love, they've got hate. They all eventually die."

"Just die?" I whimpered in disbelief.

"Well, there's plenty of ways. Y'wanna know?"

"Amon nino."

"C'mon, monkey man."

"Monkey man."

On our journey through the constellations I briefed the creature thus: "You can still die at birth, especially if you are poor. You have a good chance of dying in an automobile accident—"

"I know this; deal me in."

"I've got a heart attack for three."

"Floods cause drowning, psychopaths randomly kill individuals, house fires kill families. Three all."

"That's Ourth there. You see it?"

"Yeh. Shootings, bombs, wars, starvation—"

"Cancer, domestic accidents, suicide by gunshot, hanging, pills, slashed wrists—"

"Alcohol poisoning, assassination in retaliation, corporate genocide—"

"What's the score?"

"Ten-nine to me."

"OD-ing. Now, check it out."

"Club Indie."

"Karma fix."

"Y"wanna be Joe?"

"Y"wanna be DM?"

"Yeh."

"Yeh."

Inside, we joined an asinine queue, each body self-absorbed with their own sphere of existence, patiently waiting to be bleeped along.

"We've been here before," I said.

"I know, but there's no tangible memory. Maybe we've just seen it on the box."

Bleep.

"We've never had to queue before."

Bleep. We shuffled forward.

"Supply and demand," replied Joe. "We all wanna get bananas these days. Don't think the Pope doesn't do it either. He's prob—"

A "bleep" moved us on.

"I can't connect, Joe."

"We're getting closer."

"Bleep."

"What?" we said simultaneously.

"Bleep."

"Whattaya think, Joe?" I asked in all seriousness.

"Bleep."

"You still there, Joe?"

"Bleep."

"Bleep."

"Mr Manion. We were going to send out a search party," came jocularly from the tin-pot machine, TUM3. "5 Reeto."

"Bleep."

TUM3 vended the greyish tablets, pausing before a metal pill-like object clunked out.

"Bleep. And a new stabiliser."

I took them all in my sweaty palm and hurried out.

"How do you feel, Joe?" I asked.

"I don't know, make something up," he replied.

"We're karma-fixed-up," I said encouragingly as we placed ourselves in the thick white smog. "All you need to know is I'm gonna alter your perception."

Bleep.

"Set your controls Joe. Squeedgy your third goddam eye. We'll get out of this."

Bleep.

Bleep.

"No, we won't will we?"

Bleep.

"This is immortality: endless." Bleep. "We can't imagine anything new." Bleep. "We'll make the same mistakes." Bleep.

Bleep.

Bleep.

"Y'wanna monkey again?"

Bleep

Just keep monkeying around. We're gonna live forever. Bleep. Live for bleeping ever. Keep bleeping. Bleep, bleeps, and bleep 'n' bleep. All philosophies are bleeps. In the updated index of infinity you'll find me. Bleep on the barcode and you'll find "Earth"; a short paragraph acknowledging my existence. I was one of "them", one of "those". Our instinctual nature killed us in the end. Bleep. "Greed" got a general reference. Bleep. That's about it. You can bleep on all the possibilities, find other short paragraphs on planets who've made a more positive contribution. Bleep. But that isn't gonna change what we were, are, or could be. Only we can do that. Bleep. And all the great thinkers are comatose. Bleep.

Bleeep.

Bleeeeeeep.

THE END

About Bill Hicks

With American comedian Bill Hicks there was always an awareness of other people, of how our society links together. With this came an idealism and a vision of what the world could be. But first he had to slay all the "fevered egos" polluting the planet. He saw himself as a flame, Shiva The Destroyer, using comedy as a weapon to expose truths and show people how governments are screwing us every day of our lives. He also happened to be achingly funny, such was the accuracy of his comedy. At the age of thirteen Bill Hicks did his first gig. Six weeks before his death, aged thirty-two, he did the last. In the intervening years he frequently did over 250 gigs a year. He tried to reach as many people as possible, to put them in touch with inner and outer space in a majestic flight of one consciousness thinking. Those he inspired haven't lost the ability to take a ride.

People use and misuse the word "tragedy" all the time. It seems to accompany the death of anybody famous. But the real definition of tragedy evokes a sense of loss and poignancy, a sense of someone dying before they really gave everything they had to offer. Without hyperbole, Bill Hicks' death was a tragedy, for there was so much still to come from this creative, imaginative talent. When he died in 1994 the world lost a rare talent, but his spirit and philosophy still live on.

"As long as one person lives in darkness then it seems to be a responsibility to tell other people." This encapsulated Hicks' philosophy; that we are all one consciousness, that it is the role of every individual to do something to enhance the human condition. Unlike those we place our trust in – politicians and all manner of professionals – Bill wanted to have a lot of fun doing it.

William Melvin Hicks was born on 16th December 1961 in Valdosta, Georgia. The family (father Jim, an executive at General Motors; mother Mary, a teacher; and elder brother and sister, Steve and Lynn) lived in Florida, Alabama and New Jersey before moving to Houston when Bill was seven. They lived in the Memorial area to the west of the city, a place called Nottingham Forest, a "strict Southern Baptist ozone", as Hicks later called it. There, with friend Dwight Slade (both aged twelve), Hicks formed a comedy double act. Bill was bored with the area and mystified by the appeal of living the so-called "American Dream". "One time a friend of mine – we were nine – runs over and goes 'Bill, I just saw some hippies down at the store.' I go 'No way' and he goes 'I swear' and my dad goes 'Get off this property! We don't swear on this property!'"

In 1976 there were no comedy clubs in Houston. Bill and Dwight cycled to auditions, making tapes to send to agents. One liked a tape enough he got them a gig on Jerry Lewis' telethon, a slot from 2.00 a.m. to 2.45 a.m. They didn't have enough material, and anyway their parents wouldn't let them. It was probably a good decision at the time (they were both fourteen), allowing Bill and Dwight to develop characters like Goober Dad. There was always affection in the routines he developed around his parents; a gentler kind of comedy, the kind his parents could appreciate. Mary and Jim saw the warmth, much as audiences did. Whereas they connected with Bill as a son more than a comedian, audiences were able to connect with him on every level, not justice emotionally and spiritually, but even at the basest levels; anger, hate, lust. With experience and understanding, he could look on all subjects with the detachment of a neutral. He saw the positive and negative, the grey area.

It wasn't easy at first though. Bill's parents took him to a psychoanalyst when he was seventeen. The therapist was unable to see anything wrong with Bill; he'd pretty much enjoyed the trip Bill had taken him on and joked he was more concerned about Bill's parents.

In 1978 the Comedy Workshop opened on San Felipe in Houston. Hicks began visiting whilst he was still in High School, best friend Kevin Booth driving Bill and Dwight. Sometimes Bill was allowed to perform. When the manager, Steve Epstein, saw Bill he was amazed at the 16 year old's sharpness and confidence. He had to sneak out of his house at night, playing records loudly like Elvis Presley, Kiss, Alice Cooper and B B King, his rouse to make his parents think he was still at home. At one club anarchic comedian Sam Kinison introduced himself to Bill by jumping off the stage with a pair of red panties on his head, landing on Bill. Kinison was to prove an inspiration to Bill as they became friends, Hicks taking Kinison's anger and some of his political ideology and shaping it into something more metaphysical.

In the autumn of 1978, for five to six weeks, Tuesdays at the Workshop was for stand up, then a party at the Zipper Club (a lap dancing dive). Bill and Dwight performed five times before Slade moved away. "There is a rapport with Dwight that makes me come up with things quickly,"

Hicks said at the time. Later, he built that same rapport up with audiences, able to connect with them, confident enough to make it up as he went along. An onstage philosopher, he thought on his feet, taking off at tangents, the ideas and narrative forming and developing with ease.

Hicks was the youngest comic at Houston's Comedy Workshop, but that didn't stop him from holding back with his material. Early on there were doubts; "Sometimes you feel in control, and it's great, but sometimes you just don't feel in control and you really have to struggle to get laughs." But as his understanding and technique matured, more people came to see him.

In 1983, struggling with his art, feeling he was going nowhere, he got into drink and drugs and got angry on stage, enjoying heated verbal arguments, lambasting traditional attitudes, mocking hypocritical beliefs. Drugs helped Bill explore expanded awareness, use his intellect and imagination to travel. Kevin Booth said of Hicks, "Bill was the first person I ever met whose goal it was to become enlightened." (Together they got into meditation, astrology and telepathy.) At first it was explosive rants to bludgeon his audiences into submission. At one gig two Vietnam veterans took exception to his routine and broke his leg. At another, a heckler, unable to keep up with Hicks' returned arguments, pulled a gun on him. Hicks left the stage but it didn't weaken his determination to say what had to be said. But he got noticed because he was actually funny with it. For all the unchecked anger there was an insightful perceptiveness which simultaneously made audiences think and made them laugh at the absurdity of the situation. Hicks was in touch with aliens, he'd seen Jesus riding a unicorn, and he didn't have time for petty politics. He became one of Houston's self-styled Outlaw comics, along with Sam Kinison, Ron Shock, Jimmy Pineapple, Carl LaBoue, Fred Greenlee and Robert Barber. He indulged in a variety of substances (LSD, mushrooms, cocaine, quaaludes, ecstasy, meth amphetamine) over subsequent years, always remembering the experiences for his acts.

In 1984 Hicks got his first Letterman appearance, doing a five minute slot, then slumping down in the guest chair and lighting a cigarette. This wasn't allowed on the show, but the attitude won admiration and further bookings.

He continued partying and taking drugs; at one notorious three-day party someone brought an oxygen tank for the Outlaws to experiment with. Hicks found himself broke in January 1986 having spent all his money on a variety of substances. In 1987 Rodney Dangerfield was given a tape of one of Hicks' shows. He was so impressed he invited him to appear on *Dangerfield's Young Comedians Special*.

Hicks' first introduction to Britain came in November 1990 when he was one of eighteen comedians in *Stand Up America!*, a six week engagement in London's West End. His perceptiveness and sense of irony went down well in the UK and in 1991 he won the Critics' Award at the Edinburgh Festival. He toured Britain and Ireland extensively to sympathetic and responsive audiences. Explaining his success Hicks said, "People in the United Kingdom and outside the United States share my bemusement with the United States that America doesn't share with itself. They also have a sense of irony, which America doesn't have seeing as it's being run by fundamentalists who take things literally."

In 1993 the booze, drugs and cigarettes were behind him when he recorded the Revelations video for Channel 4 in England. But in April 1993, whilst touring Australia, Hicks was eating badly, feeling sharp pains down his left side. Still, in May he began work on *Counts Of The Netherworld* for Channel 4 in England, a show with Kansas City comedian Fallon Woodland. In it they would play two Victorian-era counts who chat and philosophise with guests.

In mid-June though Bill Hicks learned he had cancer. He only told his family, close friends and Colleen McGarr (now his fiancée), and after only a few days in hospital he left to do a gig.

By December Hicks' deterioration was evident and he knew he was dying, moving back to his parents' house in Little Rock in January 1994. On 6th January, his health clearly ailing, he played his final show in New York.

In his final weeks he played his mother music by John Hiatt, Miles Davis and Elvis Presley, showed her documentaries on Jimi Hendrix and The Beatles. He read *Huckleberry Finn* again, tried to get his father to take mushrooms. He worked on a book, variously titled *New Happiness* or *New Beginnings*. There was a sense of optimism, engendered by Bill's belief in a one-consciousness universe. He was at peace with himself and the world, calling his friends to say goodbye before ceasing to speak on 14th February.

At 11.20 p.m. on Saturday 26th February he died in Little Rock, Arkansas, buried in the family plot in Leakesville, Mississippi. At the memorial service Hicks' brother read out a piece Bill had written and requested be read: "I left in love, in laughter, and in truth, and wherever truth, love and laughter abide, I am there in spirit."

Bill's spirit then floated up into the cosmic one consciousness where he continues to enjoy the ride throughout eternity and infinity.

Since 1994 Kevin Booth has worked tirelessly on bringing more of Hicks' material to the public, two albums — *Arizona Bay* and *Rant In E-Minor* – appearing in 1997, reminding people of Hicks' great talent and inventiveness. *Rant* in particular was an apocalyptic masterpiece, what with routines on Waco, strangling Jesse Helms, killing Billy Ray

Cyrus and a savage attack on Jay Leno: "another whore in the capitalist gang bang."

There is a positivity around Hicks' legacy (for all the misanthropy he was essentially an idealist) which means his material stands up to repeat play. His themes continue to have relevance, but his great skill was always to make them searingly funny. He was fearless and there are few contemporaries to match the body of work he left behind. Now that he's jamming with Jimi Hendrix and partying with Yul Brynner and Sam Kinison in the afterlife, Earth continues to make the same fuck ups as before. But hey, it's just a ride.

Paul Outhwaite